BROKEN LANDS

BROKEN LANDS

JONATHAN MABERRY

SIMON & SCHUSTER BFYR

NEW YORK   LONDON   TORONTO   SYDNEY   NEW DELHI

SIMON & SCHUSTER BFYR

An imprint of Simon & Schuster Children's Publishing Division
1230 Avenue of the Americas, New York, New York 10020
SIMON & SCHUSTER BFYR is a trademark of Simon & Schuster, Inc.
For information about special discounts for bulk purchases, please contact Simon & Schuster
Special Sales at 1-866-506-1949 or business@simonandschuster.com.
The Simon & Schuster Speakers Bureau can bring authors to your live event.
For more information or to book an event, contact the Simon & Schuster Speakers Bureau
at 1-866-248-3049 or visit our website at www.simonspeakers.com.
Also available in a SIMON & SCHUSTER BFYR hardcover edition
Book design by Laurent Linn
The text for this book was set in Chaparral Pro.
Manufactured in the United States of America
First SIMON & SCHUSTER BFYR paperback edition December 2019
2 4 6 8 10 9 7 5 3 1
The Library of Congress has cataloged the hardcover edition as follows:
Names: Maberry, Jonathan, author.
Title: Broken lands / Jonathan Maberry.
Description: First edition. | New York : Simon & Schuster Books for Young Readers, [2019] |
Series: Broken lands ; book 1 | Summary: Gabriella "Gutsy" Gomez teams up with
Benny Imura and his gang as they seek to finish what Captain Joe Ledger started—
to find a cure for the zombie infection.
Identifiers: LCCN 2018001523 | ISBN 9781534406377 (hardcover) |
ISBN 9781534406384 (pbk) | ISBN 9781534406391 (eBook)
Subjects: | CYAC: Zombies—Fiction. | Survival—Fiction.
Classification: LCC PZ7.M11164 Br 2019 | DDC [Fic]—dc23
LC record available at https://lccn.loc.gov/2018001523

This is for George A. Romero (1940–2017).
When I was a kid I saw your first film,
Night of the Living Dead, *on its world premiere.*
As an adult, I got to work with you on the last
project you completed before you left us,
the anthology we coedited, Nights of the Living Dead.
You are the Godfather of the Living Dead, now and forever.
I miss you, my friend.

And—as always—for Sara Jo.

ACKNOWLEDGMENTS

Special thanks to some real-world people who were willing to enter the world of the living dead with me. Thanks to my literary agent, Sara Crowe of Pippin Properties; David Gale, Laurent Linn, and the whole team at Simon & Schuster Books for Young Readers. Thanks to my brilliant and talented assistant, Dana Fredsti. Thanks to Dr. John Cmar, Director, Division of Infectious Diseases, Sinai Hospital of Baltimore; Joe McKinney, San Antonio PD; Carl Zimmer, author of *Parasite Rex* (Atria Books); ethnobotanist Dr. Wade Davis; comparative physiologist Mike Harris; Dr. Richard Tardell, specialist in emergency medicine (retired); Dr. Nancy Martin-Rickerhauser; thanks to Rhian Lockard, Gail Guth-Nichols, Carmen Elisa, Rachael Lavin, Nikki Guerlain, Chris Newton, Gabrielle Faust, Rachel Maleski, and Vinessa Olp; thanks to J. Dianne Dotson; thanks to Stacey Hood, Chris Wren, Dyer Wilk, Kelly W. Collier, and K. R. Chin; Alan Weisman, author of *The World Without Us* (Thomas Dunne Books); and thanks to some of my real-world friends for allowing me to write them into this odd little tale—Solomon Jones, Randy Kirsch, Alethea Kontis, Karen Peak, Luis Alberto Urrea, and Jamie Ford.

PART ONE

NEW ALAMO, TEXAS
LATE AUGUST

THE STILLNESS

It is the secret of the world
that all things subsist and do not die,
but retire a little from sight
and afterwards return again.

—RALPH WALDO EMERSON, ESSAYS: SECOND SERIES

GABRIELLA "GUTSY" GOMEZ BURIED HER MOTHER ON Wednesday. And again on Friday.

This was the world and that's how it was.

THE SIGN OVER THE CEMETERY READ "HOPE."

Gutsy kept trying to believe in the sign, but every day it was getting harder to understand what the word even meant. Hope for what? Hope for who? Hope for where?

She stood in the road, one hand on the bridle of the weary, patient old horse; her other hand on the broad-bladed machete that hung from her belt. All the metal fittings on knife and bridle had been sanded down and painted in flat colors. There was nothing reflective on anything she wore, on the horse, or on the work cart. Reflections were dangerous this far from town. The wheels of the cart and the harness strapped to the horse were greased where they needed grease and padded where they needed padding. Reflection drew one kind of trouble and noise drew another.

"Come on, Gordo," she said, and the horse bobbed his head and followed, big hooves clomping softly on the dusty ground. He knew the way as well as she did. Maybe better, since he had taken his three previous owners here over the years. Gutsy's neighbors, Old Henry and Jackie Darling, then her mother. Twice. Gutsy wondered if Gordo would pull her cold body here someday. The horse had maybe two or three years left. Gutsy doubted she had that much time herself.

"Hope," she said. "Right."

She turned and looked at the silent form that lay wrapped in sheets in the back of the wagon.

"We're here, Mama," she murmured. "We're back."

The grave was on the far side of the graveyard, in cool shadows beneath the sheltering arms of an ancient cottonwood tree. Gutsy had picked that spot because it was quiet and there were some wildflowers growing between the tree's gnarled roots. As she approached, though, it was obvious that the tranquility had been torn apart. As the ground had been torn.

She stopped and studied the scene, frowning.

"What the . . . ?" she breathed, and a heartbeat later the machete was in her fist. Gordo gave a nervous whinny and stamped his feet.

The grave was open, yawning like a black mouth in the dark soil.

But it was wrong.

When someone came back and somehow fought free of their shroud and clawed up through all that dirt, the scene was a mess. The surface would be chopped up, dirt thrown everywhere, long scratch marks to show where the cold fingers had pulled the body out of the grave. Gutsy had seen that many times.

This was not like that.

The dirt was heaped in two piles on either side of the hole. Neat piles. As Gutsy crept close, eyes flicking left and right across the cemetery, she knew that her mother had not done this. She stopped by the edge of the grave, at the end where she had laid her mother's head down, and saw smooth patches on the sides of the hole. Shovel marks.

Someone had dug her mother up.

The soiled white shroud lay across one hump of dirt, and it had clearly been sliced open by a sharp knife. The rope Gutsy had tied around her mother's ankles, knees, wrists, and arms lay like severed snakes, their ends showing clean cuts.

Gutsy hefted her machete, the heavy blade offering only cold comfort. It would protect her—as it had many times—but not against everything. Not against a swarm of the dead. Not against a gang of the living. Not against a gun.

She turned in a slow circle, eyes narrowed as she looked at everything, accepting nothing at face value, making no foolish assumptions. Ready.

Inside her chest, Gutsy's heart felt like it had already been attacked and gravely wounded. She had barely begun to grieve for her mother, had not even taken the first steps forward as an orphan, when her mama had shown up in the yard last night. That had been bad. So bad.

If she thought Wednesday night had been the worst thing she had ever experienced or ever felt, she was wrong. Thursday night was so much worse.

So much.

And now, Friday morning was spinning out of control. A pretty morning here in south Texas had become a storm of ugliness, and it was only going to get worse. She had no doubt at all about that. So much worse.

Someone had dug her mother up, had freed her from the shroud and ropes, and either set her on the road back to town, or brought her there. The former possibility was thin because there were gates and guards, but strange things happened sometimes. The dead, though mostly unable to think, occasionally found ways back into town. That was why so many people thought there was something unnatural going on. Demons, maybe. Or ghosts.

Gutsy didn't believe in those kinds of monsters. Never had. Last night, though, she had come dangerously close to believing in the supernatural. She'd convinced herself that Mama had somehow found her way back home; that, despite being dead, Mama had known where her home was. Gutsy knew it was wishful thinking, but she'd clung to it for as long as she could.

Now, in the harsh light of day, the second possibility seemed far more likely. That someone *alive* had done this.

Normally, having solid, common-sense ground to stand on would have been a comfort; it would have calmed her. Not now. No way.

Who would do such a thing?

Why would anyone do this?

A hot breeze blew through the cemetery, picking up dust and pieces of dried weeds. It blew past her, rasping across her face and then moving on, howling its way into the Broken Lands beyond the wall. Gordo whinnied again.

Nothing else moved.

There was no one else there. It took a long time for Gutsy to accept and believe that, but after five long minutes she lowered her machete. The blade fell from her hand, landing with a dull thud. She squatted down beside the empty grave, wrapped her arms around her head, and began to cry.

Some of the tears were bitter.

Some were as hot as the rage that burned in her chest.

The world was full of monsters. Gutsy knew that as well as anyone left alive. Not all those monsters were the living dead.

That made it all so much worse.

THE MEMORIES CAME TO HER LIKE A SWARM OF monsters. Grabbing at her, holding her down, biting her, making her bleed. Making her scream.

Two days ago . . .

"I'm sorry, Gabriella," whispered her mother. "Please forgive me."
Her voice was so thin, so faint, as if she was already gone.
Gutsy sat on the floor beside her mother's cot. The air was thick with the smell of soaps and disinfectant and aromatic herbs, but the smell of dying was too strong to be pushed aside. Nothing could stop the infection. Nothing. Not alcohol, not what few antibiotics Gutsy and her friends could scavenge. It raged beneath her mother's skin, set fire to her blood, and was taking her away, moment by moment.
"It's okay, Mama," said Gutsy, careful not to squeeze too hard. Her mother's hand was hot, but it was frail and felt like it could break at any second.
Gutsy's words were muffled by the mask she wore, and she hated that the doctor made her wear gloves. No skin-to-skin contact, and even with those precautions Gutsy had to take a

scalding-hot shower afterward. Mama had insisted too, because she had been a nurse at the town hospital. Not before the End, but trained by Max Morton, the town doctor after the dead rose. She'd been part of a team of hastily trained nurses who tried to form a kind of wall between the people in the town and the constant wave of death that always seemed ready to crash down. Death never rested.

In a weird, weird way, all this might have been easier to accept if Mama had been bitten by one of los muertos vivientes.

The living dead.

At least then Gutsy could have understood and even accepted it. Kind of. When los muertos rose and attacked the living, half the population on earth had died from bites.

Not Mama. She was part of the other half. The ones who won their fights, protected their families, survived all the countless hardships, only to be dragged down by something too small to fight, too tiny to kill with a machete or club or any weapon you could hold. A disease. A bacterium.

What was even worse was that it was a disease that had nearly been wiped out in the century before the End, before the world stopped. It had begun creeping back, Gutsy knew, because so many people used antibiotics the wrong way before the End— taking them for viruses even though they didn't work for those kinds of sickness. And taking them only until symptoms went away, which wasn't the same thing as being cured. The antibiotics weakened but did not kill bacteria, and then the bacteria mutated and came back stronger.

Since the End, so many old diseases had come back in new and more terrible forms of smallpox, yellow fever, cholera, measles, so many others. And the one that was killing Mama . . . tuberculosis.

Despite the presence of Dr. Morton and two other nurses—besides Mama—there wasn't much in the way of useful medical equipment, no way to get in front of the disease. The old FEMA laboratory near Laredo was surrounded by tens of thousands of the living dead and had been overrun. The pharmacies in that town and in San Antonio had long since been stripped of drugs. The few antibiotics Dr. Morton gave Mama slowed the sickness for a while but didn't stop it. The disease kept going, attacking with the unthinking, uncaring, brutal relentlessness of los muertos vivientes *but without any of the living dead's vulnerabilities.*

Night after night after night Gutsy sat with her mother, or sat in the next room, listening to endless fits of wet coughing. Listening to labored breathing. Praying to God. Praying to every saint she thought would listen. Sometimes burying her face in her pillow so her screams wouldn't wake poor Mama.

So often her delirious mother would come out of a coughing fit, or a fevered doze, and say the same thing. "I'm sorry."

"Sorry for what, Mama?" asked Gutsy, but she never got an answer. Her mother was too far gone by then and was almost never lucid. Gutsy could feel her drifting out of reach, going away.

As often as she dared, Gutsy put on her gloves and mask and went in to sit, holding that frail hand. Feeling like a little child. Feeling old and used up.

Feeling hopeless.

That was almost the worst part. Gutsy was so good at so many things. She could fix anything, build anything, solve anything. She was a thinker and a fixer.

She could not fix her mother.

She could not think of anything to say. Or do.

All that was left to her was to be there.

To be a witness.

Then there was that moment when Mama's fingers tightened on Gutsy's and she said, "I'm so sorry, Gabriella." And this time, when Gutsy asked why, her mother seemed to swim back enough to answer, but the answer made no real sense. "The rat catchers are coming, mi corazón. *Be careful. If they come for you . . . promise me you'll run away and hide."*

It was so clear, so complete a thought, and yet it made no sense to Gutsy.

"What do you mean, Mama?" she begged.

Mama blinked her eyes, and for a moment they were clear but filled with bad lights, with panic. "Ten cuidado. Mucho cuidado. Los cazadores de ratas vienen."

Take care, take great care . . . the hunters of rats are coming.

The rat catchers.

Gutsy tried to get her mother to explain what, if anything, that meant.

Then the coughing started again. Worse than ever, as if her ruined throat was punishing her for speaking. The fit racked Mama and made her body thrash and arch. Gutsy held on, though.

She held on.

Held on.

Even when Mama settled back down after the fit was over and did not cough again. Or gasp.

Or anything.

It took Gutsy a long time to understand.

Then she pressed the hand to her chest and held it tight, hoping that she was somehow strong enough to hold Mama here, to keep her from going away.

But Mama had already gone.

Gutsy held on and on until the fingers of that fragile hand curled around hers again.

"Mama . . . ?" she whispered.

The answer was a moan.

Not of pain. But of hunger. A deep and bottomless hunger.

It was only then that Gutsy Gomez screamed.

MEMORIES WERE NOT GUTSY'S FRIENDS.

As much as she wanted to remember all the things about her life that made her happy, the wound was too fresh, the hurt too raw. There was no real closure.

Closure. That was a funny word. One she'd used so many times, just like everyone else, when death came to someone else's house. Church sermons, graveside services, the hugs from friends and neighbors, they were supposed to help the grieving get their feet back on solid ground. They were intended to remind people who lost someone that it wasn't *them* who died; it wasn't *their* life that had ended. There was more living to come, and at the end of grief there would be healing, and even joy. Happiness, like all other emotions, lived on a long street, and it only required that a person walk far enough down it to find those old emotions. There would be laughter again, and peace. None of that stuff died. Sure, it had been wounded, but it endured.

Gutsy had always understood that from a distance. She was part of the process for her friends and people on her block, and people in town.

It was different when Mama died. The hurt seemed to live

on both sides of the street, and that street was a dead end.

Over the last two days her best friends, Spider and Alethea, had tried to do for her what Gutsy had done for others: *be* there, be examples of normal life after the grieving time.

The problem was that the memories of Mama being sick were all too new.

Mama coming back as a monster last night tore the scab off any chance of healing. The shovel marks and the knowledge that someone had *done* this rubbed salt in the wounds.

Now all Gutsy had were the memories of who and what she had lost.

And the mysteries.

Take great care . . . the hunters of rats are coming.

The hunters of rats. The rat catchers.

Rat catchers?

Mama had said it with such force, such certainty, that it seemed to lift the words, crazy as they were, out of the well of sickness and delirium.

The Rat Catchers. She made it definite, like it was the name of a gang or group.

"Oh, Mama," cried Gutsy, caving forward and hammering the mound of grave dirt with her fists. "I hate you for leaving me alone."

IT WAS A DOG THAT SNAPPED HER OUT OF IT.

Gutsy heard a single, short bark, and instantly she was back in the present, eyes snapping open, hand snatching up her machete as she rose, pivoting and dropping into a defensive crouch with the blade angled in front of her.

The dog stood twenty feet away. Dusty gray, skinny, its body crisscrossed with scars old and new, with a studded leather collar around its neck and a length of frayed rope trailing a dozen feet behind it. The eyes were the color of wood smoke, and Gutsy could see that it was a coydog—a halfbreed of coyote and German shepherd.

It stared at her with frightened eyes. Its dry tongue licked at cracked lips.

Gutsy used her free hand to wipe the tears away and clear her eyes. Behind her, Gordo struck the ground with his iron hooves and gave a shake of his big head. Gutsy heard the high, plaintive call of a carrion bird, and she glanced up to see a dozen vultures circling the spot where she and the dog stood. Whether they were drawn by the silent form wrapped in sheets in the back of the cart or by the dog, who looked more than three-quarters dead himself, Gutsy couldn't tell. The moment stretched as she and the animal studied each other.

"Not going to hurt you if you don't try and hurt me," said Gutsy.

The coydog looked at her warily. It moved nervously and she saw that it was a male.

"You look like crap, boy," said Gutsy. "You got any bites on you?"

The dog cocked his head sideways as if considering those words. Gutsy saw that there was blood dried black around a deep cut on his neck below the thick leather collar. She tightened her grip on the machete. Dogs couldn't become *los muertos*, as far as she knew, but the world kept changing and it never changed for the better. There were living-dead wild hogs and stories about other kinds of animals that had crossed over and crossed right back again. Father Esteban said he saw a donkey who was dead but walking around. Spider and his foster-sister, Alethea, swore they'd seen a dead puma chase down a deer and kill it. Old Mr. Urrea said that he'd seen a bunch of *los muertos* gibbons in the San Antonio Zoo. The world was broken, so nothing could be taken for granted.

The coydog took a tentative step forward, wobbling and uncertain. He whimpered a little and stood there, trembling. Gutsy kept her weapon ready, even though the pitiful sight of the animal twisted a knife in her heart. The long scars on the dog's back and sides looked like whip marks; and the marks on his face were from dog bites. No doubt about it. Spider used to have an old pit bull who had the same kind of scars, remnants from dogfights. It made Gutsy angry and confused to think that anyone would want to make dogs fight each other, sometimes to the death. Wasn't there already enough pain and death in the world? People, she thought—and not for the first time—were often cruel and stupid.

The coydog took another step, and Gutsy held her ground. The animal was maybe fifty pounds and she was ninety, and a lot of it was lean muscle. She knew how fast she was and how skilled she was with the machete.

"Don't make me do something bad here, dog," she said.

The coydog whined again.

He took one more step . . . and then his eyes rolled high and white and he fell over and lay still.

Gutsy squatted down, the machete across her knees, and waited. Patience and observation were important to her. She hated doing anything without thinking it through. Even mercy shouldn't be allowed to run faster than common sense.

She watched the dog's ribs, saw the steady rise and fall, the slight shudder with each breath. The birds circled lower, their shadows drifting across the graves and across the dog's body. Gutsy didn't care about them, either. Birds wouldn't attack her; and even if they did, she had her weapon.

The dog continued to breathe—badly, with effort—but it was all he did.

Gutsy straightened and walked in a big circle around the animal. Twice. The first time she looked outward, making sure that the dog was not part of some elaborate and nasty trick. The second time she looked at the dog, watching for signs of movement. Dogs didn't play tricks as clever as this, not even smart dogs.

Finally she went to the cart, fetched a bottle of water and her first aid kit, gave Gordo a reassuring pat on the neck, then went back and knelt by the dog. She put on a pair of canvas work gloves before she touched him, though. Then she checked him over. As soon as she touched him, the dusty gray color of his coat changed and she realized that he was actually a dark-haired dog covered in ash. She brushed a lot of it away, revealing a coat that was almost as black as shadows. The coat made him look heavier than he was.

"You don't have a lot of meat on you, do you?" she asked. "*Los muertos* wouldn't get more than a snack off you."

A vulture shadow swept past again and Gutsy glanced up. They were close and hopeful and hungry.

"Not today, *Señor Buitre*," she said. There was no anger in her voice. Vultures were being vultures. This was what they did when they could. "Go find something else. *Vete, vete.*"

The bird didn't go away. He kept circling.

It struck Gutsy that the shadow of the vulture was actually less dark than the coydog, as if he was more of a real shadow. Some of the lines came drifting to her from an old song her mother used to sing. "Sombra." The shadow.

"No," she told herself firmly. "You are not going to name him. No way. That's stupid. Don't even *think* of getting attached."

Gutsy poured a little water on her gloved fingers and touched them to the dog's mouth, moistening the lips and the lolling tongue. The animal twitched and, after a few moments, took a weak lick. If the coydog minded the roughness of the gloves, he didn't seem to want to complain. Gutsy dribbled more water and the dog licked and licked. His eyes opened and looked at her with a mixture of fear, need, and a pathetic desperation.

"It's okay," she said. "It's all okay, Sombra."

Then she heard her own words as if they were an echo. *Sombra*. She winced. But despite her firm decision to the contrary, Sombra he became.

After a little more water she capped the bottle and set it aside, then continued her examination of the coydog's injuries. There were a lot of them, and she wasn't positive the animal had much life left in him. Maybe all he needed was a little kindness before death came whispering. Gutsy could understand that.

What mattered most, though, was the fact that none of the many injuries seemed to be from human bites or boar bites. There was no evident fever, either. Sombra was hurt, but none of his wounds were infected. Which meant *he* wasn't infected.

"Well," she said, "that's something, anyway."

The leather collar was buckled on, but the fittings were rusty and it took Gutsy a few minutes to unfasten it. Removing it revealed a vicious red band of hairless skin, and it sickened her to realize that the dog had probably worn that collar all its life. She studied it, noting the workmanship to determine whether it was from before the End or something made in the after times.

"After," she murmured, talking to herself as she often did. "Good leatherwork, though." It was two inches wide, a quarter-inch thick, and ringed by sharp studs that had been painted flat black. There was a name burned into the band between two studs. KILLER.

She gave a dismissive snort. Stupid name. The kind of unimaginative name an actual killer would hang on a dog forced to fight for its life against other dogs, and she was pretty sure that's what had happened. She thought of a few names she'd like to burn into a leather collar and cinch around the neck of whoever used to own this dog. None of them were nice names. Some of them might have gotten her slapped by . . .

Mama.

And just that fast it was all back.

The reason Gutsy was here. The grief, the bottomless pain. She closed her eyes and clenched the collar in two strong brown fists. She heard a sound and whirled to see a vulture come fluttering down to land on the wooden side of her work cart.

"No!" cried Gutsy, and without thinking about it flung the collar at the bird. She had a good arm, and both heartbreak and anger put velocity into the throw. The collar struck the bird and it squawked in pain and alarm and fled back to the sky. Gutsy ran to the cart and peered in, dreading what she might find; but the sheets were undamaged. The bird hadn't had time to peck through.

The figure inside the shroud twitched and struggled and moaned.

Mama.

Gutsy rested her forehead against the cart and tried not to cry again. She pounded the side of her fist against the wood slats. Once, twice. Again. The pain steadied her. Slowly, but it steadied her.

She pushed off from the cart and looked down at the collar, which lay almost at her feet. Whoever had made it knew what they were doing. For all that, it disgusted her. She studied the rope. It had not been cut. The end was frayed and gnarled, and she figured the dog had chewed through it. For reasons she did not understand at the time, Gutsy picked it up and tossed it into the back of the wagon. Then she turned to see Sombra struggling to get up.

She stood and watched it, offering no help at the moment.

The coydog took a shaky step toward her, paused, and gave a few small, weak, hopeful wags of its tail.

"Um, no," said Gutsy firmly, "don't even try. I'll give you some water and something to eat, but that's it. We're not doing this."

The dog continued to wag his tail.

"Not a chance," she insisted. "No way. Uh-uh."

THE DOG SAT IN THE SHADE OF THE COTTONWOOD, chewing on strips of beef jerky and taking sloppy drinks from water poured into a tin cup.

Sombra watched as Gutsy slid her mother from the cart and dragged her clumsily her across the ground to the grave, swung her wrapped legs over the edge, jumped down, and pulled the struggling, thrashing body down into the hole. The dog watched with eyes that blinked with its own pain every time it moved. The gray eyes watched as Gutsy climbed out of the grave, got a shovel from the cart, and spent two hours filling it all in and tamping it down. The coydog watched as Gutsy gathered wildflowers, tied them into a bunch with a piece of twine, and placed them on the grave. She straightened the heavy wooden cross and touched the name LUISA GOMEZ, which she had carved across it with loving care. The coydog sat in silent vigil as Gutsy sat cross-legged on the ground, dirty face in her blistered hands, and wept as if the world was cracking apart.

It was a long afternoon.

GUTSY WAS LESS THAN A HUNDRED YARDS AWAY
from the cemetery when she had an idea.

She hopped down and went around to the side of the
wagon, where she had racks for long tools and a locked chest
of supplies. Gutsy had remodeled the cart herself, just as
she'd done throughout the house where she and Mama lived.
Tools of all kinds, ready at hand; and lots of hacks—tricks
that solved everyday problems. She reached under the side of
the cart, located the lever that opened a small compartment,
and removed a key, used it to unlock the chest, and replaced
it. It was her habit to put her tools away in their proper places
so they were always where she needed to find them again.

The chest held many useful items, including several large
spools of fishing line. She pocketed one spool, took a heavy-
duty office stapler, and closed the chest. She emptied a pouch
of some useful road trash she'd collected—plastic cups, a broken flashlight, and so on—then slung the empty pouch over
her shoulder.

She paused for a while, looking around, filing details away
in her mind. There were only two entrances to the place that
could accommodate a cart. The main gate faced southwest

toward what was left of Laredo, and beyond that to the Rio Grande and Mexico. The rear gate looked northeast, toward San Antonio. *Los muertos* owned both cities. The cemetery was twenty miles from the outskirts of Laredo and more than one hundred fifty from San Antonio.

Gutsy figured that whoever had dug up Mama would have used a cart or wagon to carry her back to town. The ground on the road and at the entrances was hardpan that took no impressions from hoof or wheel. If someone returned tonight, Gutsy wanted to know from which direction they came. The rear entrance was framed by sawed-off telephone poles and a high crossbar, which also had the name HOPE painted on it. Gutsy unspooled some of the fishing line and stapled the end to one side of the post at about six inches from the ground, then strung it across and fastened the other end. The line was thin and barely noticeable in daylight, so it would be invisible at night. Then she went to one of the more recent graves and filled the pouch with loose dirt from the small mound left over after the body had been interred. She spread this loosely across the road on both sides of the fishing line. Even if the wind blew some away, there would be enough left to take a print. She returned to the main gate and repeated the process.

She trudged back to the cart, put the stapler and spool into the chest and locked it, shook the last bits of dirt from the pouch, and replaced the debris she'd collected. Gordo and the dog watched her with curious, patient eyes. She climbed up onto the seat and Gordo began walking without being told. The coydog jumped up onto the wagon and stood on the seat, his face inches from hers. He did not growl or whine or make any sound at all, but he stood there as if waiting for her to say something.

"I can't have a dog," said Gutsy. "I'm sorry."

Sombra wagged his tail, and then he lay down at her feet and went straight to sleep. Or at least pretended to.

"I can't have a dog," repeated Gutsy. Sombra began to snore.

Gutsy sighed, and the three of them left the cemetery behind. The rocking of the wagon made the coydog sway back and forth, and on each pass his fur brushed against Gutsy's leg. Every now and then he shivered as if caught in a dream of pain. A few times he whimpered softly and Gutsy reached down to pet him, though it was hard to find places to touch Sombra where it wouldn't hurt. His injuries were dreadful.

The dog woke once when the wagon wheels rumbled through a runoff wash. Recent rain had smeared the wash with mud, which had then dried hard beneath the Texas sun. When she'd come out this way from town, Gutsy had not paid much attention to the ground, but now she slowed to look at it. There were footprints in the damp earth. Human prints: all sizes, male and female, in shoes and bare feet. Not a few random prints like she often saw to mark where one of *los muertos* had passed. No, there were hundreds of sets of prints, overlapping one another in a chaotic pattern. Clearly a large number of people had passed this way, but the markings were confusing. First, why on earth would so many people go walking through muck like this? The rain had stopped in the middle of the night two days ago, which meant these marks were made right after that. Why would a crowd of people be walking through the desert at night or in the early morning?

If, she thought, *they were people.* Gutsy got down and looked at the marks more closely, and found something else. On the fringes of the mass of prints were others. Boot prints. The spacing and angles told her that the people who'd left those were not staggering or shambling, but walking with a deliberate, controlled pace. Always to the outside of the main body. Strange.

The footprints faded out completely as they left the muddy bottom of the wash and went up onto higher, firmer ground.

Very strange. Something about it niggled at her, making her feel uneasy, though she couldn't quite understand why. She climbed back onto the wagon and they moved on. Other thoughts pulled her attention away, and after a few miles she forgot about the prints.

Instead Gutsy thought about who would have done something as intensely horrible and mean-spirited as digging up her mother. A few names occurred to her, but it seemed too weird, too extreme even for some of the jerks in town. So . . . what was the point?

That speculation gave a few violent shoves in the direction of the memories of the last two nights. Gutsy was practical and strong, but she did not want to relive those memories. Not now and maybe not ever. No way.

No way in the world.

And yet that was what she thought about all the way home.

THE WAGON RUMBLED THROUGH SEVERAL ABANDONED settlements—Desert Rose, Cactus Flats, and Shelter, which was short for Field Shelter Station Eighteen. Nothing moved there but wind and dust and the slow shadows that chased the sun.

There were forty other makeshift camps Gutsy knew about scattered around out here, and the ruins of abandoned towns and cities, too. Many of these camps had been thrown together hastily during the crisis, overpopulated and under-supplied, and eventually either overrun by the dead or consumed by disease from within. There were a few other camps along the Rio Grande that were still holding on, but none as big as New Alamo.

Lately more and more of the settlements were being overrun by bigger and bigger swarms of the dead. There were also the ravagers—gangs of infected, savage men and women who were slowly becoming living dead but who retained enough of their intelligence to use weapons and organize attacks. Some people in town believed those ravagers could control the mindless dead.

The Broken Lands were broken indeed.

Some people even claimed there was a fully operational military base hidden underground, but Gutsy wasn't sure if she believed that. Why would they hide? Maybe there were reasons before the End, back when things like "politics," "war," and "national security" mattered, but why now? Why hide when people were in short supply and survival depended on working together, sharing the dwindling resources? It made no sense. Besides, Gutsy spent a lot of time out in the Broken Lands, and she'd never found a single trace of a military base. Nothing except dozens of abandoned Abrams tanks, rusting Bradley fighting vehicles, burned-out army Humvees, and a lot of skeletons. No, she concluded, the army and all the other branches of the military had died along with 99 percent of the people living in America.

That was sad for a lot of reasons. Partly because it was proof that mankind, for all its technology, had managed to lose a war against an enemy that had no weapons, no organization, no strategies. All the dead had were numbers and the fact that they terrified everyone. They weren't aliens from another planet or even enemies from a foreign land. *Los muertos* were us. That was the truth everyone had to face. The monsters those soldiers had to fight were neighbors, friends, civilians, fellow soldiers. They were anyone who died, no matter how they died. Gutsy had heard so many stories about soldiers who simply stopped being able to pull their triggers because they recognized the faces of the creatures coming to kill them.

Before this week, Gutsy could sympathize. Now, after Mama, she could empathize. She could *feel* what those soldiers had felt. She could understand how the war was lost.

She was still four miles from New Alamo when Sombra suddenly sat up and stared into the distance to the left of the road. He gave a low growl, and the hair stood up like a brush all along his spine.

"Whoa," said Gutsy, and Gordo slowed to a stop. To the dog she said, "What do you see, boy?"

The approach road to New Alamo was lined with thousands of dead cars, trucks, and RVs that had been pushed into place by squads of survivors. The entire town was protected by walls of cars. Two or three vehicles deep, with the vehicles pulled onto their sides and lashed together, with these metal walls braced by berms of hard-packed dirt. The work had taken two full years and had been brutal and backbreaking, but it kept a lot of roamers from wandering in. When rare *los muertos* somehow found their way into the corridor, those corridors funneled them toward the main gates, where armed guards were waiting.

That was the town, though, and it was miles away.

Out here in the Broken Lands, the road was wide open, with countless ruined houses and businesses in various stages of dilapidation. Most of the buildings were blackened husks, the dead leavings of fires that had swept unchecked once *los muertos vivientes* rose and all the infrastructure—police, fire departments, ambulances, and military—fell. Even though the biggest fires had burned out before Gutsy was even born, there always seemed to be a pall of dust and ash clinging like an army of ghosts. Visibility was bad at the best of times.

Slow seconds passed while she saw nothing but ruin. Everything outside New Alamo was what everyone called the Broken Lands, and the landscape earned its name. She knew that a few miles farther east was a kind of graveyard left behind from where a massive military battle had taken place. The skeletons of tens of thousands of people lay scattered in the withered grass. None of those bones belonged to the soldiers, Gutsy knew, because when they had lost the fight and died, there was no one to end their second lives. They'd all wandered off to continue their war, fighting on the wrong side forever.

So, she saw nothing.

Until she saw something.

It was a figure moving slowly through the ruined streets. Heaps of blackened debris hid it most of the time, but Sombra had heard it somehow. His low growl held anger and fear. *Smart dog,* she thought. The figure was moving in the direction of the road. From that distance it was hard to tell which *kind* of living dead it was. Monsters, as she and everyone else in her town knew, came in a lot of terrifying varieties. Slow ones and fast ones. Dumb ones and smart ones. Ones that spread their diseases through bites; others that made people sick just by being close. The ones that looked like corpses and the ones who were still mostly alive. And old Mr. Ford in town said that there were even worse mutations the farther east or north you went, including a terrifying version of the disease that slowly turned a living person into a living dead one with all of that person's memories and even their ability to speak intact until the very end. That, Gutsy thought, would be the worst. To *know* you were becoming a monster, to feel the hunger for human flesh awaken inside you, to become gradually more dead and less alive.

No one knew how the End had started, but since there

were new kinds of *los muertos* showing up all the time, whatever it was, was still happening.

She studied the shambling form and after a few moments murmured, "It's a shambler, I think."

Sombra looked at her, head cocked to one side as if asking, *What?*

"Slow and stupid," she told him.

A moment later she saw another one.

Then a third. A fourth.

"Crap," she breathed. Even if they were all shamblers, there were too many of them. If there were four that she could see, there could be a dozen she couldn't. On foot, she could have slipped past them, staying upwind so *los muertos* could not smell her, making maximum use of cover. The shamblers were easy to fool, and Gutsy had a hundred ways to do it. However, with the cart, the horse, and the coydog, Gutsy's options were limited: go back or wait. Attacking that many dead was only an option if she wanted to be lunch. Good as she was with the machete, fighting a pack of them—even shamblers—was a no-win situation because she would have to fight defensively to keep them away from the animals.

She took out her binoculars, and after making sure she was not in an angle that would let sunlight reflect off the lenses, she studied the shambling dead. There were many more of them now, though there was nothing particularly remarkable about any she saw. Their clothes made statements about who they had been when they died. A man dressed in greasy jeans, a woman wearing a waitress uniform, kids dressed for school, farmers in coveralls. Some were whole, others had clearly been gnawed on, probably while they were dying. Missing hands, missing flesh. One of them had a piece of rebar thrust through his chest. Two of them had visible bullet holes in their heads, but the shots clearly hadn't destroyed the motor cortex or brain stem. Shooting the brain wasn't enough, which was why there were so many wild stories about people who believed the common myth that all you needed was a head shot—as if every part of the brain was important to undead survival. It wasn't. Of course it wasn't. Only the motor cortex and the brain stem mattered, and to hit those you needed to know where they were and then be a really good shot. Most people had no idea and not enough skill. Gutsy, however, made sure she did. It was who she was, and it reflected her view of the world: that every problem required its own solution. Gutsy knew that firsthand.

Then she saw something that made her heart leap into her throat.

A man walked out of the shadows. She could see him clearly with the binoculars. He wasn't one of the living dead. His skin was tan, his long hair was tied back in a ponytail. The man's clothes were a mismatch of denim and leather, but they were not the same kind of filthy rags the shamblers wore. Nor were they like the leather jackets worn by most of the people who went out into the Broken Lands—leather being virtually bite-proof—because the sleeves had been cut off this man's jacket, revealing arms so muscular they looked deformed. His biceps and shoulders were covered with tattoos of laughing devils, women with absurdly large breasts, and snarling dogs. Sure, some of the dead had old tattoos, but none of them carried weapons, and this man had a rifle. He walked with the long barrel laid back on one brawny shoulder.

He looked alive. And yet he walked alongside the dead—among them—and they did not attack him. Once in a while one would make a halfhearted attempt to touch him—maybe to grab, but without intensity—and the man would simply push the hand away.

That made no sense to Gutsy, and things that didn't make sense offended her. The world, even broken like this, had what one of her teachers called an interior logic. Everything made sense. Anything that appeared not to make sense meant that the observer lacked sufficient information to understand its nature or process.

That was how Gutsy operated. Sense and order, patterns and details, observation and analysis.

This did not fit what she knew about *los muertos*.

However, what she saw did fit with something else. She remembered the boot prints made by a few men walking on either side of the mass of shamblers who'd trampled the mud at the bottom of the wash. Had they been like this man? Walking *with* the dead, maybe guiding them? Or . . . herding them?

It was a very scary thought. Inexplicable, too, though she knew any explanation she might ever discover would be a bad one.

She wondered if this was one of the ravagers. They were capable of cruelty, unlike the walking dead, who were dangerous but incapable of malice. All *los muertos* wanted was to feed. They did not and could not hate. They meant no more harm than the murderous winds of a late-summer hurricane. The ravagers often traveled in what the townsfolk called wolf packs. The fact that they were monsters who could still think made them so much more dangerous.

Was that why these living dead did not attack this ravager? Were those halfhearted attempts to grab him a reflex, or a reaction to that part of him that was still human?

Gutsy didn't know, but it did seem to make the illogical parts line up into some kind of order. Of course, that in turn opened up new questions. Why was a wolf-pack ravager traveling with a bunch of shamblers? Where were they going?

Worse still, what would happen if he saw her?

Gutsy knew the answer to that last question, but she did not dare look too closely at it.

FEAR WAS LIKE A SCORPION CRAWLING UP HER BACK.

Gutsy wanted to turn the wagon around, to get out of there, but she was afraid to move. Going back to the cemetery would be not only noisy, but also a waste of time. The sun would start going down in a few hours, and by then the longer shadows of twilight would hide any wandering dead.

So she waited. Nervous, bathed in cold sweat that seemed to boil off beneath the scorching sun.

Watching.

Gutsy's hiding place was behind an old billboard advertising coast-to-coast cell phone coverage. She had only a vague idea of what that meant. One of the things that belonged to the world that existed before the one in which she lived.

There was some cool, dark grass and Gordo, nervous as he was, never passed up an opportunity to eat. Gutsy hoped he was the only creature around who was going to be fed right then.

She got down, machete in hand, and crept to a corner of the big sign. It stood on a lattice of metal poles and there had once been an open space below, but it was choked with wild growth and provided excellent cover. Some of the flowers and plants growing wild out here were unknown and unnamed. Mutations, even among plants and animals.

The rise of the dead did more than pervert the nature of human life. There was more to it. For most of the people she knew, the collapse of society meant the end of police and military, emergency services, fire departments, and hospitals. But Mr. Ford and Mr. Urrea said that the End also meant the end of what they called "administrative oversight," which meant that no one was tending to nuclear power plants, factories that made chemicals, oil wells, and things like that.

"The nuclear plants didn't melt down," explained Mr. Urrea one day in school. He and Mr. Ford were teachers, and the best ones in town. They talked *to* the students, not down *at* them. That mattered to Gutsy as much as what they had to say. "However, the sites where they stored spent nuclear fuel rods and radioactive heavy water were no longer being tended to. And there was fallout from every nation on earth trying to stop the living dead with nuclear bombs. Power plants were blown apart, dams destroyed, factories ripped open, and fallout . . . all that fallout . . . drifting on the winds."

"Chemical storage tanks, tanker trucks, and trains transporting dangerous chemicals were left to rust," said Mr. Ford. "Which meant that they were vulnerable to metal fatigue, rust damage, and—as we've all found out—damage from hurricanes that slammed into the coast from the Gulf of Mexico. Those chemicals have to go somewhere. They don't just wash away. They soak into the ground and pollute the groundwater."

The storms were one of the worst parts of living down here in south Texas. In the years before the End, Gutsy had learned, storms had gotten worse and worse, the result of so many factories and automobiles pumping exhaust into the atmosphere. Even when the infrastructure was intact, the storms often battered everywhere they touched, causing flooding, destroying homes, taking lives.

"After the End," said Mr. Ford, "the weather didn't just reverse itself and calm down. The water temperature and salinity changed, and the storms continued. Storm surges brought seawater inland to kill farmable land, and it dragged polluted water from cisterns and sewers, mixing it into a toxic soup."

Gutsy knew the rest of the story. All that contamination, radiation, and pollution mingled together and drove Mother Nature to madness. That was how Mama had once described it, and the image stuck in Gutsy's mind. Mother Nature gone mad.

Mutations were everywhere. There was a new species of malformed cactus in the desert from which sprouted perfect yellow roses. There was grass that turned bright orange on rainy days. Strawberry plants that had mutated into towering trees, and a kind of milkweed whose sap was the color of fresh blood. Gutsy had once come upon a creeper vine that could detach itself and move like an octopus across the ground. And the scavengers who went deeper into the Broken Lands than she did said there were brand-new species of plants and flowers no one had put a name to yet.

Some of the birds had gone strange too, especially the crows, each generation of which had nearly doubled in size so that some were as big as eagles. When they cried, it sounded like someone screaming in pain. Flocks of those crows attacked cattle and could bring down a good-size calf and strip it to bones in half an hour. And yet there was a speckled mutant species of mountain lion that ate only flowers and made sounds like a mourning dove.

Strange. Dreamlike in its way; often nightmarish, sometimes quite beautiful. Always unsettling.

The location for New Alamo was picked because Mr. Urrea and Mr. Ford—who had emerged as leaders in the early days following the End—liked the isolated location, the fact that it already had a sturdy fence around it and plenty of housing. It was also far away from the worst disaster areas and had the least amount of visible pollution.

"Least amount," though, wasn't the same as "none."

The diseases in town proved that. The rates of cancer among refugees proved it. The fact that some crops grew into strangeness, yielding plants that caused new kinds of sickness.

And the living dead, in all their terrifying variety.

The breeze blew toward her, carrying the scent of bad meat from the shamblers. Had it been blowing the other way, *los muertos* would have smelled *her*.

Sombra followed Gutsy and crouched beside her, teeth bared in a silent growl.

"It's okay," she said quietly. "They can't see us."

Surprisingly, the coydog stopped snarling and looked up at her, searching her face. She smiled and touched his shoulder. Not a pat, exactly. A communication of some kind. Her instincts told her that small actions were how to deal with this battered, frightened, confused animal.

Time moved even slower than the shamblers. The ravager—

if that's what he was—stood for a while watching the dead file past, and every now and then one would start heading in the wrong direction and the man would shove it back into line with the others. The shamblers did not seem to mind the roughness and occasional kicks the man used. They did not care about anything, Gutsy knew, except feeding.

Of all the species of living dead, the shamblers were by far the most common. Ninety-nine out of every hundred were that kind. In towns like San Antonio to the northeast, it was said to be a different mix, more of the wilder mutations and smarter dead. However, this close to Laredo, right on the border, nearly all *los muertos* were shamblers.

They scared her enough, though.

An insect buzzed past her, circled and flew back, landing on the stem of a six-headed mutant daisy. It was a bee. Kind of. Instead of two bulbous eyes, its head was covered with dozens of smaller eyes. Most of those eyes were milky and sightless, and it groped its way toward the flowers with stunted forelegs. If it was aware of Gutsy and Sombra, it gave no notice. It moved with trembling slowness as if uncertain where to go despite the flowers above it.

Gutsy held out a finger and the bee crawled onto it as if it were part of the stem. She lifted her hand very slowly and held it close to the biggest of the flowers. The bee's wings fluttered and it immediately began feeding on nectar and pollen. It made Gutsy smile because despite mutation and everything, the bee was still essentially a bee, and it went about its work as bees had for millions of years. They adapted and survived. Gutsy appreciated that.

One of the living dead had the distinctive swollen belly of

a late-term pregnancy. That was a kind of horror Gutsy had heard about but never seen before. Dead mother, dead baby, wandering hungry forever.

The world was indeed insane. The shambling dead people continued to cross the road. It took nearly an hour before she was sure they were all gone, and she was very glad she'd waited. There had been twenty-seven of them, including five children.

Gutsy watched them go, and her heart did not slow to a normal pace until they had dwindled to nothing in the distance. Sombra kept vigil too, and when neither of them could see anything moving, the coydog simply lay down again. She sat for a few seconds longer, considering her new friend. He had saved her from a difficult situation.

The fact that she had found him at her mother's grave seemed somehow significant. She reached down to pet the dog, but before she did, Gutsy crossed herself and said, "*Gracias*, Mama."

Then she drove home.

A TALL, SKINNY BOY WITH DARK BROWN SKIN, SHORT black hair, and mint-green eyes stood in the middle of the street, watching her approach. He wore scruffy jeans, ancient sneakers, and a long-sleeved cotton shirt that had been hand-stitched by one of the ladies at the orphanage. There were flowers embroidered across the front and down the sleeves, and elaborate spiderwebs had been stitched between the blossoms. A single black spider dangled from a slender thread that slipped out from beneath the fold of the left front collar. His shirt was buttoned at the cuffs and all the way to the throat.

"Hey, Gutsy," he called.

"Hey, Spider," she called back.

There was a spider of one kind or another embroidered or hand-drawn on every shirt he owned. He would have gotten one tattooed on his cheek, but none of the tattoo artists in town would do it. Not until he was at least sixteen, and that was eleven months away.

Gordo angled in toward the water trough outside the big Quonset hut that had been converted to a stable and plunged his head in, gulping and splashing noisily. The sound made

Sombra stand up, and Spider arched an eyebrow as he studied the scarred, battered coydog.

"Picking up roadkill now?" he drawled.

"Something like that," said Gutsy, climbing down. She stretched so hard her joints popped. Her friend held out a canteen and she drank. As she handed it back, she caught Spider searching her eyes with his.

"Here's the world's stupidest question," he said quietly, "but how are you?"

Gutsy wiped her mouth and looked over her shoulder at the dusty road behind her. "It's been a day, y'know?"

"Wish you'd let me come with you," said Spider.

She shook her head.

Spider sighed and helped her unbuckle and unbridle Gordo. They pulled the cart into the stable, allowing Gordo to follow at his own pace. The Quonset hut was vast and there were more than enough stalls for everyone. The Gomez stall was a double because they had a cart, and because the owner of the adjoining one had been killed by the dead while on a scavenging run. As he had no relatives, there was no objection when Gutsy knocked down the thin barrier wall and expanded her own. She'd built shelves and cabinets to accommodate all her gear, and cut several ventilation holes in the walls. People were so impressed by her design and skills that she earned food credits to revamp a dozen others.

Spider took a pair of brushes from the tack wall, tossed one to her, and they began to tend to the horse, each to a side, using gentle circular motions with the curry combs. Dust and grit fell away and Gordo tossed his head, enjoying the attention there in the coolness of the barn. Then Gutsy took a hard brush and ran it from nose to tail, following the grain of the thick hair, while Spider used a pick to remove a few small stones from Gordo's hooves. Sombra sat in the cool shade and watched.

They did not speak, and Gutsy knew that Spider was allowing her some space. She appreciated it. Spider and Alethea were her best friends, and they'd both helped bury her mother the first time.

There were different rituals in town for dealing with family members who reanimated. Some used metal spikes to sever the brain stem. Others went for the more gruesome decapitation. The Catholics in town, though, restrained their dead, binding them with ropes blessed by Father Esteban, and then wrapped the thrashing bodies in white sheets on which prayers had been written. It was called "shrouding," and the people who followed the tradition believed that it was both a mercy and a religious requirement. Father Esteban preached that this process of slow decay inside the buried shroud was a kind of penance for whatever sins that person had committed in life. It was a new interpretation of purgatory that would ultimately allow the spirit, now cleansed of all sins, to ascend to heaven.

Gutsy was not as devout a Catholic as Mama had been, but this was what her mother had wanted. The process was horrible, though.

Beyond horrible.

It was probably insane, too. Maybe even cruel. People in New Alamo had been arguing about that ever since the End. Gutsy wasn't sure if she believed in purgatory. She believed in hell, though. Absolutely. That was where she lived. She wasn't the only person in town who shared her belief, that the living were not the lucky ones but rather those who, for whatever reason, had been condemned to serve out their sentences in a hell here on earth. When her own time came, Gutsy wanted a spike and then cremation. Wasn't that in the Bible too? Ashes to ashes, dust to dust?

But Mama had wanted the shroud and the grave, so that was what Gutsy did. Her friends proved how much they loved her by helping. Gutsy loved them for it, but somehow it didn't really help. It made a bad night worse, because now other people would remember the way Mama's body twisted and fought even when the first shovelfuls of dirt fell over her.

And it was Spider who had put it into the right words as the three of them stood panting beside the grave.

"The world is nuts," he said. "This proves it."

GUTSY FILLED GORDO'S MANGER WITH FRESH HAY, beet pulp, and grain, then stood for a moment gently stroking the horse's neck as he ate.

"Tell me about the dog," said Spider, standing with his fists on his lean hips, bony elbows stuck out at right angles. He was ten inches taller than Gutsy and looked like a stick bug than a spider.

Gutsy gave him an abbreviated version but mentioned the collar, the vultures, and how Sombra had spotted the living dead long before she or Gordo were aware of them.

"Nice," said Spider. He knelt and held out a hand. Sombra flinched away. "I won't hurt you. . . ."

Sombra looked at the hand, then at Spider's face, then up to Gutsy, but he didn't come closer. He began to tremble.

"God, he's scared out of his mind," said Spider.

"It's okay," said Gutsy.

Nothing. It seemed that now they were out of the desert and out of danger, the coydog's natural wariness was taking hold. That, and whatever emotional damage he'd sustained from what he'd been through.

"He wants to run," observed Spider. "Poor thing."

Gutsy thought about it, went to her cart and got more strips of jerky, came back, crossed her legs, and sat down on the stable floor, indicating for her friend to do the same. Sombra watched all this with frightened eyes, clearly caught between his instinct to flee and his need to stay near people.

"Whoever hurt him like that . . . ," began Spider, but left the rest unsaid. His hands were balled into fists.

"I know," agreed Gutsy. "Double that."

"What do you think happened to him?"

"Dogfights," said Gutsy.

Spider made a rude noise. Dogfights were illegal in town, but there was a traveling dogfight show that set up beyond the town limits every spring. Some of the people in town went to it. Gutsy knew which ones did and she hated them all. She and her friends had no mercy or compassion when it came to people like that. This was summer, though, so it wasn't likely to be the Cerberus Circus, as the show was called, named for the three-headed dog that guarded the entrance to hell in Greek mythology.

She tore off a piece of jerky and tossed it to Sombra, who jerked backward from it. He stood with all his muscles locked, eyes wild.

"Wow," said Spider.

They sat still for nearly four minutes before Sombra relaxed enough to take a single hesitant step forward, bushy tail tucked between his legs. He lowered his head and almost took a sniff at the jerky. Stopped, withdrew. Waited. Tried again. On the fourth try he gave the jerky a lightning-fast lick. Then he studied it. Maybe it was then that the memories of eating it in the cemetery came back and overrode his fear.

When he leaned out again, he snapped the jerky up, retreated again, and chewed it.

When Gutsy threw the next piece, there was only a small flinch before Sombra ate it.

After that he waited for each new piece. She never threw hard, of course. Then she handed the jerky to Spider. His first piece lay untouched on the stable floor for two whole minutes, during which Sombra eyed him with equal parts naked hostility and interest.

Sombra ate the jerky.

They fed him like that for almost ten minutes. Tossing small pieces, because Gutsy wanted to overcome the coydog's fear and build trust as much as she wanted to feed him.

Gutsy and Spider sat on overturned wooden buckets, not saying much, watching the dog. People walked past the open door of the barn. A few stopped to offer belated sympathies to Gutsy; others merely nodded. When a slender girl with long, gleaming black hair and cutoff jeans walked past, Gutsy tried not to look. Or be *seen* to look; but the girl gave her a brief glance as she passed. Was there a smile? Or a hint of a smile? Or was that wishful thinking?

Once the girl had walked on out of sight, Gutsy relaxed, but then heard a soft chuckle and turned to glare at Spider. "What's so funny?"

Spider nodded, showed a lot of teeth. "So . . . Alice Chung, huh?"

"Shut up."

"Does she know?"

"I said shut up."

"You ever tell her how you feel?"

"Do I have to punch you?"

Spider kept grinning. "Last week it was Corey Hale. I think he *does* know. Not so sure Alice does. Not so sure she'd be into it."

"Into what? I haven't said anything about anything to anyone."

"Yeah, yeah, Gutsy the Pure. I get it. But you're going to have to pick a side. Guys or girls."

Gutsy shrugged. "Why do I have to pick one or the other?"

Spider thought about that, picked up a couple of the tiny pebbles he'd pried from Gordo's hooves, and tossed them out into the street. He made no further comment.

That was fine with Gutsy. She was fifteen, and while she understood the whole puberty process and the biochemical imperative to procreate, blah blah blah, she preferred to put thoughts of romance and sex aside for now. And that worked most of the time. There were dreams, of course; just as there were some of her classmates—Alice Chung, for example, and Corey Hale—who were sometimes incredible distractions. Not that either of them knew it, of course. Not that Gutsy herself obsessed on them. Much. There were more important things to focus on.

After a few minutes of silent stillness inside the barn, Sombra got up, went outside to the trough, drank, and came back inside. He lay down with his head between his paws and watched them with his smoky eyes.

"About last night," Spider began. "It was really close. If the town guards found out that your mom came back, they'd have—"

"I know," she said tightly. "It's the law. If someone comes

back like that, they have to use a sp-spike." She tripped over the word.

Luckily—if luck was even a word that applied—no one but Gutsy and her friends knew that Mama had returned. Spider and Alethea had been over, sitting with her through the hours of emptiness in the Gomez house. When the two of them kissed her good night, and went outside, they'd all seen the nightmare figure in the front yard. It took all three of them to wrestle Mama to the ground, gag her, drag her inside, and tie her up again. And put a new shroud around her.

It was awful. As a thing to have to do, and as a memory that persisted with brutal clarity.

Gutsy knew Spider was reliving it too. He didn't have any blood relations, and Mama had loved Gutsy's friends, as they loved her.

Silence owned them both for a while. It was broken only by the slow, rhythmic crunching of horse teeth on hay.

"It's my fault," said Spider.

Gutsy glanced at him. "What? What's your fault?"

"Your mom," he said in a small voice. "I've been thinking about it all day. I think it's my fault. When we were getting her ready, you know? Doing her shroud and all. I was never good at knots. I—"

"No," said Gutsy firmly.

"Really, I think—"

"Listen, it's not your fault and it's not my fault. Someone dug her up," she said, and it stopped Spider's words as surely as if she'd slapped him. His mouth worked but no words came out. Gutsy nodded. "I saw the shovel marks." She described what she'd found at the cemetery. Spider gaped at her.

"That's insane. Who would do that? I mean . . . *why*?"

The heat of rage that had burned in Gutsy all day had changed. It did not go out but was instead replaced by a coldness that ran so deep it vanished into blackness.

"That," she said, "is what I'm going to find out."

As she said that, her fingers gripped the handle of her machete. Spider swallowed hard, but Sombra gave a single, sharp *whuff*. In that moment, he looked less like either a coyote or dog and more like a wolf.

PART TWO

RECLAMATION, CALIFORNIA
ONE WEEK EARLIER . . .

THE VIEW FROM
THE MOUNTAINS

Sweet is the memory of distant friends!
Like the mellow rays of the departing sun,
it falls tenderly, yet sadly, on the heart.

—WASHINGTON IRVING

THE ONLY THING ABOUT BEING SIXTEEN THAT FELT different to Benny Imura was that fewer people—living or dead—tried to kill him. He put that in the win category.

He sat in the shadow of a massive black oak with his best friend, Lou Chong. They both had bottles of root beer, and the remains of a big lunch were scattered around them like the leavings of hungry wolves. Chong held up a finger and Benny, attentive, listened to a very long, complicated, and deeply noxious belch. Benny nodded approval. They said nothing for a long time.

The tree stood in a corner of one of the newer fields in the town of Reclamation. The tree was nice, the town itself was nice, the name of the town was stupid. Benny and Chong agreed on that, as did pretty much everyone they knew. Sure, sure, it had all sorts of meaning because the people who lived here, in fact, had reclaimed all this land from what had once been called the Rot and Ruin. Now, instead of the cramped old town of Mountainside—which had been burned down after a war with the Reaper army— with its population of eight thousand people, the new town was home to twice that many, and more came in all the time. There was room for all the newcomers, too, and that had been part of the plan, to not only reclaim the land, but reclaim the concept of civilization.

Benny was cool with the concept. He'd fought very hard to make that a possibility. He'd sacrificed a lot, and Chong had sacrificed more. All his friends had.

But the name was still stupid.

"How about Kingstown?" suggested Chong, coming back to the topic they had been discussing off and on since breakfast.

"Why?" asked Benny. There were a few crumbs of hamburger meat on the plate and he was on a search-and-destroy mission, leaving no bite behind.

"'Cause we saved the town and maybe the whole freaking world, man. We're kings. There wouldn't even *be* a town if it wasn't for us."

"Yeah," said Benny, "no. I pretty much don't see anyone going for that."

Chong gave a philosophical sigh. "Small minds."

They watched their girlfriends, Nix Riley—she of the countless freckles, devious green eyes, and fiery red hair— and Lilah—the snowy-haired killer with a to-die-for smile. When she smiled, at least, which was rare, but always like a burst of sunlight on a cloudy day. They were throwing a Frisbee back and forth. Benny and Chong had bailed out of the game to eat, but the girls never seemed to tire. They whipped the flying disk at each other with incredible force, and it always looked like they were trying to commit murder. Benny's hand still stung like crazy from catching—or trying to catch—the throws.

The game was typical of the way those two always were, whether it was Frisbee, softball, touch football, or recreational sparring with bamboo swords. They were friends, but there was some kind of weird tension always bubbling below the surface that neither Benny nor Chong could figure out. Maybe it was competitiveness, or maybe they were both a little crazy. Chong said a case could be made either way. No one who watched the intensity of the game ever asked to join. The fun was likely outweighed by potential crippling injuries.

Benny looked for more scraps of food, found none, made a disgusted noise, and sipped his pop. "Boringsville," he said. "Tell me that isn't the best name for this place."

Chong thought about it, lips pursed judiciously, then nodded. "I like it."

"Or, how 'bout Mindnumbinglydullistan?"

"That could work," agreed Chong.

A few sun-drowsy bees flew past, buzzing close to the pop bottles, then flew off in disappointment.

"What I don't get," said Benny, "is why, or even *how*, we're bored. I mean . . . wasn't peace and tranquility and all that stuff why we went out into the Ruin in the first place?"

"'All that stuff,'" echoed Chong, a half smile on his lips.

"You know what I mean. We fought Saint John and Preacher Jack and Charlie Pink-eye and all those guys to get this, to get what we have now. No hordes of zoms trying to break in. No armies of religious nutbags who think the best way to serve God is to kill everyone. No maniacs forcing kids to fight in the zombie pits. I mean, we stopped that. Us. A bunch of teenagers. We stopped it and now aren't we supposed to just kick back and enjoy the peace and quiet?"

"That," said Chong, "was the actual plan."

Benny sighed. "Peace is boring."

Chong shrugged. "Peace is safe, man."

"Safe is boring too."

The boys drank. Chong belched again.

"Okay, you're not even trying now," said Benny.

"Fair enough."

The girls kept attempting to decapitate each other with the bright blue plastic disk. The day above and around them was picture perfect.

"That's not boring, though," said Benny. "Not even a little bit."

He glanced at Chong and saw him watching the Frisbee slash through the air like a weapon hurled at an enemy. Chong frowned and nodded to himself.

"What . . . ?" asked Benny.

Before Chong could answer, a shadow fell across both of them and they turned to look up. Morgie Mitchell stood there, his gold Freedom Riders sash hung slantwise across his muscular chest. He had not gone with Benny, Chong, Nix, and Lilah on their expedition beyond the questionable safety of Mountainside's fences. In fact, the last thing that had passed between Morgie and Benny were hard words and what seemed like a permanent breaking of their lifelong friendship. Benny and the others had gone looking for a jet they'd seen in the empty skies, searching for proof that Mountainside and the eight other small towns in central California were not all that remained of humanity. On that trip, Benny's older brother, Tom, had died saving their lives; and the wasteland had proven to be filled with people, many of whom were vicious, violent, or insane. The fight for survival had changed the world as they all knew it, and now they knew that there were people out there, and even a government trying to build a new America down in Asheville, North Carolina. Not many people, but some. Maybe even enough to reclaim the world.

Morgie had stayed behind, at first bitter and then torn by grief and self-loathing at the words that he'd said to Benny that day. He threw himself into the samurai training Tom had given them all, becoming leaner and much tougher than ever before. He volunteered for dangerous jobs in town, including apprentice tower guard, and Morgie's quick thinking and heroism had saved many lives. Now he rode with the legendary bounty hunter Solomon Jones and the Freedom Riders, the group that maintained order and kept the Nine Towns safe. Morgie was proud of the gold sash he wore that marked him as a "fighter" rather than an apprentice among the Riders. When Benny and his friends had returned to Mountainside hours ahead of an army of doomsday cultists led by the dangerous fanatic Saint John, Morgie stood beside his friends and there, in the fire and ash, in that furnace, a new and stronger friendship was forged.

Now he stood above them, silhouetted against the sun.

"Speak, apparition," said Chong in a theatrical tone.

"Dude," said Benny, "what's with the sash? I thought you were off today. Grab some ground and sit yourself down."

"Guys," said Morgie quietly, "something's happened. You need to come with me to the mayor's office."

"Hey, Benny," said Chong, "maybe they're going to name the town after you." He spread his hands as if describing a big banner. "Fartsville."

They both cracked up, but their laughter died away when Morgie stepped closer and sunlight showed his expression. His face was dead white; his eyes were wild with fear. Benny and Chong sat up.

"What's wrong?" said Benny so sharply that Nix and Lilah paused in their game to look in their direction.

Morgie looked sick. "Guys," he said again, "I just found out . . . we've lost contact with Asheville."

"So?" said Chong. "The satellite phone's been messing up for two weeks."

"You don't understand," said Morgie. "Solomon got a distress call. All we could hear was shouting, some screams and gunfire, and then it went dead. They checked the sat phone and it's working, but Asheville's not answering." His eyes were glassy and wet. "They think it might be gone."

"HOW CAN IT BE *GONE*?" DEMANDED NIX RILEY.

Solomon Jones winced because she said it really loud, and she had the kind of voice that could punch its way through any conversational chatter. It silenced the entire room. Solomon, who was both the head of the Freedom Riders for the Nine Towns and the interim governor of California, sat behind his desk in the communications center at the Reclamation Capitol Building. It was really a two-story wood building sandwiched between the general store and a feed-and-grain warehouse.

The town mayor, Randy Kirsch, stood beside the desk, hands clasped behind his back, head bowed, looking grim and worried. They were both middle-aged men, both of medium height, both bald, but that was where the similarities ended. Solomon was a muscular black man with very dark skin, a precisely trimmed gray goatee, and eyes that were both fierce and shrewd. The mayor was softer, with kinder eyes and less of an air of a hunting cat and more that of a golden retriever.

Aside from the two officials and Benny and his friends, there were at least fifty people crammed into the office. More choked the hallway, and Benny figured that by now everyone in town had heard the news. They'd all come swarming in.

The brief silence following Nix's outburst crumbled away as everyone began throwing fresh questions and demands for information everywhere.

Solomon held up his hands in a *calm down* gesture, and Benny saw Nix tense to launch another barrage of her own, but then she gave a harsh exhale and a curt nod. The others gradually settled down too. When there was quiet, Solomon nodded to the mayor.

"Some of you are new to Reclamation," said the mayor, "so this is where we are and what we know." He stepped over to a wall map of the United States. Hundreds of colored push-pins littered the map. He touched a green one stuck in the mountains of Mariposa County in central California. "Green pins indicate settled towns that we know about. As you can see, we have nine here in California, five in Nevada, seven in Arizona, and then nothing until we go all the way southeast to Georgia. There may be more—and hopefully many more—but we are still looking. Red pins indicate towns destroyed by Saint John's armies."

There were 107 red pins in the board, Benny knew. Chong had counted them one day and spent the rest of that week in a blue funk. And there were only twenty-eight green pins. Asheville was by far the biggest human settlement, with nearly a hundred thousand people, which was more than three times the combined population of the other towns. Asheville was the capital of the American Nation, the newly formed government that was trying to reclaim and rebuild America.

Most of the rest of the map was empty of pins because no one knew what was going on there. Same with Canada and Mexico and, well, the whole rest of the world. It depressed

Benny to think about it, but also kindled a little fire of hope, too. He imagined what Tom would have said about it. Probably something Zen like, *Just because you don't know what's out there, Benny, doesn't mean there's nothing good.*

Thinking about that made Benny's heart hurt. He missed his brother every single day.

"These blue pins," continued Mayor Kirsch, bringing him back to the moment, "indicate places where it was clear people had settled but moved on, either to escape Saint John's reaper army, or to avoid swarms of zoms. Most likely the latter, at least in recent months."

Over the last couple of years, some of the zombies had begun hunting in packs, and in places those packs had combined into massive swarms. Genetic mutations in the parasites that created the zombie plague in the first place were believed to be the cause of that, but the American Nation scientists hadn't yet mapped it all out. Scouts and scavengers were reporting new and bigger swarms, and they were getting closer to some of the Nine Towns. And there were other things—wild reports from travelers about different kinds of mutations coming from the east. Animals that some said had caught the zombie plague. That was scary because so far only wild hogs had been infected. Now there were stories—and no one in town had so far been able to prove if they were true—about monkeys and other animals who were said to be infected. Some stories hinted that there were even worse things out there, especially the farther east you went, but none of them had so far been proven. No one from Asheville, which was very far east, seemed to think those were anything more than tall tales. Benny wasn't so sure. The world

63

was broken and it kept getting stranger all the time.

"Now these pins," said the mayor, touching some of the many black pins, "are areas where we've lost contact but haven't yet verified whether it's because the lines of communication failed—bad radios, swarms blocking the new Pony Express, or other issues—or if those towns have been overrun."

The crowd stood in uneasy silence, watching as Solomon got up and crossed to the map, took a black pin from a tray on a side table, removed the green pin from Asheville, and replaced it with the black one.

"As of six thirty this morning," he said slowly, "we have lost all communication with Asheville. The satellite phone is working fine, so it's not that. We've placed calls to the other eight towns and confirmed that they've lost contact with Asheville too. We called the military station near New Haven and they haven't heard anything either. I wish I could say this is only a technical problem, but we have to face facts."

There was a collective gasp from the crowd. Benny saw Nix take Lilah's hand and squeeze it. Both girls looked as scared as he felt. Chong looked positively stricken. Morgie stood by the window, arms folded, mouth turned down in a hard line. The girl standing beside him was wiry, tough, and pretty, with a cynical half smile on her thin lips and a tattoo of roses and barbed wire covering her scalp, except where a stiff crimson Mohawk rose in dagger-sharp spikes. Her name was Riot, and she'd been raised within Saint John's army, but had rebelled and fallen in with Benny's group to fight back. She and Morgie were always trying to be a couple, but they kept breaking up. At the moment they were kind of together, but the fact that they stood a few feet apart suggested they were drifting again.

Solomon held a hand up for silence as the gasps turned to chatter. He said, "We don't know anything right now other than our belief that there was a crisis."

"You've all heard about the last call," said the mayor, "about the screams and gunfire. That's troubling, but it's not a good idea for us to speculate on the nature of the emergency or the extent of it. We are waiting for more information."

"What about Captain Ledger?" asked Benny. "Is he back yet?"

Captain Joe Ledger was an old soldier who had led a special ops team before First Night—when the dead rose—and he had been instrumental in bringing the military resources of the new American Nation to the Nine Towns. He'd also fought alongside Benny and his friends against Saint John, nearly dying in the process. Since then he and his group of rangers had begun searching for more towns. He was also overseeing the spreading of a mutagen that amped up the parasites semi-dormant in all zoms. That was risky and had to be managed carefully, because although the mutagen eventually caused tissue breakdown that destroyed the living dead, there was a brief period where it made the creatures move much faster and even restored higher brain functions to some of them. The captain was almost never in Reclamation, though; he was busy in the field, fighting a new kind of battle in this terrible war.

Benny caught Solomon and Mayor Kirsch exchanging a brief, worried look. Then Solomon cleared his throat.

The mayor said, "We . . . um . . . Captain Ledger was already on his way to Asheville."

"Wait," said Nix, "what does that mean?"

"It means," said Solomon Jones, "that he'd received a distress call from the military commander in Asheville and flew out in a helicopter. He did not share the details with us. All we know is that he and four of his rangers took a Sikorsky UH-60 Black Hawk helicopter that was fitted out. He planned to refuel twice at small American Nation remote outposts in Laguna Pueblo, New Mexico, and Searcy, Arkansas, before flying on to Asheville."

"And . . . ?" urged Benny.

"We were speaking with Captain Ledger on the sat phone when the line went dead. The call ended before he could tell us his location. We don't know if he reached Asheville or not. He may only have gotten as far as New Mexico, Texas, or Oklahoma. But whatever's happening, he may already be caught up in it. And I'm afraid there has been no further communication with him, or with anyone in North Carolina, since this morning."

BENNY AND HIS FRIENDS WANDERED BACK TO HIS house. They sat on the chairs, the rail, and the top steps. Benny was the only one who stood, leaning a shoulder against the post of the railing, arms folded, feeling about as empty as a Halloween pumpkin on November 1. He felt deflated, sick, and scared. The others looked at their hands, up at the trees, out at the birds pecking for insects on the lawn. Anywhere but at one another.

And yet the sky above insisted on being a bright blue, and cheerful puffy clouds sailed overhead as if the world was fine.

Except the world wasn't fine at all.

Maybe it never had been, thought Benny. Maybe the peace and contentment they'd all felt these last months was only a dream. Or worse, a setup to make them lower their guard. That was how it felt to him. During the fight with Saint John, Benny and his friends had become tough, hardened. They had been warriors. Young as they were, they had become the new samurai Tom had wanted them to be.

Now Benny felt like he was five years old. He felt small. Weak.

And so scared.

It was Chong who finally spoke. "What do we do?"

Nix and Morgie shook their heads. No one else said anything.

"No, seriously," said Chong, "what are we going to do about this?"

"What *can* we do?" asked Morgie, not looking at him. "Asheville is, like, forever away from here."

"So?" asked Chong. "We walked all the way to Nevada. That was over a thousand miles."

"Yeah, you guys did that," agreed Morgie, glancing at him. "And how many times did you guys almost get killed? All kinds of weird zoms—fast ones, smarter ones, packs of them. Not to mention a mother rhino that got out of a zoo somewhere who wanted to stomp you flat, a bear that tried to eat you, and, oh yeah, zombie wild boars. That's not even counting an army of psychopaths who wanted to wipe out all human life."

Benny sighed but said nothing.

"We're not dead," said Nix.

Morgie looked at her. "Nix, you've got two huge scars on your face."

"So what? They're just scars. I didn't die."

"He did," cried Morgie, pointing at Chong. "He's infected with the zombie virus."

Lilah stiffened and pointed a finger at him. "Be careful," she warned. The Lost Girl's throat had been torn raw from screaming when she was little, and the scar tissue on her larynx had changed her voice permanently to a ghostly whisper. When she spoke, though, people tended to stop and listen.

"I'm not cutting up on him," said Morgie quickly, "but face facts—what happens if we go looking for Captain Ledger and it takes so long Chong runs out of pills?"

"I'll take plenty of them with me," said Chong.

"What happens if he loses them? Or someone takes them away?"

"If someone tries to do that," said Lilah, "I'll kill them and take the pills back."

Benny had to turn away to hide a smile. Lilah wasn't joking. She barely knew how to joke. She also had about the same protective instincts as a mother cougar. If anyone so much as looked at Chong funny, she'd do very, very bad things to them. Benny knew because he'd seen it.

Morgie tried it from another direction. "Chong could fall into a river. Whatever." He shook his head and pointed in the direction of the fence. "Hey, man, I love you and all, but you shouldn't be allowed out there."

Chong turned away and stared at the birds in the yard. Lilah reached over and squeezed his knee, but Chong did not react.

It hurt Benny to know that Morgie was right. There was no way on earth to justify Chong leaving the town. He had been frail before being infected, and he was a scarecrow now. He also screamed at night sometimes. They all knew it, but nobody ever mentioned it. That was heartbreaking, but it was also something you wouldn't want a traveling companion to do if you were camping out in the Rot and Ruin.

Even though the townsfolk had renamed the zom-infested wilderness "Tomsland," it would always be the Rot and Ruin to Benny. To all his friends.

"We have to do something," said Nix after a long silence.

"Asheville's all the way across the Ruin," insisted Morgie.

"And you know what people are saying about new mutations and infected animals."

"People say all kinds of things," countered Nix. "Doesn't make it true."

"Doesn't make it a lie, either," said Riot. She spoke with a slow Cajun accent, which was deceptive because of how quick she was in wits and reflexes. Like Lilah, Riot had spent a lot of her life fighting and was nearly as vicious as the feral Lost Girl. "I seen some weird stuff and I've been farther east than any of y'all. Saw a bear once that I was pretty sure was turned. Had half a dozen arrows in him and one eye missing and he kept moving like that was nothing to him. Tell me that's natural. Y'all want to run smack into a zombie bear?"

"There's no zombie bears," said Lilah.

"How would you know?"

"I lived in the forest. The only zom animals we saw were boars, and that was in Nevada."

"Okay, sure," said Riot, "but I saw the bear in New Mexico. You ever go that far?"

"No."

"Then I guess you don't know for sure, do you?"

Lilah merely snorted. She and Riot had a lot of similarities in that they had lived rough, but they had never bonded.

Morgie said, "None of that really matters, because we don't even know how to get to Asheville. We don't know what route Captain Ledger took and he was flying, so he didn't need to worry about mountains, rivers, or overrun cities. We'd need to stick to roads, which means we won't be going in as straight a line. You're pretty good at math, Nix. Want to tell me what the odds are of us finding a safe route? And what if we get there and Captain Ledger's dead? Or turned into a zom?"

"It's not just about finding Joe Ledger," said Benny, though it caused a twinge of pain to say it. "We can use maps to plan a route to Asheville. If he took a helicopter, then we can follow as straight a line as we can, but either way, we'll make for North Carolina. We can take the quads and drive most of the way."

Quads were small four-wheeled vehicles that were, currently, the only working motorized transportation anywhere. While all the other machines had been rendered useless by EMPs, a clever mechanic in Nevada had figured out a way to repair the sporty two-stroke engines of recreational quads. Saint John's reapers had used them to create a kind of mobile cavalry, and Benny and his friends had stolen several and driven all the way back to Mountainside to warn of the impending invasion. Now the Nine Towns had a small fleet of them and would soon have gas-powered cars and trucks.

"What if we can't find gas for them?" asked Morgie.

"Then we walk the rest of the way. Or we find horses or bicycles. Look, Morgie, it's not about how tough it'll be. We know it won't be easy. No, this is all about getting to Asheville."

"Yeah? What if it's been overrun?"

"Then it's been overrun," said Nix. "Benny's right, we have to know. As far as we know, Asheville is where the world is starting back up again. People, government, industry, the military." She shook her head. "We have to find out."

"Do we?" asked Morgie. "The Nine Towns got along pretty good since First Night. We survived, we got to grow up. We were safe."

"*Really?*" said Nix, her voice suddenly going cold. "What about Charlie Pink-eye and the Motor City Hammer? What about Gameland? What about Preacher Jack? You call that safe? What about what they did to my mother? What about what they tried to do to all of us? They nearly *killed* you, Morgie. They *did* kill my mom. They put Benny and me in the zombie pits. Maybe I'm stupid or something, but how is that 'safe'?"

"That's not what I meant," mumbled Morgie.

"I know what you meant," said Nix, not letting up. "Why can't you admit that you're wrong?"

"Hey," said Benny, "come on. We have enough problems without picking fights with each other."

Nix glared hot molten death at him. "Sure. Fine. Whatever." She muttered something under her breath that sounded like *Boys are idiots*, but Benny wasn't sure.

Lilah said, "We have to do something. What good is it to just sit here?"

"Sitting here is better than going out to get killed," said Riot.

They were, collectively, a powerful group. Skilled to varying degrees, experienced in combat, scarred inside and out by what they'd been through. They were still teenagers, though. Benny just wished that the adults in town had more of a clue what to do, but no one at the meeting had a good plan. Not even Solomon.

They all lapsed into silence again.

Again, Chong was the first to speak. "Tell me something, Morgie . . . if anyone decides to go, would you go too?"

Morgie bristled. "Why, because I didn't go last time?"

"No," said Chong. "Because you're tough and we're going to need all the muscle we can get out there."

Everyone looked at him. "'We'?" asked Nix.

"Sure," said Chong, "or haven't you guys worked it out yet? The medicine I need to keep from going full zom is made in Reclamation, but the chemicals and stuff they need to make it come from Asheville. Dr. McReady, the scientist who figured it out, is in Asheville. I have enough of the drug to last maybe ten months. After that, which one of you is going to quiet me with a sliver in the back of my skull?"

No one spoke. The silence was crushing.

"So . . . yeah," said Chong, "I'm going to Asheville. I'd rather die trying than to wait here and just . . . die."

Lilah made a sound that might have been an agreement, or might simply have been a growl. Nix nodded, and for some reason she smiled. She was like that, Benny knew. Brave and a little crazy.

Riot gave an elaborate shrug and said, "Well, I guess I'm in for whatever. Heck, I never expected to live all that long anyway. Might as well go out having some fun."

Benny saw Morgie mouth the word "fun." It looked like the word hurt his mouth.

"You know I'm in," said Benny. "I kind of have to be. I mean, you're smart and all, Chong, but let's face it, you get lost trying to find the bathroom in your own house."

"This," said Chong, "is true."

One by one they all turned to Morgie. He opened his mouth two or three times to say something, stopped, shut it again. He leaned over and banged the side of his head against the tree.

Sighed.

Said, "When do we leave?"

Interlude One

KICKAPOO CAVERN STATE PARK
ONE WEEK AGO

THE HUNTER MOVED THROUGH THE FOREST.

His forest. He glided along, silent as a shadow, disturbing nothing, leaving no trace behind. Even animals rarely knew he was around. Sometimes he passed them by, leaving them to their ignorance. Sometimes they died without ever knowing that this was their last day.

Those killings were always quick. Part of it was a reflex of mercy, a desire to inflict no pain even as he ended a life. Part of it was efficiency—frightened animals screamed. Screams drew other kinds of creatures. The hunter did not want to become food for them.

And so he was quiet.

Silent as death.

He wore fatigues in a forest camouflage print, and when he stopped and became still, he vanished against the walls of the lush growth. He was very good at hiding. He was very good at not being seen. Years ago he had been the angel of death whose sniper bullets ended lives before the victims ever knew they were in his crosshairs. His rifle was seldom used now. It was noisy, and he rarely needed to kill something two or three thousand yards away. Now he had his knives and, for the direst of emergencies, a pistol with a Trinity sound suppressor, which, though not silent, was quiet.

He'd planned on spending the day in his small cabin; meditating, reading, and perhaps finishing his latest carving. A delicate little hummingbird he was fashioning out of a piece of oak. He had carved hundreds of birds, animals, and fish. The exacting precision and attention to detail kept his mind from falling into depression and numbness. Hunting was another way of staying sharp. He had many ways to keep from cracking apart in this broken world.

Those plans, however, had ended when he heard the sounds. Distant, but distinct. At first he thought it was a roar or growl of some beast, one of the exotics. A rhinoceros or elephant or musk ox. Or maybe one of the mutations. There were cattle out here that had developed a taste for meat, and a few hunting pairs of perentie—big and venomous Australian monitor lizards that had come from who knew where—and that had grown much larger even than their cousins, the Komodo dragons. They feared nothing, and in their arrogance of power tended to go crashing through the brush, stronger than anything faster, and faster than anything stronger.

Was this them? he wondered. But he didn't think so. There were so many mutations these days, more every season. The logic and predictability of nature was so badly warped that it was sometimes like living in a nightmare, or a hallucination. Sometimes the things he saw made him doubt his own sanity. He was a practical, skilled, efficient man, but he had been alone for a long time. Too long. He'd begun to speak to himself on the really bad, really long nights. That scared him. His survival and every one of his skills were wired into his mind.

The thousand things he did every day to live out here were components of the mental machine he had built since childhood, with the exacting studies of martial arts, the precision of competitive shooting, the structure of the Scouts and then the military.

He would find a rational explanation for the noise, and then he would deal with whatever made it. Destroy it, evade it, or anything necessary in order to impose logic on its existence.

The sound was too big, though; too steady and too unnatural. However, it couldn't be what it *really* sounded like because—well . . . that was impossible. There could not be that kind of noise. Not a machine noise. Things that made those sounds had died when the EMPs brought the great silence to the world.

And yet that was what it had sounded like. A machine of some kind. A helicopter, but a wounded one, with an engine that screamed as it died. But by the time the hunter got to clear ground with good elevation, the sky was empty and silent. Only a smudge of smoke in the distance, but that could as easily have been from a brush fire. There had been lightning recently during a brief squall.

Still . . .

He went looking because he had to know.

He followed a game trail, pausing now and then to listen to the woods, absorbing what the forest wanted to tell him. There were prints mashed onto the trampled grass and exposed dirt. Deer, mostly, though there were several exotic hooves. Animals from some zoo, probably. Then he saw a set of prints that made him pause. Shoe prints. Specifically *boot* prints. Not the tread of work boots or hiking boots. No . . . these had the unmistakable pattern of military boots. Size eleven or a little larger. Wide.

Very much like the ones he wore.

The hunter touched the prints. The dirt was soft. It had rained this morning, but the mud had dried. These impressions were pressed into semidry mud. Which meant they were very recent. An hour old? Less?

The gait was unusual, though. Not a steady pace. Awkward, and there was a bit of a drag to the left foot. Someone with a bad leg? The dead ones, especially the slow shamblers, often walked with limps, or walked clumsily enough to leave uneven prints. Some of the smarter ones did too, if they had been injured before they died. Maybe a gunshot wound, or bites.

And there were the packs of ravagers. Infected, dangerous, strange, and always violent. More and more of them all the time. The fact that the tread was military didn't matter, because those killers had taken down their share of soldiers, and they always stripped the dead for whatever they needed. Clothes, weapons. Meat.

The hunter moved along the path, careful not to obscure the prints. Then he saw something glisten on a leaf at about thigh height. Red. He bent and touched it. Fresh blood. Less than an hour old for sure. The color had not darkened too much.

Whoever had passed through here was injured, limping. Which meant he was alive. Or, at most, newly dead and reanimated. The hunter squatted there for almost a minute, thinking, considering. Either way whoever it was had no business being in the hunter's forest.

Moving silent as a ghost, the hunter melted into the woods, following the footprints and the trail of blood.

PART THREE

NEW ALAMO, TEXAS
LATE AUGUST

GHOST RIDERS

You will never do anything

in this world without courage.

It is the greatest quality of the mind next to honor.

—ARISTOTLE

SPIDER WALKED GUTSY HOME, AND SOMBRA LIMPED
along behind.

The Gomez place was a shotgun house. Narrow but long,
with six rooms lined up one after the other, from living room
to kitchen, with a dining room, bedrooms, and a bathroom in
between, and a narrow hallway running front to back. It was
sturdily built from cinder blocks, with a pitched tin roof, and
it was one of nearly two hundred identical homes that had
been built before the End. A big, faded sign stood at the edge
of town, its words only just legible.

IMMIGRATION DETENTION CENTER

A lot of rude and obscene things had been painted on
the sign, but that had been done long ago too, and all of it
had been nearly burned away by fifteen years of harsh sun,
dry wind, and blowing sand. Most of the kids in town didn't
know much about the origin of the town, why it was built,
who'd built it, who'd lived there, or why. That was part of
the world that had died before they were born. Gutsy knew,
though, because her mother had once told her the story about

being arrested in San Antonio and sent to the camp. That was where she lived for nearly two years while the authorities on both sides of the Rio Grande tried to decide who wanted her. Neither, apparently, did. Or maybe it was fair to say that neither tried very hard to make her welcome, and by the time the paperwork had come through for Mama to be sent across the river, the dead rose and consumed the bureaucrats, the police, the soldiers, the border guards, and the governments who used people in the same way the old men in town now used painted stones as poker chips.

The thing that made Mama laugh while she told that story was the fact that all those well-built houses were intended to be mini prisons, and when the dead swarmed through the camp, the prisoners stayed safe behind their walls while the camp staff perished. Mama said that there was justice in that, but it was so far outside of Gutsy's experience that she didn't get the joke. She also didn't agree. As far as she was concerned, there weren't many people left, so any death was a bad thing.

The world was hell and the world was crazy. That was what Gutsy believed. But there were good people, even in hell. Spider and Alethea, the two old guys everyone called the Chess Players, a few others. Good people.

There were also innocents. Babies, little kids. The livestock.

She glanced down at Sombra. He was scarred and scared, fierce and feral, but he was innocent too. Just because bad things had been done to him did not mean that he was bad.

As they approached her front door, Sombra slowed and finally stopped, looking nervous and uncertain.

"What's wrong?" asked Spider.

"Not sure," said Gutsy. "Maybe he doesn't like being inside."

She opened the door and tried to coax the coydog in, but he came no closer than the rosebushes in the front yard.

Spider sat down on one of the plastic chairs positioned in the shade of a blue tarp Gutsy had long ago rigged as a canopy. "Now what?"

"I'm thinking," said Gutsy. "He's scared and we don't want to make him feel worse, right? No one's ever scared of something without a reason, not even dogs, right?"

"I guess."

"So, trying to force him inside isn't going to help. Got to come up with plan B, or maybe even have a plan C and plan D in case."

"Sure," said Spider, "so what's the plan? Maybe he'll let you pet him and, I don't know, cuddle him? You think he'd let you do that?"

Gutsy shook her head. "I think that would be exactly the wrong thing to do."

"Why? He's scared. I like people around me when I'm scared. And when there's a storm, Alethea likes it when we wrap a blanket around both of us."

"Alethea's a person and so are you, Spider," said Gutsy. "You guys understand that you're trying to be there for each other. She probably tells you she wants to hide under a blanket with you, right?"

"Well, sure, but who doesn't need some affection?"

Gutsy knew there was a lot of Spider's own life in that question. He had shadows in his past that she knew something—but not everything—about.

She said, "Sombra's a dog. Dogs are pack animals, right? Look at how the strays in town all bunch together. They follow a pack leader."

"Right . . . so?"

Gutsy went and sat down near the coydog, but she didn't touch him, or try to pet him, or even look at him. Sombra twitched but didn't move away. "The way I see it," said Gutsy, "is that dogs react to two things—getting hurt and getting treats. Mr. Rayner's dog, Pickles, will do anything for a piece of jerky. All those tricks she does? That's all for treats, right?"

"I guess," said Spider slowly, not sure where Gutsy was going with this.

"Pickles doesn't know she's supposed to be an entertainer. It just seems to me that Pickles knows that if she does this thing or that thing, she gets a reward. So she's always ready to do a trick because that means food."

"So?"

"Sombra's scared right now. That's what he's feeling or thinking. He's hurt. If I get all goofy with him and pet him and tell him he's a good dog and all the stuff Mr. Rayner does, won't I just be training Sombra to think that being scared means getting a reward?"

Spider shook his head. "You might be overthinking this."

"Maybe," said Gutsy, "or maybe not. I read a little about dogs because Mama was going to get a puppy for me. I remember reading that you can't explain to a dog why it shouldn't be scared. You can't really tell it everything's okay or that it's safe. It doesn't understand. No, what you need to do is be calm. You need to be the leader of the pack, and the leader should always be, like . . . well . . . calm. Strong, mentally together. Like that."

She sat cross-legged on the ground and kept her tone normal. She didn't look at the dog at all, but she was aware that Sombra was staring at her. Studying her.

"All he's getting from me," said Gutsy, looking up at Spider, "is me being me. No problems, no pressure, no nothing except me in my own space. He can probably smell my scent all over this yard and knows this is my place. If he stays here, it's because he decides to be part of my pack."

Spider smiled and shook his head again. "You're deeply weird, Guts. Always were, always will be."

Sombra gave a huge yawn and lay down with his head between his paws. After a few minutes, he closed his eyes.

"I'm okay with being weird," said Gutsy.

Overhead the sun was rolling toward the edge of day, and the yard was painted with long purple shadows. The last of the day's bees moved without haste from one rose to another. From the house next door, they could hear the sound of bare hands slapping tortillas into shape. Farther down the street a little girl shrieked as she dodged two other kids in a game of tag. Cooking smoke from the first of the evening fires drifted toward them on a sluggish breeze, carrying the scent of peppers and onions—the way they smelled when they were tumbled fresh onto a hot pan.

Gutsy didn't know she was crying until the tears dropped from her cheeks onto her shirt. Spider came over, sat down, and almost put his arm around her.

Gutsy sniffed and forced a smile. "I'm not a dog, you dummy. *I* understand why."

He put his arm around her shoulder and they sat there in the yard, both of them aware that the sounds and smells of mothers making dinner would never come from inside the Gomez house ever again.

After a long, long time Sombra put his battered head on Gutsy's thigh.

GUTSY ASKED SPIDER TO COME OVER FOR DINNER.

"Sure," he agreed, "but I need a bath first. I smell like over-heated horse." He sniffed his clothes. "And horse poop."

"Go get clean. Tell Alethea, if she wants to come."

"She will. Mrs. Cuddly is making her 'wilderness stew' again. Yuck."

Mrs. Cuddly and her husband ran the Home for Found-lings, where Spider and Alethea lived. Mrs. Cuddly was, by all accounts, the worst cook in the history of dining, but her wilderness stew took that to an incredible low. No one was ever quite certain which meat served as the base for the stew. It didn't taste like beef, mutton, pork, goat, or even horse. Alethea said it was probably made from kids who tried to run away from the Cuddlys' orphanage. She was only half joking.

Spider left and Gutsy stood for a long time watching him walk away. All their lives Spider and Alethea had been the orphans and she'd been the one with a family, even though it was a two-person family. Her father had died when Gutsy was little, but Spider and Alethea never knew either of their parents. Now, of course, they were all orphans. Despite all the pain she felt, there was some strange comfort in it too, as if this meant Alethea and Spider were now her family.

Maybe they always had been. She'd have to think about that.

A quick check of the cabinets told her that she didn't have enough food for three people, so she sorted through her pockets to make sure she had enough food credits and headed for the door.

"Come on," she said to the coydog as she walked out into the twilight. Gutsy did not look to see if Sombra followed. Either he would, or he wouldn't.

It wasn't until she heard the faint click of his nails on the sidewalk that she knew. It lit a small fire in her heart. The general store was five blocks away and the air was cooling a little. There was still plenty of humidity, though, and that held the warmth.

As she crossed the street, a familiar voice called her name, and Gutsy saw two old men seated on opposite sides of an empty beer keg on the porch of the general store. A rusty Coleman lantern spilled light on them and on the chessboard that was perpetually positioned there. Gutsy walked over to where the Chess Players—Mr. Urrea and Mr. Ford—sat. They each had cups of tea. The knights and royals were scattered around the board, with a few standing idly alongside, victims of another of their devious battles.

"Hey," she said as she stepped up onto the pavement and leaned against a post. The Chess Players were both old, their faces deeply lined and jowly, but both of them had sharp eyes that sparkled with inquisitive lights. A long time ago, before the End put an end to so many things, both of them had been writers. Famous novelists. They still wrote, but their stories were handwritten into notebooks. Occasionally they would have some of them typeset and printed with a hand-crank copier, but mostly they shared their stories with Gutsy and her friends, or through readings in school.

Early on, Gutsy knew, the two writers had been heroes for a while because they'd organized several hundred survivors and led them on a daring scavenging raid to the docks in Corpus Christi. There they fought hordes of *los muertos* to secure a massive facility where big metal shipping containers were stored after being unloaded from ships. There were no living survivors in the city, so the stuff was there to be taken. Mr. Urrea and Mr. Ford helped to rig barges and load them with all kinds of stuff. It cost the lives of seventeen of their team, but the supplies they brought back probably saved a hundred times as many lives. Tons of canned food, medical supplies, clothes, and so much more. The whole expedition took two months, but that was fifteen years ago. Disease had claimed so many people in New Alamo that the tale had become almost a folktale. Not everyone believed it ever happened, or that the heroic deeds of two now ancient men were anything but exaggerations.

It was that story, though, that inspired a much younger Gutsy Gomez to become a scavenger. The tales the Chess Players told about how problems were met and solved at every stage of the Raid—as it was called—flipped some kind of switch in her, and from then on, she loved solving problems. They knew it too, and often posed logic problems for her to solve. Never scolding or mocking when she failed, but instead guiding her through the best logical steps so she wouldn't fail at that kind of problem again.

Mr. Urrea nodded to the coydog, who stood in the middle of the street, eyeing the two old men with uncertainty. "You picking up strays?"

"We picked up each other," said Gutsy, and explained about their meeting.

"He's a coydog," said Mr. Ford. "Interesting. Been a long time since I saw a tame one."

"Not sure he's all that tame," said Gutsy. "Maybe he just wanted to be around someone who wouldn't hurt him."

Both men nodded, accepting that.

"So, you're going to keep him?" asked Mr. Urrea.

"If he wants to stay," said Gutsy, "then he can stay. If he wants to go, I won't stop him."

The Chess Players liked that, too.

Then Mr. Urrea's face lost its genial smile, and he leaned forward with his elbows on his knees. "We heard about last night. About your mama. How are you?"

"And what are you doing to take care of yourself?" added Mr. Ford.

Gutsy took a long time deciding how best to answer the questions. She liked and trusted both of the old men, but her natural tendency was to keep things to herself. Spider and Alethea were exceptions, but she didn't share everything even with them. Just as she hadn't shared everything with Mama. It wasn't exactly a lack of trust, but rather a desire to reserve the right to think things all the way through, at her own pace.

"I'm figuring it out," said Gutsy. "I don't know what I feel about it yet, but I'm working on it."

The answer seemed to please them.

"If you need to talk to a couple of old farts who've been

around and seen a few things . . . ," said Mr. Ford, leaving the rest hanging.

"Thanks," she said. "I'd better get what I came for and get on home. My friends are coming over for dinner."

She went in and bought some supplies, but as she headed for the street, Mr. Urrea said, "Gutsy . . . ? Wait one minute longer, please."

Gutsy paused, looking at them both.

"Your mother was a good person," said Mr. Urrea. "No matter what, you need to remember that."

Gutsy said nothing.

Mr. Ford said, "She didn't ask for anything that happened to her."

"I know that," said Gutsy. "She didn't ask for anything that was *done* to her either."

There was sadness in the eyes of the two old men. Sadness and something else she could not identify and was not, at the moment, prepared to discover. They nodded to her, and after a few seconds she returned the nod, then walked home in the dark with a silent shadow trotting beside her. She could feel the eyes of the Chess Players on her the whole way, but when she stopped outside her house and looked back, the store's porch was empty.

"GUTSY?" CALLED A GIRL'S VOICE FROM OUTSIDE THE house. "There's a big, ugly, weird dog out here and he won't let me in."

Gutsy and Spider were seated across from each other at the small dining room table, about to eat the chicken tacos they'd prepared together.

"She wasn't home, so I left her a note," said Spider as he started to rise, but Gutsy waved him back.

"I'll go."

She walked through to the living room and opened the door. A fifteen-year-old white girl stood at the far end of the small patch of front yard. She was a little taller than Gutsy, heavier in a way that made older guys rubberneck at her and sometimes walk into walls. If the occasional jerk said she was too heavy, the girl withered them with a stare that could have stripped paint off plate steel. She wore tights that she had hand-painted so that the left leg was a sunlit desert after a rain, with all the popping colors of new flowers, while the right was that same desert under cold starlight. Over that was a T-shirt on which was written in flowing script: *Curvy Is My Superpower*. She had eyes that sometimes looked hazel and sometimes looked brown, and she insisted the color was "olive-brown." Her hair was a spill of auburn curls, and she wore a little hand-glittered tiara. Alethea had at least twenty tiaras and was never seen without one, even in school.

Sombra sat in the middle of the garden path, ears standing straight up, eyes fixed on the newcomer. He wasn't growling, but he also clearly wasn't moving.

"It's okay, Sombra," said Gutsy, stopping next to the coydog. "Alethea's a friend."

The dog looked at Alethea but didn't move. So Gutsy walked the rest of the way and gave her friend a hug.

"He's yours?" asked Alethea.

"We kind of adopted each other," said Gutsy. "Come on in. We just made dinner."

"I think he thinks *I'm* dinner."

"He's cool. C'mon." They walked past Sombra, who got to his feet, turned, and watched. Because the coydog neither barked nor growled, Gutsy said, "Good boy."

She wasn't sure if Sombra understood the words. Maybe he'd never been told he was a good boy before. But he yawned and went over and lay down between the plastic chairs. Gutsy remembered reading that dogs yawn sometimes as a way of releasing tension. He'd done it twice now at times when it was clear he was easing down from high alert. She took it as a good sign.

Once inside, Alethea kissed the top of Spider's head, as he bent over his plate assembling another taco, then sat down. Spider pushed the fixings her way.

"So," said Alethea, looking straight at Gutsy, "tell me

about the dog. No, wait. Tell me what happened last night and today. In fact, tell me everything."

Gutsy took a breath and did. Alethea had finished two tacos by the time the whole story was done.

"Whoa, wait . . . someone *dug* her up?" demanded Alethea, appalled.

"And brought her to town," said Spider.

"That's sick!"

"No," said Spider, shaking his head. "It's evil."

"Maybe. But whatever it is," said Alethea, "there's got to be a reason somebody did it." She cocked an eyebrow. "You make anyone mad at you lately?"

"No more than usual."

There was a short silence after she said it, and the foster siblings exchanged a knowing glance. Gutsy understood why. She was not the most popular kid in school and definitely not the most well-liked in New Alamo. Gutsy was, as old Mr. Urrea once phrased it, "a difficult girl." He'd meant it as a compliment. Urrea and Ford were also not very well liked. They were opinionated, occasionally grumpy, and—like Gutsy—difficult. What that meant was they seldom agreed with the way things were run, and rarely shared the same views as the majority of townsfolk. Gutsy considered herself a free thinker and tended to rely on her own judgment and preferred forming her own thoughts rather than being told what to do or think. That was not a pathway to popularity in a town of frightened people.

It made her like herself, though, and that was what mattered to Gutsy most. She seldom cared what others thought. If she did, she'd have been crippled by their criticisms that she didn't dress like a girl, didn't go to church often enough, didn't act right.

Most of that was true. She didn't "dress like a girl" because the old-fashioned Mexican village skirts and frilly white blouses a lot of the girls in town wore weren't practical for scavenging for food and supplies in towns infested with *los muertos*. Jeans, a T-shirt, and a vest with lots of pockets made more sense to her. She did not go to the Saturday evening dances at the school, because she wasn't a fan of being groped by boys. She wasn't even sure she liked boys. Some of them, sure, but not most. She also liked some girls, but not most.

If she lived long enough, then maybe she'd take that stuff down off a mental shelf and see if it made sense. Not now, though. Life had enough complications. Even on a day-to-day basis. She cut school now and then because of issues she had with some of what they were teaching. There were three schools in New Alamo, and two of them were very strict religious schools. She wasn't sure how important religion had been to people before the End, but it tended to dominate a lot of conversations since. Gutsy never slammed anyone's beliefs, even though she had issues with her own, because she had no idea who was right or wrong about how the universe was wired. She certainly didn't know. And she'd heard the Chess Players wrangle on for hours about religion, the practice of it, the politics of it, the different approaches to it, and the complex history of it. Mr. Urrea and Mr. Ford seemed to agree that everyone was right until everyone was proved wrong, and there was no way to do that. That seemed fair to her. Her open-ended tolerance won her few friends. The teachers in the two religious schools were not particularly keen on that view either.

So Gutsy talked her mother into letting her go to the town's third school. The official name was the drab New Alamo High, but even the staff tended to call it by its common nickname: Misfit High.

Mr. Urrea and Mr. Ford both taught there.

Spider and Alethea were not in a formal school but were "homeschooled" by their foster caregivers. The couple in charge of the Home for Foundlings had the hilarious names of Adolf and Vera Cuddly. They did not refer to themselves as foster parents and instead used the more generic and antiseptic term of caregiver. The Cuddlys had twenty-six orphans in their charge, ranging from toddlers to Alethea and Spider.

Cuddly, though, the couple were not. Adolf looked like he might have been a gangster before the End; he had cold, beady eyes and a lot of crooked yellow teeth. His wife, Vera, had the personality of an irate scorpion without any of that insect's warmth.

For Gutsy, being an outsider was a fact of her life, but rather than letting it make a victim of her, she'd embraced it. She was living life as much on her own terms as circumstance would allow. She only hoped that with Mama's death the town council would not send her to the Cuddlys as a new foster. No. She'd run away first. Gutsy was absolutely sure she could survive indefinitely out in the Broken Lands.

So, even though she wasn't Miss Perfect or Miss Popular, was there anyone in town who outright hated her? Gutsy shook her head. Her fists were clenched into tight balls of knuckles on the tabletop.

"I don't know why someone would do something like this," she said.

"How'd they even get Mama's body in through the gate without the guards noticing?" asked Alethea. Like everyone, she referred to Gutsy's mother as "Mama." Then she answered her own question. "Those lamebrains wouldn't notice if *los muertos* formed a mariachi band and led a parade of shamblers through the center of town."

"Which is why I hate this town," said Spider. Alethea sighed. Gutsy knew this was an old argument and a topic Spider came back to time and again. The only downside to reading so many books was that it made all three of them want to leave New Alamo and see the world. Not necessarily the broken world that it currently was, but the wider and infinitely complex world it had been. When he was ten, Spider made a scrapbook of places he dreamed of going, filling them with drawings or images cut from old magazines and catalogs from companies that were as dead as the rest of the world. The Eiffel Tower in Paris and the Statue of Liberty in New York. The snowy Alps and the lush tropical rain forests of Brazil. Easter Island to see the big stone heads and Australia to dive the coral reefs.

Alethea looked wistfully into the middle distance. "Maybe there's another town out there somewhere," she said.

Gutsy made no comment. So many of the other towns were dying out from disease, being overrun by shamblers, or torn apart by wolf packs. Much as she didn't like New Alamo either, it was the safest place in the world, as far as anyone knew.

Spider leaned over and kissed her on the shoulder.

"We'll get out of here," he said quietly. "Somehow, someday. But first we have to deal with this freakazoid stuff." The foster siblings turned to study Gutsy.

"Well . . . ?" prompted Alethea. "What are you thinking?"

"I'm trying to figure out why someone would hate me enough to want to do this," said Gutsy.

"Maybe it wasn't something about you," suggested Spider. "Maybe it was someone who was mad at your mom."

"Why would anyone be mad at *her*?" demanded Gutsy. "Mama was a nurse. She helped people."

"Everyone has enemies," said Alethea.

"Mama didn't."

"Look," Spider said patiently, "just because your mom was nice doesn't mean everyone automatically liked her."

"Being a wonderful person doesn't mean everyone likes you," said Alethea. "Or *has* to like you. I'm nice, but some girls make fun of me 'cause I'm not rail thin."

Spider looked thoughtful. "You're 'nice'? Is that really the right word?"

Alethea gave him the raised eyebrow of doom. "Would you like to limp for a month? No? Then hush, because grown folks are talking."

Spider mimed zipping his mouth shut.

"Mama, though," persisted Gutsy. "I've never heard anyone say a word against her."

"They wouldn't," agreed Alethea. "Not to your face. Maybe not to her face."

The conversation stalled there for a while.

After a short time, Alethea sat back and dabbed at hot sauce at the corner of her mouth. "Are you going back to the cemetery tomorrow to see if someone messed with the grave again?"

"Yes."

"Good. I'm going too."

"We're all going," said Spider. Gutsy did not argue. She was happy that they would be coming with her.

"There *has* to be an answer," said Alethea. "We'll figure it out."

But they didn't figure it out that night.

When everyone started yawning, Alethea asked, "Do you want us to stay?"

"No," said Gutsy. "Besides, if you're not back for head count, you'll get in trouble with the Cuddlys."

"Who cares?"

"I do." She hugged Alethea, then Spider, and walked them to the door. "Thanks, though."

Alethea nodded at Sombra. "You keeping him?"

"If he wants to stay, then sure," said Gutsy.

"He probably has fleas."

"Fleas can be handled."

Alethea smiled and shook her head. "You think everything can be handled, don't you?"

Gutsy shrugged. "Pretty much."

"You're weird," said Alethea, "but I love you." She kissed Gutsy on the right cheek; Spider kissed the other side.

Gutsy went outside to watch them walk away. They seemed to take all the light and warmth of the day with them. That was okay, Gutsy told herself. Everything would be okay.

It was a moonless night and there were ten billion stars up there, so she dragged one of the plastic chairs around to the side of the house where there was no light. Sombra followed, silent as a ghost, and lay down beside her chair.

Gutsy leaned back, propping her bare feet against the

wall, and looked upward at infinity. Her heart hurt but her eyes were dry. She'd cried enough tears and now she wanted to let all that go, at least for a while.

Gutsy liked the silence. And the dark. She understood it. It appeared to be simple, but never was; it appeared to be empty, but wasn't.

Without knowing she was going to do it, her left hand drifted down and began scratching the back of Sombra's neck. The coydog allowed it. When Gutsy became conscious that she was doing it, she almost stopped. Almost.

She almost said, *It's all right,* too.

Almost.

But she didn't want to lie to the dog, or to herself.

Above them the wheel of night turned.

GUTSY DREAMED OF BURYING HER MOTHER. NOT ONCE, not twice, but every single day of her life. That was what her life had become. Finding her mother, withered and dead, wandering in the rooms of their little house; restraining her; re-shrouding her; wrestling her improbably heavy body onto the cart; driving back to the cemetery; burying her; coming home; finding her mother there again. Over and over in an endless dance of heartbreak and horror.

When she heard her bedroom door creak open, the sound folded itself into her dream. It was Sombra, come to watch as Gutsy did up the knots again around Mama's ankles and knees, elbows and wrists. The coydog watched with eyes that burned with real fire; eyes that gave off the only heat in the whole world. Sombra was bigger in the dream, more wolflike.

The dog's presence bothered Gutsy as she slept. It was wrong. When she'd come in from stargazing, hadn't she left the dog in the kitchen, with the door closed? How could he be in her room?

The dreaming Gutsy paused in her work, the ends of rope in her hands, and turned to the dog.

Except it wasn't a dog.

Somehow her mother wasn't in the shroud Gutsy was tying.

Instead Mama stood there in the open bedroom doorway. Her clothes were torn and streaked with mud, her eyes empty of everything except a bottomless hunger, her gray hands reaching and her dry teeth snapping at the air.

"Mama . . . ?" said Gutsy in a voice that sounded like a little child's.

She wanted to wake up out of the dream, but she could not.

Because she wasn't dreaming.

And her mother was there, in her room, reaching for her.

SOMBRA HOWLED IN THE KITCHEN.

Gutsy screamed in her bedroom.

Mama moaned as she grabbed Gutsy.

The dream held Gutsy with cold, strong fingers, trapping her for a moment at the edge of waking. For a terrible fragment of a second she wasn't sure whether this was a nightmare or if the world had cracked open and nightmares spilled out into her real life.

Then the smell of rot and grave dirt and sickness dragged her all the way into wakefulness.

Though it was still a nightmare. Of a kind.

"Mama!" shrieked Gutsy as gray fingers grabbed one shoulder and a handful of her hair, and a gaping, snarling mouth lunged forward for a bite.

To.

Bite.

Her.

"No, Mama!"

Gutsy slammed her palms against her mother's shoulders so hard it knocked Mama's head forward even faster. Those teeth clacked shut an inch from Gutsy's windpipe. Cold spit flecked her cheeks. For a moment they were locked together that way, Gutsy's hands stiff and braced; Mama pulling her by hair and shoulder, and those teeth snapping, snapping, snapping.

In another part of the house Gutsy could hear Sombra going wild, barking, howling, knocking things in the kitchen over to clatter and smash.

Here in her bedroom, Mama suddenly twisted her head to one side and tried to bite one of Gutsy's forearms. With a yelp, Gutsy let go with that arm and flailed at her mother, knocking the biting mouth away. That shifted the weight that was pressing down on her, and Mama lost her balance. She slipped halfway off the bed, and Gutsy turned her hips and kicked her own body the other way. It broke the contact, though she felt a flash of hot pain on her head and realized she'd lost some hair. She kept kicking until she reached the far side of the narrow bed, and then suddenly she was falling. The floor hit her like a punch between the shoulder blades and the air whooshed from her lungs as pain exploded in her shoulders and spine. She lay there for a moment, lost in pain, dazed, desperately trying to gasp in a spoonful of air.

The slap of bare feet on the floorboards snapped her out of it, and Gutsy looked through the fireworks of pain to see her mother lumbering around the end of the bed. She did not move fast, but it was a small bedroom and there was nowhere left to run.

If Gutsy had thought her town and her life were hell before, now she was sure of it. Everything about this moment burned her, including the certain knowledge that some devil had dug her mother up twice, had brought her here twice.

Maybe hell was all about reliving the worst possible experience over and over and over again throughout eternity.

In her mind an ugly little voice whispered, *Don't fight. Let go.*

The voice tried so hard to make sense. And Gutsy's mind tried to fool her into thinking that there was a light flickering in the eyes of this monster, and that it was the spark of Mama's soul. Her need not to be abandoned, her buffer against grief, fueled her need to believe that somehow, impossible as it was, Mama was still there. Still here with her. Not gone.

Not forever gone.

Let it happen. It'll be okay afterward. You'll be with Mama. Don't fight.

For a burning moment she almost stopped fighting. For one razor-sharp edge of a moment, Gutsy simply wanted to give in. To accept a bite if it was what paid her way to where Mama was.

That flicker of light was there. It really was. Wasn't it?

Before Gutsy even knew she was doing it, she reached up and over and grabbed the handle of the night-table drawer, yanked it hard enough to pull the drawer all the way out, and flung it at the monster pretending to be her mother. Pens and notebooks and jewelry and a book of poems went flying as the drawer struck Mama's reaching arms. Then Gutsy scrambled to her feet, snatched the pillow off the bed, and thrust it forward, pressing it into the gray hands, smashing it against the biting mouth, blocking those teeth, using it as a cushion as she drove her weight forward. Mama snarled and tried to spit the pillow out, but Gutsy shoved and ran forward until the thrashing body struck the thin wall between her bedroom and the narrow hallway that ran from living room to kitchen.

The impact shook the house and pictures fell from the wall, their pine frames splitting apart as they landed.

There were other thuds as Sombra threw himself against the far wall, his bark rising into panic.

"Please," Gutsy begged as those cold fingers tried to grab her again. "Mama, please don't."

The body was her mother's, and even though Father Esteban said that the souls of the dead were still in the body, and would be until judgment day when they all rose to heaven, there was no response other than a monster's need. This was not Mama. This was one of *los muertos vivientes*. Beyond thought, empty of life, filled only with hunger, offering nothing but heartbreak and death.

Gutsy struggled with the living corpse, twisting her body so that her back was to the door. Then, with a huge cry of fear and effort, she thrust her mother back, whirled, and ran for the door. Her foot caught on a tendril of blanket that had fallen to the floor during the struggle. She went flying and landed badly halfway into the hall. She turned to see Mama coming for her, mouth snapping, eyes dead, hands clawing at the air.

"No!"

Gutsy kicked free of the blanket, scuttled backward, got to her feet, and made a fast grab for the doorknob. She gave it a desperate pull and the door slammed shut as Mama lunged forward. The loose-jointed sound of hands and knees and maybe a head striking the door from the other side was horrible. She looked down at the doorknob and saw it rattle. It took a few long, long moments to realize that it was moving with the vibrations of Mama pounding on the door, but not because it was being turned.

Some of the dead were smarter. Some remembered how to do things like turn a door handle.

Not Mama, though.

Gutsy tried to feel some comfort in that. There was none. There was nothing but pain and loss on both sides of the door.

GUTSY STAGGERED DOWN THE HALLWAY, FALLING against the walls, gasping, crying. She jerked open the kitchen door and Sombra bounded out, snarling, eyes wild, teeth bared.

Not at her, though.

The coydog raced past her, but he didn't stop to bark at the trembling door. Instead the animal ran into the living room and out into the night through the open front door.

"Wait . . . no, don't go out there," cried Gutsy, realizing that whoever had brought Mama here might still be there. But the dog vanished. She could hear his furious barks and then the angry whinny of a horse.

Gutsy, shaking with fear and pain, staggered after. She couldn't see her machete anywhere. She'd leaned it against the arm of the couch, but it was gone. However, there was an umbrella stand beside the door, filled with baseball bats, a field hockey stick, a crowbar, and a heavy metal golf putter. She snatched up the hockey stick and dashed outside just in time to hear Sombra let out a high-pitched yelp of pain.

The sound came from up the street, in the direction of the back road out of town. If it had been only herself to think about, Gutsy would have gone back inside and pushed furniture in front of the doors. She would have gone back to deal with the thing in her bedroom. She would have fallen apart.

The dog, though . . .

She clutched the stick in her hand, ground her teeth together in a feral snarl, and ran.

High-pitched squeals of pain told her the way. Along the street a few windows popped with yellow as some of the neighbors lit lanterns. One or two curtains parted, but no one came out to see what was happening. That was so typical, she thought. People hid rather than get involved. They were braver during the day, braver in numbers, but at night they trusted closed doors, locks, and the night guards to deal with problems. No one wanted to be seen wandering in the streets for fear of being mistaken for one of the dead.

Gutsy reached the end of her street and skidded to a stop, because now there was no sound at all. Sombra had fallen silent. Was he dead? That thought stabbed her, making her realize how much she already cared about the strange coydog.

She edged toward the corner of the last house on the left, one of the empty ones used for bulk storage. There were more houses than people in New Alamo. Adjusting her grip on her weapon, she leaned out for a fast look and ducked back, letting her brain process what the brief glimpse had captured.

Then she leaned out again and stared. *Sombra lay in the middle of the street.*

Beyond him, moving away from the spot where he'd fallen, were two riders on horseback. For a wild moment, Gutsy was terrified that the cannibal ravagers had somehow breached the walls. That was always the worst fear in town.

When they raided a town, they left nothing and no one alive. Not a person, not even the smallest house cat.

"Please, God," she begged, gripping her weapon, aware of how flimsy it was against killers like that.

Then the riders moved into a patch of light thrown by a streetlamp. They wore long canvas coats whose split tails flapped as they galloped. Each had an old-style cowboy hat with the brim pulled low, and they both wore scarves wrapped around the lower half of their faces. Gutsy moved into the center of the street and stood by Sombra, who was still breathing and whimpering softly. There was fresh blood on his muzzle, but his eyes were closed.

Gutsy gripped her hockey stick in both hands.

"Come back and fight, you freaking cowards," she yelled.

One of them, the shorter of the two, cut a look over his shoulder and reined his horse to a stop. The rider looked too young to be doing what he was doing. A teenage boy or . . .

No. Was it a *woman*?

That thought somehow jolted Gutsy, because she hadn't expected that. But even in the bad light, she was sure she was right. It was a woman. Slim but strong-looking, with broad shoulders. She raised a weapon and pointed it at Gutsy. It wasn't a gun, though. It was Gutsy's own machete. It wasn't a challenge—it was a message letting Gutsy know that it was she who had brought Mama back, and she who had taken the big knife.

Gutsy raised her hockey stick and pointed back at her. After a moment, the woman gave a single, short nod. Then shouts filled the air, along with the sound of people running. Townsfolk and the night guards. The rider turned away, kicked her horse, and was gone. Gutsy dropped slowly to her knees beside the dog. Sombra was alive, but unconscious and bleeding.

The thought she'd had earlier, that New Alamo was the safest place anyone knew, now seemed to come back to mock her. This town wasn't safe at all.

Nowhere was safe.

Nowhere.

BAD NIGHTS CAN ALWAYS GET WORSE.

Night guards tore past to try to catch the riders. People crowded the streets now, everyone chattering but no one saying anything she needed to hear. Then all conversation died as a series of gunshots filled the night air from the direction of the rear gate. Then the town's alarm whistles were shrieking, giving the signal that everyone in town knew and dreaded—three shorts bursts followed by three longer ones, and three more short ones. An old code, from before the End.

SOS.

A lot of people thought that it meant "Save Our Ship" or "Save Our Souls." Gutsy knew it didn't, or at least it wasn't meant to mean that when German sailors invented the signal a long time ago. The nine sounds were picked because it was an easy code, and it was the only nine-sound message used in Morse code. Something she had learned in a book.

It was used now for one purpose, and it might as well have meant *Save Our Souls*.

It meant that the dead were inside the town walls.

The people scattered like sheep. Some screamed as they

ran for home. Maybe on another night Gutsy would have run away too.

She did not.

The dog—*her* dog—was hurt and she wasn't going to leave him to be devoured by *los muertos*. No way. She'd already lost too much. And besides, she was mad. *Really* mad. It burned in the skin of her face and in the muscles of her hands. She wanted to hurt someone. The female rider, for sure, and anyone else who was with her. A shambler would do very nicely. Or a ravager.

Someone shouted for medics, and a moment later a group of men came up the street, half carrying, half dragging the two sentries who had been assigned to the rear gate. The guards were alive, but dazed and bloody from having been badly beaten when the riders entered the town. Gutsy saw Dr. Morton come running up the street, looking disheveled and out of breath.

"What happened?" he yelled. "Someone tell me what happened." Morton spotted Gutsy and paused. "You—you're Luisa Gomez's daughter, right? Gracie or something?"

"Gabriella, but people call me Gutsy."

Morton nodded. "Right, 'cause you're a scavenger. Always taking risks, always going outside the walls."

Gutsy said nothing.

"Do you know what's going on around here tonight?" asked the doctor.

Before she could answer, one of the night guards came and grabbed the doctor's sleeve. "We need you, Doc. Couple of our boys got hurt. Jimmy Quiñones is pretty bad."

The doctor gave Gutsy a smile that was more like a

wince. "Sorry!" he said, then ran off with the guard.

One of her neighbors, Mrs. Gonzalez, came hurrying over. She had a ball-peen hammer in her hand. "Gabriella, sweetheart," she gasped, "hurry. Come with me. You'll be safe at our house."

Gutsy shook her head. "My dog's hurt."

"Dog?" said the woman. "That's a . . . is that a coyote, or . . . ?"

"He's my dog," insisted Gutsy.

"Well," said Mrs. Gonzalez dubiously, "whatever he is, he looks pretty bad. I'm sorry, sweetheart, but you need to leave him and come with us." The woman tried to take her arm, but Gutsy shook her off.

"He's my dog and I'll take care of him," she snarled. "Go home and hide and leave me alone."

Mrs. Gonzalez flinched and stepped back. "You're being stupid," she said. "*They're* inside."

There were more gunshots and yelling, and some screams. The fight was invisible, though, too far down the exit road to be seen. Someone kept blowing the stupid whistle, as if it was even necessary to let anyone know there was trouble. People were running everywhere. A hand-cranked siren began wailing like an angry ghost, the cry rising and filling the air with earsplitting insistence.

Suddenly Spider and Alethea were there, appearing as if out of nowhere. The sight of her friends almost made Gutsy lose it. It was such a relief to see the faces of the two people on earth who *got* her, who understood what was going on with her. Their faces were clouded with concern as they knelt down on either side of Gutsy.

"What happened?" asked Alethea. She wore a bathrobe

over pajamas and carried a baseball bat. The words *You Only Hurt the Ones You Love* were painted in rainbow script along its length. The handle was bound in leather and the heavy end had dozens of roundheaded screws drilled into it. She called the bat Rainbow Smite. Alethea joked about being "a lover, not a fighter," but she was fierce with the bat. Very fierce.

She had her tiara, though, and despite how insane everything was, it made Gutsy feel like the world still made sense if—in the middle of a crisis—Alethea had paused long enough to put on her tiara. It was as if it was a statement that said, *Don't worry, there's still time. Take a breath.*

Gutsy took a breath.

Spider wore only Halloween-pattern pajama bottoms with tarantulas and bats on them, and, for no reason Gutsy ever discovered, big floppy rubber rain boots. His weapon of choice was a *bo*, a sturdy wooden staff. Despite his skinny arms, Spider could spin that staff into a blinding whirlwind of destructive force.

He studied Gutsy for a moment, frowning as he looked into her eyes. "What's going on?"

"Not now," she said urgently. "We have to get Sombra home. He's hurt and I can't leave him out here."

"I got this," said Alethea, straightening. She turned toward a burly adult man who was standing in the street, clutching a sledgehammer as if ready to take on the world. "You!" she cried, pointing at him with Rainbow Smite. The man almost snapped to attention as if the command had been given by an actual princess and not a teenage girl. He even looked surprised by his own response. "This is my friend's dog. Pick him up."

"I—"

"*Now.*"

He did. The burly man handed his sledgehammer to Spider, squatted down, and lifted Sombra as easily as if the coydog was a puppy.

Despite everything, Gutsy had to turn away to hide a smile. Alethea could make people—teens or adults—do almost anything she wanted.

"This way," said Alethea haughtily, and waggled fingers at him as she started off toward Gutsy's home.

Spider began to follow, but Gutsy grabbed his arm. "Listen," she said urgently, "my mom's in there. In my room. I closed the door."

He gaped at her, aghast. "What? *How?*"

She told him the bones of what had happened and he looked sick.

"Oh my God," cried Spider. "Come on."

They hurried to catch up with Alethea and the man carrying the coydog.

THE MAN BROUGHT SOMBRA INTO THE HOUSE AND laid him on the couch. He looked around, seeming confused as to why he was there.

"Go away now," said Alethea with a wave of her hand.

The man cleared his throat, mumbled something, and left without waiting for a thank-you or explanation.

Outside, the all-clear whistle was blowing. Two long notes, a space, two more. *All clear my butt,* thought Gutsy. She closed the door behind them, turned, and leaned against it. Spider and Alethea looked at her and then slowly turned toward the sound of muffled thumps down the hall.

"Who's making all that racket?" asked Alethea, and then she stopped and jerked upright. "No. No. No way. Don't tell me that's . . ." She couldn't finish the sentence.

"Yes," said Gutsy. "They came here and they brought me a present."

It was a bad attempt at ugly humor, and no one laughed. Alethea closed her eyes for a moment as if fighting back a scream. Her whole body trembled with rage.

"That is beyond sick," murmured Spider.

The thumping was louder now, and they could hear moans.

The three of them stood and listened for almost a full minute.

Then Alethea whispered, "But . . . *why*?"

Gutsy merely shook her head.

"The woman rider," said Spider, "the one who stole your machete, did you recognize her at all?"

"I couldn't see anything but her eyes," said Gutsy. "If I've seen her before, she didn't make an impression on me. But if I see her again, I'll know her for sure."

"If we bury Mama again," said Spider quietly, "they're just going to dig her up and bring her right back, aren't they?" Gutsy said nothing. "Would they do that if she was . . . ?" He didn't finish the sentence, because they all knew what he meant. Even the Catholics in town had a supply of spikes and a good hammer. Everyone did.

On the couch, Sombra whimpered and all three of them snapped their attention to him. The thumping was one problem. The people who'd done this was another. The dog . . . he needed their help right now.

Alethea fetched the first aid kit from the shelf in the kitchen, hurrying past the shuddering door to Gutsy's bedroom. Spider began examining the dog's head and neck. He knew more about animals than the other two, having done a lot of after-school work on farms.

"I need water and clean rags," he said.

Gutsy fetched them, and she and Alethea stood by and watched as Spider cleaned the blood away with infinite gentleness and care. There was a lump on the top of Sombra's head and some bloody welts on his neck and right shoulder.

"I think they beat him with something heavy but not sharp," he said as he studied the wounds. "Like a whip handle, maybe, but with something heavy at the end of it. Weird. It knocked Sombra out, but I don't think it broke his skull. A concussion, maybe."

"Poor baby," said Alethea, stroking the dog's back and hips. Sombra was still unconscious, though he twitched and whined.

"Is he going to die?" asked Gutsy.

Spider shook his head. "I don't think so. I've seen farm dogs who were kicked by donkeys and cows worse than this who were okay after a while." He cleaned the wounds and applied a little of Old Mabel's Get-You-Right Salve, which was made by one of the women in town. It was an antibacterial ointment that had some herbs in it to reduce swelling and soothe hurts. Everyone used it.

When he was done, they left Sombra to sleep and went down the hall, past the bedroom, and sat at the kitchen table. Gutsy put the kettle on. The pounding never stopped.

There was so much to talk about. The people on the horses. Who were they? Why had they brought Gutsy's mom back from her grave? Twice? Why had they let *los muertos* into the town through the back gate? Why do any of that? There was the injured dog. There was the tragedy of the origin of that incessant pounding.

The night asked so much of them, demanding answers, demanding actions. They sat at the table and drank hot tea and tried to work their way through everything that happened.

After a while Sombra came limping along the hallway. Gutsy heard the soft click of his nails on the floorboards and turned as he walked slowly into the kitchen.

"Hey, boy," began Spider, but Gutsy shook her head.

The coydog came up to Gutsy and sat beside her chair, licked her ankle once, and then lay down. He was asleep within seconds. *Her* dog was asleep by her side. Gutsy could feel the shift inside her as that thought became her truth.

Gutsy stood up, crossed to the cabinet over the sink, and removed a hammer and a metal spike. According to the hardware store from which Gutsy had scavenged the spike, it was officially known as a hot-dipped galvanized four-inch nail. The hammer was actually a mallet with a rubber head. Simple, efficient, and brutal.

She opened a drawer and removed a bundle of heavy-duty canvas work gloves and took two.

"No," said Spider.

She looked at him, sighed, nodded, and took two additional pairs from the bundle and handed them to her friends. There were leather jackets in the closet. Gutsy had only two football helmets, though. Hers and her mother's. She gave them to her friends and wrapped a bath towel around her own head and face so that only her eyes were exposed. She secured it with a colorful bandanna.

They stood there, dressed for horror, outside the bedroom door.

"When it comes to it," said Alethea, reaching for the hammer, "I'll do that part."

"No," protested Gutsy, but Alethea overrode her.

"You're already freaked out, girl," said her friend. "You don't need to make it worse."

Spider nodded. They hugged. They opened the door.

They stepped into madness.

BOLDNESS BE MY FRIEND

Only those who will risk going too far can possibly

find out how far one can go.

—T. S. Eliot

"WHAT DID THEY SAY?" ASKED NIX AS BENNY WALKED slowly up the garden path to the porch. He had gone off to plead the case for the six of them—Benny, Nix, Chong, Lilah, Morgie, and Riot—to mount an expedition to Asheville.

Benny stopped, shoved his hands into his pockets, and sighed. The words still rang in his ears from the meeting he'd had with Solomon Jones and Mayor Kirsch. They were both sympathetic, they were both good guys, but they were both acting like adults. Not in a good way.

"Benny," said the mayor, "you got lucky last time. With Charlie Pink-eye. With Saint John and the Night Church. You took some stupid risks and got lucky. You're still only fifteen—"

"I'm sixteen," corrected Benny.

"Okay, whatever, sixteen. You're a kid. I can't let a minor go stumbling across the entire United States toward what is almost certainly his own death. You may be tough for your age, but you're not your brother. And besides, Tom died out there."

Solomon Jones was a little less condescending. "I called a meeting of the officers of the Freedom Riders and the mayors of the Nine Towns. We'll work out a strategy and we will find the answers."

"How long's that going to take?" asked Benny, keeping his frustration off his face.

"The meeting is set for next Tuesday."

"That's almost a week from now."

"It's the soonest we can get the right people together."

Benny shook his head. "My friends and I could be halfway there by then. Maybe all the way, if we can find enough gas between here and there."

"Not a chance," snapped the mayor. "There's no way on earth I'm going to let you and your crew take six quads and—"

There was more. There was shouting. It all amounted to the same thing.

"They said no," Benny told his friends.

"Of course they did," said Chong, who was sitting in the shade of the porch. He had been weaving a broad-brimmed straw hat and had a piece of the straw between his teeth. A compound bow and a full quiver of arrows was propped against the wall nearby.

"Solomon, Mayor Kirsch, all of them," said Benny. "They said they were working on a plan. They said they'd handle it. They said we should try being kids for a while and stop messing in stuff."

"What'd you expect?" asked Morgie, who sat cross-legged on the porch floor surrounded by a dozen knives of various lengths he'd arranged like a starburst. He ran a whetstone along the edge of an old pre–First Night army bayonet.

"Pretty much expected them to say all that," said Benny.

Everyone nodded.

"Even after all this," said Nix. "Even after everything we

went through and all the stuff we did, they still think we're just kids."

Lilah sat next to Chong and was busy with strips of tough rawhide that she was using to secure a double-edged knife to the length of black pipe she used as a spear. She was smiling as she worked. She often smiled when she worked on her weapons.

Nix and Riot sat on the porch swing. Nix was cleaning and oiling a Glock nine-millimeter pistol that used to belong to Tom, while Riot was sorting small metal ball bearings into the pouches of a green military web belt.

Benny went over and sat near Morgie, shrugging off the strap of the *kami katana* his brother had given him the night he'd been murdered. Benny eased the gleaming sword from its scabbard and studied the blade. There was so much history in the weapon. Tom had gotten it from Joe Ledger a long time ago when the two of them were hunting for monsters—human and zom—in the Ruin; then Tom had used it as a paid bounty hunter, giving closure to the families of the living dead; and then it came to Benny, who avenged Tom and then carried that sword through the war with Saint John. So much history, so much blood. It was a warrior's sword. It had never once been used for selfish or cruel purposes, despite the horrible work it had done. After Tom had died, the mayors of the Nine Towns had wanted to put the sword in a museum. Benny declined.

Without looking up from his work, Morgie slid a bottle of oil, a rag, and another whetstone toward Benny.

They sat there and worked as birds sang in the trees.

After a while Nix said, "Riot says she can pick the lock on the shed, so we can get to the quads. Once we're ready we can just push them out into the field. We'll mess with the other quads so by the time the guards fix them, we'll be gone."

Benny nodded.

"We can take three trailers, too," added Riot. "We can tow enough gas to get us to Arizona. Maybe Texas."

Benny nodded.

"Got enough dried meats, canned vegetables, and protein bars to last for a couple of weeks," said Chong. "Carpet coats, first aid kit, and the rest are in bundles hidden where we can grab them."

Benny nodded.

Morgie glanced at the others. "They'll try to stop us."

"They can try," said Lilah.

The birds chattered between the leaves, bees and dragonflies drifted among the flowers, clouds tumbled across the sky. The six of them worked.

Nix watched the clouds and didn't even glance down as she reassembled her pistol. Her hands moved quickly, smoothly, expertly. When she slapped the magazine into the handle, it startled the birds and a few leaped into the air.

Benny glanced at Nix. She was smiling. She was almost sixteen and the scars on her face were only now beginning to fade from rose red to ice white against the tan of her skin. Nix caught his eye and they studied each other for a moment, sharing a conversation that didn't need words. Her smile was so much older than she was.

"Dawn tomorrow," said Benny. They all nodded.

And continued working.

THE QUADS WERE UGLY, CHUNKY LITTLE MOTORIZED machines with four fat rubber tires and a kind of saddle for the driver. On flat roads, they could tear along at forty miles an hour; and even over rough terrain, the quads could travel an astounding twenty-five miles per hour.

During the terrible weeks-long battles that, collectively, were known as First Night, the military had tried a lot of different extreme measures to stop the growing armies of the dead. When everything else failed, some maniacs had tried using nuclear weapons. That still astounded Benny, who'd learned about it in school. The nukes had destroyed some of the zoms, but they'd also killed hundreds of thousands—perhaps millions—of the living who were trapped inside the targeted cities. Those who didn't die in the blasts were exposed to radiation. The cancer rate among survivors of First Night was ghastly.

What made it worse was that there were two effects that turned a war into a defeat. The people killed by the blasts, along with countless living dead, became radioactive, and that was as deadly a weapon against the living as their bites. Mr. West-Mensch, the history teacher at Reclamation High

School, said that dropping the nukes insured that the dead won. Partly because of the devastation and radiation, but mostly because of the EMPs. Electromagnetic pulses were massive discharges of energy that burned out nearly all electrical equipment, from cell phones needed to call for help to the engines of emergency responder vehicles. The world went quiet all at once. Communication between people was gone. Planes fell from the skies. Even the tanks and weapons of the military ground to a halt.

"We were losing the war," said Mr. West-Mensch, "but the shock was wearing off. If we'd used the time we had, then any groups that were temporarily protected by natural barriers, like rivers or mountains, might have survived. If not on their own, then long enough for authorities to reinforce them while mustering a counterattack. Smarter leaders would have risen inside the crisis to take charge. Had the EMPs not destroyed all cell phone, radio, and Internet communication, we would have been able to share information and strategies, offer and ask for help, make plans. Let's face it, the zoms are simple. Within days we knew the rules of the fight. Don't get bitten. Everyone who dies reanimates. Destroying the brain or brain stem kills them completely. They can't think, they can't organize or plan. They can't adapt. We can. They can't use weapons. We can. They don't learn from what we do, so any good plan becomes endlessly repeatable. No . . . they didn't win the war, we lost it."

What really galled Benny was a belief spread among the survivors that somehow technology itself was partly to blame for the dead rising. Benny didn't know who'd started that rumor, or why people accepted it as completely as they did, but for fifteen years no one even tried to repair the old machines. Except for a few hand-crank generators, there was no electricity at all in Mountainside.

Then Benny, Nix, Chong, Lilah, and Riot had come riding out of the Ruin on motorized vehicles. No one could say that those machines were anything but a blessing. They allowed Benny and his friends to outpace the reaper army and warn the towns. Even though the reapers had many quads, their army traveled only as fast as the soldiers on foot and the swarms of zoms they brought with them.

After that war, the Nine Towns had nearly two hundred working quads, and Solomon Jones had polled the citizens to find anyone with mechanical knowledge. A massive plan was underway to bring technology back. Technicians from the American Nation helped. There were protesters to this, of course, and even some bits of sabotage perpetrated by a radical few who still believed that technology would restart the war with the dead, but Benny knew that technology was coming back.

It pleased him that technology was also going to help his crew get out of town fast.

BENNY AND NIX MOVED THROUGH THE PREDAWN
darkness like ghosts, keeping to the black shadows thrown
by the double-wide trailer used as a guardhouse. They
reached the foot of the tower without being seen because
the guards, true to their duties, were looking out, not in.
If these had been enemy sentries, Benny would have sent
Lilah and Riot to take care of them. Both of them were stone
killers. But the guards working the midnight-to-eight shift
on the south tower were neighbors. Jenny Thomas and her
uncle, Chas.

Since the reaper war, each of the Nine Towns had built
much stronger defenses than the fragile chain-link fences
they'd relied on before. The guard tower now looked past the
fences to a field six times wider than the old one. Beyond that
was the tree line of a thick forest.

They took off their shoes and began to climb, making no
sound at all on the wooden rungs. Benny went first and Nix
was a ghost behind him. The tower was tall, but the climb was
easy, and they reached the lip of the platform in less than a
minute. The door to the boxy guard station was closed, but
that wasn't a problem, because it was never locked.

There was a muffled sound of conversation from inside, and Benny pressed his ear to the door to listen. The two guards were talking about Asheville, and he could just make out the words.

Chas: ". . . leave them to their own problems. We got enough to deal with here."

Jenny: "What about the cure?"

Chas: "Ah, the cure, the cure, that's all I ever hear about. We only have their word that it even works."

Jenny: "Of course it works. Look what it did for Lou Chong."

Chas: "What did it do? He looks like one of *them*. Kid creeps me out."

Jenny: "He's a good kid, Chas."

Chas: "Maybe he is, but if he looks at me the wrong way, I'll put him down and won't cry a tear about it."

Before Benny could give Nix a signal, she stood up, opened the door, and walked in.

"Hey," gasped Jenny, surprise making her voice jump an octave, "what are you—?"

There was a metallic sound that was absolutely distinctive. Nix had racked the slide on her Glock. *Oh boy*, thought Benny, and then he went in after her. Jenny and Chas were standing there, staring at the gun in Nix's small hand, confused smiles on their faces.

"Put your hands on your heads," said Nix in a voice that was as cold as winter ice. "If you try anything, I'll blow your kneecaps off."

Chas bristled and puffed out his chest as he took a threatening step forward. Benny's sword was out of its scabbard in a tenth of a second, and the tip of it against Chas's chest stopped him cold.

"You heard her," he said.

"What's this all about?" gasped Jenny, fear igniting in her eyes.

"Hands on your heads," repeated Nix. "Fingers laced. I won't ask again."

They did as she ordered. Jenny was visibly trembling and Chas looked ready to kill. But he was no fool.

Benny resheathed his sword and removed a ball of strong hairy twine from his pocket, pulled their hands down behind their backs, and very quickly but efficiently tied their wrists, looping the line through their belts. He ordered them to sit down, and bound their ankles. Then he produced rags from another pocket. He balled some of the rag and stuffed it into their mouths, then wound more cloth around their heads to keep it secure. Once he was sure they could breathe, he straightened, then leaned over and scanned the field. It was completely empty. He waved his arm to Lilah and Morgie, who removed the bar from the gates. Lilah pushed the gate open as Riot and Chong came out of hiding, pushing the first two quads. Lilah and Morgie ran to get two more. When all six machines were outside the gate and the trailers hooked up, Morgie signaled Benny. It all took less than four minutes.

"They're done," said Benny quietly. He turned and looked down at Jenny and Chas. "Okay, here's the deal. We're leaving, and we don't want anyone to stop us. The next shift starts in an hour. We'll bar the gate again from outside, so don't worry about zoms getting in or anything.

Sorry for all this, but you know you'd have tried to stop us."

Chas said something very obscene, but the rags muffled most of it.

Nix smiled at him as she released the magazine from her pistol and showed it to them. It was empty. She dropped it on the floor between the captives, then slapped a fully loaded magazine into the weapon and pulled back the slide to load a live round into the chamber.

They started to go, but then Benny paused and turned. He bent over Chas and very quietly said, "Chong's my friend. What happened to him isn't his fault. He takes his meds and he's fine. You have no idea what he went through to save this town, including you and your whole family. If I ever see you again, and if you ever say or do anything to him, you and me are going to have a problem. Sure, I'm only sixteen, but do you think that's going to matter?"

Chas glared defiantly up at him.

"Chong's worth ten of you," Benny said. He straightened, turned, and followed Nix down the ladder.

Before joining the others, Benny touched Nix's arm and bent close to her.

"We're in trouble now," he said. "Solomon and Mayor Kirsch are never going to understand why we did this. Why we *had* to do this."

"It's done," said Nix. "Can't go back now."

"I know, but . . . we *are* doing the right thing," Benny said. "Right?"

Nix took two handfuls of his shirt and used the grip to pull him down a bit as she stood on her toes. She kissed Benny very sweetly on the lips. He wrapped one arm around her waist and tangled his fingers in her wild hair, and the kiss deepened.

Finally they stood for a moment, touching foreheads, leaning into each other's energy.

"Last year," he murmured, "after the fight with Saint John . . . I thought I'd lost you, Nix. I thought I wasn't ever going to be enough for you."

"I guess we kind of lost each other out there," said Nix. "We got so busy fighting that we stopped paying attention."

"To what? To us?"

"No, to the people we were turning into," said Nix. "I'm not the little girl from town anymore. You're not that boy who complained about everything and hated your brother. Let's face it, Benny, the world hasn't been very nice to us. We've almost died more times than I can count. So . . . falling in love and all that romantic stuff, that 'being a couple' stuff almost didn't survive." She paused and stepped back, glancing at the night-shrouded town behind them and out through the open gate. "And now we're leaving again and maybe we'll get hurt out there. Or die. Or whatever. We'll change, though, I know that much. We'll change for sure."

Benny licked his lips. "Then we'll change."

She started to go, stopped, turned back. "Benny, I don't know how to tell the future, so I don't know what will happen to us. Not just all six of us, but *us*. You and me. I don't know. All I do know is that you gave me some time and some distance after we got back last year, and if you had pushed me, you'd have pushed me all the way away." She smiled, and it was a little sad. "I love you, Benny. Maybe I don't say it enough, but it's how I feel. I love you, and one way or another, you're always going to be in my life. Always."

He felt a knife turn slowly in his heart. "I love you, too, Nix. Always will."

He was keenly aware that they were not saying exactly the same thing.

"Hey," called Morgie in a harsh whisper, "are you two monkey-bangers coming or not?"

Nix gave Benny another kiss. Quicker, lighter, but still real.

Benny adjusted the *kami katana* strap that slanted diagonally across his chest, reached up over his shoulder to touch the handle of the weapon for good luck, then followed Nix.

There were heavy iron sockets on both sides of the doors. Once they were outside, Morgie helped Benny lift the ten-foot oak beam and slide it into place. It had been put there in case the town became overrun and fleeing survivors needed to trap the zoms inside. The next shift of tower guards would have to exit through a key-locked access door to get out here and remove it. That would take time. For now, it would slow down pursuit. Benny smiled. The exterior bar was one of a hundred new precautions Captain Ledger had recommended. One of a hundred ways the old soldier had made life safer for the people of the Nine Towns. It galled Benny that Ledger had risked his own life, over and over again, for the people behind those gates; and now they were being too slow about doing as much for him.

Morgie patted the beam, nodded, and then punched Benny on the shoulder. "We're good," he said.

They ran to join the others.

The six of them pushed their quads all the way to the tree line and then another hundred yards down the main trader's road. By now the sky was turning a bloody red, and it threw its lurid light across their path. If anyone felt uneasy at the gory hue of the morning, no one dared mention it.

When they were a mile from the town, they climbed onto the saddles, fired up the engines, and drove away from home.

Interlude Two

THE HUNTER FOLLOWED THE BLOOD TRAIL FOR TWO miles.

There were blood smears on leaves, on tree trunks, against a big rock. And one big bloody handprint on the fender of an ancient Mustang convertible that had likely been abandoned long before the dead rose.

The hunter was annoyed by how sloppy his quarry was. Either the man was dazed from whatever catastrophe had befallen him, or he had no idea how to move in the woods. The man moved like he did not care that anyone might follow. That was stupid, because these woods were filled with dangers. Some that hunted on four legs, others that went on two. Alive and dead.

The hunter claimed these woods as his own, and predators who came here had to earn their right to share this forest. The hunter allowed the big hunting cats from the zoo to prowl here. They frightened off most of the scavengers and those infected who hadn't yet lost their minds. Those cats occasionally took down the dead. Not to consume them, but for sport. Leopards were like that. They, like house cats, were among the few animals who hunted for the joy of slaughter.

Many humans were like that. Even some of the soldiers the hunter had run with once upon a time had not been drawn to an idealistic sense of honor or even the sense of empowerment that came with bearing arms. Some wanted to spill blood, walk through blood, see blood, and know that it was they who had spilled it.

The hunter understood that mind-set because it was important to know how minds work. It was not, however, how his mind worked. He had killed so many times that he'd long since lost count. Sane people do not keep that kind of tally. Not unless they want to ruin themselves. As a soldier, as a sniper, as a leader of men and women through the valley of the shadow of death in battlefields around the world, he had spilled blood. And now, here in the wasteland of what had once been America, he killed nearly every day. Animals for food, the dead for protection, and humans for various reasons. He never once enjoyed it.

He killed to survive, but never for sport. There had been too much senseless death in the world. Everyone he knew was dead. Friends, family, brothers-in-arms. Dead. The world had become a graveyard.

If the wounded man was benign, then the hunter would offer help. First aid, some food and water, and precise directions for leaving this forest. For going elsewhere. If the man was hostile, then he would die. There wasn't a lot of give in the hunter. He set strict rules and lived by them. There were a lot of graves hidden among the weeds and wildflowers in these woods.

The hunter moved on, going faster now because this fool did not merit a more skillful chase. The footprints wandered on, and then he slowed as he saw something odd. The prints suddenly seemed different. Deeper. The hunter paused and knelt by one of them, touching the dirt to see if it was wetter or spongy with moss. It wasn't.

Then he saw something else that was wrong. The print was smeared a little. The tread marks looked blurred, doubled, as if the foot had stepped, lifted and stepped down again in the same spot. Almost perfectly, but not. And the weight distribution was wrong. A person walking forward lands heel-heavy. These had that, but he saw that the ball of the foot was equally deep. As if the person had stepped back into his own print and walked backward. Which made no sense unless . . .

The barrel of a pistol touched the back of his neck.

"Hold it right there, sparky," said a cold voice. "You even breathe wrong and I'll kill you."

THE RAT CATCHERS

I don't think of all the misery
but of the beauty that still remains.

—ANNE FRANK

SPIDER DROVE THE WAGON TO HOPE CEMETERY, WITH Alethea seated beside him and Gutsy in the back with her mother. This time the shroud was still, without sound or movement except the rocking of the wagon. Sombra lay with his head on Gutsy's lap, looking at her with his pale, wise dog eyes.

It had taken a lot of persuading to get the day guards to let them take the wagon outside that morning. Two of the night guards had been badly beaten by the masked riders, and a half-dozen of the dead had been turned loose in town. Luckily, the response to the whistle calls had been quick and efficient, with scores of people rushing out to do as they had been trained. They circled each of the living dead, using big T-poles to push them back. The T-bar at the end of each pole was a yard wide, and when two or three people worked together, the bars created a barrier. With a couple of strong men holding each pole and other folks using smaller T-poles to shove, a group of five or six could easily maneuver a dead person into one of the many pens positioned around town. Everyone knew how to do this, and everyone had to practice the drills a few times each month.

Once the dead were confined in the pens, handlers wearing head-to-toe body armor would go in, wrestle each *muerto* to the ground, bind them securely, and wrap leather muzzles around their mouths. The dead were then put on display to allow people to see if anyone knew them. Families would claim their loved ones and bury them according to preferred customs. The unclaimed would be taken by the guards out of town, spiked, and burned where prevailing winds would blow their smoke and ash away.

The efficiency of it always pleased Gutsy, who liked a good process. A few times, though, she had made suggestions for doing it better, and was typically ignored. Being fifteen was a pain in the butt sometimes. She also got told off for being "too smart for her own good," an expression that never made sense to Gutsy.

As for the riders, the marks on the ground made it clear that they'd ridden away west. The cemetery was in the other direction. Six heavily armed teams of guards went out to patrol the area around New Alamo, and plans were being drawn to beef up town security.

Gutsy had to explain that the riders had brought her mother back from the cemetery, and that led to a broader explanation that felt to her like a trial. The woman in charge of town security, Karen Peak, hammered her with questions, and rather than being "too smart," Gutsy played it dumb, pretending not to know much. Spider and Alethea chimed in to say that it was all a mystery—not far from the truth—and to assure the authorities that Mama Luisa Gomez was now fully dead. Father Esteban and Dr. Morton were called in to confirm it.

It was all unpleasant and it took forever. In the end, though, Karen Peak allowed them to go, but only on the condition that they return before dark. A patrol rode with them about halfway and said they would be working the area, just in case. Gutsy thanked them but was happy to see them ride off.

When they were alone, Spider said, "This is what I hate about this town. I mean, you *told* them that the riders dug up your mom, but they didn't send any trackers out to the cemetery to start a hunt? Is it just me, or are they all a little stupid?"

"It's not you, honey," murmured Alethea. "I think everyone over . . . like . . . twenty-two is weird."

"Why twenty-two?" asked Spider.

"If they're twenty-two, then they were seven when the End happened. That's old enough to remember things."

"I can remember things from when I was three."

"You're interrupting me, Spider. Shhhh, now," she said, patting him on the knee. "The older a person was when the End happened, the more they were messed up *by* the End. Littler kids probably just cried their way through it and got over it."

"Does that make sense?" Spider asked, directing the question to Gutsy. She just shook her head.

Alethea continued as if he hadn't spoken. "So, people who were teenagers or, worse yet, adults, when the dead rose, are really messed up. They have a condition. I think it's called postal stress disorder."

"Post-traumatic stress disorder," supplied Gutsy.

"That's what I said. So it's not their fault that they're all messed up. I mean, how could they not be? Their whole world went *poof!*"

"I thought 'poof' means it blew up," said Spider.

"Okay, then their world got *eaten*. Thanks, Mr. Literal. You're missing my point. They are all in the same kind of permanent shock. All you have to do is look around to see it. We have the weirdest set of rules and laws in town. I read about laws in books, and ours are freaky. Some are crazy overprotective, and some—like letting us actually go to the cemetery where these rider guys kept digging up Mama Gomez—well, that only makes sense if you're, y'know, damaged."

Spider came back at her with how it wasn't right to make fun of people who had mental or emotional problems, and they got into a long discussion that turned into a fight. Gutsy tuned them out and instead tried to make sense of what little she knew. But it refused to be made sense of.

The riders. Digging up Mama and bringing her to the house. Why? If they wanted to kill Gutsy, they could have cut her throat while she slept. What was the point of going to all the effort of bringing her mother home to do it? That was sick and it seemed like a lot of effort for no good reason.

Except that everything had a reason. Gutsy firmly believed that.

So, if there was a reason and it was completely beyond her, then it meant she didn't have enough information. Gutsy could accept that as a fact. It gave her a purpose, and purpose helped her shove her emotions to one side. She tried never to let emotions interfere with solving a problem.

Work the problem and the answers will come. That was something Mr. Urrea told her once. It seemed like an offhand comment, but it was one of the most important things she'd ever learned. It made so much sense to her.

She chewed on it. After a while she heard her friends laughing. Their fights, no matter how intense they seemed at the time, never drove a wedge between Spider and Alethea. It was like arm wrestling for them. A lot of effort and growling and determination to win, but once it was over—it was over.

As they approached the cemetery, Spider stood up and said, "What the . . . ?" Then he tugged hard on the reins. The wagon rumbled to a stop. Alethea and Gutsy were standing now too.

"Oh man," breathed Alethea.

Gutsy cried out, leaped down, and broke into a dead run.

"Wait," cried Spider, but then he was pelting behind her. Alethea, slower than the others, hurried after. They ran past dozens of graves, then slowed and stopped by the open mouth of Mama's grave. That one they knew would be empty. There were dozens of shoe prints around it. Horse hoofprints too. Around her empty grave and around dozens of other empty holes.

Gutsy and her friends turned in a circle, staring slack-jawed and wide-eyed.

Many of the recent graves in Hope Cemetery had been dug up.

All the coffins had been pried open, and all the dead from those graves were gone.

THE THREE OF THEM WANDERED THROUGH THE defiled cemetery, stopping to peer into open graves, shaking their heads. Lost.

The graveyard was big and old, but not all of it belonged to New Alamo. There were huge sections from before the End, and a quick examination showed that none of those graves had been touched. Only the sections where people who'd died after the End were buried had been disturbed. Not all of them, though, but a lot. Too many.

Sombra limped along with them, sometimes ranging ahead to follow some movement, but it was always a piece of torn shroud blowing in the wind, or a startled lizard, or nothing at all.

They drifted back toward Mama Gomez's grave and stood for a while in a clump, staring down into the shadows at the bottom of the empty hole. Sombra circled them, sniffing the ground.

"Okay," said Alethea after taking a few deep breaths, "you're the one who likes puzzles, Gutsy, so what the *heck* is going on?"

When Gutsy didn't answer, Alethea snapped her fingers in front of Gutsy's face.

"Uh-uh, girlfriend," said Alethea sternly, "we're not doing the whole 'I'm too shocked to think' thing. I'm scared green and I *don't* like puzzles. So, do whatever you need to do to go all Sherlock Holmes on this. Tell me *something*."

They had all read several Sherlock Holmes short stories last summer, and Gutsy had figured out some of the mysteries before they'd been revealed.

Spider, who often disagreed with his foster sister, waved his arms to indicate the whole cemetery and said, "We seem to have a lot of clues."

"Clues," echoed Gutsy. "Right. Clues."

She rubbed her hands over her face and closed her eyes for a long moment. When she opened them, she tried to see everything as if for the first time, tried to pull all her previous opinions and judgments out and put them to one side.

"What's strange," began Gutsy slowly, "is that not all the graves are open."

They went through and counted them. Out of more than five hundred graves in that part of the cemetery, ninety-seven had been opened.

"Maybe that's all the time they had," suggested Spider. "Maybe they'll do more tonight."

Gutsy considered that but shook her head. "I don't think so."

"Why not?"

"Well, look at where they dug. A few here, a couple over there. The open graves are scattered all over. If they were going to dig up everyone, why not work one section at a time?" She walked a few yards away and stopped by an overturned grave marker. The name Jorge Ramirez had been painted onto a little wooden plaque nailed to a heavy cross.

"Skinny Jorge?" asked Spider.

"The one with the weird teeth? He was a farmer," said Alethea. "His family lived over on the far side of town. I only knew him because his oldest son, Diego, hits on me all the time."

Gutsy nodded. "How'd he die?"

Alethea shrugged. "He got the flu, I think."

Spider nodded.

They walked on and stopped to read the names on every single grave marker. Most were crosses, because there were so many Mexicans and Mexican Americans in the town. Leftovers from the relocation camp, and some people who had fled north from Mexico. Of those, about fifty were Catholics. Their crosses were each marked with the name of a saint. Other people buried there were a mix of Protestants, Jews, Muslims, one Hindu, and some people who had nonreligious markers. Gutsy spoke each name aloud, and they tried to remember something about the person whose body had been stolen from their place of rest. Of the ninety-seven missing bodies, the three of them knew seventy-one, which was a higher number than Gutsy expected.

There were more than four thousand people in New Alamo, but there had been many more. However, the town was dwindling down. Not because of shamblers or ravagers, but constant waves of diseases—flu, mumps, tuberculosis. More than half the people in town had died over the last four years. Twelve years ago, when the town guards were organized and the defenses reinforced, there had been twenty-two thousand people. They were not all buried here, though.

During the worst outbreaks of disease, the town council had used death carts to carry loads of corpses out to fire pits. That had created its own problems, of course, because in their panic to burn all the infected bodies and clothes, the townsfolk hadn't thought about wind patterns or the effect of ash soaking into the ground during the rains. While it was true that fire purified, not all the bodies were completely consumed, and some diseases survived. The pollution and diseases that got into the water table killed more people in New Alamo than *los muertos*.

"I'm no Sherlock Holmes," said Alethea as they stood in front of the last empty grave, "but I'm starting to see a pattern here."

"What pattern?" asked Spider, looking back the way they'd come.

"The names," Gutsy said, and Alethea nodded.

"What about them?"

Gutsy bent down, picked up the marker that had been kicked over by the grave robbers, and showed it to Spider. The name was Lucy Dominguez.

"So?" he asked.

"So, that grave over there is a Cantu and the one next to it are the Santiagos. And down there, that was old Mr. Diaz. Most are Spanish."

"Okay, so that's freaky. It's six Spanish names to every one that's not." He cut the girls a look. "You trying to say this was about race? I mean . . . come on, we learned about that in school, but there's not enough people left for that kind of stuff anymore."

Gutsy took a moment with that. "Maybe not, but New Alamo wasn't always a mixed-race town. Remember, my mama and a lot of the people here were prisoners. Undocumented. Nobody really cared much about them."

As if in answer to that, Sombra gave a single, sharp bark.

"OH, COME ON," PROTESTED SPIDER, "THERE'S GOT TO be more to it than someone being racist."

"Of course there is," agreed Gutsy, "and I could be totally wrong . . . but you have to admit it's weird."

"Everything's weird," said Spider. "Why would some bigots dig up all these bodies? Why would they bring your mom back to your place? How would they even know which body buried here *was* your mom? Those riders don't even live in our town."

"What makes you think that?" asked Gutsy.

"They rode away."

"Sure," said Gutsy, "but while they were in town, they wore masks to hide their faces. The one who stole my machete pointed it at me. She knew who I was."

Spider shook his head. "I don't know, Guts, it sounds like a stretch to me."

"Let's keep looking," interjected Alethea. "Maybe we'll find something that makes it make sense."

They spread out to make their own investigations, calling information back and forth every time one of them saw something.

"I'm seeing like . . . fifteen, twenty different sets of prints," Gutsy observed. "Same kind of boots, though. Same tread patterns. Different marks of wear—cuts, nicks, whatever— on them, so we could maybe match the prints to the specific boots." She stopped to consider. "Whoever these guys are, there's a bunch of them."

"I don't think they were all guys. Take a look at this." Alethea placed her foot into one of the prints, and it was almost the same size. "Either that's a guy with an awfully small foot, or it's that woman you saw in town."

They kept looking and found single-wheel tracks inside the front cemetery gate and several sets of wagon wheel tracks out on the road; and there were none at all at the rear gate. It suggested that the people who did this had used smaller carts inside the cemetery and loaded the bodies onto big wagons outside, and then gone northeast. Surely not as far as San Antonio, though the wheels all rolled in that direction. Gutsy knew the terrain nearly all the way to that distant city. There wasn't much there. Ghost towns, overgrown farms, dead factories, and a lot of *los muertos*.

"Who are these freaks?" Spider wondered aloud, but no one had an answer.

There were marks from single-wheeled carts all over the place. That told Gutsy that the grave robbers were using wheelbarrows. It made her sick with anger to think that the bodies were being torn from the ground and dumped into wheelbarrows for transport out to the wagon. The lack of respect for the dead was horrible. Inhumane.

The wagon tracks out on the road were thicker, and it was clear they were using old car tires. A lot of people did that because there were plenty of tires around, and even though the weather had rotted a lot of them, good ones weren't that hard to find.

Sombra came out and sniffed the tire tracks, uttered a low growl, and promptly peed all over the marks.

"Well," said Spider, "I guess that says it all."

Alethea bent to give the coydog a gentle scratch in one of the few undamaged spots on his smoky hide.

Gutsy walked to the cart, giving Gordo an affectionate pat on the withers, then stopped and leaned on the wooden slat rail to stare at the form lying silent and cold inside the shroud. Her friends came and stood on either side of her.

"We can't bury her here," said Alethea as she came to stand beside Gutsy. "Not after this. Which sucks so bad."

Gutsy nodded.

It took her a while before she answered. "You know, I'm getting a little tired of being pushed around by all this."

"So we turn it over to Karen Peak or the town council and let them handle it," said Alethea. Then she shook her head. "Ah . . . I know that look, Guts. That's not what you're going to do, is it?"

"No."

Spider looked confused. "What else is there *to* do?"

Gutsy smiled. From the way her friends recoiled, she knew that it wasn't a nice smile, or a pretty one. It made Sombra sit up straight and show his teeth. "I've got a plan."

"A plan?"

"Yeah," she said, "and you're not going to like it."

THEY FINISHED FILLING IN MAMA'S GRAVE IN UNDER
an hour.

It was sad work, but the anger kept them all at it. The sun
fried them and the wind scoured them, but it got done. Gutsy
used the flat of her shovel to hammer the cross into place.

"Now what?" asked Alethea, dripping with sweat and
leaning heavily on the upright handle of her shovel. She took
a yellow bandanna from her shirt pocket and mopped her
brow, then offered it to Spider.

"Eww, gross," he said, pushing it away. He used a sleeve to
wipe sweat from his eyes.

Gutsy used her shovel to smooth the dirt, then laid the
handle over her shoulder and marched back to the wagon.
Spider and Alethea exchanged a look, shrugged, and followed.
They caught up to her as Gutsy was stowing the tools, and
she took theirs and secured them all, then fetched two bowls,
filled them with water, put one down for Sombra, and held
the other so Gordo could drink.

"Well . . . say something," said Alethea, giving Gutsy a
small shove. "I left my psychic powers in my other tiara."

Gutsy leaned forward to touch her forehead to Gordo's,

and they stood like that for a moment. She wished all of life was as simple and pure as this. Horses were smart and they had their own quirks, but unless they were deliberately mistreated, they weren't mean. Dangerous, sure, but any animal can be dangerous. That was nature. But not mean. She kissed the old horse and hunkered down next to Sombra, who was lapping up the last of the water in his bowl. The coydog flinched when she tried to touch him, then seemed to think better of it and allowed her fingers to stroke his head. She was careful not to touch the big bruise, which looked better but still not good. Sombra was not mean either. He probably had a right to be. His true nature showed through and there was a gentleness, a sweetness beneath the fear and distrust. Whoever had hurt him tried to turn him into a brute, a monster, and maybe they had, but not completely; and perhaps that damage could be undone over time. Gutsy hoped so.

She knew her friends were getting impatient, but that was okay. They would wait for her, despite what Alethea said.

Finally Gutsy straightened and wiped her hands on her jeans. In a voice pitched so that only they could hear her, she said, "There's a chance they have someone watching the cemetery. You know, to see if anyone shows up. No, don't look around. Act natural."

"The riders?" Spider stiffened. "How do you know?"

"I *don't* know," she said. "Not for sure. They've been here a couple of nights in a row—first to dig up Mama and then to do all this."

"Then why do you think they're watching us?"

"'Cause it's what I would do," said Gutsy. She glanced at Sombra, who had moved to sit in the shade beside the wagon.

"They're not close, though, or he'd be barking. So, maybe a scout with binoculars. Plenty of cover in the hills. Plenty of places they could stand downwind so Sombra can't smell them."

"So . . . what do we do?" asked Spider.

"Sun'll be down by the time we get back to town," she said. "We're going to head that way. You guys can take the wagon all the way in, but I'm going to bail near that old Abrams tank." The vehicle in question was a relic of the last battle with *los muertos*. It was a monstrous metal machine, twenty-six feet long, not counting the cannon barrel; twelve feet wide and eight feet high. All the smaller weapons—the machine gun and other gear—had long since been stripped off it, but Gutsy had stored emergency supplies inside, including water, dried meats wrapped in plastic and aluminum foil, and weapons. Sadly, no extra machete. "I'll hide out there," she continued, "then come back here when it's dark."

"You," said Alethea, "are completely out of your mind. You know that, right?"

"Get back to town before you get into trouble," said Gutsy. "The Cuddlys will freak if you don't show up, and you know it. Besides, no offense, but I can move faster and quieter alone."

"Yeah?" said Spider. "What about *los muertos*? They're pretty quiet too, until they take a juicy bite out of you."

"I've been out here at night before. I can handle the dead."

It was clear Alethea and Spider wanted to talk her out of her plan, but it was a lost cause and they both knew it. So they loaded up and set off toward home. Twilight and a drifting cloud cover were already darkening the day by the time they reached the rusted old tank.

As they approached, Gutsy said, "Don't slow down."

"What happens if they see you?" asked Alethea. "Not here, I mean, but back at the cemetery. You can't expect to fight them."

"Jeez, I'm not that crazy. I'll hide, watch, see what I can see, and then get out of there," said Gutsy. "They'll never know I was there, and I can get back into town through one of my special routes."

Gutsy had long ago worked out crawl spaces between the crushed and stacked cars that formed the town wall. She'd reinforced each of them with rebar and other sturdy pieces of metal so that even if the wall shifted while settling, her hidden passages were safe. Spider had been through a few of those with her; Alethea had not, claiming it was beneath her dignity.

"I'll be totally safe, don't worry," Gutsy told them, and even managed to keep a straight face when she told that lie. "I'll see you at my place for breakfast."

Gutsy fished a rough horse blanket from under the bench seat and wrapped it around her and Alethea. It was getting chilly, as deserts do very quickly in the evening, and this action would seem normal. As agreed, Alethea kept her right arm straight out to the side to make it look like there were two people huddled together for warmth. Gutsy bent low and tumbled off the wagon, rolled quickly and was deep in the shadows beside the tank in under two seconds.

Sombra leaped after her. Gutsy tried to warn him back, but the dog wriggled in tightly beside her as if he understood the need for concealment. The wagon rolled on and Alethea kept her arm out, selling the fiction until they were far away.

Gutsy let out a sigh of relief, then turned and scowled through shadows at the coydog. "You're a dummy. You could have been safe and warm at home."

She couldn't see him very well, but she heard his wagging tail thump against the steel tread of the army tank.

They lay there and waited for night to own the world.

THEY CAME BY MOONLIGHT.

Four of them, dressed in long yellow canvas coats—dusters, Gutsy thought they were called—with hats pulled low. The hats weren't like the cowboy style the riders in town had worn; these were like ball caps with curved bills and old American flag patches sewn on the crowns. One wagon carried them all, two up front and two in the back. They entered through the main gate and went straight to Mama's grave. It confirmed what Gutsy suspected about the cemetery being watched.

Gutsy and Sombra hid between two mounds of dirt heaped next to a pair of open graves, a thin blanket of dark wool pulled over them. She'd smeared her face and hands with dirt. Sombra was invisible beside her. His body rippled with nervous anxiety and a mix of other emotions she could not begin to define. Gutsy leaned close and whispered, "Shhh," to him.

The wagon stopped beside the grave and the four got down. It was soon apparent that there were three men and one woman. The gibbous moon was bright and she could see their faces clearly. The woman was maybe fifty years old, very fit, with black hair cut into a short, almost masculine style. She had dark eyes and an air of cold command. From the way she spoke to the others, it was clear she was in charge.

Without doubt this was the woman rider from the previous night. Same eyes. Same coldness.

There was a very large black man standing with her. He had wide-set eyes and a handsome face except for a small, pinched mouth. He wore steel-rimmed glasses and seemed to be second in command to the woman.

The other two were very similar except for race—one white, one Latino. Both were average weight, average build, very fit, and in their late twenties or early thirties. They did whatever the woman or the black man told them to do.

As they milled around, turning on a lantern, checking the area and so on, they spoke very little, but enough so that Gutsy would recognize their voices again. She heard the white man call the woman "Cap," and the Latino man called the black man "Loot." Since they had a definite military air about them, Gutsy reasoned that the nicknames were short for captain and lieutenant. But . . . of *what*? There were people in town who used to be soldiers, of course, but none of them were active. How could they be? There was no army anymore. No air force, navy, or marines. And yet these four acted like there was an active chain of command, and they moved with precision.

Gutsy found that curious but also deeply disturbing. Then they removed their dusters and she saw that all four of them were wearing identical military uniforms. Neat, new, and professional.

"What the . . . ?" she murmured, then caught herself.

The soldiers did not hear her, though. Gutsy hunkered down and studied them, making sure to commit every line, every detail to memory. These people were strangers to her. They did not look like maniacs, and definitely not ravagers. They looked calm, intelligent, and they moved with efficiency and purpose, but they could not be good people. Not if they were here, sneaking to her mother's grave under cover of night. One of them tossed shovels to each of the others.

"Let's dig this rat up and get back," said the woman.

The words hit Gutsy with a one-two punch.

This rat.

Rat?

Gutsy felt a fierce and deadly outrage at the cold contempt they showed toward her mother's body. That immediate reaction was swept away by a deeper realization triggered by what that word meant. Rat. Her mother's dying words came back to hammer at her.

"The rat catchers are coming, mi corazón. *Be careful. If they come for you . . . promise me you'll run away and hide."*

Mama had been terrified when she said that.

"Ten cuidado. Mucho cuidado. Los cazadores de ratas vienen."

"Oh my God," breathed Gutsy as she realized that Mama's words had not been conjured by the dark magic of a dying mind. Even while teetering on the edge of the drop into the big black, Mama had used her last breaths to try to warn her daughter about a very real threat. A real terror.

Take care, take great care . . . the hunters of rats are coming.

The Rat Catchers were real.

The Rat Catchers were the riders in town.

And the Rat Catchers *were here.*

PART SIX

**RECLAMATION, CALIFORNIA
ONE WEEK EARLIER . . .**

ROADBLOCK

And I will show you something different from either

Your shadow at morning striding behind you

Or your shadow at evening rising to meet you;

I will show you fear in a handful of dust.

—T. S. ELIOT, *The Waste Land*

THE SIX QUADS DID NOT TEAR ALONG AT FULL SPEED.

This was the Rot and Ruin, after all, and it was not their world. They lived in it, but it belonged to a much larger, stranger, colder, and vastly more dangerous population. Calling it Tomsland did not mean that the gentleness and optimism of Benny Imura's older brother somehow magically transformed everything out here into a garden full of hummingbirds and bunnies. Of that Benny was positive.

Once they were away from the trade routes that had been cut through the forests around Reclamation, they turned onto Route 140 West. That route took them away from the sprawling Yosemite National Park, because there were recent reports of swarms of zoms sweeping that area. Then the six of them made small turns onto various roads, heading toward Route 99 South, which they'd be on for over 130 miles. It was the clearest known route to go south to avoid the swarms and then east toward North Carolina. It also kept them well away from the nuclear wasteland of ash that was all that was left of Los Angeles 250 miles away.

Driving at half speed created a good balance between being able to outrun anything that came up behind them and being able to spot trouble ahead in time to react. The noise of the quads was a problem, though. The living dead were attracted by sound and movement.

Each of the six riders wore a carpet coat made from salvaged rugs and banded with leather, old electrical wire, and pieces of metal to protect the most vulnerable places. Lilah was the only one who wasn't wearing hers and instead wore a heavy denim work shirt with dense plastic elbow, shoulder, and knee pads. They had football helmets strapped to the backs of their quads, ready to grab if things got weird.

Between the harsh sun and the carpet coats they were all sweating heavily, and that bothered Benny. Before setting out they'd each dribbled a few drops of cadaverine on their clothes and any bits of exposed skin. Cadaverine was a nasty-smelling molecule produced by protein hydrolysis during putrefaction of animal tissue, which was a survival fact they'd learned in school. The chemical made people smell like rotting corpses, and that usually—but not always—kept the hungry dead from targeting them as prey. As food. Zoms didn't eat one another.

Sweat and the friction of the wind into which they drove at high speeds diluted the cadaverine, weakening it. They could only obtain so much of the chemical without raising eyebrows at home, and they had a long, long way to go. Every drop they used would be one less for the rest of the trip to Asheville.

Benny was driving point, leading the others by fifty yards, with Nix directly behind him. Lilah followed last to watch their backs. They all switched roles every two hours to allow fresh eyes in front and behind.

So, it was Benny who saw the problem first.

He slowed and raised a clenched fist. The drone of the other engines diminished at once and the convoy drew into a cluster, engines idling low.

"What is it?" asked Morgie, shading his eyes with a flat hand.

"Trouble," said Benny.

Trouble it was.

There was a cluster of buildings on either side of the road ahead. On one side, there was the burned-out shell of a building with the cartoon heads of three smiling men on a sign above the words PEP BOYS. Several cars had long ago been pushed across the entrance to the parking lot, and there were enough scattered skeletons to tell Benny that someone had put up a good fight there. Or tried to.

On the other side of the street was a Shell station, a Starbucks, and a Denny's. Benny knew what they were from the journey he, Chong, Nix, and Lilah had taken from home to Nevada. Gas, coffee, and food. All of them had been damaged by fire and were partially collapsed. Between the two scenes of destruction on opposite sides of the road were zoms.

At least fifty of them.

Some were dressed in the rags of ordinary clothes, a few wore the faded threads of old uniforms, but most of them—two-thirds at least—wore dark clothes with distinctive white symbols painted, drawn, or sewn onto their chests. Angels. Benny knew that even without having to use binoculars. Those zoms also had shaved heads covered with elaborate tattoos.

"Jeez," breathed Chong.

"Reapers," said Morgie.

"Dead reapers," amended Chong, tugging at the neck fittings on his carpet coat. Sweat ran in lines down his cheeks, and his oddly colored face had flushed from grayish yellow to a kind of purple.

"Doesn't make them any less scary or dangerous."

"No," agreed Chong, "it does not."

Lilah's lips moved as she counted them. "Sixty-three."

"No," said Riot, "there's not that many . . . oh . . . wait . . ." She dug out her binoculars and swept the area, then saw another bunch standing in the shadows of a faded brown UPS truck. "Crap."

Nix made a low hissing sound and they all turned toward the forest on their left. Fifteen years ago it had been the manicured decorative green space around a large, one-story white building. Only pieces of the walls still stood amid the aggressive weeds, young maples, scrub pines, and wildflowers that had escaped the boundaries of the landscaping, torn up the asphalt with root growth, and become a young forest. Nature was patient but unstoppable. The weeds were eight feet tall in places, running wild and reaching for the sky. An inexperienced eye would think they shivered as winds blew through them. None of the six teenagers was inexperienced. The movement was not in harmony with the pattern of the wind.

Zoms were coming toward the sound of the quads and maybe the smell of fresh meat.

32

"WE HAVE TO GO BACK," SAID MORGIE.

"We can't," said Chong, pointing with a bony finger. "We can't go back. Look."

The others swung their binoculars back the way they'd come. Vague forms moved in bunches, their bodies distorted by heat haze. Zombies. So many zombies. The dead who had come shambling to the road because of the engine roar and who kept following the sound. A slow scan of both sides of the road revealed more zoms, seeming to come from everywhere.

To their right, Benny saw the hulking shape of a big blocky gray building behind a chain-link fence.

"Chong," he said, "see the sign over by that building? What's it say?"

Chong peered at it. "Valley State Prison," he said slowly.

"That's not good," complained Morgie.

"Better than staying here," said Benny.

Morgie pointed to the exhaust smoke curling up from the back of Benny's machine. "Smell that? It's all over us, and it stinks worse than the cadaverine. I don't know that we'd make it through those biters."

"Then we'll need to go really fast," said Riot. When Morgie tried to say something else, he was drowned out by the roar as Nix and Lilah revved their engines. He and Benny turned to see the girls exchange identical wild grins, slap the visors down on their helmets, turn their quads, and go roaring off across a field.

"Wait," yelled Chong urgently. "Lilah—put your carpet coat on!"

But the Lost Girl could not hear him over the roar of her engine. Chong revved hard and kicked his machine forward, racing desperately to catch up. Benny shot Morgie a weak smile of encouragement and followed.

For a moment Riot and Morgie sat there on their machines, watching the others go.

"We're all going to die out here," said Morgie.

Riot laughed as she pulled her helmet off the back and fitted it over her bald head.

"Everybody dies somewhere. Don't be a baby."

Then she was gone.

Even so, Morgie lingered, looking at his friends, then back in the direction of home.

"Damn," he breathed, and gunned his engine just as the weeds parted beside the road and three dead reapers stepped out, reaching for him with gray hands. He left them in a cloud of smoke and kicked-up dust.

THEY BUMPED AND THUMPED ACROSS THE FIELD, cutting around the wrecks of dead cars, avoiding the reach of dead hands. There were old bones hidden by the weeds, and Benny heard them crunch and snap as his wheels rolled over them.

The chain-link fence looked mostly intact, and the gates were closed. That could mean that they'd be safe once inside, but nothing was certain. The prison could be filled with thousands of the dead, either locked in their cells or wandering free.

"Benny," cried Nix, "*watch out!*"

Benny twisted in his seat as something rushed at him from behind the corner of an overturned golf cart. There was a flash of milky-dead eyes and the snap of gray teeth, but he ducked under it and bashed his arm upward and back, knocking away the hands that tried to snatch him from the quad. The zom stumbled back into the path of Lilah's machine, but the Lost Girl let go of her handlebars, raised her spear, and slashed as she cut sharply to the left. The empty eyes of the zom showed no trace of pain or surprise as the head leaped into the air. The body collapsed at once and the head rolled into the weeds.

The Lost Girl immediately released one hand from the weapon and grabbed for the handlebar, but it was too late. The right front wheel of her quad struck the edge of a thick, half-buried thigh bone and that side of the machine lifted, trapped by momentum. The engine roared as the quad leaned drunkenly over on two wheels. Lilah leaned hard to the right to try to save it, and Chong zoomed up and bumped his quad into the left rear of her vehicle. Lilah's quad thumped down hard onto four wheels, but the jolt pitched her out of the saddle. She spun in the air, screaming, the spear pinwheeling over her. She crashed down between two of the dead, who spun toward her, reaching for the meal delivered to them with such unexpected force. The spear struck point-first into the ground and stuck quivering, ten feet too far away.

Benny saw all this over his shoulder, immediately jammed himself into a sliding, skidding, shrieking turn, and was blinded by his own dust plume. He jumped free of his quad and whipped his sword from its scabbard in an overhand draw that drew a line of silver fire through the dust. A hulking gray figure, naked except for one work boot, lunged for him and Benny cut through both arms below the elbow, then pivoted on the balls of his feet as he ducked low and sliced through both shins. The blade was razor sharp and Benny had trained hundreds upon hundreds of hours since inheriting the sword from Tom. The zom fell and Benny leaped over it. Quieting it could come later; Lilah was in danger right now.

As he burst out of the cloud and into the clear air, he saw how bad it was. Lilah was down in the weeds, wrestling with one zom and trying to fend another off with savage kicks of her sneakered feet. Blood completely covered one side of her face, and her mouth was twisted with pain and fury.

The truth of what was happening hit Benny like a baseball bat upside the head, and it meant that his earlier fear had come true. The cadaverine had worn off. The zoms came at them without hesitation and with a ravenous, unstoppable aggression.

Chong was nearby, fighting against a zom who must have been a basketball player before he died. Somehow he had lost his helmet, and his eyes were wild. The creature was nearly seven feet tall and moved with unnerving speed to not only try to grab Chong, but to evade counterattacks. Benny's heart sank. This was one of the rare faster zoms, the ones either fully or partially infected with the mutagen. There was thought, planning, intelligence—however primitive—in its actions. Chong's bow and arrows were still on his quad, and he fought with a bokken—a hardwood training sword. Unlike Nix and Benny, Chong preferred the wooden sword to sharpened steel.

Nix was fighting her way toward Chong, but there were zoms coming in from everywhere. Most were slow.

Some were not.

None, though, were as fast as the giant who was winning its fight against Chong.

The other quads were spaced out across the field. Riot and Morgie were way over to the right, more in line with the prison gate but farther back. Benny was torn between helping Lilah and rescuing Chong. He was sure they were both going to lose their fights.

"Nix!" he screamed as he peeled off toward Lilah. She was fighting two of them and was clearly hurt. As he tore across the bone-littered ground, Benny prayed that he hadn't just killed his best friend.

Then he had no time for thinking.

There were three zombies closing in on the struggling form of Lilah. Of the two on the ground with her, she'd kicked one in the face so many times that its jaw hung loose and shattered, with rotted teeth falling all around. And yet it still tried to bite her.

The other zom had one handful of Lilah's hair and with the other was pawing at her, trying to grab her throat.

Benny launched himself into a flying kick, catching the left-most zom square on the belt buckle. The impact propelled the zom backward and Benny landed on the balls of his feet, nearly fell face-first into the dirt, used his sword as a momentary brace, and turned a fall into a run. How he managed to keep hold of his sword he could never tell. He slashed with the blade, and the broken-jawed zom reeled back with the top three inches of its skull leaping up to expose a worm-infested brain. It collapsed down and Benny spun to try to take the other, but with her feet free, Lilah rolled onto her upper back, locked her ankles around the other zom's neck, and snapped downward with such force that the creature's neck broke like a dry stick. Lilah got to her feet, snatched up the spear, and with a series of cuts so fast they were nothing but a blur, tore the zombies apart.

Then she screamed as she saw Chong go down behind his quad, crushed beneath a wave of the dead.

"If he dies," she snarled at Benny as she broke into a run, "I'll kill you."

Fair enough, thought Benny, and ran to catch up.

The day, spinning downward, continued to fall.

LILAH ROARED OUT A SCREAM LIKE A VIKING
warrior from one of the old books Benny had read. Her
clothes were in tatters, her face was painted bright red with
blood, her pale hair whipped around her as she leaped into
the air with her spear. The blade slashed down before she
landed, the cut powered by her dropping weight and furious
muscular strength. A zombie head flew and a zombie arm
fell. Lilah spun the spear into a lateral cut that sent another
undead monster toppling away, its jaw sheared off. Lilah
kicked another in the side of the head, knocking it away from
the struggling form beneath it.

The giant zombie fell back with a deep cut through the
muscles and tendons of its right thigh, but it did not go all
the way down. It swiped at Lilah, and there was a terrible light
in its eyes as if the sight of someone so unprotected awoke
the darkest of hungers. Lilah shifted away, engaging one of
the zoms still trying to bite Chong, and the giant's fingers
closed—for the moment—on empty air.

Then Benny was there, and so was Nix, who seemed to
come out of nowhere. They chopped at the living dead like
fiends, like demons, and the dead fell before them. Benny cut

a zom in half above the waist and shouldered another out of the way. He saw Chong's face, gray with terror, eyes wild as he held his bokken like a barrier to push a snapping set of teeth way from him. Benny dared not cut again so close to Chong, so he kicked, and kicked again, and again until the weight pressing down on his friend shifted. Then he grabbed Chong by the tough collar of his carpet coat and heaved backward, aided by Chong's frenzied kicks. Nix and Lilah tore into the zoms who tried to snatch at Chong's ankles.

Benny caught Chong under the armpit and hauled him roughly to his feet.

"Where's your helmet?" yelled Benny.

Chong looked around but couldn't see it.

Suddenly Chong was snatched backward and up and Benny reeled in horror as he saw the giant, on its knees holding Chong in both hands, pulling the screaming teen toward a mouth filled with jagged, broken teeth.

Lilah and Benny both screamed as they rushed in, but another zom—smaller but just as fast as the giant—launched itself through the air and bore Lilah down. A fallen zom caught Benny by the ankle, using the grip to hold him while pulling itself forward for a bite. Benny let it bite, feeling the pain of teeth closing around his calf but trusting to the heavy indoor-outdoor carpet to protect his flesh. He used the pain of that bite to fuel his next slash, and the edge of the *kami katana* sheared through the giant's leg above the knee. Cutting tendons wasn't enough—he wanted to chop off the leg. That should do it. But the blade chunked into the heavy femur and jolted to a stop so abrupt it tore the handle from Benny's grasp.

The giant toppled sideways and crashed down backward,

dragging Chong with it. Benny turned and stamped down on the biting zom, crushing its skull and ending its unnatural life. Then he darted forward, grabbed the *katana* again, and worked the blade out of the giant's leg bone with a careful but fast seesaw motion. Samurai swords were tough when cutting or slashing, but brittle when turned at the wrong angle. The blade came free, but as it did the giant reached up and smashed a huge right hand into Benny's back. He fell, losing the sword again, losing all the air in his lungs. The slow zoms weren't smart enough to punch, and Benny had spent too much of the last year fighting them. It was stupid to forget that some of the fast ones could really fight back.

It was maybe a fatal mistake on his part.

The giant rolled over onto its side and swung again. The carpet coat could stop a bite, but it did next to nothing to smother the foot-pounds of impact. Benny felt crushed, unable to drag in a spoonful of air. Helpless. He felt the world spin around him in a sick, dizzying dance. There was suddenly too much light, and it was all swirling like a cluster of fireflies while everything around that light was fading into blackness.

Another punch came that he had no power to block, and this time the giant's fist struck the side of Benny's helmet with such shocking force that he heard the dense plastic shatter and a crack jagged through his visor. It looked like the whole world had broken in half.

I'm going to die, he thought weakly, feeling himself fading. Leaving. Going. His neck hurt and his head felt like it was full of bees, all swarming frantically and escaping through splits and fissures in his skull.

The snarling monster zombie raised its fist once more,

and Benny could no more evade or block the attack than he could leap into the air to fly. He felt as helpless as a scarecrow that had fallen from its perch.

The huge fist swung again.

I'm dead.

But there was something wrong with the giant's fist. It seemed to be rising rather than falling. And . . .

And it wasn't connected to anything.

Benny's dazed brain struggled to make sense of something that made no sense. Not to him, anyway.

Something thumped across his chest and Benny raised his head as far as he could—maybe half an inch—and looked down to see what it was.

An arm lay there. Still attached to a shoulder, but without a forearm, or wrist, or hand. He forced his head to turn sideways and watched with helpless fascination as Chong, standing wide-legged, his bokken gripped in thin hands, bashed the head of the giant over and over again.

"Well . . . ," said Benny in a voice only he could hear, "that's good. . . ."

Then he collapsed, and all the lights in the world went out.

THE DAY DARKENED FOR BENNY, THE LIGHTS WENT
out. He felt himself tumble backward and downward into a
darkness that was at first terrifying and then soft and gentle
and sweet.

If I'm dying, he thought, *then this is okay. It's not bad.*

He fell down and down.

Is Tom down there? Or up there? Or out there?

He fell and fell and never felt himself land.

And then the lights clicked back on. It felt like only a
moment to Benny.

It wasn't, though, and somehow he now understood that
with a strange clarity. With the insight of someone who had
been close to death before. Very close.

He could see the light through his closed eyelids and did
not want to open them. Not yet.

What will I see if I look? he wondered. *Tom?*

A soft hand touched his cheek.

Nix . . . ?

Like an after-echo, he heard his voice say her name aloud.
It surprised him. He thought he'd only thought it. It confused
him too, because Tom belonged to the land of the dead, and

no one was more alive than red-haired, green-eyed Phoenix Riley.

His eyelids opened. Blinked. Saw.

He stared upward, not at the blue sky but at a ceiling made from yellowed acoustic tiles and strips of metal. The light flickered, and when he turned to his left he saw a small fire burning in a metal trash can.

"He's awake," said a voice, and he turned to his right to see Nix and Chong standing there. Their faces wore identical expressions, which were equal parts concern and relief. There were wet tear tracks cut through the road dust on Nix's cheeks. They overlaid older tear tracks, as if she had been crying off and on for a long time.

"Say something," said Chong. "Do you know your name?"

"Of course I know my name," said Benny. His voice sounded like it belonged to an old man who'd spent his entire life chain-smoking cigarettes. He coughed to clear his throat. "I know my name."

Better.

"Well . . . ," said Chong, "what is it?"

"Thomas Imura," Benny said. He saw their expressions sharpen into unfiltered anxiety. "Wait. No. I . . . I, um, don't know why I said that. My name's Benny. Benny Imura. Tom is . . . no . . . Tom *was* my brother."

Nix looked marginally relieved; Chong not so much.

"What town do you live in?"

Benny had to think about that. "Mountainside? No . . . that burned down. I mean *we* burned it down. We, um, live in . . . Reclamation?" It came out as a question.

Chong sighed. "Okay. Here's a hard one to find out if you

remember *everything*. Was Tom your only brother?"

"Yes. Wait . . . no. He was the only brother I ever knew, but I had another half brother. Sam. He was a lot older than me. I never met him. He was a soldier and I think he died during First Night. Not in California; back in Pennsylvania. He called Tom and told him what was happening. Told him to get home to Mom and Dad."

"He remembers," said Nix. She touched his cheek again.

He tried to sit up, messed it up badly, and had to wait for Nix and Chong to each take an arm and help him do it. "Ouch, ouch, ouch, ouch," he said.

He swung his legs over the edge of what he realized was a desk. The room did a wild and sickening dance around him and he had to hold on to the desktop to keep from sliding onto the floor. His stomach tried real hard to do a backflip, and it took a lot of what little strength he had not to throw up everything he'd ever eaten in his entire life.

Nix poured water from a canteen into a small plastic cup and offered it to him.

"There is no way I can drink that," he said. Then he took the cup and drank all of it. And two more cupfuls. The room stopped doing its dance, and his stomach grudgingly and slowly settled down.

Benny looked around.

"Are we . . . ? I mean . . . where are we?"

"What do you remember?" asked Nix, taking and holding one of his hands. Her fingers were cold. The room was cold too, but Benny knew that her hands always got icy when she was scared.

It took Benny a long time to figure that out. His body

hurt, but nothing seemed to actually be broken. He touched his stomach and felt deep bruising in his abdomen, and some tender spots between his ribs. His chest burned, but the sternum seemed to be all there. When he touched his head, it was like doing an inventory of all the ways the individual parts could hurt. Gums, teeth, the hinge of his jaw, cheekbones, all around his eyes, his brow, the top of his head, and his nose. The only things that didn't hurt were his ears and his hair.

"I . . . I remember stopping on the road," he said, then glanced around. "I don't remember this place. Where are we? And what happened?"

"Do you remember the fight in the field outside the prison?" asked Nix.

Benny stared at her. "Um. No. That sounds like something I *should* remember, though. I mean . . . prison? What prison is—?"

Before he could finish, Nix leaned in to kiss him. It was very, very nice, and it made him not care much about his aches.

Chong seemed to become interested in the pattern of the wallpaper. "Oh, look," he said as if holding a conversation with someone, "wildflowers. How interesting. Very detailed."

Nix stopped kissing Benny but ignored Chong. She held Benny's face in both hands and whispered, "Don't you ever, ever—*ever*—do that again."

"But what *did* I do?" Benny gasped.

"You almost died, you idiot," she growled. "And you're not allowed."

Then she kissed him again.

When she was done kissing him, and while he caught

his breath, Nix and Chong told Benny everything, starting with when they'd stopped on the road all the way up to them breaking the locks on the gate and using the quads to bring Benny inside.

"Lilah and the others had to quiet a few more zoms so we could get the fence closed and secured," explained Nix.

"Is everyone else okay?"

Chong nodded and half smiled. "Lilah lost her shirt and Nix yelled at her for not wearing a carpet coat. She told Lilah that you getting hurt was her fault. Lilah was pissed because you helped her instead of helping me, and said that that's why you got your head bashed in. They had a real doozy of a fight."

"Cut it out," muttered Nix.

"People accuse us of using foul language," continued Chong, "but I was taking notes during that exchange, I can tell you. Nix has a real mouth on her. I'm seriously impressed. Wow. She called Lilah a—"

"Cut it out," warned Nix again, and this time there was serious menace in her tone.

Chong pretended to zip his mouth shut, but then leaned close and said to Benny, "I'll tell you later."

They bumped fists. Nix glared at them so hard it made her freckles glow.

Benny looked around. "So . . . what's this? The warden's office?"

"Yes," said Nix. "We couldn't get into the infirmary. It's locked, and they have steel doors with wire mesh over the windows. We came in here thinking there might be some keys, but there weren't."

"Riot's looking for them," said Chong.

"What about the quads?"

"All good," said Chong. "We have five inside the fence and the sixth—yours—is still out there, but we figure the zoms aren't going to ride off with it. Not even the fast ones."

"Yeah, speaking of which," said Benny, "were there really fast ones out there?"

"Four of them," said Nix, shivering at the memory. "And two that were smarter than the others. R2's and R3's."

Benny's blood went cold.

"Oh my God," he breathed.

R2'S SCARED BENNY. R3'S ABSOLUTELY TERRIFIED HIM. And for good reason.

When the American Nation was getting itself together, one of their most important projects involved researching reports of mutated zoms. For Benny and the other people from the Nine Towns, there was only ever one kind of living dead—the slow shufflers. They had been designated as R1's by the American Nation scientists. Reaper One was the official label, because they were the result of the dispersal of a mutagenic biological weapon called Reaper, which the scientists hoped would combat the older bioweapon, codenamed Lucifer 113, which had been accidentally released in Pennsylvania and spread by storm winds and the movement of populations around the world.

Lucifer 113 had originally been created during something called the "Cold War"—when the old United States and Russia, then called the Soviet Union, teetered on the brink of nuclear war. Bioweapons research had been done, against all international laws, on both sides. The Soviet scientists had developed Lucifer 113 as a weapon to be dropped into enemy territory. It had a 100 percent infection rate and an equally high mortality rate. You got it, you died. The kicker was that the dead reanimated as aggressive hosts for a cluster of genetically engineered parasites. The plan was for the infected to continue attacking everyone around them until all of the enemy were infected. Then the parasites were supposed to die off, leaving all physical assets—property, missile bases, computers—undamaged. It was intended to be a weapon more effective than nuclear bombs but without the radiation and devastation.

That was bad enough.

Then fifteen years ago a former Soviet scientist who had defected to the United States and been given a job as a prison doctor after the Cold War ended decided to play God with the bioweapon. He tweaked it so that the parasites did not die off and would actually keep the dead host in a state of living death for decades by reducing all unnecessary body functions. The host occasionally had to eat living tissue to get the protein to sustain itself.

The doctor's intention had been to use the disease to punish serial killers so that after their executions they would reanimate in their coffins and be trapped but alive, so their suffering would go on and on. It was a sick, twisted, and cruel plan, and like most bad ideas, it failed in a spectacular way. Homer Gibbon, the first death-row inmate infected with Lucifer 113, was not buried fast enough. His body was claimed by a relative and reanimated in a county funeral home. He woke up very confused, very frightened, very angry, and very hungry.

The plague, having mutated once more after passing through Homer Gibbon's bloodstream, was now communicable by bite, or by exposure of infected blood to mucous membranes or open wounds on the victim. It had become a serum transfer disease, spread through saliva or blood.

That was where the zombie plague started. In a small county called Stebbins in western Pennsylvania. That was where Sam Imura, Tom's older brother, had gone with his team of special ops soldiers known by the nickname the Boy Scouts. It was where Sam vanished as the plague spread uncontrollably.

Years after the end of nearly everything, the last living scientists began looking for a way back from the edge of human extinction. When reports of mutated zoms began coming in, they sent teams to capture and study them, and discovered that Lucifer 113, long believed to be an absolutely stable engineered disease, was changing. Apart from the slow and predictable R1's, there were the quicker and more coordinated R2's, and the far deadlier R3's, who were capable of problem solving, coordinated action, and even using simple tools.

Surviving scientists from the American Nation later learned that the mutation was not Mother Nature's long-hoped-for response to the plague, but was yet another bioweapon, this one created by Dr. Monica McReady and her team, hidden away in a secured facility at Zabriskie Point in Death Valley, California. They had infected some hogs with the plague and then exposed them to an experimental compound that hyperaccelerated the life cycles of the parasites. This made the infected zoms faster for a short period of time but then burned them out, killing the parasites before they could mature and reproduce. The zoms would then begin to decompose and fall apart.

"How many more zoms are out there?" asked Benny.

Nix and Chong took too long to answer.

"Guys . . . ?"

"Too many," said Nix.

She went over to the window at the other end of the office. Benny stood up to follow but swayed and would have fallen if Chong hadn't caught him. Nix whirled and rushed over to take his other arm. Together they walked Benny to the window so he could look out.

The sun was lower in the sky than he thought it should be, which told him that he'd been unconscious for a while. That was scary, and his head felt bruised and wrong. A concussion, almost certainly.

Then he looked out through the tough wire mesh that covered the windows, and all concern for his own pain dried up and blew away. His mouth went dry too, and inside his battered head he could hear his pulse hammering and hammering.

Outside he could see the field and all the way back to the road.

"Oh no . . . ," he whispered.

There were zoms out there.

There were thousands of zoms out there.

Interlude Three

KICKAPOO CAVERN STATE PARK
ONE WEEK AGO

The hunter did not move. Not a muscle, not an eyelid.

"I want you to use two fingers to take your sidearm out of its holster and place it on the ground," said the man who held a gun to the hunter's neck. "You're going to keep your other hand on your head and do everything with your left. We clear on this, sparky?"

"Yes," said the hunter, lifting the Sig Sauer gingerly.

"Good. We're doing fine here. Place it on the ground." He repeated the process with the hunter's other weapons—hunting knives, a bayonet, and a slender steel strangle wire. He missed absolutely nothing, and that both impressed and frightened the hunter. It also reinforced the hunter's belief that this soldier was not a member of a ravager wolf pack. A ravager would have shot the hunter or cut his throat.

"I'm going to take three steps back," said the soldier. "You move, you're dead. You so much as sneeze, you're dead. Are we communicating here?"

"Yes," said the hunter.

The gun barrel moved and the hunter heard three quiet steps. The steps were uneven, confirming the hunter's guess that the man was walking with a limp.

"Hands on your head, fingers laced. Do it now." The hunter did as ordered. "Turn to face me. Pivot on your knees. Stay down."

The hunter turned very slowly in the soft mud. He did not look at the gun, but instead looked past it. The man was tall, muscular, fit, and covered in dirt and blood. He wore black military fatigues, but the clothes were torn and scorched, with flaps hanging down to expose burned skin. Gray-blond hair was pasted to the man's head by crusted blood and dirt, and one eye was bloodshot and the other puffed nearly closed. A long, shallow cut ran from mid-cheekbone through both lips and along the chin. Two pieces of metal were strapped to either side of the stranger's left leg, held in place with what looked like pieces of a seat belt.

The hunter took in all the details about the man. That he was military was obvious. The trick he'd used—walking backward in his own prints in order to double back and lay a trap—was a classic. On reflection, the bloody handprint had probably been a trick too—something to suggest that he was either very injured or unskilled at woodcraft, or both. It worked, too, fooling even the hunter.

The man smelled of sweat and blood and dirt and smoke. All of that made sense. What he did not smell like was rot. *Los muertos* stank. The half-zombie ravager mutations stank. And his clothing, except for recent damage, looked new.

"Who are you?" asked the hunter. "Where are you from? What was that sound I heard this morning?"

"Hey, how 'bout I ask the questions?" said the man. "Okay with you, sparky? Good. Let's start with the obvious one. Why are you tracking me?"

"What makes you think that's what I was doing?"

"If I shoot you in the leg, will I get a straight answer to my question?"

The question, although said in a joking manner, was no joke, and the hunter knew it.

"You are in my woods," he said. "I wanted to know who and what you are. I needed to decide if you were still alive."

"Okay, fair enough," said the soldier. "Thing is, there aren't a lot of us humans left. You could have verified that I was alive by asking."

"You could have lied."

"Last I heard, zoms don't speak, and that means they can't lie."

"What's a zom?"

"Zom? Short for zombie? Dead guys that seem to think the living are part of an all-you-can-eat buffet. We had the whole zombie apocalypse thing fifteen years ago. Maybe you heard of it? It was kind of a big thing."

"I know the dead rose," said the hunter. "Never heard them called 'zoms' before. And zombies were from old black-and-white movies. Are you saying this started in Haiti, with all that voodoo stuff?"

"Not saying that at all," said the soldier. "This isn't some kind of black magic. Might have been better if it was. No, this whole thing was a bioweapon, and people started using the nickname 'zoms' for the biters."

"We call them shamblers," said the hunter, making conversation because he was looking for an advantage, waiting for a moment to make his move. "Or *los muertos vivientes*."

"The living dead," said the soldier, translating it. "Good a name as any. But let's get back to the point, shall we? I don't look or smell like one of your *los muertos* and yet you were hunting me. I'd like to know why."

"There are a lot of bad things out here," said the hunter. "And a lot of bad people. All sorts of mutations, and some of them can talk."

The soldier stiffened. "Okay, that's scary as all heck."

"Are you going to kill me?" asked the hunter.

"I'm keeping my options open." The pistol barrel was an unflinching black eye that did not waver. "Right now I'm enjoying our little chat. Mess with me, though, and I don't like your odds, feel me?"

The hunter nodded. "I heard a sound. In the sky. And saw smoke. Now you're here and your leg is splinted with pieces of metal. You're dressed like a soldier."

"Those are statements, sparky. What's the question?"

"Were you on a . . . helicopter?"

The soldier smiled. There was something dangerous in his smile, but not threatening. It was dangerous because for a split second he looked oddly familiar to the hunter. He looked like someone he'd known a long time ago. Someone who was definitely dead. Which made the feeling of unreality swirl inside his head even more.

"Yes," said the soldier, and his smile faded. "A Black Hawk. Well . . . not anymore. Now it's a pile of junk. I got out. Maybe my combat dog too. Not sure. My friends weren't so lucky."

"*How?*" begged the hunter. "There hasn't been anything flying since the EMPs."

The soldier gave him a quizzical look. "Boy, are you out of touch. The EMPs knocked everything out, but it's been a lot of scared people keeping them grounded. Some folks seem to believe that it was the machines that made the dead rise. Or make the dead come after us. Or something. Lots of crazy theories, and you can really hurt yourself trying to make sense of 'em. Truth is, pretty much anything that's busted can be fixed. Where I come from we have planes, choppers, all sorts of stuff. Nothing new, of course. It's all rebuilt or repaired. But we're fixing more of the stuff all the time."

The hunter licked his lips. It was so dangerous to simply accept this as real. Machines had been dead for so long they'd become like extinct animals to everyone. Like dinosaurs. Real once upon a time, but not part of this world. To accept their present reality required a leap of faith, and the hunter had so little to spare. He studied the big soldier.

"You set a trap for me," he said. "You doubled back on your trail and came up behind me. No one's been able to do that to me in a long, long time. Since before the End. You're no ordinary scavenger. You're a soldier. Or were."

"You're quick, sport. Did the uniform give me away?"

"I was a soldier too."

"Yeah, from the way you moved I figured you had training. What kind of soldier?"

"Special forces," said the hunter. "I was a sniper."

The soldier studied the hunter's face for a long time. Really studied it, and the hunter knew the man was trying to see past the grizzled gray-black beard and long hair. The soldier narrowed his eyes as if trying to carve years off the hunter's face. Deep vertical lines appeared slowly between his brows, and there was doubt and confusion in his blue eyes. "Do I . . . do I *know* you . . . ?"

"No," said the hunter bluntly.

The soldier kept staring at him, and then he jerked as if he'd been slapped hard across the face. He blinked several times, and the barrel of the gun, which had been rock steady, began to waver.

"Wait . . . ," said the soldier. "No . . . that's impossible. I can't . . . I can't . . ."

The soldier suddenly lowered the gun and sat down hard on the ground. He looked like he had just been punched in the face. The pistol tumbled from his hand and landed in the dirt.

"I'm losing it," the soldier said, and he grabbed his head with both hands. "I'm totally losing it. I . . . I . . . I . . ."

He never finished the sentence, because the hunter launched himself through the air and tackled the soldier.

THE GRAVE ROBBERS

The secret to happiness is freedom,

And the secret to freedom is courage.

—THUCYDIDES

GUTSY WATCHED THE RAT CATCHERS DIG. AS THEY worked, she felt something happening to her.

At first it was only a physical thing. Her fists closed into knots, her stomach clenched, her jaws locked as she ground her teeth. It felt like fear, at first. It felt the way it did sometimes when she was running from the smarter, faster kinds of living dead. Or how she felt when a party of rough-looking Broken Lands travelers nearly trapped her out on the desert. Fear of what could happen to her; of what *would* happen if she wasn't fast enough or smart enough.

As Gutsy always did, she looked inward to try to understand *what* she was feeling. The Chess Players sometimes talked about the difference between a "knee-jerk" reaction and a "considered" one. Knee-jerk reactions were instant. Sometimes they were a reflex inspired by nothing more than a simple emotion—fear, anger, need, hunger, insecurity. Other times they were copied reactions, like one dog starting to bark after another one started. *Considered* reactions were different—they were how people responded once they'd had time to think things through. It was how smarter or more experienced people reacted, basing what they did on what they'd learned, what they knew, what they thought about things.

Gutsy looked for those two kinds of reactions in people and found that it was useful to understand the forces at work in a person. It told her a lot. It gave her compassion, when that was needed, usually after someone said something or did something that they would later regret. But it also taught her a lot about how someone *really* was. If someone was kind as a reflex, that was great, like someone stepping aside to hold the door when they saw an old person going into the general store at the same time. A "reflex of courtesy," Mr. Ford called it. Or the way Mama used to snap at her when Gutsy did something dangerous, jumping to anger to hide the fear.

Then there were the times she was so mad that her face flushed and her throat burned and she felt like just rushing at someone and beating their brains out. Like the time Nicky Cantu pantsed Spider in front of everyone at the spring fair. Or when Mrs. Osborne across the street kicked the neighbor's twelve-year-old half-blind yellow Lab for pooping on her lawn. Those times were raw, unthinking anger. The kind that Gutsy always had to fight back, to stuff into their closets and lock the doors. They were knee-jerk reactions.

This, though . . . this was different.

What she felt as she watched them throw shovelfuls of dirt out of the hole was different from all those feelings.

This wasn't a reflex, and it wasn't the heat of anger. This

wasn't even rage. It went beyond that. It went the whole way past that into a place Gutsy had never been before. A place she *thought* she'd been, but now that she was there, she knew that these were her first footsteps into that strange and ugly landscape.

This, she knew, was hate.

THE RAT CATCHERS LABORED OVER THEIR UGLY WORK. The white woman and the tall black man stood watching as the other two dug. An owl hooted from a nearby tree. It was like a scene from *Frankenstein*, a book Gutsy had read last autumn.

"Make it quick," said the lieutenant to the two men with shovels. Then, in a quieter voice, he addressed his captain. "Have to admit, Bess, I'll be glad when this phase is done."

The woman raised an eyebrow. "Losing your nerve?"

"Being realistic. We're taking a big risk here."

"We're doing our job, Simon."

Gutsy took note of the names. *Bess and Simon.*

"Sure," said the lieutenant, "we are, and we're nearly done. That's great. But you've seen the reports, you've heard what the scouts have been saying. What if they're right? What if *all* of them are getting smarter? What if they're really getting organized?"

"They're not. The scout teams haven't found a thing."

"C'mon, Bess," said the big man, "you can't say that with a straight face. Not one of the scout teams we sent out in the last three weeks has come back. The writing's on the wall. We need to shut down the lab, clear out the base, and get out of here and head east while we still can."

"You're overreacting," said the captain.

"Am I? You've known me for a long time. When have I ever overreacted? I just know when retreat is the smarter choice."

"The research has to be completed before we even think about leaving."

"That's what you said last year, and the year before that. Are we really any closer to cracking this? I don't think so. I think we're fooling ourselves. All the science team gives us is mumbo jumbo and empty promises. Can you really stand there and tell me they've made progress? No, better yet, can you look me in the eye and tell me they haven't made it worse? And I mean a lot worse. Those things are *organized* out there."

"According to rumor."

Simon made a disgusted sound. "Yeah, well, what's your plan? Wait until those 'rumors' come waltzing up and bite us all on the butt?"

"Keep your voice down," snapped Bess.

"Okay, okay," said Simon more quietly, "but be reasonable. You have to know that this is going to fall apart. Don't forget, there's a heck of a lot more of them than there are of us. All that talk about the Raggedy Man—"

"Don't say that name," she hissed, cutting a worried look at the soldiers digging the grave and then out at the night. She stood chewing her lip for a moment. Then she took Simon by the arm and led him farther out of earshot of the diggers, but closer to where Gutsy lay. "Listen, officially we've got this under control. But . . . personally, I think you're right. A few of us agree. And I have something worked out if the worst happens."

"What do you mean 'worked out'?"

"The second it looks like things are falling apart, we're gone. Me and a few others." She rattled off some names that were meaningless to Gutsy. "We have transport, weapons, and supplies. We just need to grab the research from the lab and let everything else go. I'm inviting you in, Simon, but you can't tell anyone, you understand? We could use some extra muscle, and I'd rather that be you than those two." She nodded in the direction of the digging soldiers. "Stay close to me and if this blows open, then we head east to Ashe—"

"Hey, Cap," called the white soldier from the bottom of the grave. "Think we got it."

The officers abandoned their covert conversation and stepped closer. Gutsy ached to know what they'd been talking about and to hear the rest of what the captain was going to say, but now everyone was focused on Mama's grave again.

"Biohazard gear on," ordered the captain, and they all removed white surgical masks from their pockets and pulled on thin rubber gloves. "Okay, Duke, dig it out."

Duke, the white soldier, began digging with renewed vigor. "Give me a second to . . . Hey, wait . . ."

"What's wrong, Duke?" asked the Latino soldier.

"What the heck is this?" growled Duke. "Mateo, hand me the lantern, there's something hinky down here."

The Latino soldier took a lantern and jumped down next to Duke. The two officers crouched down to peer into the open grave. Gutsy held her breath.

"What in the . . . ?" began the big lieutenant, but his words petered out too. Gutsy smiled thinly.

She watched as they hauled out the shroud, now filthy

and streaked with dirt. Duke and Mateo struggled to lift it, and then the lieutenant reached down and together they heaved it onto the side of the grave. The soldiers scrambled out and crouched on either side of the shroud. There was the slithery sound of a knife being drawn, and then the captain knelt down and cut a long slit in the shroud. She reached her other hand inside and drew something out.

It was a rock. The lieutenant lifted a corner of the shroud and more rocks fell out onto the ground; some thudding to a stop in the soft mound of dirt, others bouncing off the edge and dropping out of sight. The captain pulled her mask off and dropped it.

"What's going on?" asked Duke.

Instead of answering, the captain rose quickly to her feet. She still held the knife in her left hand, but now there was an automatic pistol in her right. The draw had been so fast and smooth that Gutsy never saw it. The lieutenant drew his weapon too.

"We're compromised," said Simon. The two gravediggers immediately grabbed automatic rifles from their duffel bag.

Sombra was trembling again. At first Gutsy thought he wanted to run away, but then she saw a trace of lantern light on his bared teeth. Dogs, it seemed, could hate too.

"We're being played," said the lieutenant.

The soldiers looked scared. Terrified. Even the captain seemed shaken. They stood in a circle, weapons pointing outward.

Mateo crossed himself the way some of the more devoted Catholics in town sometimes did. *"Ay, Dios mío!"* he cried in a terrified whisper. "It's the *Ejército de la Noche*."

The Night Army? wondered Gutsy. Who or what was that?

"Maybe it's only the townies," said Duke. "Maybe they figured it out."

"Both of you shut up," ordered the captain. She stepped away from the others and turned in a slow circle, studying the area. Then she slid her knife into its sheath and bent to study the ground around the grave. The others stood with their guns pointing out into the night.

"There," said Bess, and they all looked down at a set of footprints exposed by the yellow glow. The prints began at the far side of the grave and moved off toward the cemetery entrance. "Stand down. It's not the Night Army . . . and whoever did this, they're not here."

Simon knelt by his captain and looked at the footprints. "One set. Small. A woman?"

"No," said the captain, "this was a girl. Fifteen years old. Mexican."

"How could you know that?" asked the big lieutenant.

"Because," said the woman with a sneer, "I know who it was. Damn. She always said her daughter was smart."

"Wait," said the lieutenant, frowning, "are you talking about Luisa Gomez's kid? You think she figured out it was us who brought her mother back?"

"That's exactly what I think," said Bess. "And she buried these rocks for us to find in case we came back."

"Excuse me, ma'am," said Mateo. "Why would the Gomez girl do this?"

The captain holstered her gun. "Because even rats can be smart. This one thinks she's really smart. She's trying to play some kind of trick on us."

The men said nothing.

Even at that distance, Gutsy could see the captain's face in the glow of the lantern. The woman was pretty, but her expression made her ugly. There was no trace of humanity, no spark of compassion on the woman's features. That expression was every bit as cold as the deep hatred Gutsy felt in her own heart.

"Get the gear," said the captain. "We're done here."

Mateo and Duke sketched quick salutes and ran to collect their tools. The hulking lieutenant lingered with his commanding officer.

"Bess," Simon said quietly, "you don't think Luisa told her daughter about the project? About us?"

The question clearly troubled the captain. "Luisa didn't know all that much."

"No, I don't mean anything Luisa might have suspected before. I mean after. Do you think she told her anything *after* we dug her up?"

The captain stood for a moment considering the question, head cocked to one side, lips pursed in thought. "I don't know," she said slowly. "But we can't take any risks, can we? Come on, let's get back."

They climbed into their wagon and it rumbled away.

When Gutsy was absolutely sure she was safe, she stood up. She did it slowly, and the act felt like her body was pushing against a huge, crushing weight. The night had been clear and quiet, and she was sure she'd heard every word without distortion or mistake.

Do you think she told her anything after *we dug her up?*

"What?" she asked of the night. Sombra came and stood

next to her, growling at the figures now being swallowed by the distance.

Tears burned in Gutsy's eyes, but her fists were hard as hammers. Cold as stones.

"What?" she demanded, needing to understand what she had just heard.

The darkness, that deceitful place of shadows and mysteries, held its secrets and told her absolutely nothing.

GUTSY AND SOMBRA WALKED THROUGH MILES OF shadows, back to the Abrams tank.

So many thoughts crashed and tumbled through her brain.

The Night Army. Who or what were they? The soldiers seemed scared of them. Were they the ones the captain and her lieutenant were talking about? The ones who might overrun their base?

She thought about all the rumors she'd heard around town and from scavengers about a base. There were lots of theories about what it was and where it might be located, but until now Gutsy hadn't taken any of them seriously. Travelers often told tall tales in the hopes of interested listeners buying them a meal or offering to let them bed down in a spare room. Now, though, Gutsy new that some of them had to have been telling the truth. There *was* a base. And also something the soldiers called "the lab." Where were they? *What* were they?

The information was so big, so confusing, and felt so vastly important that it threatened to kick down the walls of the world as Gutsy knew it. The Rat Catchers were clearly part of something very large, very scary, and completely mystifying.

They had known her mother's name.

"Mama, please," she pleaded to the darkness. "What's going on?"

There was no answer in the endless night. Sombra walked beside her, silent as a ghost. The cool desert wind blew toward them, bringing faint moisture from the distant Rio Grande.

When they were still five hundred feet up the road from the Abrams tank, Gutsy heard the faint but unmistakable sound of a horse nickering and then the sharp "Shhhhhh" as a female voice told him to be quiet. Sombra answered it with a single *whuff*.

Gutsy had her knife out in a heartbeat, ready to fight. *Oh God,* she thought wildly, *the Rat Catchers followed me here.*

Panic flared in her chest, and Gutsy realized how stupid all this was; how insane a risk it was to think that she could outwit trained professionals. She crouched, weapon ready, determined to take at least one or two of them with her. To make them pay for what they did to Mama.

I'm going to die, she thought. *I'm stupid and I'm going to—*

And then Spider stepped out from behind the tank, his hardwood staff in his hands.

"Oh, hey, Guts," he said with a bright smile.

She gaped at him. "Spider . . . ? I could have *killed* you. What on earth are you *doing* here?"

Even in her shock and surprise, Gutsy pitched her voice to be quiet but not whispering. Whispers, especially the *s* sounds, carried farther than normal speaking at low tones. That wasn't part of her own collection of specialized knowledge—it was one of the things people learned quickly after the dead rose.

"Waiting for you," said Spider. "What's it look like?" He ground the heel of his staff on the dirt and leaned on it. "Don't worry . . . we were careful."

Gutsy saw the faintest glimmer of silver light, revealing the presence of some of her fishing line stretched across open ground a dozen yards from the tank, and she nodded approval. The previous summer, when they had all snuck out at night, Gutsy taught Spider and Alethea to string the line between rocks, cacti, and the wreckage of any old vehicles or debris. Small metal cans filled with pebbles hung at intervals along the fishing line. If those lines were touched, the ensuing rattle would alert her friends to approaching danger. Place them at a sensible distance and the warning allowed enough time to climb out of sleeping bags and grab weapons. Personally, Gutsy would have strung her lines even farther away, but now wasn't the time to nitpick.

Alethea appeared with Rainbow Smite resting on her shoulder. "Hey, sweetie," she said as if this was a bright, sunny afternoon in the town square.

"I thought I told you guys to go back home," snapped Gutsy.

Alethea arched an eyebrow. "You did, but I don't remember you being appointed Queen of All That Is . . . and you're definitely not the queen of *me*."

"I—"

"We got halfway home then decided to come back and wait here for you."

"And by talked about it," amended Spider philosophically, "she means that she told me that was what we were going to do, because she apparently *is* the Queen of All That Is."

"Princess," corrected Alethea. "I'm not that egotistical."

"You're going to get in so much trouble," Gutsy protested. "The Cuddlys will—"

"Yeah, yeah, yeah, the Cuddlys," said Alethea, flapping a hand. "We've been in trouble with them before—"

"And will be again," said Spider quietly.

"And will be again. Who cares?" Alethea stepped closer and glared at Gutsy. "Besides, who do you think we are? Do you think we'd leave you out here all alone? Do you think we'd just stash Mama in the barn like you said and then drift off to have happy dreams of unicorns and puppies? No? No. We either do this together or we don't do any of it. End of discussion."

When Gutsy turned to Spider, hoping he'd be the voice of reason, he gave her a bland smile. "Her Majesty has spoken."

Gutsy knew how to spot a fight she wasn't likely to win. Trying to convince Alethea to do something she didn't want to do was a lot scarier than a whole pack of *los muertos*.

"Okay, okay. Thanks, guys." She looked around. "Everything been okay here?"

Alethea adjusted her tiara. "Been pretty boring, actually."

"Which is good," said Spider.

"Whatever. What about you, girl?" demanded Alethea. "You were gone a long time. I chewed my fingernails all the way to the elbow."

Gutsy looked around. "Any visitors?"

"Couple lizards," said Spider. "And about a zillion mosquitoes. No shamblers."

"Good."

"Hey, do I have to beat the story out of you?" asked Alethea, waggling Rainbow Smite in her direction.

Gutsy took a drink of water from the bottle Spider handed her, and stared back the way she'd come.

"I think we're in trouble," she said. "A whole lot of trouble."

GUTSY TOLD THEM EVERYTHING.

There was enough starlight to read the emotions that came and went on her friends' faces. Shock, horror, anger, and confusion.

"Whoa, whoa," said Spider, "they know who you *are*? They actually said 'the Gomez girl'?"

"Yeah," said Gutsy. "They're the ones who brought Mama home. No doubt about it."

"That's . . . that's . . . that's . . ."

"Yeah," agreed Gutsy, "it really is."

"How do these Rat Catchers even *know* you?" asked Spider. "How'd they know your mom?"

"Beats me," Gutsy admitted.

Alethea scratched at the knob of Rainbow Smite with her fingernail, lips pursed in thought. "You said they called Mama a 'rat'?"

"Yes," said Gutsy, and the memory of it made her lip curl into a silent snarl.

"Is it wrong that I want to beat on them for, like . . . a year?" Starlight glittered off the metal screwheads jutting out from the business end of Alethea's baseball bat.

"I'm okay with it," said Spider. Then he shook his head as if chasing off buzzing flies. "But who *are* they? No, more than that, why would they want to dig up all the bodies? Why dig up Mama twice and bring her back to your house, Guts?"

"That's what I have to find out," said Gutsy.

"That's what *we* have to find out," said Spider and Alethea at the same time.

Despite everything, Gutsy smiled. "We," she agreed. "Look, from what I can figure, these people belong to some kind of group. They're really organized. A captain and a lieutenant, and two guys who I guess are soldiers. It's like how the military used to be, at least from what people say when they talk about before the End."

"If they belong to some actual organization," mused Alethea, "then what kind is it? And why don't people know about them?"

"Yeah," said Spider, "if that secret base thing is real, why hide it? I mean—why make it *secret* at all?"

"He's right," said Alethea, shaking her head. "What would be the point? And why hide all these years?"

No one had an answer to that.

"And what's the lab?" asked Spider. "A lab for doing what? And why hide that, too?"

No one had any answers.

After a while, Alethea asked, "What now? You weren't able to follow them, I guess. Any idea where their base is?"

Gutsy sighed. "I watched for a while, and they headed east."

"To where? San Antonio?" asked Spider, but then he shook his head. "No. Too far. Too many *los muertos* there, anyway."

Alethea nodded. "Are you going to follow the road tomorrow when you can look for tracks?"

"No," said Gutsy, "I don't think I need to."

"Why not?"

"Because," said Gutsy. She glanced over at the wagon, where her mother's body lay still and cold, covered by a canvas tarp. "I'm pretty sure they're going to come to me."

Alethea gaped at her, and then pointed to the body in the back of the wagon. "Please do not tell me you're seriously going to use Mama as bait? Don't tell me you think you're going to set a trap for these Rat Catchers."

Gutsy scratched Sombra's head but remained silent.

"You," said Spider, pushing her shoulder with a stiff finger, "are out of your mind."

"Well, say something," demanded Alethea.

Gutsy climbed into the wagon and lay slowly back with her face pointed to the cold and distant stars. She reached under the tarp and took one of her mother's hands and closed her fingers around it. The shroud had been removed and filled with rocks, so all that was left was a weather-stained old piece of canvas. Gutsy tried to be practical about it, telling herself that Mama was past caring. Even so, it felt wrong. But then again, nearly everything felt wrong.

Holding Mama's hand, though, was different. That felt right. It was precious and powerful to feel the reality of her mother. Now that Mama was no longer a monster, she was merely dead. It was as if some measure of dignity had been returned to her. Mama felt real in a way that she hadn't while she had been one of *los muertos*. Somehow it made the loss more real, too.

"These Rat Catchers are soldiers of some kind," Gutsy said quietly. "People become soldiers to go to war, right? Well . . . if it's a war they want, then that's what they're going to get."

A piece of ancient space junk—a meteorite or a dying satellite—burned across the sky. It looked like someone scratching a kitchen match into flame. Sombra looked up at it and, after a long moment, leaned back and howled at the night.

THEY BURIED MAMA GOMEZ IN A SMALL GROVE OF trees south of the Abrams.

The three of them shared the task. No one spoke while they worked. Not a single word. The only sound was the *chunk* of shovels biting into the earth and the sigh of dirt being tossed onto a growing mound. When the hole was deep enough, they wrapped Mama in the stained canvas and lowered her down. Then they filled in the grave. Gutsy used a rake to break up and distribute the leftover dirt, and when it was all done, the ground was smooth.

Spider collected stones and placed them at the four corners of the plot, and Alethea gathered wildflowers. Sombra sat watching all this and listening to the night, alert to predators of any kind. There were none. Not then, anyway. Gutsy knew that the darkness hid thousands of dangers, and she was glad to have the coydog there to smell and hear what she could not.

When it was all done, they stood together at the foot of the grave. Spider held Gutsy's hand and Alethea stood behind them, leaning her cheek on Gutsy's shoulder.

"*Dulces sueños*, Mama," said Gutsy.

Sweet dreams.

Her friends said it too.

Those were the only words spoken.

A small wind blew past them, swirling the dirt on the grave, touching their faces and then blowing on toward the south. The breeze smelled of flowers and spices. It smelled like Mama's kitchen when she was cooking. There was nothing in that lonely place to account for those smells. Nothing. They all smelled them, though, and exchanged looks.

All three of them had tears in their eyes. All three of them were smiling.

The wind took the smells of better times and whirled into the infinite darkness. Going south. Toward town. And past that, toward Mexico. Gutsy did not believe in much, but she knew what that was.

It was Mama, going home.

PART EIGHT

VALLEY STATE PRISON
CHOWCHILLA, CALIFORNIA
ONE WEEK EARLIER . . .

CHOICES

Being deeply loved by someone gives you strength,

while loving someone deeply gives you courage.

—LAO TZU

THEY STOOD ON THE ROOF OF THE PRISON AND looked at the sea of gray faces.

"Well," said Benny quietly, "that's not good."

Morgie snorted. "Rough count, maybe four thousand of them."

"At least," said Riot.

The zoms milled around, bumping into one another, walking in wavering lines to and fro. Many stood still, their eyes fixed on nothing, hands slack at their sides. Benny's quad stood in the middle of an ocean of death. Some of the dead were dressed in ordinary clothes, many in rags that had been military uniforms. Some were children. Many looked like they had been older when they died. And some, Benny saw, were Reapers. Had *been* Reapers.

"How come we didn't see them when we drove up?" he asked.

"I'll show you," said Chong. He tapped Benny's shoulder and led him all the way to the far side of the roof, brown gravel crunching under his shoes. Chong stopped and pointed down. Benny knelt on the edge of the roof and leaned out a little to look down. There were hundreds of dead cars, trucks, buses, motorcycles, and vans scattered around the back of the prison, all of them half-consumed by a hungry sea of weeds.

"Nix thinks that people came here during First Night," said Chong. "Strong walls, bars, locks, guns, and guards, you dig?"

Benny nodded.

"Now . . . see that?" Chong pointed, and Benny leaned farther out. A large section of wall had been crushed inward by a massive rusted yellow bulldozer. Chunks of debris half covered the machine, all of it thick with weeds and even a few small saplings. "Way I figure it, someone busted in to try and free the prisoners. Wouldn't have been people trying to find shelter, because it wouldn't make sense to ruin the wall. But something stopped whoever drove the dozer from letting the convicts out. Nix, Lilah, and Riot all think that by the time the wall was knocked in, the people who came to hide here had already turned. There's some places inside here where there was obviously a big fight, and a couple of rooms had been used as infirmaries. Lots of old, bloody bandages."

"People didn't understand the rules," said Benny. "Not during First Night. Maybe they brought people with bites inside and they turned."

"Yeah, that's the theory," said Chong. He pulled Benny back from the edge. "When the bulldozer knocked in the wall, the zoms inside swarmed them. And after that the nukes went off and the EMPs killed all the cars. If there were any survivors, then they either got away on foot, or . . ."

Benny winced. Everyone alive knew what "or" meant in these kinds of stories. "I guess some of them used to be prisoners? Though in old comic books, didn't they always wear orange jumpsuits? Do you see any of them?" When Chong didn't answer, Benny glanced at him. "What . . . ?"

CHONG SHOWED HIM.

They went back down into the administrative wing of the prison and then through several interconnected offices, down several corridors, and into a bleaker, darker part of the building. Lilah used wooden chair legs, rags, and gasoline to make torches.

"I found the keys to the cellblocks," said Riot, jangling a thick ring.

"I think everything was supposed to work electronically," said Morgie. "There are printed instructions on how to open the security doors to each cellblock, but in case the power went out, there were keys. But . . ."

"But what?"

"Go take a look," said Riot as she unlocked a door to one of the cellblocks. Lilah handed him a torch, giving him a strange look. Her face was always hard to read because for so much of her life she'd lived alone and didn't have any reason to show emotions. Now he thought he saw a deep sadness in her eyes but had no idea why it was there. When Benny turned to Nix, he saw an identical expression. Actually, all of them looked like they were at a funeral.

"What's wrong?" he asked. "What's in there?"

No one answered him.

So Benny took the torch and went into the cellblock.

There were cells on either side of a concrete walkway. All the cell doors were locked.

None of the cells were empty. Figures in filthy orange jumpsuits stood inside each one. They were bearded, wasted, withered. Some had collapsed and lay twitching on the floor. A few gripped the bars with leathery hands. Some thrust arms at him, but they could not reach him; and they probably did not have the strength to do much if they did. In a few cells figures stood draped in cobwebs and dust, and only their wax-pale eyes moved to follow Benny.

"God . . . ," he breathed. That one word echoed in the still-ness, and it made him wonder how many of these prisoners had cried out to God for help, for their freedom, for mercy.

"None of them have bites," said Chong. "Not one."

Benny nodded. He'd seen that too.

Morgie joined them. "The people who busted in could have let everyone out. They raided the kitchen and the armory. But . . . no one opened the cells or fed the prisoners."

"I think the people who burst in here saw them and made a choice," said Riot.

"What *kind* of choice?" asked Morgie in a pleading tone.

"There was food here," she said. "But only so much. You saw all those cars. There were a lot of mouths to feed. People came in here to survive, and they had their families with them. They were scared. The world was falling down, and I guess they knew no help was coming. Then those EMPs blew out the lights."

They all stared at the zombies. Every single one of them was skinny, wasted. All their prison uniforms looked too big, and each of the six teenagers had seen enough zoms to know the difference in how bodies looked if they were skinny to begin with or wasted away after death. These living dead had all starved to death.

"The people who came in here made a choice," repeated Riot. "Between them and these prisoners. I sure ain't saying I agree with it, but I understand it."

"It's insane," said Morgie.

Riot studied him. "What choice would *you* have made?"

"Not this," he cried.

"Really? If it was your family? If it was you and a bunch of kids, old people, people you needed to protect," she said coldly, "you want to stand there and tell me you wouldn't even consider doing this?"

Morgie turned away, but everywhere he looked there was more evidence of a kind of cruelty he'd never seen before. Benny put his hand on his friend's beefy shoulder. He had been deeper into the Rot and Ruin and seen many more horrors. This, though . . .

"God," Benny murmured.

"God was never here," said Morgie wretchedly.

"How many prisoners are there?" asked Benny.

Riot looked sick and sad. "According to the papers we found in the guard's office . . . thirteen hundred and fifty-three. Why?"

He just stared at her, and she began shaking her head.

"You're out of your mind. There's mercy and then there's being stupid."

"She's right," protested Morgie. "Besides, we have a mission, and this would take forever."

Nix drew her sword with a slithery rasp that seemed unnaturally loud in the cold silence of the cellblock. After a moment Benny drew his, too.

It did not take forever.

It took a day.

It took a long, bad, wretched day.

Interlude Four

KICKAPOO CAVERN STATE PARK
ONE WEEK AGO

THE HUNTER SLAMMED INTO THE SOLDIER, DROVE him back, smashed him down to the ground.

He did not pause to pick up his knives or guns. He did not need them. The hunter had killed many men and many *things* with his hands; he was a superbly skilled fighter. Deadly, fast, and brutally efficient. His father had taught him jujutsu as soon as he could walk; his mother taught him karate and aikido. He'd studied those and other fighting arts in gyms and dojos around the world. Those skills had been sharpened like a sword in special forces, and honed further by having to use them in combat on every continent, even in the frozen wastes of Antarctica.

The hunter had never lost a fight. Never. Not outside of a dojo or training hall. Never when his life depended on it.

Until that day.

In his woods.

With an injured and possibly dying old man.

His lunge bowled the soldier over and drove him hard into the dirt, but the big soldier did not fall the way he should have. He wasn't crushed into helplessness.

No.

Instead the soldier seemed to absorb the attack, yielding to the sudden mass, turning with it as he fell, sloughing off the foot-pounds of impact by turning like an axle. The hunter was whipped around and it was he who hit the ground hard enough to drive the air from his lungs with a great *whoosh*. It was a movement so precise, so sophisticated that it appeared simple. And it was fast. God almighty, the soldier moved with shocking, blurring speed.

Then the soldier was atop him, parrying the hunter's strikes, and then delivering counterstrikes, hitting the hunter in the biceps, the inside of the deltoids, the centers of each pectoral, the nerve clusters beside his nose. Fast, fast, fast. The soldier used precise one-knuckle punches, hitting for effect rather than trying to merely smash. A series of small explosions seemed to detonate inside the hunter's body and he felt his arms go dead, his chest turn to fire, his shoulder sag.

Then suddenly the soldier was behind him, kneeling as he swiftly pulled the hunter into an awkward sitting position, limp arms hanging as a thick arm wrapped around his throat in a *kata gatame* judo choke that was so beautifully executed that the hunter could not break it. He fought to breathe, but there was no air left except what was trapped in his lungs. He knew three different counters to this move, but the strikes to his pressure points had robbed him of the strength and coordination necessary to use any of them. He was caught. Trapped.

Helpless.

The world spun toward blackness as the choke hold blocked air and blood to his brain. The hunter knew that this hold compressed both carotid arteries. He would be totally unconscious in eight seconds.

After four seconds the soldier bent close, his lips brushing the hunter's ear, and spoke two words. Two impossible words.

"Sam," cried the soldier. "*Stop.*"

Sam.

The hunter had not heard his own name spoken in over a decade. No one in this part of the country knew it. He had almost forgotten that *was* his name. Like so many things, "names" seemed to have lost their importance.

And yet . . .

"Sam, please," begged the soldier.

The hunter raised one hand, weak and clumsy as it was, and tapped the forearm of the choking arm. Tapped to admit defeat.

Tapped to signal release.

Sam.

Dear God.

The soldier eased the pressure. Very slowly, with great care, with suspicion and an implied threat of punishment for a trick. "Easy, Sam . . . ease it down," he murmured. "It's okay, Sam. It's all going to be okay."

And then the soldier released the hold and fell back, covering his battered face with both hands. The hunter—Sam—turned painfully and got to his knees, then fell back hard on his butt and sat staring at the old soldier. The soldier lay there, totally vulnerable. Sam rubbed his aching throat and stared. Their legs were still touching; they were still within range of a lethal kick. Neither took that advantage.

The fight was over.

Sam reached out a hand, fighting to make his arm work, and he gripped the soldier's wrist. Pulled. The hand came away, revealing half a face. Sam pulled the other, and he looked into the soldier's eyes. There were tears there. And pain. So much pain, and none of it had to do with his wounded leg, of that Sam was positive.

"How . . . how do you know my *name* . . . ?" he begged.

The soldier, against all sense and reason, smiled. A great big smile filled with an unvarnished joy of a kind the hunter had not seen in many years.

The soldier brushed years from his eyes. "You're saying that you don't recognize me? After everything we went through? All those years? All those fights? Come on, Sam . . . it's *me*."

Then Sam suddenly saw it.

In a flash of insight and recognition he saw through the bruises and the blood, past the dirt and gray hair and the distortion of years. He cried out in alarm and scuttled clumsily backward.

"No!" he gasped, and he could feel the whole world began to crack and tear and come apart. The fractures in his mind turned to fissures, and he wanted to scream. All the years of fighting to stay sane in an insane world crumbled away and here—right here in front of him—was proof that his mind was already gone. "You're dead. You're *dead* . . . you have to be dead."

The soldier tried to stand but hissed in pain and collapsed back. There was fresh blood on his injured leg. He spoke through the pain, and his voice was kind, gentle, almost pleading. "I'm not dead, Sam, but it's not like the world hasn't been trying."

The hunter shook his head, still unwilling to accept it.

"Sam," said the soldier gently, "it's me. It really is. I didn't die. I'm not a ghost. This is happening. It's really me, Sam. I'm Joe Ledger and you're Sam Imura. And boy do I have some things to tell you."

PART NINE

NEW ALAMO, TEXAS
LATE AUGUST

RUMORS OF WAR

Victorious warriors win first and then go to war,

while defeated warriors go to war first

and then seek to win.

—SUN TZU, THE ART OF WAR

THE GUARDS ON THE WALL ASKED GUTSY AND HER friends a lot of questions but didn't make too big a thing of the fact that three teenagers had spent a night outside the wall. Not after Alethea spun a convincing tale about them bedding down in an old gas station that had secure windows and doors. The guards said that they would have to report it anyway, but Gutsy doubted they would. A lot of people went into the Broken Lands for days at a time. As long as they didn't come back infected, the guards seemed blasé about it. Well, more like *if anything happened, it was on you*. It wasn't really much of a relief. Not that Gutsy wanted a fuss made, but the fact that it was all waved away so easily made her uneasy. Alethea, who was driving, wasted no time getting the wagon in through the gates.

They stowed the wagon, took care of Gordo, and walked the long way to Gutsy's house, making sure to avoid the Cuddlys' place.

As they went into the house, Spider asked, "You think those soldiers are going to come back here?"

"Probably," said Gutsy, "but not in broad daylight."

Morning light sparkled through the windows and there

was birdsong everywhere and hummingbirds droned happily from one rose to another in the yard. Sombra immediately went over to the couch and jumped up on it.

"Hey! Off," said Gutsy sternly. She pointed down the hall. "Kitchen."

Sombra got down and trudged out of the living room.

"That was mean," said Alethea.

"He's filthy and he stinks. We all do. You two are also in trouble. The Cuddlys probably reported you to the town council by now."

"Yeah, yeah, whatever," said Alethea, though Spider looked nervous. The Cuddlys never used corporal punishment on any of the foster kids—though they threatened it when they were mad—but there were always tons of extra chores for anyone who broke a house rule, the worst of which was cleaning the bathrooms. A few dozen orphans could do a lot of damage to a couple of bathrooms, especially when they knew one of the house "weirdos" had to clean it up. Spider once said that he would rather floss the teeth of a dozen *los muertos* than clean those toilets again. From the look on his face now, Gutsy knew that he was imagining long hours of disgusting work.

Gutsy had been so glad her friends were with her when they put Mama into the ground for the last time. They'd been there when Mama's ghost kissed her face with that soft wind and went free. However, most things have consequences. Everything was a process of cause and effect, as the Chess Players so often said.

"You want to clean up here before you go home?" she asked. They were all covered in dirt and dried sweat.

"No, thanks," said Spider. "Probably should get this over with."

Alethea gave a nod and a bleak stare. The Cuddlys, unlike most adults, were not people she could order around. Gutsy wondered, though, if that would change when her friend turned seventeen. After that no one could tell any teenager what to do. It was a year and a half away, though, and Mr. and Mrs. Cuddly could make life miserable for her until then.

They hugged each other, and Gutsy stood in the doorway to watch her friends trudge home. Most likely she wouldn't see them for a day or two. House arrest, as Mr. Cuddly, called it, was part of the punishment for rule breaking. She tried hard not to wish a full-out living dead attack on the Cuddlys, but . . .

Then she closed her door, stripped off her vest, T-shirt, and pants, and went into the kitchen in her underwear. Sombra lay in a patch of sunlight by the window, looking at her with suspicious eyes as Gutsy opened a closet and removed the same soap and sponges she'd used on the dog the day before. Sombra whined and closed his eyes as if pretending to be asleep.

"Nice try," she told him. "Come on."

With great reluctance, as if walking toward his execution, the coydog followed her into the bathroom and climbed into the tub. He whined piteously as she soaped and scrubbed him and even howled a few times.

"Stop being such a baby."

He contrived to stare at her with large, liquid, accusing eyes. Gutsy couldn't help but grin. Sombra may not have spent much time in houses with people who cared about him, but he was learning fast how to manipulate.

Once the suds were gone, Sombra looked skinny, battered, and unhappy, but he smelled of soap and wet dog. It was a nice smell. Gutsy patted him dry, pausing to examine his injuries, all of which were healing nicely. She wrapped him in a towel and he curled up on the bathroom rug while she rinsed the tub and filled it for her own bath. Gutsy heated some water on a little wood-burning stove she'd installed in the corner of the bathroom, and when it was perfect, she stepped out of her underwear and sank gratefully into the steaming water.

It was the single best feeling in the world.

She lay there for a long time, thinking things through. There was no guarantee that the Rat Catchers would think that she'd brought her mother home. There was no guarantee they'd come to steal her body the way they'd stolen all the others. It would be a dangerous thing to do. Risky. After all, they had to believe Gutsy would tell the town council about what happened.

Gutsy hadn't, though, and she had her reasons.

She thought about the fact that they'd brought her mother back twice. There were many weird things about that, and she began cataloging them in her mind. Many questions, too.

The riders had attacked the night guards the second time, but not the first. Why?

Why bring Mama's body back at all?

What did Simon, the big lieutenant, mean when he asked the captain: *Do you think she told her anything* after *we dug her up?*

Did he expect Mama to actually say something? Gutsy knew that there were many different versions of the disease that made the dead rise. As far as she knew, though, the only infected who could speak were those people who had the version of the disease where they slowly turned into monsters. That wasn't what happened to Mama, though. She'd died of tuberculosis and had none of the symptoms of the wasting mutation Mr. Ford told her about. She wished she'd asked him about it, and decided to go find him later and ask.

Do you think she told her anything after *we dug her up?*

Even if Mama could think and talk, Gutsy mused, what on earth did they think she might have said?

Why and how did the Rat Catchers know her?

She looked over at Sombra, whose gray eyes peered out at her from inside his towel nest. "What are they doing with all those bodies?"

The dog, the house, and the day had no answers.

Yet.

THE TOWN OF NEW ALAMO WAS THE ONLY PLACE
Gutsy had ever lived, but it was strange.

It wasn't like the places she read about in books. It always
felt awkward to her . . . though she admitted that it might be
that it was she who was awkward. Or both. Hard to say.

After cleaning up, fixing food for Sombra and herself,
and doing other busywork that wouldn't interfere with the
thoughts running through her head, she went out. Her list
of questions had grown very long, and now Gutsy wanted to
start making sense of things. The problem, as she saw it, was
that she wasn't sure who to talk to first. Or if talking to anyone was safe. The fact that the Rat Catchers had brought her
mother into town the first time without causing any distur-
bance with the guards worried her. Either they had a secret
way in—in which case, why hadn't they used it the second
time?—or they had friends in town, possibly among the
guards.

Before she left her yard, she asked Sombra, "What would
Sherlock Holmes do?"

The coydog wagged his tail.

"Exactly," said Gutsy. "Let's go."

Her first stop was the porch where the Chess Players were always to be found. Mr. Urrea was asleep, his straw hat pulled low over his face, arms folded over a comfortable belly, legs stretched out, and ankles crossed. He was usually barefoot, as he was now.

Mr. Ford was awake and he sat cross-legged, polishing the little chess pieces and putting them into place on the board, ready for another game. There was a set of wooden shelves against the wall on which were more than forty chess sets of different kinds. They were specialty sets salvaged from abandoned towns or obtained through barter with traders. The sets had themes, with the figures carved from wood or stone or cast in metal, and included both World Wars, the Civil War, Napoleon and Wellington, the Lord of the Rings, Harry Potter, Disney and Warner Bros. cartoon characters, classic monsters and monster hunters, and others. The Chess Players loved to share the stories behind each set and often regaled Gutsy and her friends with memorized scenes from those based on novels. The *Wizard of Oz* set was one of Gutsy's favorites, though it was missing three flying monkeys and two Munchkins, and so was seldom used. The set currently sitting atop the chessboard was based on the old stories of Robin Hood and his Merry Men against the evil Prince John and the Sheriff of Nottingham.

"Well," said Mr. Ford as he polished a Maid Marian queen, "you clean up pretty well. More like a girl and less like a Dickensian waif."

"Thanks. I think." Gutsy wore old but clean blue jeans, a plain green T-shirt, and another of her many fishing vests. Since her machete was missing, she instead wore a broad-bladed farm knife that was as close to her favorite weapon as she could find. It was a bit too heavy, and the handle was a little large for her hand, but it would do until she found a replacement. Gutsy had one of her mother's favorite scarves threaded through some holes she'd punched and grommeted in the vest. The scarf was pink and orange with some swirls of sea green and blue.

"You have a look of terrible purpose writ large upon your countenance," said Mr. Ford in a mock theatrical voice.

"Can I ask you a question?" she said, stepping onto the porch.

"You know you can ask nearly anything," said Mr. Ford. It was how both he and his friend always answered that kind of question. *Nearly* anything. So far Gutsy had never asked anything they refused to answer, but it often made her wonder where that line was. And why it was there.

"Do you remember when you told me about how some people got sick and turned into *los muertos* over time instead of dying and coming back?"

"Sure."

"You saw my mom before she died, right? Is there any way she might have had that same kind of sickness?"

Ford stopped polishing the chess piece and set it down. There was a look of curiosity and concern on his weathered face. "Why do you ask?"

"Can you just answer the question first?"

The old man's eyes narrowed. "No," he said.

"No, you can't answer or—"

"No, that's not what she had." Ford picked up a different chess piece. Friar Tuck, a fat monk.

Gutsy took a half step closer. "How do you know?"

He cocked his head and studied her. "What makes you ask?"

It felt like a bit of a standoff. Gutsy didn't want to tell him about what had happened at the cemetery or at her house, because he was an adult and he might tell the town council on her. That would probably get her in trouble, and maybe even sent to the Cuddlys' Home for Foundlings.

"Can't you just tell me?" she asked. A few slow seconds shambled past while the Chess Player thought about it. When he didn't answer, Gutsy folded her arms and gave him a flat, hard stare. "What are you hiding?"

A voice drifted up from under the hat on Urrea's face. "Busted."

"Go back to sleep," Ford told him, but Urrea plucked the hat off his face, yawned, and sat up. He did not look at all like he'd been asleep. His face wasn't flushed and his eyes were crystal clear.

The two old men looked at each other for a five-count, and then Urrea nodded and Ford sighed. But then Ford looked up and down the street, to where people were going to and fro, doing their daily business. "Not here," said Ford, "and not now."

"Why not?"

Ford stood. "Do you want an honest answer to your question? About the sickness, I mean? Yes? The school. My classroom. One hour."

Then he stretched, scratched his stomach, clapped Urrea on the shoulder, and wandered into the general store. Urrea got up too, gave her a sly wink, and followed him, leaving

Gutsy standing on the porch feeling very confused. But also excited.

What do they know?

She ached to find out, and an hour was forever away.

Gutsy stepped down off the porch and thought about it, then smiled and headed off toward the rear guard post.

THE SOUTHERNMOST PART OF NEW ALAMO WAS called Cargo Town, because it was where large quantities of scavenged supplies were kept under guard.

The Raid had been the first expedition to Corpus Christi, but there had been others, and also plenty of raids on warehouses and factories scattered throughout that part of Texas. Those survivors who knew the area worked with scouts and mission planners to set up the raids. Most of the time those raiding parties found buildings that had burned down, been stripped of everything useful, or were so thoroughly overrun that it would cost too many lives to justify an attempt. Some of the warehouses had been taken over by scavengers. A few had become small communities, and no one in Gutsy's town wanted to go to war with other survivors.

And then there were the plague towns: places where whole populations had been wiped out by disease. Early attempts to scavenge goods from those unfortunate places had brought death to New Alamo in waves.

It was getting harder to find stocks of clean bulk food, like canned goods that hadn't swollen with botulism, or sacks of grain, rice, and other staples that weren't so thoroughly infested by bugs as to be useless.

On the other hand, there were other items in bulk that were worth the effort to bring home. Pots and pans, building supplies, clothes, toilet paper, books, furniture, and supplies of things like aluminum foil, clean plastic bags, tons of baking soda, and more. One raid on a mile-long derailed train yielded two hundred tons of toothpaste, mouthwash, roll-on deodorant, bar soap, and hand sanitizer. The daily diet in New Alamo might not have much range, but everyone had great teeth, and hygiene was remarkably high for a postapocalyptic settlement.

Big Quonset huts were set along the walls and crammed with supplies, and there were guards in each. The area directly around the gate was clear except for a corral of horses and a line of trade wagons. There was a flat catwalk that ran around the entire town atop the stacked walls of cars. Two sentry towers had been erected at each of the town's gates, and the gates themselves were made from stacks of rubber tires on long vertical poles, lashed firmly together and mounted on a series of heavy-duty sets of truck wheels to make them easy to move. When closed, the gate could withstand a wave of *los muertos*.

Gutsy and Sombra walked up to an old Winnebago permanently parked inside the wall. It was used as an office for the security supervisor. She peered in through the window to see who was on duty and was relieved that it was Karen Peak, the mother of Sarah, one of Gutsy's friends from school. Or at least Sarah used to be a school friend. Because of a severe allergic reaction to something inside the school,

Sarah had been taken out and was now tutored at home. Sarah was a pretty girl who used to be funny and popular, but now she was sickly and withdrawn, clearly not fully recovered from being sick. Gutsy rarely saw her anymore, though both Karen and Sarah had come to visit the morning after Mama died.

Gutsy tapped on the door and went in. Karen rose and came over to give Gutsy a hug. Mrs. Peak was an athletic woman of about forty, with straight blond hair framing a pretty face. Like a lot of the adults in town, there was a kind of permanent sadness in Karen's eyes. Gutsy knew that it was an emotional scar that marked anyone who had lived through the end of the world as they had all known it. Eyes that had seen too much and lived in a world full of reminders.

"Hey, Gabriella, how are you doing, sweetie?" asked the supervisor. Karen always called Gutsy by her given name, Gabriella, but Gutsy didn't hold that against her.

"Okay, I guess," lied Gutsy. "Getting by."

Karen looked past her to the coydog standing uncertainly in the open doorway. "Who's that?"

Gutsy introduced Sombra and made up a story about finding him wandering in the desert. She did not mention Hope Cemetery or the collar the dog had worn. Karen listened and made sympathetic noises, but Gutsy could see the supervisor's sharp eyes roving over the many injuries, old and new. The expression in her eyes let Gutsy know that Karen was making some of the same judgments about Sombra she had herself.

All Karen said was, "Poor pup's been through the wringer."

"Lot of that going around," said Gutsy. "I heard that some

of your guys got hurt the other night. What was that all about?"

"We're, um, still sorting that out," said Karen. Her eyes shifted away for a moment. Was she embarrassed? wondered Gutsy. Or was there something else? "Jimmy Quiñones is in the hospital with a cracked skull, a broken leg, and some other injuries. Roberto Cantu was knocked out, but he'll be okay."

"Who were those people on the horses?"

"No one knows. Ravagers, probably."

"How'd they get in, though?"

Shutters seemed to drop behind Karen's eyes. "We're looking into that."

There was some kind of warning in her expression and Gutsy didn't push it. Instead she asked, "Were they working the night before?"

Karen looked surprised. "No, why?"

"Who was?"

"Trey Williams and Buffy Howell worked that shift. Why?" The suspicion was very evident in her tone.

"Oh, I just wondered if they saw anything before," said Gutsy quickly. "I mean, were the riders from a wolf pack or something?"

It was a little clumsy, and Gutsy wished she had prepared better for this kind of conversation; however, it seemed to work. Karen's tone was milder when she answered.

"Nah. Trey and Buffy didn't see anything. No one on the day shift did either; and we've had our own riders out on patrol all week, but no one's seen a thing. We don't understand what happened the other night."

"Really? What's with the patrols?" Gutsy asked, and nearly winced because it was too quick, and it put Karen back on the alert.

"Why are you asking about all this?"

Gutsy took a breath. "I . . . I guess I'm just scared is all. What with Mama dying and being alone. Being a *girl* alone . . . you know?"

That did it. Karen's expression softened and she gathered Gutsy in for a hug of the kind that could only be called "motherly." Very tight, very long, with lots of pats and soothing words. Woman to girl.

"It's all right, sweetie. We've doubled the guards and I have mounted and foot patrols round the clock. I'll make sure they check on your house tonight, don't you worry."

"Gosh . . . thanks," said Gutsy, disentangling herself and forcing a smile onto her face. She almost panicked when she realized that her attempt to defuse Karen's suspicions might lead to a hastening of an official response to Gutsy being a minor living alone. She thanked Karen and got out of there as quickly as she could.

Doubts and fears seemed to nip at her heels as she walked through Cargo Town. Not just because of the risk of being sent to foster care. That was an issue, but not the biggest one at the moment. No, there was something strange about the guard thing. Very strange.

How had the Rat Catchers gotten past Trey and Buffy? How was that possible?

They stopped at a horse trough so Sombra could take a drink, and Gutsy leaned down to give his head a thoughtful scratch. People were moving around as they always had, attending to their own business, a few of them nodding or smiling at her. Where once that might have been completely normal, now every nod seemed to suggest a meaning, and every smile looked suspicious.

"I think I'm getting paranoid," she told the dog, who raised a dripping muzzle and glanced up at her. Then an old line from a book she'd read occurred to her. *Just because you're paranoid doesn't mean they aren't out to get you.*

She shivered despite the afternoon heat.

"Come on," she said, and they headed off in the direction of the school. Gutsy did not take a direct route, but wandered up and down streets, in and out of stores, glancing around to make sure she wasn't being followed. Where, she wondered, was the dividing line between paranoia and practical caution?

It was a very important and extremely dangerous little question.

GUTSY AND SOMBRA DRIFTED IN THE DIRECTION of the Home for Foundlings. She wondered what kind of trouble Spider and Alethea were in. So she headed that way. As she approached, she saw Vera Cuddly sitting on a beach chair outside, watching with a stern and unfriendly eye as Spider and Alethea sat on stools and peeled potatoes. A mountain of unpeeled spuds stood between her friends, and a large tub of peeled ones was at their feet.

Before Gutsy could say a word, Mrs. Cuddly growled, "You keep on walking, missy. There's no one here needs to talk to the likes of you."

Alethea gave Gutsy a guarded smile. Spider mouthed the words, *Kill me now.*

Sombra growled at the stern-faced woman, which made her flinch, but Mrs. Cuddly reached behind her beach chair for a shotgun and laid it across her meaty thighs. The coydog gave her an evil look and the woman gave it right back.

"Go on now," she said—either to Gutsy or Sombra. "Git."

Gutsy hurried on, feeling the weight of Mrs. Cuddly's disapproval all the way down the block. At the corner, she looked back and saw that the mean old woman was still glaring at her. Gutsy rounded the corner and walked straight into someone. She staggered back and nearly fell, and the other person *did* fall. Hard. Into a big, steaming pile of horse droppings someone had swept against the curb.

It was Alice Chung.

The look of absolute horror and disgust on Alice's pretty face tore holes in Gutsy.

"Oh God, I'm so sorry," she cried, and grabbed Alice to pick her up. Gutsy tried for a good grip, got a bad one, and tore Alice's lovely blue hand-embroidered blouse open. A long piece of it hung from Gutsy's hand like a dead snake. There was a T-shirt underneath, but that was hardly the point. Alice was one of the best seamstresses in school and took great pride in the delicacy and complexity of her work. That blouse was the envy of everyone in school. It was gorgeous, a work of art.

Now it was ruined.

Alice sat there, legs sprawled, skirt tangled around her knees, smack in the center of forty pounds of sunbaked manure, with her blouse ripped.

Gutsy stood there, the piece of blouse still in her hands. People on both sides of the street had stopped to stare. Two boys from school burst out laughing. So did a gaggle of girls from the next grade up. Everyone who saw it cracked up, and there suddenly seemed to be a lot of people around. Gutsy wanted to die right there, right then.

"I'm sorry, Alice. God, I'm so sorry."

The look in Alice's eyes told her everything. Hurt, anger, humiliation, loathing, disgust. She got up very slowly, clumps of stuff falling from her skirt. When Gutsy offered a hand to try to help, Alice stared at it like it was something more foul than the mess she'd fallen into.

"Don't touch me," she said in a tone that was ten degrees below freezing. "Don't you dare touch me."

Gutsy pulled her hand back as quickly as if she'd been burned. Her face burned too. People were laughing at Alice. But everyone knew that it was Gutsy's fault.

With great dignity and open contempt, Alice turned around and walked back the way she had come. Going home. She did not try to wipe the mess off her skirt. That would have been worse. It would have been pathetic. Instead she stiffened her back and walked away, dragging all light and cheer from the day.

Not that there had been much to begin with.

Gutsy turned away from the grinning spectators and looked down at Sombra. He wagged his tail. He, apparently, thought horse poop was a wonderful thing.

Without meeting anyone else's eye, Gutsy slunk away with her battered dog in tow.

MISFIT HIGH WAS ONE OF THE FEW BUILDINGS IN
New Alamo that was not either a Quonset hut or one of the
blocky dwellings built as temporary housing for people like
Mama—the so-called "illegal aliens." The school was a former government multipurpose administration facility, half
of which was empty. The building was two stories tall and
sprawled in all sorts of unlikely directions, as if the architect
and the builder were not on speaking terms. In the burning
heat of late August, the school was closed except for a few
summer school classes, but they were all held in the morning.

Gutsy circled the building, relying on her eyes and Sombra's nose to locate any lurking threats. There were none, so
she entered through a side door that had a faulty lock. She
knew because she'd rigged the lock so she could slip inside
with Spider and Alethea after hours. Not to steal or vandal-
ize, but because Misfit High had the best library in town.
They would sit in the cool darkness of the basement, lost
among acres of books, eating oranges and figs and apricots
they'd picked on the way. There were thousands of fruit
trees in town. Then, inside, they would spend whole eve-
nings reading in silence, or sometimes reading aloud, while

camping lanterns bathed them in blue-white illumination.

The door closed silently behind them—Gutsy kept the hinges oiled for that purpose—and they stood listening. It was one of the few places she could go where there was no sound at all. The walls and windows were thick, and not a bird's peep or a cricket's chirp could be heard. No human voices either, which was nice. Except for her two friends, and occasional conversations with the Chess Players, Gutsy preferred silence so she could listen to her own thoughts. Sombra walked a few yards along the hall, sniffing at the floor or lifting his head to sniff the air. His body language told Gutsy that he was calm. Good.

The classrooms used by Mr. Ford and Mr. Urrea were on the second floor, and Gutsy moved like a silent ghost along the halls and up the stairs. The coydog's nails made small sounds on the marble floors and stone steps. She cut him a look halfway up the stairs and was surprised to see that he was climbing easily. His limp had gradually gone away and he no longer moved as if he was pushing through walls of pain. She had no idea how fast dogs healed, but Sombra seemed to have a core of strength and vitality. Nice.

At the top of the stairs she paused again, listening once more. Gutsy was seldom in a hurry and tried to never move faster than her ability to study and analyze her surroundings. That had kept her safe many times out in the Broken Lands. That natural caution, amped up by acquired knowledge and lots of practice, kept her from running afoul of shamblers, wolf packs, and other dangers. It was why she was alive when some other scavengers were either bones in the weeds or walking corpses.

Now, more than ever, she knew that caution was crucial. The Rat Catchers were cautious too. Smart, organized, and dangerous. She had to be all that and more.

A door stood open down the hall, and lamplight painted a yellow oblong on the floor. Mr. Ford's classroom. She drew her knife, and at the sight of it Sombra changed his body language, hunching his shoulders and lowering his head as if stalking a wild rabbit. Or getting ready for a fight. Moving with total silence now, they crept closer.

Gutsy stopped at the doorway and knelt to peer around the frame. Mr. Ford sat in his chair behind the desk, and Mr. Urrea, leaning on his cane, stood by the blackboard. They were deep in a quiet conversation. Gutsy listened, straining to hear what they were saying, but she couldn't quite make it out.

The old men were alone in there, so Gutsy rose, slid her knife back into its sheath, took a breath and exhaled it, then stepped into the room.

The conversation died as first Ford and then Urrea turned toward her.

"Miss Gomez," said Urrea quietly, "I guess you'd better come in."

She held her ground. "There's some stuff I need to know. About my mama. About what happened in town. About something that happened out at the cemetery."

"Yes," said Ford. "And I think it's time we talked about what's really going on around here."

Gutsy and the coydog walked across the classroom and stopped in front of the desk. She placed her palms on the edge and leaned forward, glaring at the old men.

"You *know* what's going on?" she asked coldly.

They exchanged a look. Urrea gave Ford the tiniest of nods.

"Yes," said Ford. "But . . ."

"But what?"

"You're not going to like it," said Ford.

"Tell me anyway," she said.

PART TEN

VALLEY STATE PRISON
CHOWCHILLA, CALIFORNIA
ONE WEEK EARLIER . . .

DIRTY WORK

It is the part of a good man

to do great and noble deeds,

though he risks everything.

—PLUTARCH

IT WAS A LABOR ASSIGNED IN HELL AND CARRIED OUT with the diligence of the damned.

The prison had huge tanks of water, so there was no shortage for washing. But even the harshest soaps and torrents of water could not sponge away the things they had done that day.

It had all been done according to a strange and nearly silent routine of action, and though they worked in pairs, there was no conversation except for what was needed in the moment.

"Open the door."

"Here's the key."

"He's done."

Like that.

When it was done, they each drifted to the shower rooms to get clean. There were a lot of shower stalls and no one wanted to share. No one could look at anyone else.

Alone in a far corner of the guards' locker room, Benny stripped to the skin and spent the next half hour washing every inch of his body.

Again and again.

· · ·

Chong found Benny an hour later.

"You need to get dressed," said Chong.

Benny looked away. Chong came in and sat down next to him. The floor had long since dried. Neither spoke for nearly five minutes.

Then Benny said, "What if it's like this in Asheville? What if Captain Ledger never even got there? What if he's dead? What if they're *all* dead?"

Chong took his time before he said anything. "Y'know, man, all my life I've tried to steer away from looking at things as either black or white. There always seemed to be a third choice. A gray area, I guess, because in every case there was more information, additional details that had to be considered."

Benny snorted. "How's that working out for you?"

"Right now? Not all that good." Chong sighed. "Look, we either go back to Reclamation or we go to Asheville. If we keep going . . . there might be more stuff like this."

"I—I can't do this again," said Benny. "I don't think we should have *done* this. The zoms don't care. They're not in pain anymore. But I am. *We* are. This . . . really messed me up, dude. I'm not sure I want to . . ." He let the rest hang.

Chong turned and looked at Benny. "You know I *have* to go, though, right? You get that?"

Benny closed his eyes and said nothing.

"While I was in the shower," continued Chong, "I cooked up three different plans for me sneaking out with my quad and leaving some elaborate and heroic note about how you all should go back and let me do this alone. About how it wasn't yours to do because *I'm* the one who's sick. About you being needed back there a lot more than you needed to come with me on what's probably a suicide mission."

"And . . . ?"

Chong shrugged. "Truth is, I'm too scared to go alone. And I can't go back home because all that would mean is me waiting to die, with all my friends hanging around like some death watch. Like being at my own funeral for ten whole months. That would suck."

"That would suck," agreed Benny.

"Sure, going to Asheville might be more of this kind of thing," Chong said, waving his hands to indicate the entire prison, "but I still have to try."

After a long, long time, Benny nodded. "Have to try."

Chong cleared his throat. "Any chance I could talk you into putting on some clothes? I have enough problems in my life without seeing you naked."

"Hey, you're the one who came into my shower and sat down."

"I'll add that to the long list of things I will forever regret," said Chong.

They both burst out laughing even though it wasn't all that funny.

They laughed too loud and too long.

Chong got to his feet and opened the door; then, without looking back, he recited a fragment of an old poem. "'But I have promises to keep,'" he said softly, "'and miles to go before I sleep.'"

Benny got slowly and heavily to his feet, used the last bucket of water to rinse off the dried soap, toweled off, and got dressed. He walked over to where his *kami katana* stood leaning against a wall. He picked it up and held it out in front of him, supporting it horizontally with both hands, the way a samurai would. He bowed his head.

Not bowing to the weapon, or even its potential. He wasn't sure what he was bowing to. His eyes were dry and they burned, and his heart was a lifeless stone in his chest.

Benny slung the long strap over his shoulder and angled the handle so that he could reach up and over and draw the weapon. Like he had done every day since Tom handed the sword to him with the very last of his life's strength.

The words Chong had recited seemed to echo in the air.

But I have promises to keep, and miles to go before I sleep.

"Yeah," said Benny to the empty room. Then he went to find his friends.

THEY ATE, SLEPT BADLY, AND WOKE IN THE COLD light of morning, ready to go and needing to be gone. As Benny helped prepare breakfast, he could feel the oppressive weight of the ugly place bearing down on him, as if it was becoming *his* prison. It made him feel claustrophobic. Memories of what they had done yesterday made him feel like a criminal.

Over breakfast they studied the maps and made plans. The one highlight of the previous day had been the discovery of the locked armory. The key had been among those Riot had found, and when they opened the heavy steel door, they stared slack-jawed at what was inside. More weapons and equipment than they could ever use.

"How come no one looted this stuff before?" wondered Chong.

"Because people are stupid," was Lilah's gruff response. It was hard to argue with, because there were enough weapons and ammunition in there for a small army. Benny thought it was more likely that the plague had spread too fast inside the prison. It also suggested that the guards who worked here must have simply abandoned the place during First Night, maybe before the refugees ever got here. Most likely they went home to see to their loved ones and were washed away by the tidal surge of the Lucifer 113 infection.

Whatever the reason, finding that armory made their mission to Asheville suddenly seem possible. Within half an hour they were all kitted out in black Kevlar limb pads, ballistic helmets, and vests that would stop a bullet and—Benny hoped—a bite. The carpet coats were an extra layer of protection to cover any areas left exposed—wrists, waists, and so on. It was all dreadfully hot and heavy, but at that moment Benny would have wrapped himself in cast iron because of what lay ahead of them. They debated whether to use the cadaverine as yet another bit of protection. Lilah and Riot argued against it, citing their limited supply. Benny, Nix, Chong, and Morgie overrode them, and they each smeared a little on their armor.

They took as much as they could carry or cram into the quads. Riot and Morgie rounded up all the remaining food, too. Then they peered out through the cracked windows of the loading bay, where five of the six quads were stored. The sixth was way out in the field, mostly hidden by tall weeds and too many zoms.

"Getting Benny's bike's not going to be easy," observed Chong.

"Nah," said Morgie. When everyone glanced at him with expectant eyes, he said, "Those weeds are dry. We can use some fuel from in here, make a firebomb . . . the weeds will go right up and we'll burn 'em out."

"What about my quad?" asked Benny.

"We can—" began Morgie, but Riot cut him off.

"Morgie," she said caustically, "you are so dumb you could throw yourself on the floor and miss."

"Huh?"

"The wind's been blowing strong and it's blowing north. You start a fire and it'll march all the way to Reclamation and keep on going. You want to set fire to all of California?"

Morgie flushed a deep red and kept his opinions to himself.

Lilah tapped the glass with a finger. Despite her facade of toughness, Benny saw that she was back to biting her nails all the way down.

"We fight our way through," she said. "Four quads go off in different directions, heading to the road. Revving high to draw them. Riot takes Benny to his quad and waits while he gets it going. When the zoms clear off, Benny gets dropped and Riot gives cover until he's mounted and has the engine on. That's the plan."

It was not said as a suggestion, and everyone nodded. It was a scary plan, but a practical one.

And that was what they did.

As soon as the gear was loaded, five quad engines roared to life. Benny opened the door, then jumped back as the machines burst from the shadowy garage into the bright sunlight. Riot slowed to let him jump on. The line of quads tore across the weed-choked field. There were zoms out here, too, but only a dozen or so, and these were spread out. The five quads zoomed into the field, spreading out as they accelerated, drawing as many zoms away as they could while Benny tried to start his quad. The engine coughed and choked but did not catch.

The quad was out of gas.

THE QUAD HAD BEEN LEFT RUNNING AND HAD burned through its fuel before sputtering and dying out in the field.

Riot skidded to a stop, hurried over, and pushed Benny out of the way. "Watch my back and don't let me get bit."

Benny drew his sword and stood ready, but he kept glancing over his shoulder as Riot worked. Unlike the others, she was very familiar with the mechanics of the chunky machines, having used them while still part of the reaper army.

She opened the lid of one of the hard-shell saddlebags on the back of the quad and removed the fuel tube beneath the tank to release air. She immediately began fueling from the spare tanker attached to the back of the quad. As soon as there was enough in the tank, she gave the throttle a couple of pumps, opening it all the way and closing the choke. Then she turned the key. The motor screeched in protest as if wanting to stay asleep. She tried again, and for a moment Benny thought it was going to start, but then it faded. Riot kept trying, and on the fifth try the sturdy little machine growled to life. The whole process seemed to take an hour, but he knew it was less than a minute. Time was as broken as the world. Riot kept working to adjust the choke to settle the engine into a normal rhythm.

"You waiting for an engraved invitation?" she barked. "Or did you rub steak sauce all over yourself this morning?"

"What . . . ?" Benny looked around and saw a whole bunch of zoms coming around the corner of the prison and shamble toward him. He ran to meet the ones in front and the sword wove a pattern of destruction that left five of them dead and two more crippled. Benny backpedaled until he was near the two quads again.

They remounted and took off across the field, heading back to the road to where the others waited. Now that they were on the road again, Benny could feel the time burning off around him. If Captain Ledger was in danger when they'd set out from Reclamation, then he was probably long dead now.

Regret was an ache that cracked his chest open.

He gunned the engine and roared down the road.

Interlude Five

KICKAPOO CAVERN STATE PARK
ONE WEEK AGO

THEY SAT THERE. TWO GROWN MEN, SCARRED FROM lifetimes of battle. Both of them killers. Sitting in the mud, staring, tears running down their faces.

"Joe . . . ?" said the hunter, his voice hushed to a whisper. "Are you . . . *real*?"

The soldier grinned. "If you are, then I am."

"How? They said you were dead."

"Heard that about you, too, brother."

They sat there. Birds and monkeys chattered in the trees around them.

"How are you here?" asked Sam.

"Here, as in right here, right now? Or here at all?"

"I don't know. Either. Both."

Ledger sighed. "Yeah, well, that's a long story. Short version? The world ended when I was off the clock. I was coming back from a job in Southeast Asia, and by the time I reached the States the devil was off the leash and everything was falling apart."

Sam nodded. "I know. I was in the middle of it. My team was sent into a quarantine zone in Stebbins County, Pennsylvania. A Cold War bioweapon had been released and—"

"Lucifer 113."

"If you know about it already, then—"

Ledger shook his head. "I know parts of it. Bits and pieces. I know Dr. Volker used the pathogen on a death-row prisoner. Homer Gibbon. Volker was psycho when it came to punishment for serial killers and wanted to make Gibbon suffer. His new version of Lucifer 113 was supposed to make Gibbon aware of his own body rotting in the coffin. Didn't work out that way and Gibbon, he woke up hungry in some small-town mortuary. I got that much from the news. Some bozo reporter named Billy Trout was doing these field reports. 'Live from the apocalypse.' Stuff like that."

"Billy was a good guy," said Sam. "A bit of a bleeding heart, but decent. He and his girlfriend—"

"Dez Fox. Stebbins County Police Department."

Sam punched the ground. "You *do* know the whole story."

"No, I don't," said Ledger. "I met Dez Fox and Billy Trout about six months after the outbreak. They're the ones who told me you were dead. I helped them out of a jam. They had a convoy of school buses filled with little kids. Couple of your team were with them, heading down to Asheville." He grinned and shook his head. "Guess the reports of your demise were a bit exaggerated."

"I was wearing body armor," said Sam. "Kevlar limb pads, chest protector, ballistic helmet. I got buried under a bunch of the dead. By the time I crawled my way out, the buses were gone. I looked but never found them. Tell me they made it."

"Hope so," said Ledger, "but I lost track of them. Heard some rumors, even followed some leads, but if they're alive, I don't know where."

"This is insane," said Sam, shaking his head. He was still unsure whether this was even real. He hadn't seen Joe Ledger in nearly twenty years. A long time ago, nearly three decades before, when Sam was in his early twenties, he'd been the sniper for Echo Team, one of the world's most elite counterterrorism squads. They had taken down one terrorist group after another, trying to keep the world from falling apart. But then, five years after the last time Sam had seen his old team leader, the world had, indeed, fallen off its hinges.

He and Ledger went back and forth, sharing histories, filling in a few blanks, leaving other parts unsaid or unknown. While they talked, Ledger retied the bandages on his leg. The wound was bad. Deep and ugly. It would need cleaning and stitches.

"Hey," said Ledger, "I don't suppose you saw a big dog around here."

"Lots of stray dogs around, Joe."

"Not like this one. He's an American mastiff. Two hundred and fifty pounds, wearing spiked armor and a helmet. Name's Grimm, and me and him have some history. He was with me on the chopper and I pushed him out over a stream before we hit. Thought I saw him splash down. If it was a shallow stream, Grimm might be alive but hurt. If it was deep, he could have drowned with all that armor. Either way, I'd like to know."

"I can look for him," said Sam. He got to his feet, offered a hand to Ledger, and pulled the older soldier carefully to his feet. "I need to get you to my cabin and take a better look at that leg."

Sam wrapped an arm around Ledger's waist and they began making their way back along the game trail.

"How are you here?" Sam asked. "I mean right here, in my woods?"

"I was on my way from California to Asheville, North Carolina," said Ledger. "That's where the new government is based. We have about a hundred thousand people, give or take. An army. A new government. The whole works."

"In *Asheville*? That can't be right."

"Why not?"

"Because Asheville was completely destroyed," said Sam. "It was nuked."

"Says who?"

"Says some soldiers I talked to."

"When was it supposed to be nuked?"

"Oh . . . years ago."

Ledger shook his head. "Then they lied to you or they repeated bad information. I've been to Asheville as recently as six months ago. It was never nuked. It's intact and fortified." He narrowed his eyes. "Who are these soldiers who told you this junk?"

"There's a small facility down near the Mexican border, about two hundred miles south. A hardened facility, so they still have lights, generators, and a fuel store. The Laredo Chemical and Biological Weapon Defense Research Facility."

"I heard about that way back before it all fell apart. A black budget site?"

"Yes," agreed Sam. "Reduced staff before the dead rose, and then one of several sites trying to find a cure. Maybe the last one."

"There was one at Zabriskie Point in Death Valley," said Joe. He told Sam about rescuing Dr. McReady and her research. Sam was impressed and felt a flush of excitement at the thought of a cure.

"It's more of a treatment," corrected Ledger. "Keeps infected people alive if they take their pills. Works different on full-blown zoms, though. Accelerates the life cycle of the parasites. They get fast and then they die. But listen, if the soldiers at Laredo told you Asheville was gone, then they lied to you. Asheville survived the end of everything else, and they got their act together. A government, a president, a Congress—kind of—and a lot of scientists and engineers working their butts off to fix stuff. I was heading there when my bird went down."

"What happened?" asked Sam. "Engine trouble?"

"No," said Ledger. "Someone shot us down. We took an RPG in the tail rotor. To say we did not see that coming was an understatement. Been a lot of years since I was in an aircraft that took enemy fire."

"Someone shot you down?"

"Yeah. Who knows, maybe it was one of your soldier friends. I didn't see the shot. I was on a call with some guys in Reclamation. We'd just gotten word that something was happening in Asheville and then suddenly—*boom*. Odd timing, though, and you know how I hate coincidences."

"I don't know the soldiers," said Sam. "I know *of* them. And I don't know why they'd fire on you."

"Yeah," said Ledger slowly. "I'd kind of like to ask someone that question. Not sure I'm going to be very nice about how I ask. But . . . frankly, man, I'm kind of surprised to hear that there's an active base here in Texas. I'd also like to know why they haven't been in touch with Asheville. If they have power, then they had to have working satellite phones. So, something's hinky."

Sam shook his head. "I really don't know. I've never been

to the base. The impression I got was that it was operational but not doing very well. Don't know the details and haven't really cared to find out. I, um . . . moved *away* from all that, Joe. I've been living alone here for years. I see a few people now and then, do a little trading for goods, but mostly I stay to myself."

"Like a monk," said Ledger.

"I guess. Doing penance for old sins."

Ledger shook his head. "Anything you did was for the greater good."

Sam shook his head again. "Don't lie to a liar. I've had a lot of time to think about everything I've done, every trigger I've pulled, every life I ended. You can't tell me that we were always the good guys in spotless white hats. You've never been that naive, Joe."

Ledger sighed but said nothing for nearly a mile.

"Listen, Sam," he said at last, his voice tentative, "there's something I need to say. Your family . . . your brothers . . . do you know what happened to them? Did you ever try to find them?"

Sam flinched as an ancient ache stabbed him. "I tried, Joe. But the nukes, the radiation, the dead . . . . I called my stepmom. She told me that Dad came home hurt. Bitten . . . you understand? She dropped the phone. There were screams. I could tell what was happening. They're all dead, Joe. My parents. Tom, little Benny. It's crazy, but I never even saw Benny. Just baby pictures and e-mails, you know? Facebook posts. But I never actually *saw* him. Poor kid never had a chance."

When he caught Joe's expression, Sam stopped. "What is it? I'm talking about my family and you're smiling. . . ."

"Sam," said Ledger in a voice that was fragile with emotion, "I have a lot to tell you. God . . . where do I even begin?"

PART ELEVEN
NEW ALAMO, TEXAS
LATE AUGUST

SECRETS AND LIES

By a lie, a man . . . annihilates

his dignity as a man.

—IMMANUEL KANT

"I GUESS THE BEST WAY TO START THIS," SAID MR. URREA, "is to ask what you already know."

"Know about what?" demanded Gutsy.

"About *Los cazadores de ratas vienen*."

She stiffened. "The Rat Catchers. I know some."

"Some, huh," said Urrea, shooting a look at Ford.

"Question is," said Gutsy, "what do you know? I mean, do you know who these Rat Catchers are and why they're acting like they're in some kind of military when there *isn't* any real military left?"

That seemed to jolt the two old teachers. Urrea studied her with intense eyes. "Gutsy," he said stiffly, "you really do need to tell us everything you know. Everything."

"You first," she countered.

"No," said Ford.

When she still hesitated, Urrea said, "Please."

Gutsy folded her arms. "How do I even know I can trust you two? Because right now you're scaring me, and I'm getting tired of being scared." As if picking up on her emotions, Sombra stood up and glared at them. He did not exactly snarl, but there was clear menace in the way he stood—straight, ready, his muscles tense.

The dog's high state of alertness, coupled with the marks of violence all over him, seemed to flick some kind of switch in both of the old men. Ford got up and crossed to the door, closed it, and locked it. Urrea pulled the shades down on all the windows, plunging the room into amber shadows. Then the Chess Players sat down at students' desks and waved Gutsy to another. She pulled hers around to face them, and Sombra lay like a sphinx in the space between.

"If you've ever trusted us," said Ford, "then trust us now. Tell us what you know. Leave nothing out."

Gutsy took a while to think about it. Mr. Ford and Mr. Urrea had always seemed like good guys. Smart, insightful, fair-minded and . . . honest? She hoped so.

"Okay," she said, "but you'd better not be messing with me."

They gave their words, and Urrea even put his hand over his heart.

"If you think we're lying," he said, "then you can sic your coydog on us. I give you full permission."

"I don't," said Ford, but Urrea ignored him.

Gutsy considered them both, then nodded to herself. She told them all of it, and even surprised herself by keeping nothing back. Everything Mama had said on her deathbed; the two times the Rat Catchers had brought horror back from the cemetery. The desecration of all those graves. The captain, lieutenant, and two soldiers. The Night Army. The lab and the base. The bizarre question about whether Mama had told Gutsy some kind of information *after* she'd been brought back from the grave.

Partway through her tale, Mr. Urrea took his pipe from a pocket, cleaned it slowly, and put the stem between his teeth. As far as Gutsy knew, the old man never actually smoked the pipe. Something to fidget with, she figured. Something to keep nervous hands busy.

Mr. Ford, on the other hand, sat still and barely even looked like he was breathing. Only his eyes were fully alive.

By the time she was done the noonday sun was baking all of New Alamo.

"Okay," said Gutsy. "Your turn."

"THERE IS A BIG DIFFERENCE BETWEEN WHAT WE know for sure," began Ford, "and what we've guessed."

"We have theories," agreed Urrea. "We've heard things, but we can't prove much."

"Tell me anyway," she insisted.

Ford nodded to his friend. "You go first. It started with you."

Mr. Urrea took his pipe out of his mouth and studied the bowl with raised eyebrows, as if surprised to find that it was empty. Then he looked up at Gutsy. "I was a writer before the End. You know that, of course. Ford was too. We were at a writers' conference in San Antonio when it all started."

"What's a writers' conference?" she asked.

"Bunch of self-important writers trying to convince a bunch of earnest wannabes that they're all going to make it big." He paused. "Look, before the End people like us made a living—even a good living—writing books. That's one of those professions that died when the world changed. Along with movie stars, web developers, nuclear engineers, airline pilots, and a whole long list of other jobs that don't make any sense to someone like you."

"How does this matter?"

"It matters, because Ford and I were more than just writers," said Urrea. "We were working on a project together. Something kind of secret and something very dangerous. There's a thing called 'investigative journalism.' That's when a reporter or writer digs into something that other people maybe want to keep hidden. Stuff like crimes, bad politics, corruption. You understand?"

"Sure. Like the stories Mr. Golden writes for the paper."

Mr. Golden printed several hundred copies of the weekly *New Alamo*, which mostly ran ads for trades and swaps, notices about store hours and town council meetings, and recipes, but also had a column called The Whisperer. Everyone knew Mr. Golden wrote the column—he wrote every word of the paper—but it was supposed to be written by a mysterious person called X. The column was a lot of gossip, most of it stupid, almost all of it questionable. Like when X said that Trapper Halls sewed small pieces of scrap metal into the corners of his feed sacks in order to give short weight on what he sold. People tore those bags apart and didn't find a thing. Or that other time when X claimed that Nancy Fowler was having an affair with Hack Santiago, when everyone who had two brain cells knew that Hack was gay. Rumors and gossip that got people talking but were usually hurtful, sneaky, and mean-spirited. Nobody Gutsy knew liked Mr. Golden. However, everyone she knew—including Mama—read that column every week.

Ford snorted again. "Gus Golden wouldn't know the truth if it crawled up his pants leg and bit him on the—"

"Ford . . . ," said Urrea quietly.

"I get the point," said Gutsy.

"Real investigative journalists care about the facts," said Urrea. "They want to uncover the truth. Not lies, not hearsay. They want the cold, hard facts. The case we were investigating had to do with how undocumented immigrants were being treated."

Gutsy felt her attention sharpen.

"We'd talked to a number of the undocumented who had been in this very camp. People who had been processed out of here and sent back to Mexico but who came back across the border."

"How?"

"Oh . . . various ways. Tunnels, or across the Rio Grande, in glider planes, over the wall. Sometimes across the Gulf of Mexico. People always found ways in. I knew several because of my own history. I was born in Tijuana, Mexico, but went to college in the States. In San Diego."

She cocked her head to one side, reappraising the old man. "You don't look Mexican."

"My mother was American. I have her blue eyes and I used to have sandy blond hair."

"You used to *have* hair," said Ford.

"In Mexico," continued Urrea as if his friend hadn't spoken, "as a kid, I was the outsider because I looked American. In America I was the kid with the Mexican accent. I wasn't welcome on either side of the border. Then I began writing about immigrants—legal and illegal. And about the need to cross borders, cross lines, change the definition of who you are to fit who you want to be. When I caught wind of something very bad happening here, I told Ford about it. We got ourselves invited to the writers' conference in San Antonio and used it as a cover to start poking our noses where they didn't belong."

"We didn't expect the world to end," said Ford.

Gutsy frowned. "Yeah, but what was it you guys were investigating? And how does that have anything to do with the Rat Catchers or what happened to my mom?"

"It has everything to do with it, I'm afraid," said Urrea, and Gutsy could hear pain and maybe fear in his voice. "You see, the rumors we followed weren't just about the way undocumented persons were being treated here. Not only about that. No, the story we were investigating had to do with things that were happening to some of those people in the lab down here."

"*Lab?*" gasped Gutsy. "What lab? You mean the FEMA place near Laredo?"

"No," said Ford. "That was set up during the crisis. Everyone knew about it because they wanted people to be able to find it. Unfortunately, some of the people who went there for shelter had been bitten. And . . . well . . . you know how that turned out. We came looking for a *secret* laboratory that was supposed to be around here."

She folded her arms. "I've been all over the Broken Lands. If there was a base, I'm pretty sure I would have found it."

"Wouldn't that depend on how well it's hidden?" asked Mr. Urrea. "I mean, the Rat Catchers said they had a base, right? That's what you overheard. Then the base exists. Trust me, kiddo, the military were always very good at hiding things. Before the End, there were all kinds of rumors and urban legends about hidden bases. A lot of people believed there were even bases where they hid wreckage from crashed UFOs."

"Ri-i-i-ight," said Gutsy. "Mr. Golden writes about that, too. He thinks that the whole reason *los muertos* rose is because of aliens. Or . . . radiation from some kind of space probe. Or something like that. Crazy stuff. Are you going to tell me that this secret base was hiding little green men from outer space?"

"No," said Urrea. "Be almost nice if that was the case."

"Be better than the truth," said Ford.

"Why better?" asked Gutsy.

"Because the truth is so much more frightening than that," said Urrea. "And it's so much uglier than space aliens or cosmic radiation. If it was something wild like that, then it would have all been totally beyond our control. It would have been something done *to* us."

"You're saying it's not?" she asked.

"No. This plague . . . the whole end of the world was something done *by* us."

When she said nothing, Mr. Ford quietly said, "And it's not over."

"What do you mean?"

"He means," said Urrea, "that the people who started this whole thing are still out there. And they're still playing God with what's left of the human race."

"IT REALLY STARTED WHEN I MET A MAN NAMED Juan Cruz," began Mr. Urrea. "I was giving a talk at a library as part of a book tour. The book was about a family of immigrants who are trying to reconnect north of the border and build a life for themselves as part of the American Dream. Do you understand any of that?"

"I'm good," said Gutsy. "Keep going."

Urrea nodded. "My book was being adapted into a TV series. Juan heard about me and looked me up on the Net, found my list of appearances, and was in the audience for that talk. I focused partly on the plight of people who risked everything to come to America because their country—Mexico—had always suffered through poverty, a shortage of decent-paying jobs, and none of the advantages that would allow a working man or woman to provide comfort for their families."

"He also talked about politics," said Ford, "and went on a rant about how unfair the immigration system was, and how immigrants in this country were used for cheap labor and then disposed of when some politician wanted to be elected on an 'America first' platform."

"You weren't even there, Ford. You didn't hear my lecture."

"No, but every time you talked about immigration, that's where you always went."

Urrea looked like he was going to argue, then smiled faintly. "Fair enough. Anyway, after I gave my lecture, I took questions from the audience. Juan Cruz stood up and said, 'You give a lot of statistics about how many people sneak over the border, how many manage to eventually become US citizens, and how many are captured and sent back. Where do you get those numbers?' It was a fair question, and I cited a number of sources that included government agencies and public watchdog agencies."

"What are those?" asked Gutsy.

"Groups that tried to make sure the government was doing the right thing and telling the truth," supplied Ford. "Some of them in defense of immigrants, and some dead set against them. People didn't always agree about how many people should be let into this country, how many should be allowed to become citizens, how many should be sent back to wherever they came from. There were plenty of fights about it. Not just in state and national Congress, but actual fights in the streets."

Gutsy nodded. She knew a lot about this part. New Alamo had, after all, been a detention and relocation camp for illegal immigrants. Some of the people in town had been survivors from among the guards and staff of the camp, though they were now a minority. She remembered Mama once telling her that after the End, when the old camp was being turned into an actual town, many of the former undocumented people who'd been imprisoned there had wanted to force the old staff members out. But it was the Chess Players who stood up to argue against it. They made a case for mercy and forgiveness among all the survivors, citing that they were all badly outnumbered by *los muertos* and that there was strength in numbers. Not only physical strength, but by polling the crowd at a big town meeting they proved that each person there—American, Mexican American, or Mexican—had some skills or knowledge that made them useful to the whole. Carpenters and builders, hunters and farmers, engineers and designers, clergy and psychologists, cooks and tailors, and on and on. The more knowledge they had, the more of the best parts of the old world they could retain, and the more of the structure of society they could maintain.

"I told Juan about how I'd collected the statistics he asked about," continued Urrea, "but there was something about the way he looked at me that bothered me. It wasn't that he didn't agree with me or didn't believe me. No, from the look on his face it was obvious he *knew* I was wrong. His certainty really rattled me, and after the lecture I looked for him. He was gone, though, but when I went out to walk back to my hotel, there he was. Scared the heck out of me, because I've had trouble before because of speaking my mind. Juan Cruz was angry because he said that I was making statements without knowing the truth, and he said that made me complicit. You know that word?"

"I remember it from class," said Gutsy, nodding. "It means to be involved with people who were doing something illegal."

"Good girl," said Urrea, beaming. "Yes, that's what it means, and that's what Juan meant. However, he came to me because he believed I had been fooled, that I did not know the whole truth." He paused and studied his pipe for a moment. "I have a lot of faults. We all do. But I have a great respect for the truth. I've never been comfortable with an 'accepted truth,' as some people call it. That's not truth. It's a distortion caused by opinion or misunderstanding or some other factor. The truth can't have a 'version.' I know you get that, Gutsy, because you have that kind of mind. Always have. That's why people don't always trust you: because they can never be sure you'll side with them or back the 'version' of the truth they insist is real. You're not a follower. You're not even a pack animal, despite your friends Spider and Alethea. You're more like Sombra there."

She said nothing. Gutsy never needed her ego stroked and generally felt uncomfortable with compliments.

"Get on with it, man," said Ford quietly. "Tell her what Cruz told you."

"I'm getting there," Urrea said.

"Glaciers are faster."

"Okay, okay. So, after Juan and I went back and forth a few times, with me defending the statistics because I'd double-checked them while researching my book, and again while working with the TV people, and *again* while prepping for my lecture tour, he said that I was wrong. He told me that he was an illegal. He said that he and his family had been arrested in Corpus Christi and sent to a relocation camp. He said that he had spent weeks there and been tested, photographed, fingerprinted, blood-typed and everything else. The same with his family. And then he said that I could look for him in the system, that I could check every record and I wouldn't find him. Or his family. When I asked him what he meant, he surprised me by taking a flash drive from his pocket."

"A what?"

"It's a little device about the size of your thumb, but flat. It was part of the computer world and it stored data. You've seen computers—"

"Only dead ones. But I know what they were."

Computers always amazed Gutsy, and she wished they still worked. The thought that almost all the world's information had been available on a little metal and plastic box . . . that was incredible. She thought about how quickly and hungrily she devoured books and tried to imagine how easy it would be to lose herself completely in an endless ocean of things to know.

"The information on the flash drive Juan Cruz gave me," said Urrea, "included his complete medical history, and also the medical files on his family. Every test done in the US and in Mexico, every procedure, all of it. He'd been a computer expert in Mexico and was an excellent researcher, so he collected an incredible amount of information. He said that he'd hacked the information—stolen it from government computers— and he had proof that some of the undocumented people who had been detained were being used for some kind of medical research. Not legal stuff, though it was hidden behind various labels and lies. Because of the spread of viruses like Zika and other pathogens, all those people were being *tested* for the presence of diseases that might pose a threat to the United States population."

Gutsy heard how Mr. Urrea leaned on the word "tested." "You're saying that's not what happened?"

"Oh, they were being tested," said Ford, "but not to

prevent the spread of diseases. Oh, sure, some of the doctors at the camps were doing that, but not the ones Juan told Urrea about."

"No," said Urrea. "There was a special group working for a department within the government that had no official name. It was one of many sections hidden behind bland titles or simply unnamed. They were known as 'black budget' groups; projects paid for by tax dollars but whose nature was never made public. Juan said that they were using those people to test the spread of different kinds of diseases."

"What's so evil about that?" asked Gutsy. "Wouldn't keeping tabs on people with diseases help to prevent outbreaks?"

"Sure," said Ford, "if you're talking about tracking existing diseases. That's not what this program was about. This was a covert biological weapons research program tasked with implementing field applications and tracking outbreak models through controlled release of infected vectors."

"What . . . ?"

Ford's smile looked like a wince of pain. "When secret government labs created bioweapons, this group infected people with them and then tracked them in order to measure how fast these designer diseases spread. It was part of something called biological warfare."

"They made people sick?" Gutsy demanded, appalled at the thought.

"Oh yes," said Urrea. "But these weren't doomsday diseases. Nothing that would, say, endanger the general US population. No. This was much more insidious. These were diseases that already existed—mumps, measles, pertussis, rubella, tuberculosis . . . all kinds of diseases that modern medicine had either eliminated or controlled. These were new strains. Nothing so radical that they would *look* like designer diseases, because the misuse of antibiotics had already created mutations. And maybe that's where the scientists in the program got the idea in the first place. Who knows? Juan didn't know either. However, he believed that he and his family had been part of this program. His wife died of whooping cough. His three-year-old daughter died from a new strain of the mumps. All of them had been at the relocation camp. Juan found all their records. None of the other families in the same barracks as his family got sick. So . . . how did they? Why did they?"

"I don't understand," she said, then held up her hands. "What does any of this have to do with what's happening now?"

"Because," said Mr. Urrea, "even though the department didn't have a name, the research team did. Groups like this use code names. Want to take a guess what their code name was?"

Gutsy felt her mouth turn dry as dust, and there seemed to be a distant ringing in her ears. The room felt strange, as if it—or maybe the whole world—was beginning to tilt.

Even so, she forced herself to say the words. "The Rat Catchers."

It wasn't a question. It was a statement. And both the men nodded.

"Oh my God," breathed Gutsy.

"It gets worse," said Urrea softly. "The program Juan Cruz told me about was conducted partly at the camp. *This* camp. And partly out of a government facility hidden in a fortified bunker somewhere near here. That bunker is still there, still in operation. And, I guess, all overseen by the lab, wherever that is."

"How do you know that?" demanded Gutsy.

"We don't *know* all of this," admitted Ford. "A lot of this is a patchwork of bits of information, things we've picked up or overheard, and a whole lot of guesswork."

"We've had years to put this much together," said Urrea.

"We have to tell someone about it," cried Gutsy.

"There's more," said Ford. "You know about the ravagers, yes? You know what they are?"

"I know what everyone else knows," said Gutsy. "They're infected with a different kind of disease. They're turning into *los muertos*, but a lot more slowly. They're like the living dead except they know what they're doing."

"All of that is true," said Ford, "but like most things, there's more to the story."

"Like maybe they're herding *los muertos*?"

"What?" asked Urrea. "Where did you hear about that?"

"I saw it," she said. "I didn't tell you that part, because it didn't seem to have anything to do with Mama or the Rat Catchers." She told them about the footprints in the wash and the smaller group of living dead with one of the ravagers moving them along.

Urrea turned away and walked over to the window. He stood for a moment peering out through the blinds. "So, it's true . . ."

"What is?"

Ford answered. "It's true that the ravagers are infected, but it's not with the same plague that created *los muertos*. They're not going to become shamblers. They've already become what they are. They are living dead, but their minds aren't gone. They can think and talk."

"I don't understand."

"Gutsy," said Urrea, "the disease they'd been infected with was not a bioweapon, not like the one that started this whole thing. They were given something that was intended to be a cure."

"A *cure*? But they're monsters."

"Oh yes," said Ford. "They are the scariest monsters in the whole world. They are the most dangerous by far. Do you want to know why?"

"Because they can think?" she ventured.

"No," said Ford, "because they can remember."

"What do you mean?"

Urrea turned away from the window. "They were soldiers once. Probably good soldiers. They fought the dead in a losing battle from Western Pennsylvania all the way to San Antonio. They fought an enemy that people didn't really understand. Not at the time. And while they fought, many of them were bitten and became infected. The scientists at the lab that's somewhere around here were supposed to try and help those soldiers. They gave them treatment after treatment that they swore would save their lives. But the scientists lied to those poor soldiers. They had no cure. All they had were a series of radical and experimental treatments. Many of those soldiers died. Badly. Screaming in agony, turning wild, attacking their fellow soldiers. It was a bloodbath. It was horrible, because they couldn't understand what was happening to them. All they knew was that after getting a series of shots they were different from the other infected."

"The later generations of the treatments upset the chemical composition of the soldiers' bloodstreams," said Ford. "Somehow the attempted cure merged with the original plague and totally warped their brain chemistry. They developed tumors and cysts that corrupted their minds. The soldiers became incredibly violent, uncontrollable. It turned them into homicidal maniacs with an unbearable need to kill and consume."

"The treatment drove them mad," said Ford, "but it didn't kill them. Eventually those test subjects revolted. They slaughtered most of the medical staff and broke out of the lab. The chemicals in their systems continued to warp their personalities. Now there are hundreds of them out there, and there are crazy rumors that one of them has emerged as a leader among them."

"The Raggedy Man," supplied Urrea. "Not sure who or what he is, but the ravagers are reported to worship him like a god. And that, young lady, is a truly terrifying thought. A god of the living dead."

"Raggedy Man . . . I heard that name," said Gutsy. "The Rat Catchers seem to be scared of him. Is he a ravager too? And how is he a 'god' to them?"

"Urrea's being dramatic," said Ford. "From what I've heard, he's more like a king or a general."

"Equally terrifying," said Urrea, and Ford didn't dispute his statement.

"We don't know anything reliable about him," continued Ford. "As for the ravagers, though, either they learned how to manage their madness, or the disease mutated further still. In either case, there have been reports that they can communicate with the shamblers and other mutations. They attack settle-ments and camps, but they also attack the soldiers from the base. All they want to do is kill anything that is not like them."

Urrea sighed and shook his head as if unbearably weary from all of this. Gutsy couldn't blame him.

"The soldiers at Mama's grave," she said slowly, "they were afraid of the Night Army."

"Yes. The Night Army is real, and they're the ones follow-ing this Raggedy Man. It's his army. We have our walls here in town to protect us, and the base is hidden, but the Night Army is looking for a way in to both places. They won't give up because they can't. We've left them nothing else worth having. All we've done is give them a reason to want to wipe us all out." He paused and closed his eyes. "We damaged this lovely green-and-blue wonder of a world, we squandered this beautiful gift. But our extermination is not because of nature rebelling, it isn't Mother Nature's revenge. No. We've done this to ourselves. We created our own boogeymen, and now they're hunting us."

"Was it the Rat Catchers who made Mama sick?" asked Gutsy. "Could they have done that?"

"I don't know," said Ford, "but we have to accept the pos-sibility."

"And their lab is around here somewhere?"

"Yes. Urrea and I know people who swear it's still in oper-ation. The Rat Catchers never stopped their work, even after what they did to their own soldiers. They are still trying to find a cure, but now they're using the people in New Alamo as their lab rats."

She stared at them and the tilting room began to spin.

"My mama died from tuberculosis," she said.

"Yes," said Ford.

"I didn't catch it."

"No," said Urrea.

"They killed her, didn't they?" she said in a voice that was no more than a hoarse croak. "They killed her because they knew she'd come back as one of the living dead. They killed her so they could try a cure on her." She looked at them. "Didn't they?"

Neither man answered. Which was answer enough.

Gutsy looked at them, and away, and around, as if she could see the whole town and the endless miles of the Broken Lands. Nothing looked right. None of the parts that made up the places she knew seemed to fit anymore. The day was the same, but the world had changed.

She walked over to the window. Stumbled, fell against the sill. There was not enough air in the room. Not enough in the whole world. Then she bent and laid her face atop her balled fists. She did not cry. The horror was too great to allow that. The rage was too cold to allow it.

Sombra stood up behind her. She heard his nails on the floor.

He did not whine or bark.

He howled.

After a moment, Gutsy threw back her head and she, too, howled.

PART TWELVE

CENTRAL CALIFORNIA AND POINTS EAST
TWO DAYS EARLIER . . .

STRANGE HIGHWAYS

I had crossed the line. I was free;
but there was no one to welcome
me to the land of freedom.
I was a stranger in a strange land.

—HARRIET TUBMAN

THE SIX QUADS DROVE ALONG SLOWLY, EACH OF THE riders more watchful now than they had been before the prison fiasco. Experience was a harsh and unrelenting teacher. Even though their attempt at mass quieting was behind them, it felt fresh and raw to Benny. Everyone else was processing it at their own speed. No one was happy. No jokes, no smiles. But also—no tears. He wondered what the processing was doing to them; what it was turning them all into.

Although the engine roars drew wandering zoms to the sides of the road, the six of them could see the creatures coming in plenty of time to go off-road when necessary to evade encounters. By midafternoon, even at a reduced rate of speed, the prison was many miles behind. They followed Route 426, skirted Bass, and headed south, past a spot where a military jet lay crumpled amid a sea of bones. All the trees around the crash site were younger than fifteen years, and Benny figured that the jet's fuel tanks had probably exploded, burning down the older growth.

They stopped at the deserted Bass Fork Mini Mart, where people had clearly lived for a while, but there was no one alive to greet them. Just bones. Meals were mostly conducted in silence. Their route took them along North Fork Road to where a campground was littered with tents and RVs that were completely covered with creeper vines and kudzu. They saw many zoms, but those dead were trapped by the endless coils of vines, unable to give chase. It was a sad, strange place and Benny was happy when they found open road again.

They rode and rode and the hours melted away, and then days.

The six of them avoided any area where they thought zoms might naturally have gathered. Towns, food warehouses, hospitals, malls, military bases. Places where people would have gone seeking food, shelter, and protection during First Night. Those places became feeding grounds for the dead.

It struck Benny how little borders meant in the Rot and Ruin. The maps and compasses they brought with them insisted they'd left California and entered Nevada, and then passed below the border of Utah into Arizona and then into New Mexico, but it was all wasteland to Benny. They saw thousands of zombies. Young and old, torn or seemingly whole.

They found no living people at all. Not one.

It saddened Benny. He kept hoping to find outposts, settlements, camps of traders or scavengers, and in truth they did find many of those, but they were all empty. Some had clearly been abandoned years before. Others looked newly deserted, and of these, every one of them was marked with the clear signs of violence. Spent shell casings, dried blood, some bodies too badly mangled to reanimate.

All dead, though.

They came to a place where a train had derailed, spilling all kinds of chemicals from ruptured tanker cars. They stopped for a while, though, and gaped at what they saw.

All along the train tracks, and growing wild between the tumbled cars, were trees. But they were all wrong. The chemicals had worked some kind of sorcery on the genetics of the plant life and twisted what had probably been scrub pines and piñon trees into towering monstrosities, with bark that looked more like the scaly hide of some dragon. Strange, ugly fruit hung where pinecones should have grown, and swarms of deformed wasps buzzed in clouds, warring with one another, filling the air with insect rage.

On the ground, where those fruits had fallen and split open, thick yellow worms feasted on the body of a five-legged deer. Roaches the size of mice teemed over the side of one tanker, and Benny could see something pale and obscene moving inside the ruined metal container. It looked like a praying mantis, but it was far too large.

"No," said Nix, and that was all that needed to be said. They backed their quads away, careful not to make any noise that would attract those insects. Then they headed south as fast as they could.

Their plan had been to go north of Albuquerque, but they stopped again when they encountered the first of several signs that been erected across Route 40. The signs had been hand-painted on bedsheets and hung on trees and on the sides of overturned vehicles. The signs read:

NUCLEAR REACTOR MELTDOWN

DON'T GO THIS WAY

"Won't the radiation have, I don't know, faded by now?" asked Morgie.

"Not for another ten thousand years," said Chong. "Let's get the heck out of here."

They got the heck out of there.

That afternoon, when they stopped to eat, Chong said, "Chemical spills, radiation, all of that . . . I always wondered what it would do to the animals and plants. Now we know."

Riot shook her head. "Nah, we only seen a bit of it. I heard stories going back ten years about the things that were happening out east. Not just to the birds and the bees, but to people. And maybe to the zoms, too."

They all looked from her to the far eastern horizon. The direction they were heading. They ate the rest of their meal in silence.

They kept finding more signs for the meltdown, which drove them farther south, but by the time they left the last warning sign behind them, they began seeing massive swarms of zoms. It hurt Benny to have to waste more time going even farther south, but once they were on Route 285 in New Mexico, it was clear driving. That road took them through empty towns that even the dead had abandoned. However, every attempt to shoot due east again ran them into more of the swarms.

South and south and south they went.

They paused at the junction of 285 and Route 10 in Texas, hid their quads behind an overturned tractor trailer that stood amid an abandoned community of campers, and watched as a river of the zoms came staggering past. They all doused themselves with cadaverine, because this was no time to conserve.

And they watched. The swarm was massive. Chong tried counting them, but gave up after he reached seven hundred. Benny figured there had to be ten times as many as that. Nix crouched beside Benny, her body trembling with fear. This was the largest horde of the dead they'd seen since Saint John's reapers herded thousands of them against the Nine Towns.

"Why are they doing this?" asked Morgie, who hadn't seen flocks of zoms except during the war with the Night Church and the groups clustered around the prison.

"It happens out in the Ruin sometimes," said Benny. "I thought it was only because of the reapers and their whistles."

The reaper army had learned that the ultra-high-pitched shrill of a dog whistle would attract the zoms. They coated their own clothing with a chemical similar in effect to cadaverine and walked among them like drovers working a herd of cattle. There were no drovers here, though.

Or so they thought.

Lilah suddenly tensed and pointed around the rear of the overturned semi. Here and there, scattered throughout the endless mass of zoms, were people who were still clearly alive. They were ugly and rough-looking, dressed in heavy leather jackets, jeans, and boots; and they all had chains wrapped around their arms or waists. They were filthy and unkempt, but they weren't zoms, because they talked to one another, calling out crude jokes and sometimes cursing at zoms who strayed out of the main army.

They were not reapers; of that Benny and his friends were certain. However, they were doing exactly the same thing—driving the dead. Not with dog whistles, but through some other means that was not evident. The men were herding the staggering, shambling, rotting army toward the south of Texas, following Route 10.

It took a long time for the swarm to pass, and when it was gone, the six teenagers emerged from behind the semi and watched the receding dust cloud.

"G-god," breathed Chong as he nearly collapsed back against one of the campers. He pushed up his visor with fingers that shook so badly he fumbled the simple action twice.

Lilah stood beside him, and even her legendary calm was shaken. She nibbled at her fingernails as she stared at the mass of zoms. "Too many," she whispered softly.

Riot and Morgie stood in total silence, unable to speak.

Nix pushed up her visor and wiped at some tears. Her hands did not shake as badly as Chong's, but there was a fever brightness in her green eyes. Benny shook his head, swallowing at the thought of how hopeless it would be to get caught by a swarm like that out in the open.

Then Nix turned around and gave a sharp cry, and when the others turned they saw more of the dead coming along the same road. This second swarm was smaller, but the third, following half an hour behind them, was the biggest yet. If the first swarm was a river, then this was an ocean.

"H-have to be thirty or—or—or forty th-thousand of them," stuttered Chong once they were gone.

"Where are they going?" demanded Morgie, who was gray with fear. "What's down that way?"

Benny consulted the map. "San Antonio, I think."

They waited another half hour, but there were no more zoms, and darkness was falling.

"We can't risk going back the way we came," said Nix.

"We take that road," said Lilah, gesturing to Route 10.

Chong nodded. "And we sure as heck can't go north because of that meltdown."

"Way I figure it," said Benny, poring over the map, "is we go straight all the way south to the Mexican border and follow that. That'll take us far enough away from San Antonio to stay out of whatever those swarms are all about."

They moved away from the wrecked truck and that stretch of the road, found an abandoned service station, and made it their home for the night. There were two zoms in the place, but Lilah and Nix quieted them without fuss. Chong and Morgie used drop cloths from the mechanics' bays to block the windows, and they took turns standing watch.

Deep in the middle of the night they heard another swarm pass.

And another.

And another.

"Wherever they're going," said Benny, "I'm glad we're not going anywhere near them."

They slept badly and the night was long.

THEY DROVE ALL MORNING AND REACHED THE BANKS of the Rio Grande by noon.

It was a wild area and much more overgrown than Benny expected, considering the barren terrain through which they'd ridden for many miles. It was as if nature had gathered all its strength and burst forth with lush new life on both sides of the winding river.

Down here they saw all kinds of wild animals, many clearly the descendants of creatures that had either escaped from zoos or been turned loose. A small herd of zebras grazed on dandelions. Monkeys screamed and taunted them from the branches of a thousand trees. Tapirs rooted in the grass, kangaroos stood in clusters and watched them with dark eyes. Pythons slithered away from the sound of their motors, while an old, bony, weary-looking tiger watched from within the shadows beneath a towering pine. A huge tortoise crossed the road in front of them, and they all stopped to allow it to pass. Then they drove on without comment.

A weathered sign told them they were entering the Las Palomas Wildlife Management Area, and as they approached the edge of the forest, the last of the crumbling towns faded away completely and the huge woods loomed up like something out of one of the fantasy novels Benny loved to read. Fangorn Forest, maybe. Shadows seemed to crouch beneath the boughs of those trees. It looked like a hungry place to Benny, and even as they thundered toward it he felt as if they were making a very bad decision. He did not know why he said nothing to the others. Maybe because it had been his plan to come this way and he felt trapped by the decision. Or maybe this was where all his roads inevitably led. To this dark and unforgiving place.

They drove into the forest and it swallowed them whole as shadows turned bright day into purple gloom. The road was long since gone, cracked apart by roots and choked with dead tree limbs and nameless debris. They saw a single zom wandering toward them, but Riot used her slingshot to fire a ball bearing at it from fifteen feet. The zombie's head snapped back and it fell into the undergrowth, vanishing as completely as if it had never existed. The six of them moved on, slowing to little more than a fast walk.

Inside the forest the air felt different, much more humid and alive with buzzing insects. Birds sang in the trees, though only in front and behind them, with their songs falling silent as the quads rolled along. The birds yielded grudgingly to the noisy machines and resumed their gossip as soon as the engine roars faded.

Nix came up and rode side by side with Benny. Her face was bright with sweat, and the flush darkened her freckles and the two long scars. On another face, on someone with less personal power, those scars might have been ugly; they might have been something for her to turn away to hide. Or hide behind. Not Nix, though. She owned them as proof of what she had been through and of how she had come through it. She was, as Chong once phrased it, the best example of herself. Aware of her own strengths and weaknesses. The quiet and introverted girl she'd been once upon a time had burned off, or been shucked like a cocoon to reveal a more evolved person. Loss had stolen some of her laughter, and trauma had ignited strange lights in her eyes, but experience had taught her that she owned courage, and situations had revealed her compassion.

Benny loved her with his whole heart. And if that heart was in danger of being broken because there was no certainty of any shared future, then he knew he was luckier than he deserved for the time they had together.

"It's beautiful here," she said, shaking him from his thoughts. "Not how I imagined Texas."

Benny looked around, trying to see the forest through her eyes. She had never liked growing up behind the fences of Mountainside. It had been her need, her desire that had fueled the quest to leave home last year to find out if there was anything beyond the fence. She viewed the world differently than he did. Differently than Chong or Morgie or anyone did, but once in a while Benny caught a glimpse of Nix's version of the world. Sometimes it was beautiful. Sometimes it was scary and frightening.

They drove for half a mile in silence, each of them looking at the forest and *seeing* it, which was never quite the same thing. Stones in the veil of tree-thrown shadows were soft with moss. Vines hung in soft curves between neighboring tree trunks. Little puffs of mist coiled up from deep inside clefts in the ground, and a gentle breeze brushed the grass and weeds so they leaned over as if weary.

"Yeah," Benny finally replied, "it's pretty."

She cut him a look but didn't comment. They drove on.

After half an hour, though, the light was beginning to fail and it became harder to determine whether objects ahead were zoms or tree stumps, so Benny began looking for a place to camp. It was Lilah who found it, zooming past them and cutting off to the right, going deeper into the woods. At first Benny couldn't understand why, but then he saw light dancing in the shadows and realized that it was flowing water, and that she'd found a small tributary to the larger Rio Grande. He signaled to the others and they all turned that way, following the Lost Girl's quad for several dozen yards over lumpy ground. Then one by one they pulled to a stop and cut their engines.

The scene before them was truly beautiful, and even Benny had to admit it without reservation. A ribbon of blue meandered past them, the waters kissed by beams of sunlight that slanted between the tall pines. Blue-white wading birds of a kind Benny had never seen before stalked through the rushes on the far bank, and bullfrogs thrummed from their hiding places in the mud. There was enough moisture in the air that the sunlight looked like bars of gold leaning slantwise on the tree limbs.

"Wow," said Morgie. "This is incredible."

"It's defensible," said Lilah bluntly. She dismounted, plucked her spear from the makeshift rack on the back of the quad, and began stalking along the bank. Riot, without saying a word, headed in the other direction. Both of them had spent a lot of the last few years living in the wild. Benny had no illusions about the gulf between what he knew—and what he'd learned from his short trips with Tom—and what *they* knew. He stayed where he was until they came back and said that it was safe.

Then they got to work.

Each of them had brought long spools of plastic-coated wire scavenged from an old store that sold radio and computer equipment. They created a network of trip wires around the camp, so that it formed a half circle, with the stream at their backs. Chong collected the empty tin cans everyone had in their saddlebags, filled them with pebbles, and hung them on the wire, using small black metal binder clips to secure them. One set of wires was strung at waist level, the other at knee height. A small animal could pass without creating a racket, but a zom of any size would be heard even in the dead of the darkest night.

Morgie and Riot were the best cooks, and they began preparing a simple meal of beans and beef. Lilah slung a game pouch over her shoulder and vanished into the forest, returning forty minutes later with the pouch filled with summer berries, edible roots, and some nuts. They sat to eat.

Benny noticed that Chong turned half away when he took his pills. It hurt Benny that Chong was embarrassed by what he called his "condition." He caught Benny looking and gave him a weak smile. Benny shook his head to tell him that it was all good, no judgment. Chong looked down at the campfire and did not meet his eyes again.

Since leaving the prison, there had been very little conversation among them. However, as the sky turned black and the stars came out, they began to talk.

It was Lilah, usually the least talkative of them, who broke the silence.

"Captain Ledger is alive," she said in her spooky whisper of a voice. She said it with such certainty that for a moment no one seemed willing to offer a contrary opinion.

Until Riot did. "Look, I like the old geezer as much as y'all do, but I don't know that I'd bet a broke-leg hunting dog on that, Lilah. Maybe Captain Ledger got to Asheville and it was all so bad he couldn't get out. I mean, c'mon, if someone like him was okay, then wouldn't he have found some way of reaching out?"

"He's alive," grumbled Nix. Benny started to say something, thought better of it, and gave her an encouraging nod.

"Something could have happened to the, um, wires," said Morgie, who Benny knew did not really understand how satellite phones worked.

"They had satellite phones and they had radios," countered Riot. "We ain't heard nothing."

"Maybe we have," said Nix. "We've been gone almost a week now—for all we know there's been a hundred calls from Asheville."

"Really?" said Riot. She nodded to Benny. "Why don't you ask your boyfriend if there's been a call?"

Everyone turned to Benny.

"What is she talking about?" demanded Lilah.

"Yes," said Nix coldly, "what is she talking about?"

Benny glared at Riot, then got up, threaded his way through the wires to his quad, opened the saddlebag, removed a black object, and brought it back. He showed them what it was. A satellite phone, and the small green power light was lit.

"I saw it when I was looking for the fuel line to get his bike going," said Riot.

"Why didn't you tell us?" asked Chong.

Benny sat down with a heavy sigh. "I wanted to. I snuck into the mayor's office while you guys were sleeping and stole it. I . . . I guess I was hoping to be able to spring some good news on everyone. At first I didn't say anything because we were stuck in the prison. Then, after we left, I rode point so I could use the earpiece to check it when you guys couldn't see."

"Why?" asked Nix. She did not look happy. "Why hide it?"

"Because the other night, when I was standing guard, I heard some chatter from home. Solomon Jones made a general call. One of those conference-call things where a lot of people listen in at once?" The others nodded. "He was talking about maybe sending an expedition east because there hasn't been any word at all from Asheville. Nothing."

For a long time, the only sound in the world seemed to be crickets and cicadas and the lonely call of some night bird. Then Chong bent forward, put his face in his hands, and began to weep.

THEY HUDDLED AROUND CHONG FOR A LONG TIME.
Offering comfort, telling him that the factory making his
drug was going to be there, that it would endure. That there
was some *other* reason for the silence from Asheville.

It was a pack of lies. They all knew it. Even Chong knew it.
Sometimes lies are the only mercy, the only kindness people
have to offer. Benny knew that. When Tom died, the others did
as much for him. They told him that *it's all going to be okay*. Lies.

Kindly meant. They were shields, they were warm blankets
in the cold wind of reality. The speakers of those lies needed to
hear themselves say them as much as Chong or Benny or anyone in the stranglehold of pain needed to hear them.

As Benny sat with his arms around Nix and Lilah, who
hugged Chong, he realized this with a kind of clarity that
would be impossible in the absence of experience.

The night was a big, violent bully that pushed at them,
shoved them, gave them no real peace, and only the tight
clutch of a half-dozen teenagers kept it from winning. They
huddled together for more than warmth.

And so the tears, the terror, and the night passed.

THE MORNING WAS COLD AND DAMP, WITH A THICK mist cover that transformed the forest into a dreamscape painted in shades of green and gray. Insects buzzed but were invisible inside the haze.

Benny had taken a late watch, turning in just before dawn, but sleep had eluded him and he lay with his eyes closed and his curled back pressed against Nix's. He heard her moan and turned to see her twitch, lost in a dream of something ugly. When he leaned over, he could see that there were deep lines in her face that formed a grimace of fear and pain. He knew she was not in actual physical distress, but remembered pain always feels real in dreams; and Nix had felt so much hurt. Physical, mental, and emotional. He heard her murmur a word. A name.

"Mom . . ."

Benny closed his eyes and felt the old ache tear itself open, because he knew what she was dreaming about. Her mother's murder. The loss. All of that.

He bent and kissed her head very gently. Her body froze for a moment and then the lines on her face softened, her shudders subsided. Not all the way, but some.

Enough.

She drifted deeper, maybe swimming down below the level of those particular memories. That was something.

Benny glanced over at Morgie, who sat hunched over, whittling a stick as something to do while staying awake to stand his watch. Benny sighed, lay back, closed his eyes, and tried to fall asleep.

His mind wandered instead. Wafting like a ghost but going nowhere. Then he heard Nix moan again. It pulled him wearily back to the surface. And as he rose to wakefulness, his mind replayed that sound. That moan.

A moan.

But not Nix's.

Benny was instantly awake, scrambling to his feet, snatching up his *katana*, whipping the blade from the scabbard.

"Zom!" he cried.

Even as he shouted it, there was a din of stones rattling in tin cans. Morgie leaped to his feet, knives in each hand. "Get up," he bellowed. "Everyone get up. Zoms!"

Everyone was already in motion. Benny's cry had snapped the spell of sleep, and they grabbed weapons and turned toward the perimeter.

Everything around them was a big white nothing. Even the massive tree trunks were ghosts lost in a sea of fog.

"Where—?" began Nix, but Benny cut her off.

"Quiet," he snapped, and they all froze. Listening, straining to see. The cans rattled to their left, and they all pivoted in that direction. The mist itself was moving, drifting like ghosts around them. A zom had to be out there, though. Benny had heard it, and something had touched the trip wires. He sensed more than saw one of the living dead, and he pivoted silently on the balls of his feet to track something as yet unseen. Nix turned too.

"Where?" she repeated quietly.

Benny raised his sword, pointing with the silver tip.

The mist swirled and swirled.

Nothing emerged.

The rattling of the cans slowed, slowed . . . and stopped. Silence dropped over everything, and even the buzz of morning insects faded into silence.

"Is it gone?" asked Chong, his voice low and frightened.

"I think so," said Nix.

Morgie nodded.

Lilah took a few steps forward and stopped next to Benny. They exchanged a look. She shook her head, confirming what he thought. They moved forward together, ten feet apart so as not to interfere with each other's weapons. Crouched, stalking with maximum care, maximum readiness.

A sound stopped them in their tracks.

It was what had awakened Benny. It was a hoarse, plaintive, hungry sound. Not a moan, though. Not exactly. This was different. It didn't sound like anything Benny had ever heard before. Almost a grunt, but with the same need to satisfy the undying, unbearable hunger.

"What *is* that?" asked Morgie.

"Shut up," said Lilah. "Listen."

They listened.

Another grunt, and this time there was a crunching sound. A heavy foot on fallen twigs. It sounded somehow sneaky. Careful. Benny felt his blood turn to ice. God, was there an R2 or R3 out there? Smarter than other zoms, stalking them? Being careful? Maybe even stepping over one of the lines of strung cans?

"It's coming," he said, and again Lilah nodded. She had her spear in a two-handed grip, ready to fight. A faint creak behind him told Benny that Chong had nocked an arrow and pulled back on the string. A rubbery creak suggested that Riot had pulled tension on her slingshot. Everyone was ready for whatever was out there.

He hoped.

The grunt again.

Deeper this time. Louder.

Closer.

The cans rattled once more, and there was a sharp *snap* as one of the lines of strung wire snapped. The cans thudded to the ground, coughing out their pebbles. Falling silent.

And then the mist changed. It was as if the droplets of water suspended in the fog abruptly coalesced into a physical shape. But it was the wrong shape. Not slender from emaciation. Not upright and shambling.

Not human.

Instead the thing that came slowly toward them was bizarre, brutish, monstrous. It was hunched forward, walking on all fours like an animal. But even with that there was something wrong. The rear legs were too short and the front legs were much too long. It had a massive, shaggy head and huge shoulders. At first Benny thought it was a zom that had been some kind of body builder, with hugely overdeveloped arms and chest and something wrong with its legs. Walking on its knees and hands; or on the stumps of severed calves.

As horrible as that would have been, it would have been better than the creature that finally emerged from the mist. The arms, shoulders, chest, and body were completely covered with dark brown-gray fur. The fur was torn and some hung in ragged strips, revealing gray skin or pale reddish striated muscle. The head was hideous, with a high crown and sloping brow, eyes that burned with hunger and hate, and deadly fangs. It reeked of rotting meat and a totally unnatural vitality.

It was not a person.

It was not anything Benny had ever seen except in a book. Or a nightmare.

It was a full-grown silverback gorilla.

And it was a zombie.

Interlude Six

KICKAPOO CAVERN STATE PARK
ONE WEEK AGO

They talked all through the afternoon and into the evening.

While they talked, Sam cleaned and sutured Joe's wounds. They were still talking when the morning painted the sky with the first pink colors of dawn. Sam Imura, former sniper and soldier, former special ops killer and survivor of the apocalypse, was no longer alone. He had his old friend and former boss, Captain Joe Ledger. The only guest who had ever visited Sam's little camp hidden away in the depths of the forest.

Sam had that, which was more than he'd had since coming this far southwest after the world died.

But he had more than that.

Sam had a *brother*.

A half brother. Benny. Sixteen years old. Smart, tough, honest, and brave. An actual hero, who'd helped save the lives of tens of thousands of people in central California. Sam had never met Benny, though he'd seen baby pictures. Sam had always assumed Benny was dead, along with Benny's mom—Sam's stepmother—and their dad.

And Tom.

It hurt Sam so much to know that his brothers had survived, but that a killer's bullet had taken Tom's life less than a year ago. Tom had died saving children—little ones and teens—from a nightmare called Gameland, where the kids were forced to fight for their lives in zombie pits. Ledger described how Tom had burned down the first Gameland, rescuing many that time; and how he had gone hunting when he learned that two men—Charlie Pink-eye and the Motor City Hammer—had rebuilt it. There had been a terrible battle. Tom had allies—other tough men and women like him—and they fought alongside Benny and his young friends, whom Tom had trained to be a new breed of samurai. Together they'd destroyed Gameland forever.

At the cost of Tom's life.

When Ledger told him that story, Sam bowed his head and wept. Ledger wrapped his arm around his friend's shoulders and he, too, wept.

Later Joe said, "Straighten me out on the age thing. Benny's sixteen. Tom died when he was thirty-five. And you're my age . . . how's that work?"

"First off," said Sam, "I'm ten years younger than you. My mother had me when she was eighteen. I was supposed to be an only child, but when I was twenty she had Tom. I always felt more like an uncle than an older brother. Guess it was hard to be close to a kid that much younger. Then Mom died and Dad married someone way younger than himself. Guess it was a midlife crisis thing, dating someone so young. Whatever. They seemed to be in love and I was out of the house by then. Barely knew her, to tell the truth. I guess we had a hard time getting along because we were nearly the same age. Anyway, I was running with Echo Team when they met. Missed their wedding. Missed almost every Christmas. And by the time Benny was born, I was running my own crew . . . and that was when the world fell apart."

"You'd like Benny," said Ledger. "He's a little goofy at times, but he has heart and he has nerve. Real good in a fight. He's more or less the pack leader of a group of young butt-kickers Tom trained. The new samurai. Little corny, but the training was righteous. And I taught Benny and his friends a few of my dirty tricks."

He told Sam about the Night Church and the reaper army.

"Night Church, huh?" grunted Sam. "Sounds like something we have going on around here. Not a church, though. I do some trading with people in farms and settlements throughout this part of Texas. There are some rumors that the ravagers are getting organized, turning themselves into an actual army. The Night Army, though I don't know if that's what they're calling themselves or something spooky tagged onto them."

"Night Army?" snorted Ledger. "I think somebody was watching too many episodes of *Game of Thrones* before the dead rose."

"You wouldn't joke if you saw them, Joe. The ravagers are part of that outfit, and they have serious numbers."

"Any chance they can use something like an RPG?" asked Ledger.

"Probably, if they knew where to find one," said Sam. "I hope it doesn't mean they found one of the weapons caches."

"*One* of them? How many caches are there?"

"Two that I know of," said Sam. "A small one that was part of a forward outpost during the last battles, and the big one somewhere near Laredo. I could probably find it if we go look."

"You never went there?" asked Ledger.

"Why bother? I've looted enough dead soldiers, hunters, and cops to have enough rifle and small arms ammunition to last me the rest of my life." He sucked a tooth for a moment, considering. "If they only found the small one, then it's bad, but probably not enough for them to take New Alamo."

Ledger nodded. "How big is the big one?"

"Very."

"So, maybe we should go take a look," said Ledger. "If this Night Army—and, by the way, I'm having a hard time taking that name seriously—is really out there, then we need to get some weapons to those people in New Alamo."

"It's not as easy as that," said Sam. "From what I've been told, the cache is buried underground in an ultrasecure facility, and the whole area is swarming with—what did you call them? Zoms?"

"Yeah. So what, though? We've both been dealing with zoms for a lot of years now."

"Not like these."

"Why? What's different about them?"

"These 'zoms' used to be part of a circus," said Sam.

"So . . . zombie clowns . . . ?"

"No," said Sam. "Lions, and tigers, and bears."

"Oh my . . . ," breathed Ledger.

"And elephants. You haven't really lived until you've been chased by twelve thousand pounds of living-dead elephants."

Ledger was about to comment when a monstrous howl split the morning. A huge hulking shape filled the open door of Sam's cabin. Sam lunged for his rifle, but Ledger grabbed his wrist.

"*No!*"

The creature stalked inside, barely able to fit through the doorway. It was huge and completely covered in bands of metal and chain mail, with razor-sharp spikes sticking out in all directions. The armor was splashed with blood—red and black. A dented helmet was strapped to its head but it was twisted and hung low, blocking one eye. The animal stopped inside, looking from Sam to Joe and back again. It bared its teeth at Sam.

"Oh, stop showing off, you big goof," growled Ledger.

Grimm, who had been through a hundred battles with his master, bounded like a puppy toward Joe Ledger. Sam found himself laughing—something so rare for him that he'd come to believe himself incapable of it—as Ledger, the most dangerous man he'd ever known, was trampled and licked into submission by a dog.

Sam's laughter began to crack, though, as he thought of his family. Stepmom and dad, gone. Brother Tom, gone. And Benny . . . ? What was he like? And would he ever see him? Sam didn't think so. The world was not that kind; the universe was never that generous.

Or was it? He watched Ledger remove the dog's armor and check the animal over for injuries. It was clear Grimm was family to Ledger. The dog had been thrown out of a crashing helicopter and here he was—alive. Against all hope, despite all probability, alive.

Maybe, thought Sam, the defining characteristic of the universe *wasn't* cold cruelty.

Maybe.

And maybe, he knew, was a dangerous word. Maybe was another word for hope.

"Joe," he said. "Listen . . . we'll rest for today, and then tomorrow I think we need to go find one of those weapons caches. Maybe both of them. Clean them out before the Night Army finds them. If you need to stay here and rest your leg, I'll understand. This isn't your fight, so . . ."

The smile on Ledger's face made Sam's words trail off. He knew that smile from long ago. It was not a friendly smile, not a tolerant smile. It was the smile of a killer.

"Sam, old buddy, this has always been my fight."

Sam Imura smiled too.

PART THIRTEEN

NEW ALAMO, TEXAS
LATE AUGUST

HUNTING THE HUNTERS

There is no hunting like the hunting of man,
and those who have hunted armed
men long enough and liked it,
never care for anything else thereafter.

—ERNEST HEMINGWAY

WHEN SHE TURNED AROUND—WHEN SHE *COULD* turn around—the Chess Players were sitting where they'd been. But they looked frozen in place. Shocked. Terrified for her, and maybe of her. Sombra stood between Gutsy and the two men, looking at her; then he turned toward them too.

Gutsy pushed off the windowsill and walked over. The room no longer spun and the floor felt steady beneath her feet. There was a time for panic and there was a time to get back to work. There was a time to be a scared kid and there was a time to be who she was, undefined by age or gender or race or anything. The icy hatred she'd felt before was still there, just beneath the surface. It was so powerful, and it focused her like sunlight through a magnifying glass. It did not own her, and she hoped and prayed it would never define her.

When she spoke, her voice sounded calm. Way too calm. She thought she probably should have been worried about that. It wasn't something to be calm about. Inside her head, she felt fractured. Her broken heart was like two pieces of old lava rock. Hard, sharp-edged.

"Where is this lab?" she asked, her voice harsh and cold.

"We don't know," said Urrea.

"What about the base?"

"We don't know," said Ford. "We've looked, we've asked questions—"

"That's not good enough," roared Gutsy. "You've had *fifteen years* to find it."

Urrea quickly said, "Gutsy, we think that the lab is somewhere near town, maybe near what's left of Laredo. But it's a lot of real estate, and the two of us are not as nimble as we once were at escaping swarms of shamblers or fast-infected. We haven't really gone out much to poke around."

"We even had to be careful with asking questions," said Ford. "Other people asked about the base, and some of them went missing over the years."

"Or turned up dead," said Urrea.

Gutsy frowned. "That doesn't make sense unless someone in town is connected with the Rat Catchers and . . ." Her words trailed off, and both men began nodding. She straightened and said, "The guards. When the Rat Catchers brought Mama back the first time, there was no fuss. No riders in the streets. No one got hurt. That never made sense to me unless someone let them in."

"You always were a smart girl," said Ford.

"But there was a fight the next time."

"Which means what?"

She thought about it. "Different guards. The first night it was Trey Williams and Buffy Howell on the rear gate. Karen Peak said that they hadn't reported any problems. But the other night it was Jimmy Quiñones and Roberto Cantu. They both got hurt, but nothing happened to Trey and Buffy."

"And that's something you know but can't prove," said

Ford. "Logic and supposition don't always come with evidence."

"Wish they did," said Urrea with a sigh. "Now, as for why the Rat Catchers attacked Roberto and Jimmy—we can only guess. You reburied your mother. Maybe that upset their plans, or upset some kind of timetable. They took a risk in bringing her back home, even though it meant having to brutalize the guards."

"Why, though?"

"Ask yourself the same question," said Ford. "You told us what the soldiers said. They wondered if Mama had told you something."

"She was already dead."

"Yes, she was," said Ford, his eyes glittering with strange lights. "So what does that suggest?"

"It doesn't . . ." She stopped. One of the things the Chess Players always stressed in their classes was to avoid knee-jerk reactions. Only considered opinions mattered. She cut a look at one of the many small signs framed on the walls around the classroom. THINK BEFORE YOU SPEAK. Gutsy was aware of them watching her, and of them following her line of sight. Both old men nodded. "They did something to Mama," she said after a while.

"Yes."

"They made her sick. She died because of it. I don't know how. And I don't understand why she didn't spread it. Tuberculosis is so contagious and, sure, we all took precautions once we knew what it was, but before that . . . How come it didn't spread at the hospital and all through the town?"

"Very good questions," said Ford.

Urrea frowned. "There are all kinds of mutant strains of diseases. Maybe this was one that wasn't easy to catch. Just because Mama caught it doesn't mean it's something that *could* have spread quickly."

Ford gave him a pitying look. "So, after everything we've seen you're erring on the side of a best case scenario? You've been out in the sun too long."

But Urrea stood firm. "No, it has to be something like that otherwise Gutsy would be correct, it would have killed half the town. And, don't get me wrong, I'm not saying this was a *natural* mutation." He studied Gutsy.

She thought about it some more, then shrugged. "I honestly don't know. I mean, if these people just wanted to kill her, there are a lot of easier ways. They could have come in on a night when the right guards were working and killed her while she slept. Could have killed both of us."

The Chess Players nodded.

"So . . . maybe *killing* her wasn't the point," said Gutsy slowly, pushing past her heartache and the other emotions that kept wanting to derail her train of logic. "They brought her back . . . brought her back. Twice. If they wanted her to kill me, they could have done it easier. So that can't be it." She chewed her lip as she fought to recall the exact words spoken beside her mother's grave.

Do you think she told her anything after *we dug her up?*

After.

Gutsy grabbed Mr. Urrea's wrist. "They did something to her," she gasped. "They kept bringing her back because they thought . . . they thought . . ." She could not bring herself to say it.

So Mr. Ford did. "Gutsy, I think these people did something to your mother that they thought would reawaken her dead brain. Something that would bring at least that part of her back to life."

Gutsy looked from one to the other and back again. "But . . . *why*?"

"It's all about finding a cure," he said. "It's always been about that."

"That's not a cure! She was a monster."

"If it worked," said Urrea gently, "if Mama had been able to talk with you, if she'd known you, then maybe she would not have attacked you. Maybe that's the whole point, Gutsy, to find a way to stop the unthinking *aggression* of *los muertos*."

"And why dig up all those bodies in the cemetery?" asked Gutsy. "Why steal the dead?"

Neither of them had an answer to that.

The three of them sat there with the horror of it all surrounding them. To Gutsy it was as if the classroom was filled with ghosts. Maybe Mama's ghost too. All trying to speak to her, to tell her dark secrets. To tell her truths that were wrapped in broken glass and barbed wire.

After a while, Urrea sighed and said, "As far as Ford and I figure, at least half the town guards are in on it—whatever this actually is. And probably some key members of the town council, too. Otherwise more action would have been taken. We've seen how the council reacts to rumors about the hidden lab. They downplay any rumors very quickly. Far too quickly, in my opinion. We've thought they were trying a little too hard to dispel those rumors, and there's no good reason why they should bother, unless they're involved."

"So you're going to need to be very careful about who you talk to in town," said Ford.

"Is there anyone we can actually trust?" asked Gutsy.

They took a long time with that. "Well . . . us," said Ford.

"Your friends, Spider and Alethea," added Urrea. "As long as you think they can keep their mouths shut."

"They can."

"Would you risk your life on that?"

"Yes," she said without hesitation. The Chess Players nodded.

Ford shook his head. "Offhand, I don't know how many others *I* would trust."

"Trust is hard to come by in this world," admitted Urrea sadly.

"That makes three teenagers, a scruffy dog, and two scruffier old men," said Ford. "Hardly what I would call a force to be reckoned with."

"It's what we have," said Urrea.

Gutsy kicked the desk hard enough to move it six inches. "What do we do about it, though?"

"You shouldn't do anything," said Ford. "You're fifteen and you're likely to get hurt. Or worse."

She gave him such a withering look that he held up his hands in surrender.

"Oooo-kay," he said slowly, "can you at least promise us you'll be smart and careful?"

Gutsy nodded. "Guess I'm going to have to be. Otherwise they'll stop me, and I don't want to be stopped. They killed my mother. They disrespected her. They tried to use her to kill me. Or hurt me. Or something. Whatever it was, whatever they meant to do, it was cruel and . . . and . . ."

"The word you're looking for," said Ford quietly, "is evil."

Gutsy looked at him and at the word, as if it hung burning in the air.

"Evil," she said, tasting that word. It was bitter and wrong and didn't fit comfortably in her mouth; and yet she knew it was exactly the right word. A thought suddenly occurred to her, and she knelt and held out a hand for Sombra, who came over and allowed her to scratch his head. She felt herself smile one of those smiles that made people flinch.

"What is it?" asked Ford. "You have an idea. I can see it."

"You won't like it."

"Would you like a comprehensive list of all the things I don't like?"

"No, thanks."

"What's your idea?" Urrea asked her.

Gutsy leaned her head forward and touched her brow to the coydog's. He allowed it and then leaned in. The way Gordo so often did. Without breaking contact, Gutsy said, "When we were in the cemetery last night, Sombra wanted to attack those soldiers. He was afraid of them, but he wanted to hurt them too. I think he knows them. I think maybe he used to belong to one of them."

"I don't like where this is going," said Ford.

Gutsy stroked Sombra's smoky fur. "I bet he knows how to find them."

"That's insane," gasped Urrea.

"Maybe."

"You'll get killed."

"Maybe I won't."

"They'll take you. Arrest you. Make you disappear," warned Ford.

"Only if they see me coming," she said. "Only if they can catch me."

"You're *fifteen*!"

"Stop saying that. They didn't care that I'm fifteen when they brought my mother back to my house. Twice. Besides, maybe they think my being fifteen means I'm just a kid, that I can't do anything. That I'm not a threat to them." She paused. "They're wrong about all of that. They won't think I'll come after them. They'd never think that for a moment. They'll try and come for me instead."

The Chess Players kept protesting.

Gutsy fell silent but kept smiling.

Sombra growled, low in his throat. As if he understood. As if he approved.

GUTSY TALKED WITH THE CHESS PLAYERS FOR A WHILE longer, mostly building a list of people in town they thought might have some knowledge of who the Rat Catchers were, or who had spoken out in the past about the base.

Then she left them and slipped quietly out of the building with Sombra, keeping to the shadows. Fear seemed to crouch on her back like a parasite, though. Her heart kept hammering and did not want to settle down, and chilly fear sweat dampened her clothes. Every face she saw seemed to be turned toward her with suspicious, guilty eyes. Every mouth seemed to be set in a sneer, every glance was an accusation. It irritated her to feel that kind of paranoia, because it distorted her perceptions. Knowing that did nothing at all to help shake the feeling that she was in a town filled with potential enemies.

There were spies in town. There were scientists in a secret lab somewhere. There were soldiers in a hidden base. And there were insane wolf packs of infected killers trying to build an army of living dead.

Gutsy wanted to find a rock and crawl under it.

Gutsy wanted to find the people who did this and kill them.

Gutsy wanted her mama to be there to make it all okay again.

She walked on, feeling the world fracture a little more with every step.

Her route back home was a wandering one, allowing her to surreptitiously check to see if someone was trailing her. If they were, they were better at it than she was at spotting it. Sombra didn't bark, whine, or growl, however, so that was a comfort.

Not having Spider or Alethea to talk to hurt.

"Mama," murmured Gutsy, "why'd you have to go away?"

Sombra whined softly and leaned against her for a moment as they walked. Once more Gutsy wondered if Mama had somehow *sent* the coydog to her. It was a silly thought, she knew, but it seemed impossible to shake.

It spooked her and it felt good in nearly equal measures.

She passed the Chung house and flinched when she saw a familiar figure standing in the yard, hanging freshly washed clothes. The skirt Alice was pinning to the line was no longer smeared with horse manure. The torn blouse was nowhere in sight. As if sensing her approach, Alice lowered her arms and turned. She was pretty and slim, with hair as black and glossy as a crow's wing. As black as Gutsy's own, though longer. Some people in town thought Alice was Mexican with strong Native American blood, which wasn't that much of a stretch. The Asian influence in the Indios was evident in a lot of people Gutsy knew. She even had a bit of it herself. Mr. Urrea had talked about what he called the "global genetic melting pot" that was the Americas. However, Gutsy's skin took a deeper tan and Alice's face was pale. And lovely. Always so lovely. She'd even looked pretty when she was mad.

Gutsy stopped by the small wooden fence. Alice stood where she was, a clothespin in one hand and a basket of laundry at her feet.

"Hey," said Gutsy. Not the world's most clever opening, but it was what she had.

There was a beat before Alice said, "Hey."

And a whole bunch more beats as Gutsy sorted through a thousand possible things to say, ranging from clever to apologetic. All them sounded lame.

"Earlier . . . ," she began.

Alice blinked once. Very slowly. Like a cat.

"You're never clumsy," she said.

"Um . . . what?"

"You," said Alice, "you're always quick on your feet. In gym class, in lacrosse practice. Even when we were little and everyone was playing living and dead in the school yard. I never once saw you trip or crash into anyone."

Living and dead was a game of tag in which the person chasing everyone pretended to bite whoever he—or she— caught. Kind of gross, looking back on it, but fun at the time.

"I . . . um . . . okay . . . ," Gutsy said, definitely tripping now.

"But today you bump into me so hard you knock me down into horse poop."

Gutsy looked down at her shoes. "Sorry," she mumbled. "It . . . it was an accident."

Alice dropped the clothespin into the laundry basket and walked slowly over to the fence. She smelled of soap and flowers.

"Look at me," said Alice.

It took a lot, but Gutsy did.

"Remember back in third grade, when I always had my hair in braids?" asked Alice. Gutsy nodded. "Do you remember why I stopped braiding my hair?"

"No."

Alice said, "Bobby McNeal was always pulling my braids. He was always sticking stuff into them because he sat behind me. Feathers, straw, dandelions." Gutsy nodded again. "He was always playing tricks like that. Pretending to sneeze on me and tossing cooked pasta on my blouse like it was a booger. Putting snails in my shoes. He did all kinds of stuff when we were little. Do you know why?"

"Bobby McNeal's a jerk."

"No," said Alice, "he's not. Not really."

"He was bullying you, Alice. There's nothing cute about that."

Alice frowned. "Look, he wasn't really trying to be a jerk in third grade. He was trying to say something and didn't know how."

Gutsy stared at her. "Say what? That boys can do whatever they want because they're stronger and girls just have to take it?"

"No," insisted Alice, getting flustered. "Bobby really liked me. He still does, I guess. He wants me to go to the fall dance next month. He doesn't mess with my hair or put snails in my shoes anymore. And he apologized, like, a thousand times for doing it back then."

"Doesn't make it right."

"Well . . . no. But I think he gets that now."

"Maybe," said Gutsy dubiously, "but he's still trying to get you to notice him."

"Sure, Guts, but he's not doing anything like he used to. People can change."

Gutsy gave a reluctant shrug. "Maybe. Why'd you bring him up? He and I aren't even friends."

"I brought it up because back then, he was hitting on me the *wrong* way because he was going through a lot of bad stuff. Don't forget, his dad was killed by shamblers in the summer before third grade. And his uncle, too. Bobby was all screwed up."

"So . . . ?"

Alice put her hands on the edge of the fence. She seemed to be standing very close.

"Look," she said, "I know your mom just died. That's horrible. My dad died two years ago and I'm still not over it. I think about him every night. I dream about talking with him and sitting in the living room sewing side by side, talking about stuff. About anything, really. Just *being* together. I miss him so bad. So I know what you're going through. And while I was washing my clothes, I kept wondering if that's what's made you weird lately. If that's why you walked into me like your head was totally somewhere else."

"I . . ."

"But," said Alice, leaning a few inches closer, "if you want to get my attention, maybe try it some other way."

"What?"

Alice smiled. "Flowers are nice," she said, "and they smell better than horse poop."

"I—I—"

Alice looked up and down the street, then darted forward and kissed Gutsy. It was very, very quick. It was on the lips.

And then she turned and walked back to her laundry and did not so much as glance back in Gutsy's direction.

Gutsy had no idea how long she stood there.

She had no idea how she even got home.

Floated, maybe . . . because Gutsy did not remember her feet touching the ground at all.

61

"WHAT ARE YOU SMILING ABOUT?" ASKED SPIDER AS he and Alethea came up her garden path.

"Smiling?" asked Gutsy. "Who's smiling?"

"You are," said Alethea, scowling at her.

"Am I?"

Her friends plunked down on chairs on either side of her. They looked exhausted and smelled like sweat and vegetables. Even the black widows on Spider's shirt looked limp and listless.

"We have to be back no later than an hour after sunset," Alethea said. "And we have double chores all week."

"Sorry," said Gutsy, meaning it. They were in trouble because of helping her. She didn't remind them that they did not have to stay out all night. That would be a slap in their faces, because they'd done it out of friendship and love.

They all sat in silence for a while, looking down the street, looking at nothing. Looking inward, really. Spider reached down to pet Sombra, and the coydog stood and laid his head on Spider's thigh, eyes closed, tail wagging back and forth very slowly. In another world, in another time of her life, this would have been a nice moment. Maybe, she mused, it was like the eye of a hurricane. Calm for as long as it lasted, but there was destruction behind and ahead.

Keeping her voice quiet so only they could hear, she said, "I talked to the Chess Players."

"Oh?" asked Alethea.

"They know about the Rat Catchers."

"Oh," she grunted.

Gutsy told them everything; and as she did, the happiness of talking to Alice melted away and left her with the cold reality of the Rat Catchers, the lab, the base, and the Night Army. Her friends listened without comment, but their mouths slowly fell open and their eyes bulged wide. Finally another silence settled over them as Alethea and Spider digested the details.

Spider eventually said, "Whoa."

"Yeah," agreed Gutsy.

Spider said, "This is bad."

"Thank you, Captain Understatement," said Alethea.

Gutsy looked up at a family walking past. Father, mother, two little kids, all talking and laughing at some joke. The father cut a look at the three of them and the dog sitting in the shade of a canopy. He smiled and moved on. The smile looked creepy. Suspicious.

"Okay," said Spider, "I officially don't trust anyone."

"Sweetie," said Alethea, "glad you finally caught up to where I've *always* been."

"I don't want to be like this, though. I *like* people."

Gutsy and Alethea exchanged a quick, small, sad look. Spider was without doubt the nicest of the three of them. Most people treated him like he was a weirdo, but he never seemed to mind. Gutsy was sure he noticed, but it didn't matter to him as much as being himself. It had to hurt on some level, Gutsy knew. It was tough to be disliked for no good reason. It probably made Spider go deeper into himself. It sure as heck made *her* do that. And Alethea, tough as she was, as uncaring as she always seemed to be, had her own scars from cheap shots.

Unlike Spider, Gutsy didn't automatically like people. She was much more calculating in that she had to have a reason to like someone. Maybe that was a flaw, or maybe it was how she was wired, but it was a fact of her life. Now, after talking to the Chess Players, she was even less enthusiastic about bonding with the people in town.

Well, with a notable exception. She could still feel that kiss. Quick as it was, Gutsy knew that it had made a permanent mark on her. She wanted another one. A longer one. And about a million hours of conversation, preferably under a tree or somewhere quiet.

"You're smiling again," said Alethea in a definitely accusatory way. "How can you smile with everything that's going on?"

"Um . . . ," began Gutsy.

Alethea straightened, seeming to come to point like a bird dog. "Alice Chung!"

Gutsy blinked in surprise. "What? How? I mean . . . how did you know?" She looked sharply at Spider. "You told her, didn't you?"

"He didn't need to tell me anything, girl," said Alethea, puffing out her chest and raising her eyebrows. "You talked to Alice, didn't you? Come on, don't lie. It's written all over your face. I have only ever seen you blush three times in your whole life, Gabriella Gomez. Once when Corey Hale told you how pretty you looked at the Christmas party in school. And twice when you saw Alice Chung on the street. You were redder than a fresh-picked tomato then and you are twice as red now, which means it was more than seeing her on the street. You *talked* to her, didn't you? No . . . you told her how you feel. Come on, out with it. Don't make me beat it out of you. I can go fetch Rainbow Smite and we can do this the old-school way. . . ."

Gutsy had to laugh.

"Wait," said Spider quickly, "you mean you *did* tell her?"

"Not exactly."

"Well, what *exactly* happened?" demanded Alethea.

Gutsy told them. When she got to the part about the accidental collision and Alice falling into a pile of steaming manure, Spider laughed so hard he choked. Alethea gave him a hearty thump on the back that knocked him out of the chair so that he nearly crushed Sombra, but the coydog scampered away and stood wagging, tongue lolling, excited by the laughter though confused by it as well.

By the time Gutsy finished her story Alethea was nodding as if it was all something she'd foreseen.

"Well, it's about time. You only had like months to say something to her."

"I . . . almost did," said Gutsy weakly. "A few times. I mean I thought about it . . . but I didn't know how she'd react. Her mom's so proper and—"

Alethea held up a hand to stop her right there. "Proper? *Proper?* What's that supposed to mean. Are you saying that you talking to Alice isn't proper? Who says? What's *im*proper about it?"

"No, I mean . . . I didn't want to offend her."

"Offend? God, I am so going to smack the stupid off you."

"You know what I mean," said Gutsy. "How could I know Alice was bi?"

"Actually," said Alethea, "Alice Chung is *not* bi."

Gutsy stared at her. "What . . . ?"

"*You're* bi, sweetie," said Alethea. "Alice is a lesbian. She only likes girls."

"Wait, what? Since when?"

"Since always, I expect. It's not like something you catch. Pretty sure you're born that way, unless everything I ever read is wrong, and it isn't."

Gutsy gaped at her. "But . . . but . . . how do you even know?"

"How do you *not* know?" Alethea said with a laugh. "Have you ever seen Alice talk to a boy about anything except the time of day? Have you ever seen her kiss a boy? No, you have not, and you're not likely to. She likes girls, Guts, and for some reason she likes a particular girl who I find occasionally annoying."

"She was just being nice."

"No, seriously, I really am going to have to smack you." Alethea rolled her eyes. "You knocked her into a pile of crap and she was *still* nice to you? She kissed you. Her. No one's *that* nice. Not unless they like you enough to make something like that not matter." She shook her head. "I'm straight as an arrow and I can see that. How can you be bi and not see it?" She sighed, then adjusted her glittery tiara. "Gutsy, you may be able to fix anything and find anything, but when it comes to figuring out how your own heart and mind work, you are dumber than a box of rocks."

That stopped Gutsy in her tracks. She looked at Spider, who was rocking back and forth, laughing so hard he couldn't make any noise. His brown skin was now a violent brick red. Sombra looked at Gutsy and gave a single, happy bark.

"See," said Alethea, "even your weirdo dog knows."

LAUGHTER, EVEN THE WEIGHTLESS AND UNBURDENED laughter of good friends, fades away in time. When it faded, the weight of reality dragged them all down.

"The Rat Catchers," said Spider. "What are we going to do about them?"

"What *can* we do?" asked Alethea glumly. "Much as I want to beat their heads in and keep beating them until I feel better—which might take a while—there's a lot of them and they have guns."

"We have to find out about them," insisted Spider.

"Sure," said Alethea, "and then what?"

"What do you mean?"

"I mean, once we find out, what do we do? If those two old farts are right and half the town council and some of the guards are in on it, what can we do without getting in more trouble? This isn't one of your comic books, Spider. We don't have super-powers and there's no one we can call, like in those novels you read. When you can't trust the cops, who do you call?"

"Not all the guards are involved," said Gutsy. "Karen Peak is cool. And the guards who got beaten up. They can't be in on it."

"Don't make any assumptions," warned Alethea.

Spider nodded. "Besides, even if they're all innocent, that's only three people, two of whom are in the hospital. Really some army we're putting together. Maybe we can get old Mr. Kilroy and his blind cat, too."

But Gutsy shook her head. "First things first. I want to go talk to Karen and see what she knows. Then Sombra and I are going hunting. I bet between his nose and what the Chess Players told me, I can find that lab."

Spider leaned forward and studied her, his face screwed up with concern. "And then what?"

"I don't know yet," said Gutsy. "And before you ask, I can't even work out a rough plan because I don't have enough information. Investigate first, plan next."

"What book is that from?" asked Alethea.

"The Book of Gutsy," she replied.

KAREN PEAK WAS JUST LEAVING HER OFFICE TO head home when Gutsy and Sombra caught up with her.

"Got a sec?" asked Gutsy, falling into step with her.

The security officer smiled. "Sure. What's up?"

There was no one on the street, so Gutsy took a chance and asked, "Karen . . . what do you know about the Rat Catchers?"

Karen stared at Gutsy with wide eyes that were instantly filled with fear. "*What?* How do you even *know* that name?"

Gutsy faced her and felt a tightness in her chest. "Then you *do* know them? Who are they?"

Karen went pale. In a fierce whisper, she said, "Listen to me, Gabriella, you can't say that name. You can't ever mention them. You've never heard of them and you won't ever talk about them. Do you understand me?"

"No," said Gutsy, "I don't. I want you to tell me who they are."

Karen shook her head. "I . . . I can't."

"Can't or won't?"

The panic in Karen's eyes gave her the answer. She was too terrified of the Rat Catchers to talk about them. That much was obvious; but Gutsy thought she saw something else. Karen was afraid, but she didn't look guilty. Or angry. Or hostile. Just scared. Did that mean she knew something but wasn't involved?

Sombra stood next to Gutsy, glaring up at the older woman.

Karen looked at the dog and chewed her lip nervously. "You never told me where you found that dog."

"Does it matter?"

"It, um, might. The people who own him could come looking for him."

"People? You mean the Rat Catchers, don't you? He belonged to them, didn't he?"

Instead of answering, Karen said, "You should turn him loose. He'll find his way back and no one will be mad at you for taking him in."

"I think the Rat Catchers are already mad at me."

Karen said nothing.

"Karen," said Gutsy evenly, "let me tell you what I think, okay? I think the Rat Catchers are soldiers working for some secret lab hidden outside town. I think the lab is doing medical experiments. I think those people made my mother sick. I think that's why Mama died."

Karen shook her head, but it was clear that it was more a matter of not wanting to have this conversation than denying what Gutsy was saying. The woman did not turn and run away, though. There was that.

"The other night," continued Gutsy, "when the riders came into town, that wasn't the first time, was it? They were here the night before, too."

"No . . . ," said Karen hoarsely. "You don't know that."

"Yes, I do. And you know what they did that first time? They brought Mama home."

Karen's face, already pale, turned the color of ash. She backed a half step away and put her hand over her mouth.

"I took Mama back to Hope Cemetery and buried her again," said Gutsy. "Do you know that? Can you imagine how that felt?"

Karen said nothing, but she kept shaking her head.

"Then two nights ago the Rat Catchers brought Mama back and put her in my bedroom," said Gutsy, and she had to fight to keep from snarling. "In my *bedroom*. I had to fight my own mother, Karen. I almost died."

"You didn't report anything like that. . . ."

"Of course I didn't," snapped Gutsy. "Your night guards didn't stop them the first time and they got hurt the second time. What good would telling you anything do?"

"I could have helped."

"Really? Against the Rat Catchers? You almost fainted when I said that name."

"Gabriella, please . . ."

"My name is Gutsy," she snapped. "Gabriella was the little girl you used to babysit. She's gone now. It's just me. Gutsy Gomez." She took a step closer. "I went out to the cemetery *again* yesterday to bury Mama, and those Rat Catchers had dug up nearly everyone who died in the last few months. The Santiagos, the Cantus . . ." She rattled off a list of names. "All of them dug up and their bodies stolen. If I'd buried Mama again, they would have taken her body too."

"What did you do with . . . ?"

"It doesn't matter what I did," said Gutsy viciously. "I took care of my own. She's safe and they'll never find her. Besides, don't change the subject. You're supposed to be the head of the guards, which means everyone in town is *your* own. Why aren't you taking care of us?"

Karen Peak said nothing. Her face was pale but her throat was bright red, and small red poppies seemed to bloom on her cheeks. "You don't understand," she said weakly.

"You're right. I don't. That's why I'm talking with you, Karen. I'm giving you a chance. I want to understand. I need to. So, why don't you help me?"

"Help you? *Help you?* You want me to help you? Fine," said Karen angrily, "then listen to me. Go home. Never mention this again. Not to me or anyone. Don't tell your friends. Don't speak of it. Put it out of your mind."

"You really think I could do that?"

"You have to."

"I can't and I won't," insisted Gutsy. "Want to know why? Because I think that whatever happened to Mama has happened to a lot of people. And I think it's going to go on happening unless someone stops it."

"You *can't* stop it."

"How do you know what I can and can't do?"

"Gabriella—Gutsy—please . . . you can't get involved. You can't stop this."

"I can't if you don't help me by telling me what you know," Gutsy countered, "but even if you don't, I'm going to try."

"That's insane. You'll get hurt."

"Don't worry about me. I can take care of myself."

"No, you'll get killed," said Karen. "They—"

"If you don't help me," interrupted Gutsy, "and I get killed, then it's on you. But if you do help me, if you tell me what you know, then maybe they won't do anything to me. Maybe I'll be able to stay a step ahead of them. And maybe I'll stop them from hurting other people."

Karen Peak laughed. It was a short, shrill laugh. "You have no idea what they are. You don't understand why they're doing this. You have no idea how many of them there are."

"Then *tell* me." Gutsy almost yelled it. Sombra growled and showed his wickedly sharp teeth. Gutsy believed that if she told the coydog to attack, he would.

Karen backed away again, shaking her head. "No. I can't. I have a family. I have my own daughter to think about. I . . ."

She suddenly whirled and ran away. Actually ran.

Sombra quivered with a desire to give chase, but Gutsy stood her ground. Fists balled, jaw clenched.

For maybe five full seconds.

Then she and Sombra were running.

64

KAREN PEAK WAS FIT AND QUICK AND RAN WITH desperate energy.

Gutsy caught her less than a block away.

Quick was fine; fast was better, and Gutsy Gomez was very fast. They were still on a deserted street, but someone could come along any moment. No time to waste. She clamped a hand on Karen's shoulder and jerked her backward with such force the woman backpedaled five steps and then sat down hard on the pavement. Gutsy had to fend Sombra off from pouncing on her.

"What are you doing?" cried Karen. "I'm the head of the town guard, I could have you arrested for—"

Gutsy slapped her across the face.

It shocked Karen to utter, aghast silence. Before she could recover, Gutsy leaned in close and spoke in a fierce and uncompromising whisper. "You shut your mouth and listen to me. We're done with you being the responsible adult and me being only a kid. You know something about what happened to Mama or you know what's going on with the Rat Catchers, and you're going to tell me. You don't want to know what I'm willing to do to make you tell me."

Beside her, Sombra growled with eloquent promise.

"You're out of your mind," gasped Karen as she climbed angrily to her feet.

"Maybe so. If I am, then that's even more of a reason not to mess with me." Gutsy put her hand on Karen's shoulder again. The woman was a few inches taller, but it was clear that she knew who held the power. Gutsy was angry, but this also made her sad. She liked Karen; she liked her daughter, Sarah, too. But she was not going to back down. Now or ever. That line had been crossed and by crossing, it had been eliminated. Now they were in a strange new territory with no clear set of rules. Fine. That meant that the person in power had to make new rules, and for the moment Gutsy was in power. Even so, she did not want to be totally ruthless. "Listen," she said, "I know you're scared. I'm scared too. The apocalypse happened, the dead rose, there are mutants and wolf packs and bad guys. People are dying all around us. Who isn't scared? But being scared isn't an excuse for standing back and looking the other way. You know who these Rat Catchers are and you're going to tell me."

"My daughter . . ."

"Yeah, your daughter. You love her, right? What makes you think Sarah will be safe just because you keep a bad secret? The Rat Catchers are hurting people. Making them sick. Killing them. They tried to kill me and I was somebody's daughter. They—"

"Gutsy, you really don't understand," interrupted Karen. "Sarah's sick. She's . . . *infected*."

That jolted Gutsy. "Infected? With what? One of the diseases like what Mama had?"

Tears broke and fell down Karen's cheeks, and in that moment, Gutsy understood.

"She has the plague?" she gasped.

"Yes."

"How? Sarah never goes outside the walls."

The answer was there in Karen's silence and in her eyes. It chilled Gutsy to the marrow.

"The Rat Catchers made her sick?" she whispered. "They gave Sarah the plague? How?"

"They're scientists. Maybe they injected her, maybe some other means. I don't know. All I *do* know is that my daughter is infected and they have the only medicines that can keep her alive. And they'll do that and worse to you and to me, and to anyone who interferes with their research."

"What are you talking about?"

Karen glanced around. They were alone on the street, but even so the woman was clearly terrified. She leaned in. "Not here. Not out in the open. I can't."

"Okay, fine," said Gutsy. "My house. Two hours."

"No, I—"

"Want me to come to *your* place?"

Karen shook her head.

"Okay, then, like I said, two hours. Come in the back way. I'll leave the door unlocked. You'd better be there, Karen. I'm not joking."

With that she turned away. Sombra looked back a couple of times, but Gutsy did not. She didn't want to see what her words and her threats were doing to Karen. She was angry, she was filled with hate, but she wasn't that cruel.

GUTSY LOOKED UP AT THE SUN AND JUDGED THAT
she had about an hour of good daylight left before the slow
summer twilight.

She and Sombra did not head home, but instead took
another circuitous route back to Misfit High. However, Mr.
Urrea and Mr. Ford were already gone. Gutsy took a sheet of
paper and wrote a quick note, paused, considered, and wrote
a second one. She folded them both and left the school.

Spider and Alethea were out front of the Cuddlys' place
again, though now they were shaving carrots. Mrs. Cuddly
was inside, but even so Gutsy didn't slow down or do anything more than say, "Hey."

One of the notes fell beside the basket of unpeeled carrots. Gutsy and Sombra walked on.

The Chess Players were on their shaded porch, deep into
a game, with pieces scattered across the board and cups of tea
steaming beside them. Neither of them glanced up at her as
Gutsy stepped onto the porch and leaned against the rail.

"Who's winning?" she asked casually.

"I am," said Ford.

"You wish," said Urrea.

When Ford flicked a glance at her, Gutsy showed him a small corner of the note she had concealed in her hand. She raised a single eyebrow. Ford moved his bishop, and when he reached for his tea, his hand brushed the spine of an old paperback, knocking it to the floor. Gutsy bent to pick it up and saw that it was a dog-eared copy of T. S. Eliot's "The Waste Land," a frightening epic poem inspired by the legend of the quest for the Holy Grail and the story of the Fisher King, both of which had been taught in school. Gutsy covertly slipped the note between the pages and handed the book back. She lingered there and watched Ford advance toward checkmate and then left, pretending to look bored.

She stopped at the butcher shop to buy a beef bone for Sombra, then went home.

While the coydog attacked the bone with savage glee, Gutsy used the bathroom, washed her face and hands, went into the kitchen, made a light meal, ate almost none of it, and waited.

The windup clock on the wall ticked through what felt like ten million seconds.

That was fine.

It gave Gutsy lots of time to think.

66

THE KNOCK ON THE DOOR WAS LIGHT AND QUICK. A nervous, tentative sound. Even so, Sombra leaped to his feet and barked.

"It's okay," soothed Gutsy, and the coydog immediately fell silent, though he stayed alert.

Gutsy opened the back door. Karen Peak stood there, dressed in dark clothes with an old man's porkpie hat pulled low. She pushed her way inside and closed the door.

"No one saw me," she said. "I was careful."

"Good," said Gutsy. "Come on. We can talk in the kitchen."

She led the way, but as soon as they entered the kitchen, Karen cried out and backed up, her hand moving toward a pistol she now wore in a leather holster clipped to her belt.

"What is this?" she demanded.

At the table, Spider, Alethea, and the Chess Players looked at her. Only Alethea was smiling, but it was a nasty smile. Rainbow Smite lay on the table, with the studded end pointing toward Karen. Gutsy, who stood very close to the officer, darted out a hand and snatched the pistol from the holster before Karen could stop her. She ejected the magazine and racked the slide to remove the chambered bullet, and then she handed the weapon to Mr. Urrea, who placed it on the table.

"Sit down, Karen," said Ford, waving his hand toward one of the two empty chairs.

"This is insane," said Karen. "I'm not going to—"

Gutsy shoved her toward the chair, and she wasn't very nice about it.

"Sit down," she said. Sombra snarled. Karen looked around, but there was not a friendly eye in the room.

She sat, perching like a nervous bird on the edge of the chair. Gutsy sat next to her.

"Here's how we're going to do this," she said. "My friends all know what I know. I told them what little you told me. They know about Sarah."

"And our hearts break for you and your daughter," said Urrea.

"But we all need to know what you know," continued Gutsy. "You're going to tell us."

"As a measure of trust," said Ford, "we'll tell you what we know. All of it. Understand, Karen, if we thought you were the enemy, we wouldn't do that. We'd hold back key facts to see if you tried to lie or twist the truth. But we've known you since the beginning. You were with us on the Raid. You're brave and tough and, for the most part, honest."

Gutsy saw Spider mouth the words, *for the most part*.

"We're giving you the benefit of the doubt," added Urrea. "You told Gutsy that Sarah was sick and intimated that the Rat Catchers were responsible. That's beyond horrible, but it makes a kind of sense. It sounds like they needed a way to put a leash on you, and everyone knows how much you love Sarah."

"Then you know why I can't talk about this," insisted Karen.

"It's a risk," said Gutsy. "Sure. I don't care. Something bad is happening here and it's getting worse. I care about Sarah too, but I nearly died the other night. The Rat Catchers know that I know something about them. They're probably going to come after me. Maybe as soon as tonight."

Alethea drummed her painted fingernails on the handle of her bat. "Which means that you have to tell us everything, 'cause you don't want to find out what's going to happen to you if anyone puts a finger on Gutsy."

"Let's not resort to threats," said Ford, but Spider gave him a withering look.

"Yeah, Mr. Ford, I think threats are what we need right now. I mean . . . what else do we have?"

"We have trust," said Urrea. He looked at Karen. Everyone did.

She closed her eyes and sat in silence for several seconds.

"Okay," she said, opening her eyes and turning to Gutsy. "But you won't like it."

"People tell me that," said Gutsy, "and they're usually right. So, no, I don't expect to like it, but I think I need to know it."

Karen nodded.

Ford and Urrea told her what they'd told Gutsy. Then Gutsy, Spider, and Alethea retold their part of it, going into great detail. Karen listened without interrupting, nodding occasionally. Sometimes dabbing at tears that tried to form in her eyes.

67

"YOU'RE RIGHT ABOUT A LOT OF THINGS," SAID KAREN, "but there's so much more to the story. Even I don't know all of it, but . . . well . . . I know a lot."

"How do you know?" asked Gutsy.

"Some of it was stuff I knew from when the town council was formed. They know too. Half the guards know. Some of the people in town, too. Some are in on it, and I mean really in on it. They're not really townsfolk. They're spies, plants. Or maybe they're watchdogs. A little of all of that." Karen folded her hands on the tabletop. "Other stuff I pieced together from things I heard or saw. And some of it was told to me because of my job and they needed me to be able to cooperate."

Everyone nodded.

"The stories about a hidden base are true," said Karen. "It's here. The official name is the Laredo Chemical and Biological Weapon Defense Research Facility. You won't have heard of it. It was what they called a black budget site. Actually illegal according to a whole lot of treaties with other countries. All bioweapons testing was supposed to have been stopped by the major powers, but none of them ever really stopped. They kept going in secret on the assumption that other countries would still be developing their biological warfare weapons, and if we stopped doing research we wouldn't be prepared. They fudged their way through congressional budget hearings by saying that their whole purpose was to study bioweapons in order to create vaccines and countermeasures." She cut a look at the teenagers. "Do you understand any of that?"

"Enough," said Alethea. "We've had pretty good history and science teachers."

The Chess Players gave her small nods and smiles.

"Okay," said Karen, "so the base was already here. Secret, hidden. Then the End happened. It wasn't an attack by another country, but the plague that was used had been developed in Russia back in the 1980s, during the Cold War. It wasn't a virus or a bacterium. It was a parasite like the green jewel wasp and some others. They wanted a bioweapon that would not only infect the host, but drive the host to aggressively spread the parasite larvae through bites. They also engineered it so the infected would feed on animal proteins in order to keep going, even while shutting down a lot of the body's unnecessary functions—higher reasoning, natural human reproduction, and like that. They wanted a host that was all about protecting and perpetuating the bioweapon, and that's what they got. The inventor, Dr. Herman Volker, made it worse, though, because he genetically reengineered the parasites so that they no longer had a normal life cycle. Like some jellyfish and these tiny freshwater animals called hydra, the parasites were designed to endlessly regenerate. All they need is protein, and not much of that. When they don't get protein, they go into a kind of hibernation, which is why you sometimes see *los muertos* just standing there, year after year. Never quite rotting all the way to nothing. Everything the living dead do, everything they are, was designed into them."

"What is the basis for the plague, then?" asked Urrea. "What are the parasites?"

"They used different kinds of parasites found in nature," explained Karen. "The bioweapon was called Lucifer, and there are a lot of different versions of it. The one that started the plague was Lucifer 113, the one Dr. Volker redesigned after he defected to the States."

She explained about Dr. Volker's warped idea of punishment for a serial killer at a prison in Western Pennsylvania. She explained how the unfortunate arrival of a major storm slowed down the police and military attempts to control the spread of the outbreak, and how it then went on to spread around the world as people fled the area. Movement of populations via cars, trains, and planes helped it spread.

Gutsy felt like she'd been punched in the face. She glanced around at the looks of horror on the faces of everyone at the table. Even Karen. Or maybe especially Karen, since this was knowledge she had been carrying around with her.

"After the End," continued Karen, "the base here kept working, and they established a field lab too. Both of them are still here. All this time they've been trying to come up with a cure, with treatments for those who are infected but not yet turned. They're also trying to modify the behavior of the fully infected."

"Modify?" asked Spider.

"I'm getting to that. Originally they scrambled to come up with a mutating agent to disrupt the parasite life cycle in the hopes that Lucifer 113 would become inert. They tried different versions on animals, trying to find a species that could be infected, but they didn't have much luck. That was part of the design of the bioweapon, because the last thing they wanted was infected flies, mosquitoes, rats . . . or any of that."

"People have been talking about *los muertos* wild pigs," said Alethea.

Karen nodded. "Sure. Pigs are biologically close to humans. So are monkeys, and there were a lot of test animals at the base. Didn't work, though. The wild boars escaped from the lab somehow and since then have attacked everything, including other pigs and even other animals. I heard something about them hoping that if the infected mated with or infected wild boars it might result in the wild boars developing some kind of immunity. But no. It was all a mess. What did happen out there was that some other kinds of animals survived the bites. All kinds of species, and the mutated strain in the hogs somehow broke through the resistance and caused interspecies infection. And some of them had babies. The babies were different. They carried the disease in radical new forms, and none of them were benign. It seemed that every generation, every new strain, was either just as dangerous as the original, or more so."

"All kinds of animals?" asked Spider.

"I doubt anyone knows the answer to that. The base had small testing stations all over, mostly disguised as small settlements of refugees, but most of them have been wiped out."

"By the wolf packs?" suggested Ford, and Karen nodded.

"And that's where this gets even worse."

Alethea gave her a sour look. "Speaking for everyone here,

I don't particularly like 'worse' when we're talking about the apocalypse. We already have *los muertos*, half infected, mutant animals, wolf packs, and the Rat Catchers. Is there a 'worse'?"

"Before I answer that," said Karen, "let me say this. I'm not defending what those people are doing, but I understand why they're doing it. And maybe I even understand why they're being so cold and brutal about it."

"Oh, I need to hear this," said Alethea.

Karen gave her a hard look. "Think about the problem, then. The plague killed most of humanity and turned them into flesh-eating monsters. There were *billions* of living dead and only thousands of us left. Every single person who dies, no matter how they die, comes back as one of *them*. There's no government left, not much in the way of resources, and the clock is ticking. If you were one of the scientists in the lab, and you believed—actually *believed*—that it was on you to find a way to save humanity from becoming completely extinct, tell me, Alethea, how far would you be willing to go?"

"I wouldn't make healthy people sick," said Alethea firmly. "I wouldn't spread other kinds of diseases, like the one that killed Gutsy's mama. I wouldn't let anyone else die, because that would just make the problem worse."

Karen shook her head. "It's more complicated than that."

"Then uncomplicate it," said Gutsy. "Why did they give Mama tuberculosis?"

Karen's hands balled into fists. "For the same reason they gave the plague to my daughter, Sarah."

"*Why?*" demanded Spider, Ford, and Gutsy all at the same time.

"Because they needed to control us," said Karen. "With

me, they needed to put me on a leash, but at the same time they wanted me healthy enough to do my job."

"And Mama . . . ?" asked Gutsy quietly.

"She was a threat to them. Most of the hospital staff aren't part of this. Your mama wasn't a part of any of it. But she was smart and she was putting some pieces together. Making you sick wouldn't have been enough, so they made her sick instead. They did it with a disease she was exposed to anyway at the hospital. It took her fast, though. Way too fast for ordinary tuberculosis. We were told it was a naturally mutated strain, but she didn't believe that. Though before she could do much about it, she was too sick to even move."

Gutsy sat in a well of silence, unable to move or speak. Alethea and Spider got up and came around and hugged her. The Chess Players sat immobile. Karen looked down at her hands.

"There's more to it," said Karen slowly. "Some of it I know, and some I don't know."

"Tell me," whispered Gutsy. "Tell us all of it."

"I OVERHEARD SOME THINGS I WASN'T SUPPOSED to hear," said Karen. "I was in the hospital one night to get medicine for Sarah and I heard two people talking behind a screen. One of them was the woman soldier you saw. Captain Bess Collins. She runs the base and oversees security at the field lab. I report to her, so I recognized her voice."

"What was the substance of the conversation?" asked Urrea.

"I only caught parts of it because they were talking in hushed voices, but from what I was able to piece together, they've been working on a new generation of the mutagen. It seemed pretty clear to me that they've just about given up on actually stopping the plague. Every attempt to do that just has resulted in a worse mutation, and I'll tell you more about that in a second. The conversation I heard was about the new thing they've been trying for the last two years. It was starting to show results that made them think they were getting somewhere. Something that, if it works, would change the nature of all *los muertos*. Lucifer 113 changed the brain chemistry so that all higher reasoning was detached from motor function. I'm not a scientist, so I can't explain the actual biochemical process, but this new plan was supposed to some-how repair that damage, restore the connection. At least in a percentage of the dead."

"For what reason?" asked Spider.

"To give them back their ability to control their bodies," said Karen. "To make them stop wanting to feed, stop want-ing to bite."

They sat with that for a moment.

"That's actually kind of horrible," said Spider. "To sud-denly wake up and know you've been a flesh-eating monster. That's their great master plan?"

"I'm explaining it wrong," said Karen. She asked for a glass of water and Gutsy gave her one. Karen took several sips, then set her cup down. "The scientists seem to think that the living dead aren't actually brain-dead. They think that the consciousness of the host is still there, and still aware, but the parasites prevent it from taking control of any actions. Think about that. The living dead do some things already—walk, some even run, a few can climb, some pick up rocks, some can turn doorknobs. There's some memory of things they used to do lingering inside. Lucifer 113 had not been designed to destroy higher function, not really, but to disconnect it from motor functions. That's what it does in nearly all of them. The ones who can still do a few things are exceptions."

"Okay," said Ford, "that is profoundly worse."

Urrea nodded. "I can't think of anything more horrible. You're actually saying every single shambler, is aware of what it is?"

"Much worse than that," said Karen, looking sick. "They are still connected to all five senses. They hear, smell, taste, feel, and see everything, but they are unable to exert any control over the physical body. That's what Dr. Volker built into the plague. He wanted the person, that serial killer, to be able to experience everything after he woke up in the coffin."

Mr. Urrea got up so suddenly that his chair fell over backward with a crash. He staggered into the bathroom and they could hear him vomiting. Gutsy sat gripping the edge of the table with all her strength for fear that she would simply fly away into darkness.

"Mama . . . ?" she whispered. "*Ay Dios mío* . . . Mama?"

Urrea appeared in the kitchen doorway, his eyes glassy with unspilled tears. "Do you know how many *los muertos* we killed during the Raid? Do you know how many we've killed since?"

Karen nodded. "I'm sorry, I didn't want to tell you any of this."

Gutsy slammed her palms down hard on the table with a sound like a double-barreled shotgun firing. Sombra leaped to his feet and began barking.

"No," yelled Gutsy, and the dog instantly fell silent. He crept over to her, tail tucked between his legs, whimpering. Gutsy turned in her chair and took the dog's head with both hands and leaned against him, forehead to forehead, the way she did with Gordo. She stayed like that for a long time and no one spoke. Then Gutsy straightened. "Is that what you heard in the hospital?"

"Some of it," said Karen weakly. "The rest . . . well . . . I heard enough to know that they were testing this new mutagen on the people in New Alamo."

"Why here?" asked Alethea. "And why us?"

Karen licked her lips. "Because they ran out of lab animals two years ago."

And there it was.

"God in heaven," said Ford.

"God may be in heaven," said Karen, "but the devil is here in our town."

"So the diseases," said Spider, "weren't really natural, right?"

"No, I don't think so."

"And making Mama sick wasn't just to shut her up?"

"No."

"They brought Mama back to Gutsy twice," said Alethea. "What did they think was going to happen? That seeing Gutsy would somehow wake her mind up?"

Karen didn't answer. She didn't have to. They all knew it was the truth.

Gutsy cleared her throat and forced herself to ask the next question. "What's the Night Army? Are they the wolf packs?"

"They are," said Karen, and now she looked even more scared. "But they're not what you think."

"What do I think?"

"That they're just another mutation. I mean they are, but they're not just that." She cupped her palms around her glass and looked down into its contents. "During the End, when our army was still fighting the dead, do you know why we lost?"

"I think I do," said Urrea. "We lost because they were us."

"Huh?" said Alethea.

"I get it," said Spider, but Karen explained.

"Soldiers were always trained to fight the enemy, and the enemy was always someone else. Another race, people from another country. It was 'us' versus 'them,' and the soldiers, the men and women who signed up or who were drafted, joined because they were fighting *for* something. Not anyone's politics, not really. They were fighting for their families, their homes, their friends. And once they were in the field, once they were in actual combat, they were fighting for the soldiers next to them. That's how it's always been. I know because I was in the Texas National Guard. I was a soldier, which is how I got the job as security officer for this town. When the End happened, we weren't fighting the Russians or North Koreans or militant religious terrorists. We were told to stop the infected—and those infected were our own people. Family members, friends, neighbors who had turned. That's who came at us. Sure, we fought, but we only fought for as long as we could. We fought until our hearts broke. I saw soldiers— tough, experienced soldiers—drop their guns and walk into the infected, arms open, trying to hug someone they knew. Accepting the consequences, because they'd rather be dead among the people they loved than alive with only their grief, or the knowledge of who took the bullets they fired."

She paused, drank, and set the cup down so hard water splashed on her hands. She made no move to clean it up.

"The people in the base never stopped their war. They had a medical triage center on the front lines, and they took as many soldiers as they could to try and help them. Or so we thought. The wounded were sent back to aid stations, except that was a lie. A lot of them were sent to the base. The scientists figured that they were dying anyway, so they used them. Experimented on them. Generation after generation of the mutagen. Hundreds of soldiers as test subjects. Some died, and I mean really died. A lot of the others turned. Some . . . *changed*. They didn't die and didn't completely transform. The scientists thought this was a sign of victory, a sign that they were making real progress, so they asked for more wounded. They called them 'volunteers,' but let's face it, no one was volunteering." She paused, thought about it, and shook her head. "Or maybe they did, who knows? Maybe they told the soldiers that volunteering for experimental treatments would lead to a cure that would save their family members—living and living dead. Now that I think about it, I bet that was what they did."

"That would be my guess too," said Urrea. "Otherwise the soldiers would eventually have mutinied."

"They did," said Karen. "Later. Way later."

Ford leaned forward. "What do you mean?"

"It did work in a way, in that the mutagen they were given allowed them to keep their consciousness. They can talk and think. But the mutagen did not stop the aggression or the need to spread the disease. It actually made it worse, because the presence of the parasite in the brain drove them all mad. They are thinking parasites. They are filled with nothing but rage and a desire to kill, but they have their intelligence. They can plan how to kill. They carry out those plans too. Which is why all those camps and settlements have been destroyed."

"That's the Night Army?" asked Gutsy.

"That became the Night Army," said Karen. "For a while they were leaderless, just a bunch of wolf packs, roving the Broken Lands. Then they started merging, forming larger packs. They started targeting the small testing stations and wiping those out."

"Why? What changed?"

"They have a leader," said Karen. "The soldiers call him the Raggedy Man, but that's either a nickname or a code name. I don't think they know his real name."

"The Rat Catchers mentioned him," said Gutsy, and told her about what they'd said at the graveside. Urrea and Ford explained about the rumors of the Raggedy Man being a god, a general, or king to *los muertos*.

"I don't know that much about him," Karen conceded. "Bits and pieces, and none of it good. All I know is that whoever he is, he'd been someone important during the outbreak, and the military went to great lengths to find his body and transport it to the base."

"His body?" asked Spider. "You mean he was dead?"

Karen cocked her head to one side and considered Gutsy. "What's 'dead' really mean these days? Whether he was a living dead or some mutant version, I don't know. All I do know is that everyone was afraid of him, but they needed him. They needed something from him, and don't ask me what it is, because I don't know. They experimented on him, and I think something they got from him helped them with the latest generation of the mutagen. That's where it all went wrong, though. Something happened and there was a mutiny at the base and all the infected soldiers got out. From what I could piece together, the Raggedy Man was either in the base and he led the revolt to break out, or he sent word for them to break out. I'm really not sure."

"The Raggedy Man did this?" asked Ford. "He reanimated?"

"Apparently. Or maybe he was never really dead. Again,

I don't know how. Either way, he's out there. And he's been bringing all the wolf packs together, and the last of the living soldiers at the base are freaking out because they think the Raggedy Man is able to control the shamblers, too."

Urrea looked stricken, and Gutsy was afraid he was going to throw up again. "You're saying he's *leading* them? You're saying that all the infected are now this Night Army and . . ."

"And he's their general," finished Gutsy.

"Sooner or later," said Karen in a hollow voice, "the army of the dead is going to go to war with the last of the living. It's why the scientists are trying everything they can—no matter what they have to do or who they have to hurt—to find the perfect mutagen that will stop the Night Army. That's why they're using so many people in town."

"Killing them with diseases?" demanded Alethea.

"Yes, because they need fresh subjects who haven't been out in the sun rotting for years. Remember, everyone who dies, no matter how, becomes a living dead. That means we're all infected already, and death allows the parasites to somehow become active and dominant."

"I want to go wash my DNA with lye soap," muttered Spider.

"If they want fresh bodies," said Gutsy, "why not just shoot people?"

"And risk an outright rebellion?" Karen shook her head. "No, if they did that, then everyone would realize what's going on, and there aren't a lot of the soldiers left to stop four thousand people if they rose up."

"Maybe a little open rebellion is what we need," murmured Urrea.

"Sure, and maybe you'd like to personally bury all the innocent people who would get caught in the cross fire."

Urrea sighed and nodded, accepting her point.

"Wait," said Gutsy, "if they're giving people diseases, then does that mean they gave tuberculosis to Mama?"

The silence that followed her question was profound and ugly and filled with thorns.

"I think so," said Karen. "I don't know how any more than I know how exactly they infected my daughter. Does it matter? The fact that they did it is enough."

"Yes," said Gutsy in a dangerous voice, "that's enough."

"There's more to it," Karen said to Gutsy. "They keep it all quiet so everyone here in New Alamo goes about their normal lives, which makes it easier to keep tabs on them. At some point or another everyone's been to the hospital, so Rat Catcher spies there have collected medical histories going back years. They apparently need that data. So, horrible as it is, the diseases people are dying of are their way of selecting candidates for new medical trials, making sure each person dies when they need them to die, and in a way that doesn't raise an alarm. And then they study them after death."

"Is that why they dug up all those graves?"

Karen frowned. "I'm not sure. I know something big is happening, and Collins and her people are acting very skittish. It could be the attacks on the settlements and the increased number of ravagers. As to why they dug up the bodies . . . maybe they want to do tests on the parasites after certain periods of time."

"Yes," said Ford, "that might fit. If they already have extensive medical histories and studied those specific dead at given intervals, that would fit a kind of recognizable scientific model."

"It's sick," said Spider.

"No argument," said Ford, nodding. "And it suggests a level of desperation. When the military acts erratically, it's usually because things are breaking down. They are all about control, and sometimes they go to dreadful lengths to maintain that control."

"Yes," said Karen. "I agree. They're very desperate, but they've done a lot of bad things all along. It's pretty clear they think that the end result—saving what's left of humanity—is worth the cost of the lives they sacrifice."

"Why us?" asked Gutsy. "Why people like the Santiagos and Cantus? Why Mama?"

Karen couldn't meet her eyes. "Because everyone they infected was either an illegal alien, or the child of one. In their eyes, you're not Americans."

"Which means we don't count?" yelled Gutsy. *"We're still people!"*

"Not to them," said Karen.

The silence that followed was profound.

Finally Karen said, "That's all I know. I have to get back to my daughter. The soldiers can't know I'm here." She started to rise.

"Where are the Rat Catchers?" asked Gutsy. "I need to find this Captain Collins and make her tell me the whole truth."

"She'll never talk to you," said Karen.

"I'll make her."

"We'll help," said Alethea, tapping her bat. Spider nodded, and even the Chess Players agreed.

"She still has to pay for what she did to my mother,"

insisted Gutsy. "So you need to tell me where to find the base."

"I don't know where it is. I know it's close, but I never went there and they're very careful about never giving a hint of where it is."

"What about the field lab?" asked Ford. "Do you know where that is?"

"Well . . . of course . . . ," said Karen.

"Then I'll start there," said Gutsy fiercely. "*Where is it?*"

Karen looked at her with evident surprise. "I thought you understood. . . ."

"Understood what?"

"This town . . ."

"What about it?"

"It's not a real town. It never has been."

"What do you mean?" demanded Gutsy. "What are you talking about?"

"This town was never a relocation center for illegal immigrants. Not really, or not entirely. Even before the End it was always a cover for something else." She looked at each face around the table. "This town *is* the lab. Everyone who lives here is a lab rat."

That rocked Gutsy.

It hit everyone. And yet . . . Gutsy could understand it now. It explained a lot about the strange rules and weird behavior.

"I don't understand," said Spider. "Does that mean the Rat Catchers live here?"

Karen shook her head. "Here? You think the handlers live in the same cage as their animals? They're at the base. Now, please let me go home to my daughter."

THEY SAT IN STUNNED SILENCE FOR A LONG TIME after Karen left.

Everyone erupted into chatter at once. The din filled the whole kitchen, but they soon realized they couldn't be heard and couldn't hear one another, so they lapsed once more into silence.

Mr. Urrea held up a hand. "Gutsy, it's your house. You go first."

She nodded and glanced down the hallway to the closed front door, as if she could still see Karen Peak. "I want to say this first," she began. "Karen could have told us a bunch of lies and—"

"And if she did, I'll knock her head off," promised Alethea.

But Gutsy shook her head. "No, that's not where I was going. Karen *could* have lied to us and done it pretty easily. She could have told us a lot less. She didn't. She told us a lot. Maybe everything she knew."

Alethea snorted. "Sure, and she could be marching right over to the town council. Or to rat us out to Captain Collins."

"I don't think so," said Gutsy.

"Nor do I," said Ford.

"Me neither," said Spider.

"Actually," added Urrea, "I think she was happy to unburden herself. Imagine how it must have felt to carry the weight of all that and have no one to tell."

"That's what I thought while she was talking," said Gutsy.

"Which means what?" asked Alethea. "Do we trust her now?"

Gutsy considered, but shook her head. "Not if anything we say or do puts Sarah in more danger. Other than that? Yes. I trust her."

She waited while the others thought about it. One by one they nodded. Alethea was last, and her nod was reluctant. "It's not that I don't trust her," she explained, "it's just that she might be forced into a spot where she has to pick Sarah or us. What do we do then? It's not like we can move to another town, because there isn't one."

It was an unfortunate truth.

"Okay," said Spider, "now that we know all this stuff—and it's a lot to swallow, I got to tell you—what do we do about it? I mean, I'd love to go find Captain Collins and kind of, y'know, beat her head in with a stick, but . . ."

"They have an army," said Ford. "We don't."

"This," said Urrea, "is the kind of conversation resistance groups have had since there have been corrupt regimes. So, like, forever. We know who the good guys are, we know who the bad guys are, but the odds are so unfair that any move we make could result in us being swatted. And I'd also like to point out that none of us have guns, and they have a lot of them."

Gutsy chewed on that, but before she could comment,

Ford spoke up. "Personally, as horrified and outraged as I am about what the scientists in the lab and these Rat Catcher soldiers are doing, I'm going out on a limb here and saying that I'm ten times more scared of this Night Army."

Alethea shook her head. "That's almost too big a problem to think about right now."

"I can't *stop* thinking about it," admitted Spider.

A lot of minutes crawled by without anyone saying much. Sombra went and stood by the back door, so Gutsy let him out, then cleaned up his mess. Back inside, she set down food and fresh water for him. All in thoughtful silence.

"Alethea's right," said Urrea.

"About what?" asked Spider.

"There isn't another town."

"Thank you, Mr. Wizard," said Ford. "Would you also like to suggest that water is wet and the sky is blue?"

"My point," said Urrea, "is that we are faced with a choice most resistance groups don't have. And that choice is no choice."

"Huh?" said Spider and Alethea.

"We have New Alamo or we have the Broken Lands. That's not an actual choice. There are no equal benefits to weigh. So, I suppose I should say that we don't have a choice of location. We have to stay here. The one choice we *do* have is whether we can risk taking action or not."

"Kind of already know that," said Gutsy, sitting down at the table again.

But Ford shook his head. "No, because even there the choices are limited. If we take no action, then—given that we are all living in the research lab—we will eventually become test subjects. Like Mama, like Diego and Maria Cantu, like Mirabelle Santiago, like all the others. Like the soldiers who 'volunteered.' If the scientists are willing to do that to their own soldiers, then what chance do we have of living full and rewarding lives?"

"None," said Gutsy.

"None," agreed Ford. "Which means the real choice is whether we accept the risk of rebellion."

"They could kill us all," said Spider, then shook his head. "No. They *will* kill us all. If we fight back, then maybe there's a chance they won't."

Clearly no one thought much of their chances.

"I agree with Spider," said Alethea. "Look, I don't have a lot of friends in town, but there are people I care about. People I don't want to see turned into lab rats." She cut a look at Gutsy. "I think we all have people we care about here." Gutsy knew Alethea was referring to Alice. They shared a private smile, but Spider caught it and gave a small nod.

"Look," said Gutsy, "the choices may be bad, but as Mr. Ford said, we don't really have any other ones to make. We die or we try."

Urrea nodded approval. "I'm glad you didn't say 'die or die trying.'"

"I don't intend to die," said Gutsy. "The situation's hopeless, but I'm not."

Everyone nodded this time.

"And," she said, "I think I even have a plan."

PART FOURTEEN

RIO GRANDE
UNITED STATES–MEXICAN BORDER
TWO DAYS EARLIER . . .

LOST ROADS

Be sure you put your feet

in the right place, then stand firm.

—ABRAHAM LINCOLN

IT WAS A CREATURE OUT OF NIGHTMARE.

Huge, immensely powerful, totally unnatural, infinitely deadly.

And dead.

It let out a roar that shattered the world around Benny. It was impossibly loud, and he screamed in pain at the assault on his ears. The gorilla pounded the dirt with two huge fists in a challenge that shook the ground. Its face was covered with long slashes and there were black holes on its chest. Bullet holes that hadn't found the right target. The ape's mouth and hands were smeared with blood, but Benny didn't think it was the monster who bled. It had just come from a fight, or a kill.

That thought darted through his head in a microsecond, because everything was in furious motion. The gorilla flung himself at Benny.

Benny backpedaled and swung his sword, but fear robbed him of precision and balance. The tip of the sword drew a line across the creature's chest but did not bite deep enough to do any real harm; and Benny's left heel caught on a tree root. Suddenly he was falling, and in a surreal moment of clarity he saw the ape go hurtling over him. The ground punched Benny in the back and the shock twitched his hand open. The *katana* went flying.

He fought to turn, to get back to his knees, but his body was spasming, his lungs trying to draw breath.

The ape struck Morgie and bore him to the ground, teeth darting forward for a deadly bite; but Lilah thrust her spear into the creature's side at the same instant Riot fired a ball bearing from her slingshot. Both weapons struck home; neither stopped the enormous beast. The ape had to be four hundred pounds, and most of that weight was in its massive arms and shoulders. Morgie screamed in pain and tried to fight, but he was helpless.

The ape howled again and then an arrow struck its head.

And bounced off the dense skull.

Even so, the gorilla wheeled around and ran at the archer. Chong scrambled to fit another arrow onto the string. There was no time at all, and he shrieked and flung himself out of the way, holding the arrow but losing the bow. The ape landed hard, rolled, and came right up again, lunging now for the nearest victim: Nix.

She had not drawn her ancient Japanese sword, *Dojigiri*, but instead stood in a wide-legged stance with her automatic pistol held in a two-handed shooter's grip. The ape howled.

She fired.

Once, twice. Again. All in the time it took Benny to close his hand around his fallen sword.

The first bullet struck the ape in the cheekbone. The second hit it in the center of its upper lip. The third punched a small black hole in the steep shelf of brow above its nose. The loads in the bullets she and Lilah used were not heavy, not intended for maximum stopping power. They were lighter loads that would prevent the bullet from exiting the skull. Any skull. Instead the round would be trapped inside the frame of the skull and bounce around until all the force was expended. The effect was to plow holes haphazardly through the soft, vulnerable brain.

Joe Ledger had taught them that. He said it was a trick used by assassins. Low caliber, maximum internal damage.

The ape did not stagger, did not roar.

It simply lost all motor function and all nerve conduction. It was a slack corpse before it flopped to the ground.

The six of them stood where they were, caught in postures of combat or flight, or lay as they had fallen. Staring at the nightmare creature they had just fought.

RIOT CAME OVER TO MORGIE AND LOOKED DOWN AT him. "You alive?"

He said, "Ughh."

She pulled him roughly to his feet. Morgie stood swaying, clearly in pain. She checked him over for bites, found none, and then gave him a harsh two-handed push.

"Hey!" yelped Morgie. "What was that for?"

"For moving slower than cold dirt."

"I didn't have a chance," he protested. "Did you see how fast that thing was?"

"Sure," said Riot, "but you're still slower than molasses in January. Could have got your dumb self chomped by a dead ape, which means you ain't even as *smart* as a dead ape." She turned away, no trace of good humor on her stern face. Morgie looked at her, and Benny could see that there was more hurt in his eyes than in his body. The cracks in the relationship between Morgie and Riot were getting deeper.

"Was anyone bit?" Nix asked.

"No," said Benny, "but for the record, I will never sleep again."

They gathered in a circle around the dead thing.

"Zombie silverback gorilla," mused Chong. "Well, that's something you just don't see every day."

"Don't want to see one again," said Nix with a shiver. She glanced around as if expecting the trees to be full of them.

Lilah knelt and touched it, prodding the skin, poking into the muscles. "Hasn't been dead long," she pronounced. "Day. Maybe two."

"How'd it turn?" asked Morgie. "I thought it was only wild pigs."

"You heard the same rumors we've been hearing, Morg," said Benny.

"Sure, but I didn't believe any of them."

"Believe them now, genius?" said Riot. Morgie colored but said nothing.

The woods were very thick, the morning mist still masking what was around them. Chong turned away and squinted through the fog. "You know, guys, we kind of should have seen this coming."

"How could we *possibly* expect a zombie gorilla?" asked Benny.

"Not that specifically," replied Chong, "but something weird. I mean, think about it. Tom was the first one who warned us about thinking we know what's out here. I remember his exact words. He said, 'People in town refer to everything beyond the fence line as the great Rot and Ruin. We assume that it's all nothing but a wasteland from our fence all the way to the Atlantic Ocean three thousand miles away.' He said we can't know for sure about anything."

"Asheville's in the east," said Morgie.

"Sure, but think about what we know of Asheville. They

turned it into a kind of kingdom. They protected thousands of acres of farmland and everyone pretty much lives inside the city. You've met plenty of soldiers and tech staff from there, Morgie. Can you remember any of them saying what was happening in Virginia, or Pennsylvania, or Maryland? No, because they've been so busy trying to create a safe place in Asheville that no one's gone looking."

"They would have told us if there were other zom animals. . . ."

"Would they? I mean, sure, if they knew, but America is huge. Something like four million square miles. All of Asheville, including all the farmland, is like sixty square miles. They don't drive out here like we're doing. They use helicopters."

"They'd have seen something like this from the air."

"Really? With all the helicopters and planes they have, how come they didn't know about the Night Church and the reaper army? I mean, okay, Captain Ledger knew some, but even he had no idea how big their army was . . . and that was an army. Some zombie animals wouldn't be even a blip to them."

"You have a point to all this or are you just talkin' to hear yourself talk?" asked Riot irritably.

"I do," said Chong. He pointed into the mist. "We don't know *anything* about what's out there. We don't know if there are more animals like this. We don't know if there's maybe a whole other place like Asheville, maybe in New England or Montana, or Canada. All that radiation we saw, and the toxic chemical spill? You saw what it was doing to the plants. Put that in the same pot with the fact that we know for sure the scientists were experimenting with mutagens, and then tell me if there isn't a real chance that a zombie gorilla isn't the worst thing we might see. Remember those lions in Nevada last year? Or the rhino in California? What if they turned zom? Maybe it wasn't zoms who overran Asheville. Maybe it's something we don't even know about yet."

"Okay, so now we're scared," said Nix. "So what? We were scared before."

"Maybe," said Chong, "we haven't been scared enough. The world here is different than where we came from and I, for one, don't want to make the mistake of *assuming* I know what's what. There could be things out here we're not ready to face."

And as if in answer to his words, a scream slashed through the mist, rising high into a shriek of unbearable agony.

It was a human scream.

DESPITE THE NEED, THE HUMANITY, AND THE URGENCY
of the scream, they did not immediately go running into the
forest. The mist was like a wall, and Chong's words of warning
had not been erased by the cry. The infected gorilla was still
there, a reminder even in death.

"Where is it?" whispered Morgie, turning first one way
and then another. He had his *bokken* in his strong hands.

"There," said Nix, pointing to their left.

"No," said Lilah, looking straight ahead. "There."

That direction was where the gorilla had come from.
Benny glanced down at the blood on its fangs and hands.
Nix and Riot did too, and their eyes met as understanding
flooded in.

"That thing attacked someone else before it came after
us," he said.

Lilah shook her head. "Or it has a mate who is hunting
someone else."

"Crap," said Morgie.

There was another scream, and this time it wasn't a word-
less howl but a definite plea in a man's desperate voice. "Oh
God . . . *help me . . .*"

Benny was moving before it finished.

"Wait!" cried Morgie, but Nix and Lilah plunged into the mist right behind Benny. Chong drew a breath, fitted an arrow, and followed. When Morgie turned to appeal to Riot, she was gone. He hadn't seen her fade into the fog. Morgie lingered for a moment longer. "We're all going to die out here," he said, repeating what he'd said before they left Mountainside. This time they felt less like a complaint to his ears and far more like a prophecy.

Even so, he gripped his wooden sword and followed.

Up ahead, Benny moved as quickly as he could through the mist, but it was like running through a dream. The screams rose and fell, and the fog distorted them, making some cries sound like they came from right where he was, while others seemed far away and in a totally different direction.

Lilah caught up and passed him, and he let her lead, trusting her judgment far more than his own. Nix touched Benny's shoulder to let him know she was beside him, and they moved together.

"Please, God . . . help me . . . oh God . . ."

The cries were continuous now, and Benny was certain they were getting closer to the source. The fog was thinning too, the farther they were from the stream. He could see trees taking shape as more than rumors, and their solidity steadied his feet and his mind. Some, though; not entirely.

Chong's words echoed in his mind. *Maybe we haven't been scared enough. There could be things out here we're not ready to face.*

"Thanks a bunch," Benny grumbled.

"Here!" called Lilah, and a split second later he heard her scream too.

"Lilah!" bellowed Chong as he appeared out of nowhere and pushed between Benny and Nix before vanishing into the mist ahead.

"Wait," cried Benny, but then he broke into a run. Nix was faster in a fight but Benny could outrun her, and he did so now, leaping a fallen log and plunging into a dense stand of vine-covered pine trees. The ground sloped sharply away and he fell three feet down a decline, skidded on moss, caught his balance and outran his own momentum so that he emerged into a clearing in a fast run.

He ran straight into the center of a bloody battle. Not with another gorilla, nor with any other infected animal. She was fighting three big *men* . . . and with a shock Benny realized that these were the same kind of men he'd seen herding the swarms of zoms. All leather, spiked gloves, and chains. One held a big logging ax, another had a pitchfork, but the third clamped the stump of his right wrist as blood shot from it with fire-hose force. His hand, finger still hooked through the trigger guard of an automatic pistol, lay on the ground at Lilah's feet, and there was fresh blood on her spear. Behind her, sprawled on the ground, was a fourth man who was covered in terrible bleeding wounds. He was different from the brutal attackers; dressed like a soldier, in forest-pattern camouflage and a military equipment belt.

The closest of the three attackers spun toward Chong and swung his ax, but Chong went into a sliding skid beneath the swing and fired his arrow while still in motion. The arrow struck the man in the shoulder, but the brute plucked it out of the thick leather without even a wince. He raised his ax for a downward killing blow.

Benny leaped into the air and slashed at him with a blow so furious and powerful that it cut the attacker nearly in half. Blood splashed the trees.

That left the wounded man and the one with the pitchfork. Nix shot the second man in the chest twice. A double-tap that knocked him back against a tree. He winced in pain, but then laughed and rushed at her.

It was so weird, so unexpected, so impossible that Nix froze for a second.

"He's . . . *he's a zom!*" cried Chong.

Benny pivoted and back-kicked the man in the ribs, knocking him sideways against another tree, and Lilah spun and stabbed him in the stomach.

The killer froze, his pitchfork falling with a thud, impaled on the heavy blade. But not dead. He grinned with bloody teeth and with a savage growl tore the spear from Lilah's hands. He tore the blade from his stomach, spun the spear in his hands as if he was familiar with such weapons, and rushed at Nix.

She shot him three more times. Twice in the chest, which did no good at all. Her third bullet, however, punched through the bridge of his nose, and he went down all at once into a sloppy, boneless sprawl.

That left the third attacker. He bled from the stump, but with his remaining hand he pulled a knife from a thigh sheath and tried to stab Lilah in the back. Then Morgie and Riot were there, closing in on him from two sides. Riot hit him in the throat with a ball bearing from her slingshot, and Morgie smashed him across the temple with the bokken. The man staggered, fought to remain on his feet, kept trying to stab.

Morgie hit him again. And again.

And again.

What was left of the man fell.

Benny started to rush over to the injured man these three killers had been attacking when something clamped around his ankle. He looked down in abject horror to see that the man he'd cut in two had an iron grip on Benny's ankle. Blood swirled around the man, and Benny could see that it was both red and black, but the two colors were not mixing, as if the human blood would not tolerate joining with the oily black blood.

It sent icy needles through Benny, because he had seen this before.

This was how the R3 zombies bled. The ones who were smarter, faster, more dangerous.

But these men had used weapons. They were dressed like fighters, like members of a gang. Even the R3's were not that sophisticated. What, then, was this?

Benny raised his sword and swept the blade down. The neck and the brain stem parted and the man's hand twitched once and then relaxed.

Morgie stared at the fallen man. "Is he . . . I mean . . . what . . . ?"

"He's an R3," said Nix, her voice hushed.

"No," said Benny, "he's something worse than that."

A GROAN MADE THEM ALL TURN, AND THEY HURRIED over to the injured soldier. It was easy to see that he was horribly injured. Dying.

"Morgie, Riot, stand watch," said Benny as he knelt beside the man.

He, Lilah, Nix, and Chong did their best with strips of cloth to stanch the bleeding wounds, but they all knew it was hopeless. There were knife wounds all over the man's body, but there were also bite marks. Human teeth. The man's eyes were filled with pain, but he blinked them as clear as he could and looked up at the faces around him.

"You're . . . you're a bunch of . . . *kids* . . . ?" he gasped, struggling to talk. "Who are you? Are you from town?"

"Town?" asked Nix. "What town?"

The man seemed confused by the question. "There's only one town. The settlements, the camps . . . they're all gone. There's only . . . New Alamo."

"New Alamo?" echoed Nix. "Wasn't everyone at the old Alamo killed in a war?"

"Look, mister, we're not from here," Benny said gently. "We're just traveling through."

The confusion lingered. "Traveling from where? *To* where?"

Benny glanced at Nix, who shrugged and then nodded. "We live in central California," said Benny.

The man gave a weak shake of his head. "No way. California's gone. They nuked it and that set off earthquakes. It fell into the sea."

"No," said Chong, "that's not true. They dropped bombs on some of the cities—Los Angeles, San Diego, San Francisco, a few other places—but it didn't cause earthquakes, as far as I know. We live in the mountains in Mariposa County, in the Sierra Nevadas."

"There's nowhere else," mumbled the soldier. "We killed the world. All that's left is New Alamo."

"Listen to me," said Benny, leaning close. "You're wrong. There are nine towns in California. Thirty thousand people. And a lot more in Asheville, in North Carolina. There's even a government. We're coming back. The world's coming back."

Blood ran like tears from the man's lacerated face. "I heard those stories," he wheezed. "About Asheville. It's not true. There's nothing there but the dead."

"We're heading there now," said Benny, choosing not to tell him about the fact that the capital of the American Nation might be as dead as this man thought it was. "But first, where's this New Alamo town? We'll take you there. Do they have doctors there?"

The man laughed. Actually laughed. "Doctors? Yeah, kid . . . they have lots of doctors." His laugh turned into a coughing fit that left his lips flecked with fresh blood.

"Who are these men?" asked Lilah gruffly. "They're zoms or half-zoms?"

"I . . . don't know what that means," gasped the man. His voice was fading and the glaze was returning to his eyes. "They're ravagers. They're . . . infected. These three . . . they were part of a pack of five. Scouting party. I . . . got one. Infected gorilla got another."

"We met the gorilla," said Chong. "It's dead."

The man blinked in surprise, then attempted a smile. "Tough kids."

"Tough times," said Benny.

"Tougher than you know," said the man.

"Why did these men hurt you?" prompted Nix. "You said these ravagers were scouts? Scouts for who?"

"For the . . . Night Army . . ."

"What's that?" asked Chong.

The man was weakening, fading, but he managed to tell them a horror story. At first Benny thought he was raving and delirious, but the more the man spoke, the more convinced Benny became of the reality of an army of infected killers backed by hordes of shamblers—which Benny took to mean the R1 zoms. He said that there was a man who was able to control all the dead. The soldier called him the Raggedy Man, but Benny was half-sure the guy was losing it, becoming delirious.

Then the soldier coughed again and this time the fit did not seem to want to end. He convulsed and thrashed and vomited blood onto the grass, then settled back, eyes glassy and skin gone yellow-gray. "Please," he said in a faint whisper, "the ravager scouts wanted to know the hidden way . . . in. To the base, I mean. There are tunnels. Tunnels into town, too. If the ravagers find the tunnels and the weapons, everyone is going to die. My friends at the base . . . the doctors . . . everyone in New Alamo."

Another coughing fit, worse than the others. Terrible to see. He was weeping when it was over.

"Please . . . you need . . . to warn them. The town. The council. They think help . . . will come." He shook his head. "They don't know what's really coming. Please, don't waste time . . . on me. I'm no good. I'm nothing. I'm a Rat Catcher. I was *part* . . . of it. I know I'm going . . . to hell."

"No, don't say that," soothed Nix, but the man gave a single violent shake of his head.

"It's funny," said the soldier bitterly, "but we believed them. The doctors. The captain. We believed every lie. They told us we were trying to save the world. They lied. *We* . . . lied." His hand caught Benny's wrist with surprising strength. "The people . . . the people in town. Please . . . tell them to run . . . while they still can. No help is coming. The only chance they have is to run. Maybe it's no chance at all. But . . . it's all they have. Tell them the Night Army is coming. . . ."

"We'll tell them," promised Benny. "Where's the town?"

"Close," he said, and his voice was noticeably weaker now. "Go straight northeast from here, you can't miss it. Big walls made from stacked cars. The Night . . . Army may already . . . be there. But listen," he wheezed, "there's a . . . way . . . in."

Benny bent closer still. "Tell me."

The man spoke for as long as he could and Benny listened. Nix and Chong leaned in, but they could not hear anything. And then Benny couldn't hear anything else. He straightened and looked down at the soldier, and saw that he was gone. Benny sighed and quieted the man.

The four of them got to their feet and told Morgie and Riot everything.

"What do we do now?" asked Nix.

"It's not our problem," said Morgie. "It's not our town. If there's an army out there, we have to get away from here right now."

"How can we just *go*?" demanded Chong.

"How can we stay?" Morgie countered. "If we do this, we might never get to Asheville. Come on, Chong, you of all people have to see that. You're going to run out of pills if we don't keep moving."

Lilah turned to Chong. "He's right. We have to go."

"Kind of agree," said Riot. "We don't have a dog in this fight."

Chong walked a few feet away and stopped, his hands pressed to the sides of his head as if keeping it from cracking open.

Benny leaned close to the others and spoke in an urgent whisper. "We can't go to Asheville. Not now. Not after what he said."

"We have to," snarled Lilah, her voice lowered but intense. "Chong can't risk it."

"Look, this isn't only about Chong," said Benny, and before Lilah could say anything, or possibly stab him, he continued. "It's not about any of us, or even all of us. This is a whole town full of people. We have to at least warn them. We can't just let them die."

"You don't even know if that man was telling the truth," said Nix with quiet ferocity.

"Come on," said Benny, "you think he was going to use his last breath to mess with us?"

"He said he was a bad guy, Benny. He admitted that he lied to people. He could have been lying to us. Or maybe he was just out of his mind."

Benny shook his head. "I can't take that chance."

"Why not?" she demanded.

"Because he has a soul," said Chong. They all looked at him. He turned slowly to face them. "You guys can't whisper worth crap."

"Chong, I—" began Nix, but he shook his head.

"Let me talk," he said. "Morgie, Riot . . . you're right. Lilah? You're right. This isn't our problem. This isn't our fight. We don't know these people and we have other responsibilities."

"That's what I mean," began Morgie, but again Chong shook his head.

"I'm infected and, yeah, I really want those pills." He smiled. "We all know that even with those pills I'm not going to live as long as you guys. Doc McReady said I could have ten or twenty good years. Okay. So, maybe I'll make it to my fortieth birthday. Maybe I won't. You always joke about how I'm half-dead already, Morg. You're not wrong. But listen to me, okay? Asheville is a long way from here. From what that man said, this New Alamo place is about an hour away by quad. If we turn and sneak off, then that defines who we are."

"The people in Asheville need us too," said Riot.

Chong frowned. "Do they? I mean, really—what can six of us do if Asheville is overrun? Other than sneak in, get my pills, and sneak out again, what are we really hoping to do? We never found Captain Ledger. We probably won't. We've nearly died a bunch of times already. One of these times we *will* die. You know it as well as I do."

No one spoke.

Chong nodded. "So, given a choice between going on a possibly suicidal and definitely selfish trip to Asheville or taking a chance of helping a whole town full of people who are still alive, then is that really a choice? That man gave us information those people need to know. I can't speak for anyone else, and I'm not going to ask any of you to go with me, but I am taking my quad and going to find New Alamo."

"What if it's overrun?" asked Riot.

"Then it's overrun. If we can get away, we will. But what if it's not *yet* overrun?"

"What if we get stuck there when this Night Army attacks?" asked Morgie.

"We have all the weapons we took from the prison," said Benny.

"Don't forget my li'l ol' slingshot," said Riot with a sour grin.

Morgie did not return her smile. "All we'd be is casualties."

"No," said Nix. She walked over to stand beside Chong. "When we found out the Night Church was taking an entire army to the Nine Towns, there were only five of us, and look what happened."

Morgie's fists were balled at his sides. "This is different."

"I don't know," said Riot. "Night Church, Night Army. Kind of has a theme. Feels like old times."

"What are you saying?" demanded Morgie. "Don't tell me you're thinking of doing this too."

"Morgie," she said, "I'm getting tired of always talking you into doing the right thing. I mean, I love ya and all, but you are a lot of hard work."

She went and stood with Nix.

Lilah bent and picked up her spear. "If my town boy wants to fight, then I'm going to fight with him."

Morgie turned pleading eyes to Benny. "Come on, man . . . you always act like you got elected leader of our gang. Maybe you can talk some sense into them."

Benny walked over to him and clapped Morgie on the shoulder. "I was on his side before he even said anything." He joined the others.

Morgie stood his ground.

"Face it, sweet cheeks," said Riot, "you know you're going to cave. You always do. You always know we're right."

Morgie slid the bokken through his belt, then bent and picked up the dead killer's timber ax and straightened, laying it over his shoulder. The others were grinning.

"No," he said.

They stared at him, and Riot wore a half smile, waiting for him to deliver the punch line to the joke. Morgie's face was stone.

"I love you, Riot," he said. "I love all of you, but you're wrong about this."

"What are you saying?" asked Riot, her smile crumbling.

"I'm saying you guys go do what you think you have to do," said Morgie. "I love you guys for wanting to do this, but it's the wrong call. There's a town here, sure, but the whole American Nation is back east. So, you do what you got to do, but I'm going to Asheville."

With that he turned and walked away, vanishing into the mist. They stood staring in disbelief. Riot took a couple of quick steps after him, stopped, looked back, and seemed caught between two terrible choices.

"It's okay," said Chong. "Go with him."

She lingered a moment longer. "I . . ."

That was all she said, and then she whirled and, light as a dancer, melted into the mist. After a long, silent minute they heard the sounds of two quads roaring to life. They turned to follow the noise as the machines moved away and slowly, slowly faded to silence.

"Oh my God," murmured Nix.

Lilah grabbed Chong, spun him toward her, and kissed him very hard on the lips, then shook him hard enough to rattle his teeth. "You're not allowed to die," she snarled. "Now or ever. If you get killed, so help me I'll . . . I'll wait for you to reanimate and then I'll beat you to death."

She shoved him back and stalked toward the quads. Nix ran to catch up.

Chong stared after Lilah in total confusion. Benny clapped his friend hard on the shoulder.

"That was pure poetry," he said. "Ought to make a love song out of it."

They walked over to catch up with the girls. Two minutes later the four quads burst out of the misty forest and turned northeast, following a dead man's directions to a doomed town.

Interlude Seven

KICKAPOO CAVERN STATE PARK
THREE DAYS AGO

THEY DID NOT LEAVE SAM'S CAMP THE NEXT morning. Or the morning after that, or for most of the week.

The wound to Ledger's leg was not bad, but the infection that set in was. A fever ignited midway through the first night, and by noon of the following day Ledger was sweaty and shivering. Sam made soups and teas concocted from herbs he picked. The first concern was Joe's fever, but he knew better than to try to reduce it. A fever is part of the body's natural way of fighting illness or infection, so reducing the fever could make the illness last longer. It could also let the causes of the illness live longer in the body. Sam's small store of pharmaceuticals were to be used with caution, he knew, because even something like Advil or Tylenol were foreign substances that needed to be metabolized and filtered by the body, and that took energy and resources better left to the job of fighting the sickness. On the other hand, Joe was suffering. So a choice was often a gamble. Sam got some low-dose anti-inflammatory painkillers into him, which helped with aches but did not reduce the fever too much.

His main approach to helping Joe was to keep feeding him fluids, whether the cranky old soldier wanted them or not.

Dehydration was dangerous; and besides, the fluids helped the body flush the illness: water, herbal teas like chamomile, peppermint, or catnip. They helped considerably.

Sam fished among his precious fruits and vegetables, found the last of his elderberries, and made them into a syrup to boost the immune system. The recipe was simple, but he had to go out several times to search for the right herbs, leaves, and tree bark. Sam knew his forest, so the process was time-consuming but not actually difficult. Grimm sat silent vigil over Ledger throughout, but now even *his* muscular body was crisscrossed with bandages.

In the evening Sam used coconut and fruit to make a kind of rough smoothie. It was ugly to look at and tasted horrible, but it had excellent antibacterial and antiviral properties. In the morning of the fourth day, as Ledger was coming out of it, Sam plied him with peppermint tea to soothe his aching and atrophied muscles.

Every night, when both were feeling well enough, they talked. Ledger talked about Asheville, about a town in Nevada called Sanctuary—long since lost to the dead—that had been a kind of hospice run by monks and nuns, and about the Nine Towns of central California. He told Sam everything about Tom, and about Benny, and the new samurai. He told him about the new version of the ancient samurai code of Bushido, the ethics of those ancient warriors. Tom's modern version was the Warrior Smart program, and like Bushido, the warrior's code never actually mentioned warfare. Warrior Smart was about kindness and cooperation, honesty and loyalty, optimism and judgment.

Sam liked to hear about these things, and he felt his own

fears melt away only to be replaced by a new dread. The Night Army was still out there. New Alamo was still under threat. And Joe's mission to Asheville was still in force, even though all communications were gone.

One evening Sam said, "I think I've worked out where the bigger weapons cache might be."

"How?" asked Ledger.

"I have some old maps from before," said Sam. "I marked them up over the years, putting in any military bases or installations that I knew about, or found, or heard about. And . . . well . . . I've *talked* to a few people here and there. People who came onto my land. Some of them were soldiers."

"You 'talked' to them?" said Ledger. "Meaning what, exactly?"

Sam's face was as expressionless as a mask. "Meaning they were on my land and some of them tried to take food and supplies from me. I didn't let them. Some of them were very willing to talk."

Ledger stared at him. There were so many ugly things unsaid but implied. After a moment Sam looked down at his hands. "It's been hard out here, Joe. Old rules don't apply."

Ledger said nothing.

Sam said, "If the cache is where I think it is, then we need to go past New Alamo. I can leave you there, if you want, and—"

"No," insisted Ledger, "if we're hunting for the weapons cache, then we do it together."

"Okay," said Sam dubiously. "But it's two hundred miles and you're hurt. Besides, that's a strange area. You have New Alamo, the biological warfare base, and the weapons cache all within a few miles of each other. From the people I've talked to, though, the soldiers keep a low profile. I don't think the people in town even know they're there."

Ledger frowned. "That's weird. Why would the soldiers not be right there to help the people?"

"I don't know."

"Doesn't sound right to me."

"No," agreed Sam. "And I know how you like to poke your nose into things."

Ledger spread his hands. "Born with a curious mind. Sue me. But seriously, what's the play? If we find the weapons, do we warn the base first or warn the town?"

"I don't know," admitted Sam. "I think we'll have to get closer and make the call then. But . . . it's a long way from here."

Ledger slowly flexed his leg. "I think I can walk on it."

"You won't need to," said Sam. "I have something else in mind."

PART FIFTEEN

SOUTH TEXAS
LAST DAY OF AUGUST

NIGHT RUNNERS

Night hath a thousand eyes.

—JOHN LYLY

GUTSY SAT AT THE EMPTY KITCHEN TABLE. SOMBRA sat with his head on her thigh, eyes closed as she scratched his neck.

Night had fallen, but Gutsy didn't think Captain Collins and her Rat Catchers would come for her this early. Urrea and Ford both urged her to sleep in their guest rooms, and Alethea said she could sneak Gutsy into the Cuddlys' place. Gutsy thanked them and said no.

"I'll take my bedroll and bed down in the school library," she said. "I doubt the soldiers will look for me there." None of them liked it, but she could not be budged. Spider and Alethea had left minutes after the Chess Players. Each of them had gone home, with a loose agreement to meet again tomorrow to decide what to do.

Now the house was quiet as a tomb, as still as death, as cold as her own heart. The weight of everything was too much. The Night Army. The Raggedy Man. The lab and the base. All of it. Too much to bear, and Gutsy felt like she was cracking and crumbling beneath it.

They are still connected to all five senses. They hear, smell, taste, feel, and see everything, but they are unable to exert any control over the physical body.

That was what Karen had said. It had been hard to hear at the time, but there was so much coming at her that the edge of it was blunted. Now, here, in the absolute, unbearable quiet of her empty house, the truth of it cut her and left her to bleed.

"Mama . . . ," she breathed.

She almost couldn't bear to close her eyes for fear of being back in her bedroom, with Mama lumbering toward her, clawing at her with dead hands, snapping at her. Gutsy had looked into those empty eyes and seen nothing.

Or had she?

Had there been the tiniest flicker?

Was that Mama in there, screaming for her daughter to run? To fight? To forgive her? To release her?

Gutsy suddenly caved forward, clutching her stomach as if actually stabbed. Was that Mama in there? Screaming? Terrified? Aware that she was dead? Feeling herself begin to decompose?

Oh God.

Please, don't let that be true.

Karen said it, though. The Rat Catchers and the doctors believed it. Sending Mama back had been part of an experiment of some obscene kind.

Before they left, Spider and Alethea had clung to her, weeping, trying to tell her that it wasn't true. Alethea could usually tell a good lie, but not tonight. Spider was never able to manage it. So Gutsy had to comfort them, help them lift their own pain and carry it out of the house.

Everyone was gone now but Gutsy and the coydog. No one had been able to suggest a plan. Mr. Ford said that they needed time to digest, to consider.

Sure. Whatever. She was glad they'd left.

And yet the house was so empty without them. The windup clock on the wall sounded wrong and Gutsy glanced at it, seeing the second hand tick, pause, tick, tremble, stop. She knew that it was only because she hadn't wound the spring, but it felt like a message. It was the universe telling her that there was no time left. Or, maybe, that her own time had run out. That wasn't exactly the same thing, but maybe both things were happening at the same time.

Gutsy looked slowly around the kitchen, down the hall, out through the window into the yard. This was the only place she had ever lived; it was home. Her home. Mama's home.

Past tense.

"Mama," begged Gutsy as she slid from her chair onto the floor, "help me."

But Mama was gone and Gutsy could not smell her, feel her, sense her. She couldn't even sense her own energy here. It made the house feel like those old dead batteries in all those rusting cars. Empty.

As useless as a stopped clock.

"A HORSE?" SAID LEDGER, STARING AT THE HUGE animal that stood in front of the cabin. It was as battle-scarred as the dog and the two soldiers, but it tossed its head and gave a healthy whinny.

"Peaches is a good girl," said Sam.

Ledger laughed. "Peaches? You want us to go riding into battle on a horse named Peaches?"

"I didn't name her."

"Who did?"

"The teenage girl who used to own her."

Ledger met his eyes but did not ask the obvious question. If the horse was here and the teenage girl was not, then the answer was equally obvious.

"I put out feed for her, but mostly I let her run wild. She always comes when I call, though." He cut a look at Ledger. "Can you ride?"

"After a fashion. I guess. Maybe. But what about you?"

"I'll run."

"You're nearly as old as I am and this New Alamo is *how* many miles away?"

Sam shrugged. "If you have a better plan, Joe, I'm all ears."

Ledger did not have a better plan. He studied the horse, who glared down at him with a rolling eye.

"I don't think she likes me."

Sam shrugged. "She's a good judge of character."

Grimm gave a deep *whuff*.

Ledger scowled and shot a harsh look at Grimm. "You can keep your opinions to yourself, fleabag."

It took some doing to get Ledger into the saddle, which was designed for a petite teenager and not a big man who was over six feet tall and better than two hundred pounds. Ledger squirmed around trying to find a comfortable position.

"There are parts of me that are going to hate this," he complained.

"Would you prefer I rig a new saddle out of fluffy pillows? And, do you want me to cut some leafy branches and fan you while I run?"

"Would you? That would be just swell."

Sam shook his head as he checked the straps and tugged the saddle blanket down to protect the horse. He created saddlebags out of two battered old backpacks connected by belts and slung them behind Joe. Water, food, and lots of ammunition. Then Sam trotted back inside and returned with two items that made Ledger whistle in appreciation.

One was Sam's military sniper rifle. Not his original one, but a top-quality gun picked up along the way. The other was a *katana* with a gleaming lacquered black scabbard, hand-carved fittings, and silk cord tied in decorative knots. Sam held the sword for a while, took a breath, and handed it to Ledger. The old soldier gave a small bow as he received it, and bent to examine the scabbard and the *tsuba*—the round hand guard—as well as the various "furniture," or fittings.

"This looks old," he said appreciatively. "Real old."

"It is old," said Sam, "and it's one of the best swords ever made. Work on it began in 1669, and it was finished in 1670 by Nagasone Kotetsu."

Ledger gaped at him. "He was one of the greatest sword makers of the samurai era."

"He was *the* greatest."

"How on earth did you get this?"

"Look at the inscription on the blade. You were always good with languages; can you still read it?"

Joe angled the blade so he could read the delicate words the sword maker had inscribed centuries before. He read them aloud, translating as he did so. "'To Ichiro Imura. May your family name endure.'" There was a signature and seal below it. "'Tokugawa Tsunayoshi, fifth shogun of the Tokugawa dynasty.'"

"It was presented to my ancestor," said Sam, "after a great battle."

"How do you even *have* this?"

"It was in my apartment in Baltimore," said Sam. "I got there a month after everything fell apart. It's the only thing I have left from my family. I've . . . used it since. Many, many times."

"I can't take this, Sam," protested Ledger. "Give me a rifle. You should keep this."

"It's not a gift, Joe," said Sam, "it's a loan. You told me that I have a brother—Benny. You told me he's been studying *kenjutsu*, that Tom was training him to be a samurai. You told me how he saved all those people from the Night Church.

Well . . . if one of us survives this, and whichever one survives, that sword needs to be given to Benny. It's his legacy. It has a name, *Atarashī Yoake*."

"New Dawn," murmured Joe. "Yeah, that fits. Or at least I hope it fits. But, man . . . I can't accept this."

"You're a samurai too, Joe," said Sam firmly. "You've been family to me and you've been family to Benny. You carry it for now. And, not to be corny, but I ask that you use it with honor."

Ledger smiled. "That is the least corny thing I've ever heard, brother."

They nodded to each other. Grimm barked loud enough to frighten the monkeys from the trees.

Ledger untied the silk cord, slung the ancient weapon across his broad back, and tied it firmly in place.

"Let's go hunting," he said.

Sam didn't answer. Instead he slapped Peaches on the rump and then ran to catch up with the bolting horse. Grimm barked again and gave chase.

LATER.

Much later, Gutsy thought back to what Mr. Urrea had said as he and Ford were leaving. He gave her a sad, concerned smile.

"Gutsy," he said quietly so that only she could hear, "I should probably be talking you out of doing anything about this."

"You can't," she said.

"I know. Even so, I feel like even discussing the possibility of doing anything is enabling questionable behavior. Your plan—if I can call it that—is dangerous and possibly even suicidal."

"I gave you all a chance to come up with a better one," she said.

"Not having a better one doesn't make this a good one."

"I'm going to do something," she said with a shrug. "Don't know what it is yet, but you can't talk me out of it."

"I know," he repeated, then sighed. "I would love to say that you're too young to be doing what you're going to do. And you are. But not really. War doesn't respect age. Children have died in war as victims and died as soldiers. I know you're fifteen and smart, and I know you're tougher than anyone I've ever known, but you are still so young. You should be allowed to grow up without knowing what horror is, or without seeing or causing bloodshed. That's what would happen in a fairy tale, but . . ."

"I read a lot of fairy tales, Mr. Urrea," she said. "The old ones, in the books you gave me. Children weren't safe in them, either. I don't think we kids were ever safe."

"You should be," said Urrea.

She patted his chest. "This is the real world, and I don't believe in happy endings."

Pain lanced through his eyes. "That is the saddest thing anyone has ever said to me."

He left, shaking his head, looking even older than his years. That was an hour ago. Since then Gutsy had worked through a lot of different ideas, refining the admittedly bad idea she'd presented to her friends, discarding other ideas one after another as unworkable, unsafe, unwise, or downright crazy. The one idea left in her mind was the craziest of all, but it persisted. She stood up. It was full dark outside, but there was a brilliant moon in the sky. Plenty to see by.

That was good. She could use that.

"I can't wait until tomorrow," she told Sombra. "I don't want to tell them, either. They'd try to stop me. Stop us."

Sombra wagged his tail.

Gutsy changed into her darkest pair of jeans, a black T-shirt, and a navy-blue vest. Black socks and sneakers, too. She filled the pockets with items from the rows of mason jars mounted floor to ceiling in her bedroom. Spools of wire, matches, water-purifying tablets, first aid stuff, small folding tools, and more. The bottom drawer of her dresser had dozens of different knives in it, ranging from boning knives for fishing to deadly fighting knives scavenged from long-dead soldiers. Gutsy strapped two different-size fighting knives to her belt and slipped a folding lock-knife into a pocket. She had no firearms and wasn't a fan of them anyway. Too noisy. In the end, she opted for a twelve-and-three-quarters-inch crowbar that weighed a little over a pound. Very tough, but light enough to swing fast. It was useful as a tool and a weapon. She slid it through her belt.

After patting herself down to double-check that she had everything she needed, Gutsy went to the kitchen, filled a canteen, and put that, along with some jerky and a bag of nuts, into a backpack, and padded them with a waterproof nylon poncho for warmth and in case it rained. The last thing she took was the field hockey stick from the umbrella stand. It was sturdy and dangerous.

Then she paused and looked down the hallway toward the closed door to Mama's old room. Empty now too. It would always be empty. Even in the unlikely event that Gutsy came back here, even if she used that room for something else— a workroom, maybe, or storage—it would always be Mama's room, and it would always be empty of her. The heartache, which simmered constantly beneath the surface, threatened to bubble up, and Gutsy almost stopped. And stayed. It was still possible.

Maybe.

That lie tugged at her, wanting her to believe it. Gutsy felt herself leaning toward it, needing to believe that everyone would be okay, that this was silly, that she could wish things back to the way they had been because accepting the truth was just too big.

But she shook her head. Even the most appealing lie can never be made real by wishing it so. That was how people broke themselves. Maybe Karen believed a lie because she had her daughter to think of. Maybe she *had* to. Maybe some of the town council believed they were doing what was best for everyone. That was the lie—or maybe warped truth was more accurate—the scientists in the lab told the soldiers. How many of them knew the real truth? How many of them believed the adjusted truth because it was the only way they could survive emotionally?

Did Mama know the truth and accept a lie in order to protect Gutsy?

The memory of her words came back harder than ever. Mama *had* known something. How much she'd known was uncertain, but Gutsy had to accept the truth that Mama knew about the Rat Catchers. It made her feel sorry for how she'd treated Karen. How many mothers—and fathers—in New Alamo knew the truth and lived a lie in order to keep their children safe?

Even the Chess Players had known something was going on.

Everyone seemed to know something except her. No . . . except the kids. The little ones and the teenagers like her and her friends. Was that how it always was? Did parents hide harsh truths from their children and in doing so accept injuries and shackles and pain? Gutsy thought back to the things she'd learned in history classes. People living in fear, living in war-torn countries. How, after all, had parents felt during the Second World War and the Vietnam War all those years ago, knowing that when their sons came of age the draft would be waiting to whisk them away? What lies had Jewish mothers been forced to tell their children while boarding the trains to the death camps? How had Mama's parents rocked her to sleep when she was little, knowing that at any minute immigration police could kick their door in and send them back to poverty and starvation?

How?

How was any of it possible? How could anyone bear it?

Gutsy thought about what she would do if she ever became a mother herself. The world was a horror show. If she held a child in her arms while dead hands beat on the door, what lies would she be willing to tell to make it all okay?

It wasn't fair. It wasn't right.

"It's the way it is," she said out loud. Her voice sounded loud and hollow and false in the empty house. And even though those words were true, she realized she'd said them to convince herself of a lie. That lie was so subtle, so tricky. By saying that things were the way they were, by trying to stand on solid logical ground, Gutsy was trying to build a case for herself—Miss Practical—to be able to deal with whatever.

Lies were sneaky like that.

Sombra whined softly, needing comfort. Like a child who did not know the truth. And yet as Gutsy knelt to pet him, she felt the scars of tooth and whip. Sombra knew. But, like her, he didn't want to know. Not really.

Not unless he could actually, truly do something about it.

"I don't think we're ever coming back here," said Gutsy to the house. Sombra opened his eyes and looked up at her.

She bent and kissed him and he licked her nose. It made her laugh, but the laugh was thin and fragile and the empty room drained it away.

Gutsy wasn't taking Gordo and the wagon, so that would simplify things. She knew a dozen sneaky ways to get through the walls, and at least three of those would work for Sombra as well.

Fine.

"Come on, boy," she said, and Sombra trotted over. "Let's go hunting."

The dog wagged his tail.

Gutsy and Sombra went out of the house by the back door, took a cautious route through back alleys to the stables, and slipped inside unseen. It was dark in there and she had to search by feel, but there in the back of the wagon was the leather collar she'd removed from Sombra. She held the collar out to Sombra, who was nearly invisible in the darkness.

"Find them," said Gutsy.

Sombra's response was a low growl of nasty intent. His tail wagged with excitement.

Gutsy and the coydog left the barn and ghosted their way to Cargo Town, slipped through one of the hidden exits, and were gone into the Broken Lands.

77

ALETHEA STOOD IN HER DARKENED BEDROOM, with Spider beside her, looking out at the moonlight. The view from the third-story room looked out over street upon street of the single-story residences that were identical to where Gutsy lived. Beyond those was the high, lumpy expanse of the wall. Spider had once counted all the 16,911 cars used to build the wall. In its way, that wall was one of the most incredible feats of engineering in human history. No mechanized cranes. It had been built by ingenuity and sheer brute strength, by careful planning and genuine cooperation.

Since the completion of the wall, a handful of guards had been able to protect the town against the shamblers, mutated variations, and even some wild animals. It had withstood every attack, and the people in town had always felt safe.

Until now.

The two foster siblings, unable to sleep, had gotten together to talk in hushed voices about what they'd learned from Karen Peak. Now the wall did not seem to be as reliable.

How could it be, when the real monsters were here in town?

Here in the lab.

Without knowing he was doing it, Spider reached for Alethea's hand in the dark. They held on to each other for dear life.

78

SOMBRA RAN THROUGH SHADOWS AND GUTSY
followed.

The moon was huge and white and colored the world
in shades of icy paleness. It was so bright that it seemed to
extinguish most of the stars in the sky. Sombra ran without
pause, moving in a straight line except to avoid rocks or old
wreckage. It wasn't exactly like watching a dog follow a trail;
she didn't have to let him smell the collar again. It was more
like Sombra understood what she wanted of him and was
eerily focused on that goal.

Strange dog, she thought as she ran. She realized that she
loved the scruffy mutt. Quite a lot. That realization threw a
little more gasoline on the fires of her hate.

Gutsy was used to running, and so the miles melted away.
Time held no more meaning out here than it did back in her
kitchen. It was as if this was the last day of her life, maybe the
last day of the world as she knew it. There was only the timelessness of night and whatever lay at the end of her chase.

How long did it take to find the base?

An hour and a half? Less? There was no way to tell. She
knew she had found it before she actually saw it. There was no

way not to know. Sombra suddenly yelped in fear and Gutsy skidded to a stop at the foot of a hill. Beyond the hill the night had suddenly turned to day.

Gutsy paused, terrified and confused, as she saw the pale blue-white of moonlight washed over with a furious yellow-red. Then she broke into a faster run all the way to the top of the hill.

And stopped. Stunned.

Horrified.

Beyond the hill and stretching as far as she could see, the desert seemed to be burning. Sombra stood with her, trembling in fear. Fires erupted from below the surface of the empty desert. Long fingers of flame reached for the night sky, as if some massive monster of pure fire was trapped underground and clawing to get out. There were explosions. Small at first, muffled, and then much louder as parts of the landscape leaped up into the air, swirling and burning, only to collapse slowly down amid whirlwinds of dust. The ground rippled as if an earthquake was grinding out its fury, but then whole sections of the desert floor folded inward and more fire belched upward.

They had found the hidden military base.

But someone else had found it first . . . and utterly destroyed it.

She could see them, painted in fiery yellow, like demons from the pit. Some of them were shamblers, and some of those were burning too, victims of falling debris. Gutsy saw ravagers, too, dressed in leather and chains. Many were holding guns over their heads, shaking them in triumph.

There were dozens and dozens of ravagers.

There were many hundreds of *los muertos*.

She scrambled forward, getting closer but staying completely out of sight. Here and there soldiers, scorched and screaming, ran in panic, firing weapons without aiming, wasting their ammunition on an enemy that required control and precision. Gutsy took her binoculars from her backpack and swept the landscape. She saw a familiar face. The soldier, Mateo, from Hope Cemetery, swinging an empty rifle like a club. She watched as a dozen shamblers fell on him. His screams rose into the air in a brief pause between explosions. He cried out for help in a plaintive shriek that rose higher than the gunfire for as long as it lasted. He prayed to God. He called for his mother. He begged for anyone to save him. The dead tore him to pieces and devoured him.

Gutsy watched in horror. Not merely for the gruesome slaughter, but because she now knew that every single one of those shamblers held a prisoner inside—the conscious and aware person they had been. Those people were in there, feeling and tasting all of it. Hearing the screams. Connected to nerve endings and taste buds and optic nerves. Witnesses to a crime in which their bodies were the murder weapons.

Crouching there, Gutsy murmured an old prayer Mama had taught her. It had lost meaning for her over the last few years, but now she hoped that someone was listening. And that whoever heard her prayer cared.

Then she saw other movement and turned to see that many of the ravagers were herding swarms of the shamblers away from the destruction. Pushing, shoving, driving them. Not to save them from the flames, but to direct them elsewhere.

Gutsy turned to stare and saw that scores of them were already moving across the desert landscape.

Not merely away from the destroyed base.

No.

They were heading toward New Alamo.

"No . . . ," she breathed, but the night said yes.

LILAH WAS RIDING POINT ON THEIR COLUMN AND ranging far ahead, picking out the best path on the moonlit terrain. They were following the directions given to them by the dying soldier, and it occurred to Benny, who was at the rear of their line, that they'd never even asked for his name.

How sad was that? To die without anyone knowing your name. It was like so many of the zoms out in the Ruin. They were just "zoms" to most people, but they'd been people once. They'd had lives, hopes and dreams, family and friends. They each had a history, and every one of them had expected to have a future. Each of them had been a person with a name.

Now . . . ?

Even to Benny and his friends, who *felt* for the people they'd been, they were nameless monsters. It felt like a crime, or maybe a sin, not to know the names of people who died when you were present. Even a man like the soldier, who claimed to be a bad guy, should have had mourners to say his name so that he did not pass out of life without an identity.

Benny knew he was being superstitious, or maybe he was losing his marbles. Probably a little of both. The deeper they went into the Ruin, the less stable he felt. And the more morbid his thoughts became.

He rumbled and bumped over the ground, grateful for once that the carpet coat and body armor were warm, because the temperature plummeted as soon as the sun went down. Ahead he could see Nix's curly hair whipping in the wind from under the edge of her helmet. Beyond her was Chong, sitting hunched as if the weight of everything was crushing him by slow degrees. And Lilah. Still a mystery to everyone. She acted so cold and tough, but Benny knew there was a heart beneath the ice and armor. It had to be breaking after what Chong had said earlier about his life expectancy.

Up ahead Lilah reached the top of the crest, and he saw her slow her quad into a skidding stop. She killed the engine and turned to the others, drawing a finger across her throat in a *kill it* gesture. They all stopped and switched off. She waved them over and then flattened herself out on the crest so she could peer over the edge. Benny caught up with the others, his heart thumping.

"Now what?" he breathed as he closed in on the Lost Girl.

The four of them saw "what."

The crest overlooked the edge of a long, flat plain of grassy ground with a few sparse trees here and there. With the engine motors stilled, they could hear the sounds from below.

Moans.

A thunder of them. A storm of bottomless need. An ache that spiraled up from within the living dead and gathered into a collective, unanswerable appeal for food. For meat.

"There's so many of them," gasped Nix.

"Look," said Lilah, pointing. "More of the ravagers."

It was true. There were dozens of the leather-clad half-zoms spread out among the swarm, and, as before, they were herding the dead.

"Um, guys . . . ?" said Chong. When the others turned, he pointed in a different direction, down the length of the crest to a point where it leveled out with the plain. Figures were moving, running toward them. Ravagers. Armed with knives, whips, and guns.

"They heard the quads," said Benny. "Run!"

They ran for their machines. There were several hollow pops, and Benny saw the limb of a stunted live oak explode in a spray of jagged splinters as heavy bullets punched into it.

"Go, go, *go*," screamed Nix as she fired up her quad and spun away, kicking up clouds of dust and gravel. She did not try to return fire. The ravagers had rifles and she had a pistol. She would be lucky to even clip one of them, let alone get a head shot. The distance was too great to waste bullets.

Chong slipped and went down to one knee, but Lilah caught him under the arm, hauled him up, and shoved him in the direction of the quad as bullets burned through the air around them. One round struck the wheel of the cart attached to the back of Benny's quad, blowing apart the tire.

Benny jumped into the saddle, started the engine, and was off, dragging the damaged cart behind him as more bullets chased him. He was hyperaware that the cart carried their dwindling supply of fuel. Even if he'd had time to detach it, they needed that fuel. On the other hand, could a hot lead bullet ignite the fuel if it struck the tank? Benny didn't know, so he opened the throttle and roared into the moonlit landscape.

He heard the other two quads coming up hard behind him; and Nix was far ahead, picking out the route. The ravagers fired and fired, and suddenly Benny felt something punch him in the back. He pitched forward over the handlebars as pain exploded all through his chest cavity.

I've been shot, he thought wildly. *Oh God, I'm shot.*

His mind wanted to go dark, to escape the pain and all that would follow. Torture. Teeth. Reanimation as a zombie.

I'm dying.

With what strength he had, Benny kept the throttle open and followed Nix for as long as he could. For as long as he was able.

ON THE LONG RUN FROM TOWN GUTSY HAD TRIED to pace herself, to conserve her strength for whatever lay ahead as she attempted to infiltrate the base.

Now, running back, she could feel all those miles in the heaviness of her legs, in small shots of pain that began shooting up her shins and across her lower back. After a few miles, she shrugged out of the backpack and let it fall. There were useful things in there, but she didn't care. The only thing she really needed was time, and she could feel it burning away. The silenced clock in her head now ticked as loud as gunshots, and instead of an empty timelessness, she was acutely aware that the seconds of her life were ticking down.

She had to reach home in time.

She had to warn everyone in time.

If only there was *enough* time.

She ran. Sombra ran with her, but even dogs are not tireless. He was panting as he ran.

The dead were coming. The only grace was that they were slow, and the ravagers moved at the speed of the shamblers they herded. It was something, but only if she could get to the town in time to alert Karen Peak and the town council.

It stabbed her through the heart to realize that those people, the ones who knew about the base, the lab, the Rat Catchers, and all of this, were the very ones she had to rely on to save them all. She wondered if the world was always that warped, that complicated. Probably, she decided, and that twisted the knife.

The glow of the fire faded behind her, and all the sounds of destruction and death, of horror and pain, became muted by distance and the sound of her own laboring breath.

Where was the town?

How far had she actually come to find the base?

Distance became meaningless.

Her mind tried to distract her by overanalyzing the facts. She cataloged every detail, from the moment of Mama's death to the things she and her friends had learned from Karen. It all fit a pattern, it had a history, and although the actions of the lab scientists and the Rat Catchers were based on rationalization rather than compassion, they made a kind of sense. Part of what it took to be rational and practical, Gutsy knew, was to be able to see both sides of any issue. That did not, as some people seemed to think, require an agreement with either side. Understanding mattered. In history class she'd read books on war, on politics, on social unrest, and she understood a lot of different viewpoints, even some that were truly vile. So it only required perspective to understand the way the Rat Catchers thought.

To them, the people interned at the relocation camp were not entirely real. They were less than fully human. Bigots had to think like that, because otherwise they'd have to face their own fears. Otherwise they'd risk being crippled by compassion.

She ran, and the ghosts of ten thousand years of civilization ran with her. Heroes and villains, conquerors and the conquered, the bad and the good, and all the countless variations of what it meant to be human. Like an army of ghosts, they ran with her, and behind them was an army of the living dead.

Ahead . . . seemingly a million miles away, she could see the lights from the watchtowers of home.

SAM WONDERED IF HE'D MADE A SERIOUS MISTAKE.

The horse walked at a brisk pace—not running, certainly not galloping—but even at a walk, it was hard for Sam to keep up. It chewed up hours and then days. Hunting in his woods demanded care and sometimes great violent exertion, but this was different, requiring an endurance that might have taxed him as a young man. Now, in his fifties, he felt all his years, all the damage that had been inflicted on him by fists, knives, bullets, and shrapnel. He felt as if he carried a thousand pounds of extra weight—a burden composed of regret, guilt, bad memories, fractured hopes, and loss.

One thing kept him going, though.

Benny.

He had a brother. He had family.

And so, he ate his pain and he ran.

The miles fell away as day turned to night and the moon hung burning like a signal flare in the black night.

But then Ledger slowed the horse and Sam stopped, leaning against Peaches's flanks, gulping in air. Grimm immediately flung himself onto the ground with a weary groan and a clank of armor.

"Are you seeing this?" asked Ledger.

"Seeing . . . what . . . ?" gasped Sam.

Ledger pointed. Sam wiped sweat from his eyes and fol-lowed the pointing finger. He was so exhausted that it took him a moment to understand what he was seeing. Then he saw it.

The sky in the distance was no longer the color of icy moonlight.

Now it was the fiery red of an open furnace.

"Tell me that's not New Alamo," said Ledger.

GUTSY DID NOT BOTHER WITH THE SECRET ENTRANCE. There was no time left for stealth.

Instead she ran into the corridor of cars that led to the front gate. She began screaming for help before she reached them.

After that it was a blur.

Guards yelling. The gate swinging open. People running. Sombra barking. Whistles blowing. Questions, questions, questions.

She sagged down and collapsed back against the fender of one of the crushed cars just inside the wall. Sombra stood shivering next to her, his eyes wild and mouth flecked with foam. Gutsy begged for the guards to fetch Karen, and suddenly the security officer was there.

"Gutsy," she barked, "what is it, what's wrong? Why were you outside the gates this late?"

Gutsy grabbed her wrists and pulled her close to speak in a fierce whisper. "The base . . . I found it."

Karen's eyes flew wide and she tried to pull away. "You don't know what you're—"

"It's gone!" cried Gutsy.

"What?"

"They blew it up. I saw it. The whole thing is burning. All the people there . . . they're all dead."

The other guards exchanged confused looks.

"What's she talking about?" demanded Buffy, and Gutsy remembered that she had been one of the two guards on duty the night the Rat Catchers brought Mama home the first time. Which meant that she had let them into town. It meant that she was one of *them*.

Even with everything that was going on, Gutsy wanted to punch her.

She didn't, and instead told Karen everything about what she'd seen out in the desert. The huge swarms of shamblers and the packs of murderous ravagers.

"They're coming here," said Gutsy.

"Here . . . ?" murmured Karen, her face going dead pale. "How much time do we have?"

"Not enough," said Gutsy.

Above her, in the guard towers, the sentries began screaming their warnings.

PART SIXTEEN

NEW ALAMO, TEXAS
LATE AUGUST

REMEMBER THE ALAMO

We must not permit our respect for

the dead or our sympathy for the living

to lead us into an act of injustice

to the balance of the living.

—David "Davy" Crockett, "King of the Wild Frontier"
Frontiersman, soldier, and politician
Born in Limestone, North Carolina
(now part of Tennessee), August 17, 1786
Died in South Texas,
the Battle of the Alamo, March 6, 1836

"I'M SHOT," CRIED BENNY, AND HE TOPPLED OFF HIS quad into the reaching hands of Lilah and Chong. They lowered him to the grass, and Nix immediately began tearing at his clothes, checking him over, looking for the wound that was going to break her heart.

"Oh God, oh God, oh God," Nix said.

Chong's worried face filled Benny's. "I don't see anything."

"B-back . . . ," gasped Benny.

"Turn him over," ordered Nix. "Careful—*careful!*"

"I see it," said Lilah.

"No exit wound," whispered Chong. "Oh no."

"How . . . bad . . . ?" begged Benny.

Nix pushed him roughly onto his back. Her face seemed to swell with emotion. Not concern, but . . . anger? For a weird moment, he thought she was going to punch him.

"You big dummy," she growled.

"Wh-what?"

"You're wearing Kevlar, genius," said Chong, sagging back and shaking his head. He looked up at the moon and laughed.

"What?"

"It's called a bulletproof vest for a reason, you monkey-banger. Probably bruised your ribs, knocked the air out of you."

"I'm not going to die?"

Nix slapped the front of his vest. "I may kill you for scaring me."

Lilah became immediately disinterested and stood up. She crept to the top of a small hill and peered back the way they'd come. Benny sat up very slowly. Kevlar or not, he *felt* shot. The pain was horrible, and he still had trouble breathing.

"Look at this," said the Lost Girl.

Chong and Nix helped Benny stand.

"We seem to be making a habit of scraping you up off the floor," said Chong.

"You can go right ahead and bite me," Benny told him.

"Not even if I was a full zom."

They looked at each other for a moment and then they both cracked up.

"Boys are idiots," said Nix to the air, the moon, or anyone who would listen. She went and stood next to Lilah. Then she snapped, "Benny, Chong, get over here."

They hurried over.

The hill offered a magnificent panorama, and far behind them they could see the ravagers trudging back to rejoin their group, having given up trying to chase motorized vehicles.

"No," said Lilah in her ghostly voice, "not there. Over here."

They looked. Chong went back to the quads and fetched their binoculars, and they all stood looking to the northeast.

"Is that a . . . town?" asked Nix uncertainly.

"Yes," said Chong, "it's a town. Big wall made of—I think—stacked cars."

The town was far away and the night created a lot of distortion.

"I see something rippling around it," said Benny. "Is that water? Like a moat or something?"

Chong studied the scene for a long time, and then slowly lowered his binoculars. "God . . ."

"What's wrong?" asked Nix.

Lilah answered for him. "It's not water."

"Then what is it . . . ?" Benny began, and then trailed off. A cloud had been partly obscuring the moon, and now it moved off and the full light splashed down, defining the roiling shapes that seemed to wash up against the rows of cars. Not water lapping at the walls. No. It was a river of zombies.

A lot of them.

There were flashes from the walls as the people in the town began firing down at them. But there were so many monsters climbing the walls. Shamblers did not have the intelligence or coordination to do this, but the ravagers did, and they swarmed upward.

So many.

Too many.

GUTSY AND HER FRIENDS STOOD ON THE WALL AND watched death come toward them.

But it was like a dream, because death did not hurtle in their direction, or even come at a fast march. It shambled. Slowly, awkwardly, but inevitably.

Hundreds upon hundreds of the living dead. Too many to count. Far more than had ever assaulted the town at one time.

"No," said Spider, shaking his head slowly. He wore his tarantula pajamas and boots and looked six years old. But he kept his strong brown hands on his fighting staff. If those hands glistened with fear sweat or trembled while he waited, Gutsy could completely understand.

Alethea wore a bathrobe over a nightgown and fuzzy slippers. She still had her tiara, though, and somehow that anchored Gutsy to the possibility of hope. Alethea clutched Rainbow Smite as forcefully as Spider held his staff. They were both good fighters; they'd both fought *los muertos* before.

Never more than one at a time, though.

Gutsy wondered how many of the people in town had fought in a war. Every adult had lived through the End, and a lot of them bragged about how many of the shamblers they'd killed. Looking around at the faces of the people in the street below, it occurred to her that surviving wasn't always the result of fighting; and stories are often just that. Could these people actually fight? They seemed to belong to another world, or maybe a fantasy world. Old-fashioned Mexican dresses, men dressed like farmers from the nineteenth century. It was part of some kind of cultural thing, reclaiming the past. Something like that. But it had never made sense to Gutsy. It was like looking in the wrong direction—backward instead of toward the future.

Now Gutsy felt more sympathy toward them, and it occurred to her that the old-fashioned clothes and some of the traditions in New Alamo were an anchor, a safety net. The people who used to wear those clothes a century or two ago didn't have to face the living dead. Was that what it was all about? Rituals and traditions?

Maybe. Probably. Whatever.

There were too many monsters, and the night was going to last forever.

Below where Gutsy stood with her friends, Karen Peak was yelling orders, pushing and shoving people into position, checking weapons, her voice cutting through the panic. Men and women with weapons climbed ladders to the catwalk. A dozen archers took up position along the wall.

"Not enough," said Gutsy.

"What?" yelped Spider.

"It's not going to be enough."

"Don't *say* that," he cried. Alethea wrapped her arm around him and pulled Spider close while glaring at Gutsy.

"Yes," she snapped, "*don't* say that. You're supposed to be the problem solver, girl. Well, as far as I can see it, this is a really big darn problem."

"I offered Karen my help," said Gutsy. "She said they had it handled."

Before Alethea could reply, there was a thud that shook the wall, and they hurried to the edge and looked down.

The first wave of the dead had arrived. They were not ravagers, but they were faster than shamblers and had outpaced the rest. There were a dozen of them, men and women, ragged and wild. They didn't moan but instead snarled like wildcats as they leaped at the wall, clawing at it for handholds, falling, slipping, trying again, relentless. Sombra snarled and barked.

Gutsy had come to the wall prepared for a fight. She had a dozen different clubs, including a crowbar. She understood enough about physics to know that hitting downward gave her extra force because of gravity; and the dead had to use their hands to climb. Waiting, though, was hard. Some of the tower guards were firing, but she saw half the bullets miss.

"Aim!" yelled Gutsy. "Pick your targets. Conserve your ammunition."

If any of the adults on the wall heard her, they gave no indication and kept firing wildly. A moment later Karen's voice rang out.

"You heard her," she roared, and added some curses that made Spider grin despite his terror. Karen gave Gutsy a nod and turned away to organize more of the defense.

"At least she doesn't treat you like a dumb kid," said Spider.

"No, she doesn't care that you're a kid," amended Alethea. "That's better."

The shamblers were almost to the town now. Gutsy looked down at the people in the streets. Most milled around as if they had no idea where they were. She saw plenty of people she knew well and some she saw only in passing. Some of her friends from school were down there.

So was Alice.

Despite every wrong thing in the world, despite her own fear, Gutsy's heart skipped a happy beat when Alice looked up and their eyes met. Alice wore jeans and a white blouse embroidered with flowers, as if this was any other evening in town. She might have been on her way to the general store or to hang out at the library. Her long black hair was pulled back into a ponytail, and she held a spade shovel in her small hands.

Alice smiled up at her and gave the shovel a strong shake, as if promising to fight like a hero. Gutsy lit up and returned the smile. Then suddenly one of the tower guards screamed and toppled backward from his post. Gutsy whirled, and only then, like an afterthought, she heard the crack of a rifle.

"Where did that come from?" she asked, and Spider pointed with his staff. Down there on the wrong side of the wall was a knot of ravagers armed with rifles. That thought made Gutsy feel faint.

"It's too much," she said, but only loud enough for her own ears to hear it. "It's too much." As if in agreement, she heard people screaming behind her. Men and women. Children, too.

And then the dead reached the top of the wall and the Battle of the Alamo began in earnest.

FOUR QUADS RACED ACROSS THE PLAIN IN A STRAIGHT
line.

They had watched the zoms approaching the town of
New Alamo and had stood helpless, their minds shocked into
blank canvases.

Chong finally said, "We're too late."

"Yes," said Nix. She looked stricken.

"There are too many of them," said Lilah.

When Benny said nothing, they glanced at him. Nix
frowned.

"Why are you smiling?"

"Oh God," said Chong. "I think he has an idea."

"Maybe," said Benny.

"We won't like it, will we?" Nix asked.

"Not even a little bit."

He reminded them of the last thing the dying soldier had
told him. Chong gaped at him. "Let me get this straight: You
want us to find the entrance to a tunnel?"

"Yes."

"That runs a mile underground."

"Closer to two miles," corrected Benny. "The soldier said it was three klicks long. Captain Ledger used that expression a lot. A klick is a kilometer, which is—"

"Point six-two miles," supplied Chong. "The actual distance isn't the issue. First we'd have to find it."

"He said the entrance was in a Texas Rose Car Wash."

"Uh-huh. Okay," said Chong patiently, "but even if we find it, you're talking about going underground, maybe through the dark, to come up *inside* a town that's about to be overrun by—oh, what's the exact number?—oh yeah, a *zillion* freaking zoms."

"Pretty much," said Benny.

"In order to accomplish what? Look," said Chong, "I'm not trying to go all Morgie here, and I know coming here was my idea in the first place, but this is kind of nuts. We came here to warn the people of New Alamo about the swarms. I think they pretty much know at this point."

"No," said Nix. "They don't. They only think they do, but they don't know what we know."

Benny nodded. "Besides," he said, "maybe we'll get lucky."

"When have we ever been lucky?" complained Chong. "No, don't answer that. We're alive. We stopped Saint John, blah blah blah. We are the souls of good luck and happy times." He sighed. "Okay. What's your plan, Benny-Wan Kenobi?"

Benny grinned. He and Chong had read a slew of old *Star Wars* novels over the summer. The Jedi knights in those books were clearly inspired by samurai.

So Benny took a breath, grinned like a wolf, and told them his plan.

True to form, none of them liked it. But they, too, wore smiles. Hyenas must have smiled like that, Benny thought.

He'd read about them, too. Then he remembered that people always had the wrong idea about hyenas. They weren't stupid, cowardly scavengers. They were predators and they were very, very smart. They didn't poach leftovers from lions; it was the other way around, with lazy lions stealing from hyenas. Hyenas were supposed to be smarter than chimpanzees.

Why am I thinking about hyenas? he wondered, but the answer was already there. No one expected them to be as tough or as smart as they were.

No one.

They ran for their quads.

THEY CAME CLOSE TO THE FIRE AND SAW THAT, NO, IT wasn't New Alamo.

"What was this?" asked Ledger. "And don't tell me it's the weapons cache."

"No," said Sam. "I'm pretty sure this is—was—the Laredo chemical weapons base."

A massive section of the ground had collapsed inward, leaving a smoking pit a quarter mile wide from which tongues of flame licked out to taste the night.

The two old soldiers approached cautiously, staying downwind of the dead who lingered there. Most of the major swarms had moved off. A scream made them turn, and they saw a pack of three living dead chasing a man who was scrambling along on all fours, his body flash-burned and one foot mangled into red ugliness.

Ledger slid from the saddle and drew the sword.

"Why bother?" asked Sam, moving to block him.

"Because we can't ask questions of the dead."

Sam stepped aside.

Two of the shamblers were dressed in civilian clothes, and the third was in a desert-pattern battle-dress uniform, clearly a new recruit to the army of the unliving. There were no other zoms within sight, so Ledger limped over and gave a quick whistle. "You, deadheads, over here."

The zoms all turned toward the big man who came striding toward them. With hisses of urgent hunger, they rushed at him. The ancient *katana* drew silver lines on the canvas of the darkness, and the dead men flew apart. It took less than a second.

Ledger snapped the sword to one side in a *chiburi* motion that whipped the black blood from the oiled steel. Sam walked up behind him, a Glock in his hands with a sound suppressor screwed into the barrel.

The wounded soldier collapsed weeping on the ground, and they knelt on either side of him. Sam rolled the man onto his back. Beneath the burns and soot, the victim was a large, muscular black man with cracked wire-frame glasses and a small mouth pinched with pain. He wore lieutenant's bars and a name tag: HOWELL. Shock glazed his eyes.

Sam touched Ledger's arm and nodded to Howell's mangled leg. It was covered with bites.

"What happened here?" asked Ledger, and the obvious air of command elicited an immediate response from the lieutenant.

"We were overrun, sir," the man said, adding the "sir" automatically. As best he could, the injured man explained how ravagers who had once been soldiers at the base led a marauding party in through a back way. The rear door used a high-tech hand-geometry scanner that read palm prints. One of those ravagers had been a security specialist at the site, and his palm print had never been removed from the security database, an oversight that proved fatal. Once the security doors were open, the ravagers led hundreds of shamblers inside. The dead soldier also disabled the alarm systems and other critical systems, including the lights. The dead can hunt by sound and smell, and in the utter blackness, the slaughter was comprehensive. The ravagers took weapons and set off a series of explosive charges that brought the whole structure down.

When Ledger asked him why they did it, Howell seemed confused by the question. "They hate us for what we did to them." Then he blinked and stopped talking, as if suddenly realizing that he knew neither of these men. He was sweating badly, and when Sam checked his pulse he felt a thin but rapid heartbeat. The infection was already raging through him. His glance to Ledger shared that info.

"Listen to me, Lieutenant," said Ledger, "you know how this works. You're bitten. You understand what I'm saying?"

"God . . ."

"Do you understand?"

"Y-yes, sir."

"We're heading to New Alamo, but I have the feeling that they're about to be the second course on tonight's all-you-can-eat menu. We'd like to cancel that party, so we're out here looking for a weapons cache. What can you do to help us?"

Howell licked his lips and looked at the two old soldiers. "Captain Collins took a squad to town, to the lab. We lost all the research here, but she went after the duplicate records." He hissed as pain lanced through him; when it passed, he said in a much weaker voice, "You have to believe me . . . we were trying to save the world."

"I don't care," said Ledger. "Help us save the town."

A hopeless expression filled Howell's face. "The Raggedy Man is coming for them. He's going to kill them all."

"Yeah, about that," said Ledger. "Who exactly is this Raggedy Man?"

"He's like a . . . like a god to them," the lieutenant said hoarsely. "He can control them. All of them. The shamblers, the fast-infected, all the mutations. Even the ravagers. I don't know how. But the Raggedy Man is coming for New Alamo. You have to . . . warn them."

Ledger had to lean close to hear because the man's voice had become the faintest of whispers. "Look, man, if you want us to help the town," said Ledger, "then tell us where the weapons cache is."

The man tried, but his voice was gone. He lapsed into a silent, twitching coma, then settled back, exhaling a final breath like a sigh of defeat.

Sam straightened, reaching for his gun, but Ledger shook his head.

"Nah," he said, "save your bullet." He drew his sword and stabbed downward. The twitching stopped.

The two of them stood for a moment, digesting what they'd learned.

"The Raggedy Man," mused Ledger. "Bad enough you telling me he's the local boogeyman. Worse when I hear it from a military officer. What do you think he meant when he said this Raggedy Man is their god? You think he has some way of controlling the zoms?"

Sam shook his head. "Let's hope not."

"Yeah," said Ledger, looking worried, "but it gives me a bad itch in a place I can't scratch."

"I know the feeling," said Sam.

They returned to where they'd left Grimm and the horse. From that vantage point they watched the last of the shamblers and their ravager herdsmen move off into the northeast. "They're heading straight to the town," said Sam.

Ledger shook his head. "They really named that place *New* Alamo?"

"Yeah."

"Any of them ever read a history book? Everyone at the *old* Alamo died."

Sam snorted. "When have people ever learned from their mistakes? I mean, look around, Joe, we're standing in the middle of the actual apocalypse. What's it going to take for people to learn?"

"A second chance," said Ledger.

"Really?" said Sam disgustedly. "And how many 'second chances' do we human beings deserve?"

Ledger shrugged. "Considering how many mistakes we make, Sam . . . I guess we need as many chances as we can get."

Sam snorted. "Since when did you become an optimist?"

"Always was, brother," said Ledger. "Always was."

They set off at the fastest speed that a tired horse, a tired dog, and two tired old soldiers could manage.

THE DEAD THING CLAWED ITS WAY TO THE TOP OF THE wall and reached for Gutsy.

"Not a chance, sweetheart," growled Alethea, and bashed it with Rainbow Smite before Gutsy could react. The creature was one of the smarter ones, and it tried to grab the bat— proving to Alethea that it was not quite smart enough. The impact sent it flying backward off the wall. "Buh-bye!" Alethea laughed out loud and swung at another withered gray face.

Gutsy did not smile as she fought. Every inhuman face she saw seemed to have a human and conscious one painted over it. Her whirling mind convinced her that she saw the pleading in those dead eyes.

And yet, she fought. There was no other choice.

Her crowbar was smeared with black and red blood, and her arm ached from each and every blow she'd delivered. She did not keep track of the number of *los muertos* she'd fought. Eight, so far? Maybe ten. Even though it was one at a time, the total exertion was incredible, and it would have been bad enough if she hadn't run all those miles in the dark. Sombra crouched beside her, terrified and furious in equal measure. Gutsy did not want him to fight, because she didn't know what would happen if the coydog bit an infected. Would he be okay? Would he become one of the living dead animals people reported seeing? Would he become a carrier even if he didn't become infected? Or would he get sick and die? It was clear the animal wanted to fight, but he obeyed Gutsy's commands. So far, at least.

The last time she risked a look over the wall to see if she could spot Alice on the street below, the girl was gone. She did see Karen and two of her guards standing firm between a group of old people and kids and a pack of fast-infected. Karen carried a pump shotgun and fired, pumped, fired, pumped, fired, getting head shots every time because the monsters were too close to miss. The children screamed and hid behind their grandparents.

There was another fight farther along the street, and Gutsy was surprised to see Mr. Cuddly walking almost casually toward some oncoming shamblers, firing a pair of what looked like old-fashioned cowboy six-shooters. His face was completely devoid of expression—not fear, not stress, not joy—as he killed a monster with each shot. He handled the guns with an icy precision, and Gutsy did not believe that his skill came only from battles since the End. Maybe the rumors about him were true, and he used to be a gangster. Maybe even an assassin. He was cold enough.

His wife was nearby, and she had a heavy meat tenderizer mallet in one hand and a meat cleaver in the other. Her clothes were splashed with dark blood and there was a trail of crumpled *los muertos* behind her.

Gutsy grinned, liking the two of them for the first time. Mrs. Cuddly looked up and their eyes met, and then she looked past Gutsy to where Spider and Alethea fought. The woman nodded as if pleased. Then she went back to killing.

It was all surreal.

Not everyone in town was doing as well. There were bodies here and there, and a few were twitching their way back from whatever dark waiting room lay on the other side of death. They rose and stalked forward to join the fight. With a breaking heart, Gutsy saw that one of them was a teenage girl a year younger than her who lived at the Cuddly place. Mrs. Cuddly hesitated before striking her. In that moment, the girl threw herself at the older woman and they went down in a thrashing tangle behind a parked wagon.

Gutsy spun away, sickened and horrified. She rushed to the other side of the catwalk and looked to see hundreds of the dead funneling through the corridor of cars. The outer gate stood open and topped by ravagers. Only the inner gate was still shut, but more of the killers were climbing up the walls. The town was being attacked from all angles. Smoke rose from fires that she couldn't see, and it was impossible to tell if the ravagers were starting fires, or if lamps in town had fallen. Either way, that created an even worse problem.

Armed guards flanked where she and her friends fought, and Gutsy was happy to see that they were picking their targets and conserving their ammunition. Panic was always nipping at the edge of everyone's awareness. There were a thousand people on the walls, but every time one fell, it left a gap through which the faster dead and the ravagers poured through.

Below, in the streets, the rest of the townsfolk fought for their lives.

How can we win this? Gutsy wondered as she wiped blood on her jeans to allow her a better grip on the crowbar. Over the years she'd thought of a hundred good ideas for defending the town, but no one ever took her seriously. Most of those ideas were long-range, requiring time and coordinated effort, like a moat around the town filled with thousands of sharpened spikes or pieces of jagged rebar. Or a network of wires and ropes that would create a kind of maze and barrier. The shamblers wouldn't have the brains to climb over them, and the smarter ones, fewer in number, could be picked off by archers or armed guards working in teams.

Dozens of ideas like that.

This was an immediate problem, though. What could she do right now?

The guard to her right suddenly cried out, and in same instant Gutsy heard a shot. She whirled to see the guard stagger, weapon falling, hands clutching his throat. He stumbled backward and fell from the wall. Into the town.

It was the third guard shot in the chest or throat. No head shots, even though the ravagers had rifles. Why not? In a flash of insight, she realized that the shot was probably not accidental. Not where it was aimed, at least.

They're not just shooting to kill. They're creating a new part of their army inside the walls.

Every person who died reanimated as one of *los muertos*, and that was math that didn't require Spider's counting skills.

We're going to lose this fight, thought Gutsy with dreadful clarity. *We're all going to die.*

88

"GUTSY," CRIED SPIDER, "WATCH OUT!"

She spun to see a pair of burly ravagers running at her. One had a fire ax and the other was inserting a fresh magazine into an assault rifle. Behind her, Spider and Alethea were desperately battling a wave of fast-infected who were swarming over the wall.

Sombra started forward, but Gutsy hip-checked him out of the way, fearing for him even though it meant she was going to die. The ravager with the rifle raised it, a nasty grin on his face, and aimed the weapon dead center at her chest. She was too far away. Even Sombra was too far away.

She snarled and rushed him anyway. If death wanted to take her, then death would have to work for it. With a howl of rage, she charged the ravagers.

Then the head of the ravager with the gun exploded.

It was very immediate and nasty and wet. The body simply puddled down and the rifle clattered to the catwalk. The other ravager paused, gaping at his comrade. There was no accompanying gunshot, but nothing except a heavy-caliber bullet could have done that much damage.

For a split second the ravager and Gutsy stared at the

corpse and then at each other. The second burned away, and Gutsy swung her crowbar at the ravager before he could raise his ax. There was a lot of fear and rage and even hopelessness powering that blow. It shattered the ravager's elbow, sending the ax flying over his shoulder. Gutsy gave the killer no time, no chance. She lashed out with a kick to the knee so savage that it bent his leg backward with a sound like a dry tree limb snapping. As he canted sideward, she jumped into the air and put every ounce of body weight behind a vicious swing to his head. He went down, smashed flat, the unnatural life crushed out of him.

Gutsy landed, turned, and rushed to help her friends but jerked to a stop as a third ravager pulled himself over the edge of the catwalk and fired a pistol at her. Or tried to. As he raised the gun, his head exploded with the same awful force.

She never heard that shot either.

Another ravager fell a second later with the whole lower part of his face disintegrating into a red-black cloud of mist.

"NICE SHOT," SAID JOE LEDGER.

Sam Imura lay on a hummock, his sniper rifle steady on a bipod. Six loaded magazines stood in a row on a clean piece of cloth, ready to hand.

Sam ignored him as he worked the slide and fired, worked the slide and fired.

"Sam, look," said Ledger, and pointed to where a very tall ravager was walking along the entrance corridor with several other ravagers flanking him like guards. "Is that the Raggedy Man, d'you think?"

"I don't know. Maybe." Sam sighted at him through his scope. "No clear shot."

"It's all good," said Ledger. He patted Grimm on his armored head, drew his sword, and said, "My turn."

THE RUSTED SIGN SAID TEXAS ROSE CAR WASH.

The place looked deserted, abandoned. It was a single-story block building squatting just off the main highway. Junked cars lay where they'd died when the EMPs blew out the fuses for the world. There were bones among the weeds. In all it looked like ten thousand places Benny and the others had seen out here in the Ruin. Proof that life had existed here once, but further proof that it had passed away.

The four teens circled it with their quads and then stopped outside. Silence fell as they killed their engines and dust clouds wandered off into the night.

The left side of the building was, indeed, a car wash, with brushes and a conveyor belt and hoses. To the right were two service bays for oil changes and tire rotations, as advertised on signs partly covered with creeper vines. The far right-hand side was an office and store with glass grimed to opacity.

"Are you sure this is the place?" asked Chong. "Kind of looks like nothing much at all."

Benny shrugged. "It's what he said."

"Yes," said Lilah. "This is the place."

"How can you be so sure?" asked Nix.

Instead of answering, Lilah dismounted, took her spear, and approached the first of the two service bays. The others followed, weapons in hand.

Chong saw it first and grunted. Benny and Nix saw it soon after.

There was a bloody handprint on the edge of the entrance. Fresh blood. Red blood. Not the blacker blood of the dead. They heard the moan a moment later and a figure lumbered out of the darkness. He wore a military uniform and held a pistol loosely in a slack hand. He was dead, much of his face and throat torn away.

A second figure moved into view behind him. A woman in a similar uniform. One of her hands had been bitten off. Moonlight could not reach very far into the service bay, but far enough to see the blood spatter from a battle. Three zoms lay on the ground, their bodies stitched with bullet holes. Beyond them, strips of pale light revealed the shape of a door that stood partly open. The light looked electric rather than like firelight.

"The entrance," cried Nix.

The two dead soldiers reached for them. Benny took one; Nix took the other. Identical flashes of silver and then heads fell with melon wetness to the concrete. They went inside. A third soldier lay on the floor, undead, but crippled by a spine injury. Lilah quieted him.

The door was one-half of a big set of double doors about eight feet wide. Benny and Chong took positions with their hands on the handles. Nix sheathed her sword and drew her pistol, and Lilah did as well. Nix nodded to the boys and they pulled the doors wide.

Behind the door was a corridor ten feet wide that ran on and angled down. Electric lights showed the way, and they showed the damage. There were bodies everywhere. Soldiers, zoms, and the leather-clad ravagers. Blood spatter marked the spots of individual deaths. It was a diorama of bloody destruction.

From far away, down deep in the tunnel and out of sight, they heard a few sporadic gunshots, plaintive screams, and the relentless moans of the hungry dead.

Benny studied the tunnel and then went outside to examine the landscape. When he came back, he said, "The soldier was right. This tunnel goes right toward the town."

Even from nearly two miles away they all heard the sounds of gunfire and screams rolling across the night-darkened desert. They could see the lights of New Alamo.

"You want us to go running down there?" asked Nix.

"No. I want us to go *driving* down there," replied Benny. "I think we can get the quads in there pretty easily."

"Only single file," said Chong. "We can't drive and fight at the same time. Not even Lilah can keep that up."

"Then we double up," said Benny. "One person drives, the other shoots. Nix and Lilah are the best shots, so you and me'll drive."

"I don't like it."

Lilah snorted. "Too late for that, Town Boy."

"We have all these guns we took from the prison," said Nix. "We can clear the tunnel and have plenty left over for the people in town. Bet they could use some."

Chong sighed, nodded, and turned around to go fetch his quad. The others ran to catch up. They buddy-checked each other's armor. Nix gave Benny a tight hug and climbed onto the back of his machine. Lilah kissed Chong hard enough to make his knees weak, then laughed while he fired his engine.

Benny leaned close to his friend. "That's what you're fighting for, dude."

"Yes," said Chong, managing a smile. "I know."

GUTSY HAD NO IDEA WHERE THE SHOOTER WAS WHO
had saved her life twice now. From the way the ravagers'
bodies jerked as they died, she was almost certain the shots
came from outside the walls. But that made no sense.

Everything around her was madness, and it made it hard
to be sure of anything at all. Screams and moans competed to
dominate the air around and above New Alamo. Shouts, too.
And the grating, mocking laughter of the ravagers.

Alethea and Spider were working as a team, each of
them covered in gore, dripping with sweat, and wild-eyed
with fear. Alethea caught her looking and gave her a manic
grin. She blew a strand of hair out of her face, straightened
her tiara, turned, and bashed a fast-infected in the face.

A scream pulled Gutsy's attention, and she raced to the
other side of the catwalk and looked down to see something
that chilled her to the bone. Five of the shamblers were
closing in around a girl who backed away, holding a length
of black pipe like a baseball bat, but caught in a moment of
indecision, clearly uncertain which enemy to attack first.
Aware that the others would fall on her at once.

The girl was Alice.

"*No!*" bellowed Gutsy, and before she knew she was going to do it, she was running for the stairs. Sombra following, barking furiously. Gutsy jumped down the last few steps, landed running. Sombra shot past her and leaped at one of the shamblers, slamming into its back to send it crashing face-forward to the hard ground. He did not bite the creature, though, and jumped at another, knocking it down.

That was when Gutsy understood that the coydog had been trained for this. Trained for combat with the infected dead. It sent a thrill of excitement through her, and she caught up and smashed the heads of both *los muertos* with her crowbar.

The other dead turned at the sound and movement, and Alice took that moment to hit one with her pipe. It was a very hard shot, but the monster was too tall and the pipe hit its shoulder, bounced up, and only grazed its skull. The thing turned and grabbed for her, baring its teeth for a bite.

Gutsy bashed reaching arms aside and hit another living dead in the forehead, driving it to its knees while beside her Sombra knocked the fifth one down. Gutsy ignored that one and attacked the monster who was clawing at Alice's clothes.

She hit that one very, very hard.

Its shattered skull snapped sideways on a broken neck and it fell away into a motionless heap. The fallen dead thing hit in the forehead started to get up, but Sombra bit down on its pants cuff and jerked it backward. It fell on its chest, and Gutsy smashed the skull.

Five seconds, five dead.

Alice gaped at her, the pipe forgotten in her hands. "Gutsy," she gasped, "you're amazing."

Despite everything and all the violent madness around her, Gutsy felt her cheeks begin to burn.

92

THEY WERE OLD AND THEY FELT THEIR YEARS, BUT MR. Urrea and Mr. Ford stepped up to face the oncoming storm of the dead.

The Chess Players were dressed in makeshift armor— Dallas Cowboys football helmets, hockey pads, SWAT team vests, and antique weapons looted from a museum. Ford carried a medieval horseman's ax, and Urrea had a Swiss longsword from the early sixteenth century. The weapons were pitted with rust, but they had been sharpened and had already proven their effectiveness. Bodies lay all around them.

They stood in the street in front of the general store. Behind them, crouching in the shelter of barrels of grain and kegs of beer, were dozens of children, pregnant women, the disabled, and people too old to fight. Fights raged up and down the street, and so far every one of the ravagers, shamblers, and fast-infected who had come hunting for the innocent had died there on the street.

"Eleven," said Ford, panting for breath during a lull.

"What?" asked Urrea.

"I got eleven. You got nine."

"What are you talking about? I killed the two crawlers," he said, pointing to infected who had been crippled in some other part of the fight but who'd clawed their way across the street to join this battle.

"You can't count them," insisted Ford.

"The heck I can't."

"Okay, so maybe those two count as one. That still leaves you with ten. I'm winning. I'm Legolas."

"What?"

"Legolas," said Ford, "Lord of the Rings. Remember the Battle of Helm's Deep? He and Gimli kept a tally? Legolas killed the most orcs."

"You're delusional," said Urrea. "Besides, I'm Legolas."

"How do you figure that?"

He tapped Ford's weapon with his bloody sword. "Gimli was the one with the ax."

"No way, José, I'm—oh crap." Ford and Urrea set themselves as a fresh wave of shamblers lumbered toward them. They both smiled like heroes from some ancient tale. If either saw the fear in the other's eyes, neither mentioned it. After all, heroes were allowed to be afraid.

THE TUNNEL MIGHT AS WELL HAVE BEEN THE ENTRANCE to the underworld from an ancient myth.

The two quads filled the corridor with thunder that drowned out the moans of the dead and the sound of slaughter.

It was quickly apparent that there were three kinds of monsters down here. Most of them were R1 slow zoms, and half of these were recently murdered soldiers. There were a few R3's—fast and devious, but no match for the four of them in their riot gear and weapons. But then there were the ravagers. They were the most dangerous and armed, but luckily, there weren't many of them; and they were all the way at the far end of the throng of living dead. Their own mindless followers kept them from using their guns effectively.

The quads were sturdy, with roll bars and crash grilles, and steel impact plates welded in place by the mechanics in town. Built for fighting the dead. Built for brutal work. Benny led the way and smashed into the shamblers, knocking them back against their fellows while Nix kept up a continuous fire. Chong was behind him, his body shifted to the right to allow Lilah to shoot past him. Even with the shotguns taken from the prison, the four of them earned every yard they gained. Nix and Lilah fired their guns dry, reloaded, kept firing.

Together they stormed the gates of hell.

94

THEY WERE LOSING AND ALETHEA KNEW IT.

Not just them, but the whole town. There were still hundreds of *los muertos* out there and dozens of ravagers. There were too many. They never got tired, they never lost heart, they did not understand the concept of despair, or compromise, or surrender.

It was like fighting a hurricane. There was simply no way to turn your back on it, no way to reason with it. It was a force of nature, and—even perverted as they were by science—so were the armies of the dead.

Spider was lighter and very fast, but even he moved as if his thin limbs were weighted down with blocks of stone. Alethea, though very strong, carried more weight, and she felt like her lungs were going to burst.

She used Rainbow Smite to ram the face of an infected, sending him backward off the wall, arms pinwheeling as he fell. Then another crawled over the edge near her and a shape pushed past her to smash its skull with a meat tenderizer. Alethea gaped at the blood-spattered person of Mrs. Cuddly. Her clothes were torn and her hair was wild, but there were no visible bites on her.

Mrs. Cuddly caught her eye and gave her a stern frown. "Don't think this gets you out of kitchen duty." Then she turned away and laid into a ravager who tried to attack Spider with a hatchet.

Alethea laughed out loud. The world was nuts, but that was fine with her.

As she turned back to the wall, she saw something below that made her stare. A big man dressed like a soldier was walking directly toward a bunch of fast-infected. He wasn't alone, though. Stalking beside him was the biggest dog Alethea had ever seen. It was massive, nearly as big as a bull calf, and it was completely covered with armor from which spikes jutted in all directions. They were down there at the main gate, and they were *attacking* the dead.

The monsters howled as they rushed at him and the man reached over his broad shoulder to grasp the handle of a long, slim sword. His reach was slow, but then he whipped the blade free and stepped into the onrush. From then on the sword seemed to become invisible, just a whisper of flickering silver. The dog slammed into the dead from another angle, using its massive bulk and those spikes and blades to tear the legs from the dead. The dead swarmed toward them, and Alethea was positive she could see the man laughing as he fought.

Fifty yards away, beyond the gate and on the other side of the wall of cars, Alethea saw a figure she hadn't noticed before climb to the top of a hill. It was a ravager, but he seemed different somehow. Bigger than the others, and there was something oddly powerful about him. He dominated the scene. She could not hear what he was saying, but it was clear he was shouting at the ravagers and to those infected who retained enough intelligence to follow orders.

It was clear that the man with the sword was fighting his way toward the tall ravager, who roared at his army to defend him. A mass of the dead that had been heading down the corridor to the attack the gate suddenly turned like a tide and washed toward the man and the dog.

GUTSY WANTED TO HUG ALICE. SHE WANTED TO KISS her. Both things were so wildly inappropriate in a moment like this that it made Gutsy doubt her own sanity. How could she think of romance when people were dying around her?

On the other hand, seeing Alice, and knowing that she was alive, made a lot of weariness fall away. Even in the heat of the moment, Gutsy was analytical enough to understand what she was feeling. Alice was something to fight for. She was someone to *survive* for. Maybe that's what all warriors needed to come home from the battlefield. And this, after all, was a war.

Thinking that nearly stopped her again. This *was* war. And war was something from the past, from history books and the stories the survivors of the End told. It wasn't really part of her experience. Like Spider and Alethea, Gutsy had grown up *after* the war. After what everyone assumed was the last war. Now, here it was. She was at war with the soldiers and scientists—if any survived the attack at their base. She was at war with the Raggedy Man and his army of the dead.

She was at war. She was in a war. Did that make her an actual warrior? Or a soldier? And what was the difference? All Gutsy knew for sure was that she could not be on the sidelines. She could not run and hide. She had to fight because she *could* fight, and because she had things—people, her home, her friends, Alice—to fight for. Gutsy almost smiled at that thought.

Then she saw two people go running across the street, heading in the direction of the town hospital. The first was Dr. Max Morton. That was normal. That made sense. But the person with him twisted the world into a grotesque shape.

Captain Bess Collins. Not dressed in her Rat Catcher clothes but in jeans and a leather jacket. She had a pistol holstered on her right hip and a familiar broad-bladed machete hanging from her left. Both of them carried big, empty canvas duffel bags and were running as fast as they could.

The words that rose to Gutsy's mouth were not ones she ever used. They were foul, vicious, hateful. Alice stared at her in shock.

"What's wrong?" she asked. "Who is that woman?"

"She's dead is who she is," growled Gutsy. "Alice—get to the general store. The Chess Players will keep you safe."

"Where are you going?"

"To catch a rat."

The doctor and the captain pushed through the crowds of injured at the hospital, and Gutsy raced to catch up. She bullied and pushed her way through the people, trying not to do more damage to the injured, but absolutely determined to catch up with Captain Collins. People pulled back from her dog as much as from her, and Sombra played his part by showing his teeth to anyone in his way.

The hospital was packed with people, and some of them were unconscious, maybe on the edge of death. One had just reanimated, and an orderly with a hammer and spike was wrestling with him.

Gutsy hurried past in time to see Collins and Dr. Morton enter his office at the end of the hall. She ran faster but skidded to a stop when she heard them speaking in urgent voices just inside.

"—all of it, Max," Collins was saying. "Everything. The files, the clinical trial data, the autopsy reports on the bodies we brought back."

There was the sound of duffel bags being unzipped and file drawers being yanked open.

"We only had time for four autopsies, Bess," said Dr. Morton.

"I don't care. Take whatever you have. But take all of it."

"This is insane, Bess. The town's falling apart. These people need me."

Gutsy heard Collins give a harsh laugh. "Since when do you care about these rats?"

"Not all of them are test subjects. I have *friends* in this town."

"Oh, well, feel free to stay and die with them, Max," sneered Collins. "Personally, I'm going to get this data to the base and then head east to the other lab."

Other lab? It was the first Gutsy had heard of that. Karen Peak hadn't mentioned it, which suggested that it was something kept secret from everyone but a select few. Gutsy wondered how the captain was planning on getting through the dead attacking the town.

"What happens if the Night Army wipes out the whole town, Bess? What then?"

Collins's voice was ice cold. "Then we'll get the big guns from the weapons cache, come back here, and wipe them out, and after that we'll have a whole town full of stage two test subjects. Imagine all you'd learn from that, Max."

She heard the doctor gasp. "You're actually insane."

"Oh, grow up," said the captain. "Don't pretend you really care about anyone here. Friends or not. Not after all you've done for the project."

"What I've done has been for the good of—"

There was a sharp sound of a hard slap and then Collins spoke in a tight voice. "Don't you dare preach to me, *Doctor* Morton. You're a monster and so am I. Monsters are exactly what we need to be. It's what we've had to be since the End. It's monsters like us who will *save* whatever's worth saving in this messed-up world. If that means killing every single person left in this state, then that's what I'll do, because right now hard choices and big-picture thinking are the only way we have even a chance of winning. Now stop whining, help me collect all the research, and let's get out to the base while we still have time."

Gutsy pulled the door open and stepped inside. The doctor and the captain froze. She looked at the half-filled duffel bags and then up at them. She knew they could see the truth in her eyes. They knew that she'd heard them.

"Gutsy," said the doctor quickly, "it's not what you think. . . ."

"Shut up," said Gutsy. "You're a doctor. You're supposed to help people. You disgust me."

She turned to face the captain, who did not look particularly worried about the presence of a girl with a bloody crowbar and a big coydog. Collins laid her hand on her holstered pistol.

"And you, Captain Collins," said Gutsy, enjoying the way the Rat Catcher's eyes suddenly flared, "if you think that you're going to be safe at your secret base . . . well . . . I have some bad news for you."

The captain narrowed her eyes. "What are you talking about?"

"I just *came* from there," said Gutsy. "It's gone."

"What do you mean 'gone'?"

"I mean gone. I watched it blow up. I watched the Night Army eat all your men. You have nowhere to run to."

Sombra growled.

The captain glanced at the dog, and again her eyes widened. "Killer . . . ?"

Sombra barked once. It was not a happy bark.

"Is this your dog?" asked Gutsy.

"It belongs to one of my men. Did you steal it, you little rat?"

"No," said Gutsy. "You're wrong. His name is Sombra and he's my dog. He's my friend."

Sombra bared his teeth and hot spit glistened on his fangs.

"Cap, it's getting bad out there, we really need to go," said a voice, and Gutsy turned as a soldier entered the room. "What's going on? Whoa, hey . . . Killer? You found my dog? Holy—"

With a snarl that sounded like a werewolf more than a dog, Sombra leaped at the soldier. They crashed backward through the door. The soldier's scream was piercing and filled with terror, confusion, and pain.

Then Gutsy heard a metallic click behind her and spun around to see Collins pointing the gun at her face.

96

THEY FOUGHT THEIR WAY ALONG TWO MILES OF tunnel. The hall became so choked with the dead that they had to abandon their quads and fight on foot.

Benny's ears rang with the noise of gunfire and screams. His sword dripped with gore. Nix and Lilah had long since run out of pistol ammunition and switched to the clumsier but more effective shotguns. Chong eventually switched from bow to long gun too. The dead could not use their weight of numbers to advantage because the whole corridor was one long choke point. The four of them fought with brutal efficiency.

It was a rhythm of mayhem, a ritual of destruction.

Never before had the training they'd gotten—first from Tom and later from Captain Ledger—mattered as much. Never before had it sunk in that the four of them were *this* dangerous.

Never before had Benny felt more like a killer. He was no fan of guns, but after a while it became clear that the only way to reach the end of the tunnel was with the shotguns. He went half-deaf from the roar and hated having to use them. Somehow, to him, they were cruder and less civilized than his sword. He was aware that this was fractured logic, but it was how he felt. He used the shotgun with as much precision as he could, and as it became easier to use and as the efficiency of it became evident, he felt himself moving forward in a machine-like way. It did the job, but it did not feel right. He understood that he needed these skills and this weapon, but it also hurt him. Maybe because it detached him from the act of quieting far more so than the sword. Each of the infected still mattered to him on a deep level, on a human level. In other battles, Benny had felt himself losing pieces of his soul with every undead life he took. There was even one time when he simply wanted to stop doing harm, even harm to these unfeeling monsters, and just let them take him. That had been a black moment in his life, and he carried the memory of it with perfect clarity.

Even with that, he fought.

The dead fell and he moved on.

There were far fewer of them now, and beyond the last dozen or so, Benny could see a heavy metal door. The last ravagers were trying to force it open, but so far had not managed it.

They passed stacks of supplies. Cases of bottled water, tanks of propane and other fuels. Pallets of canned goods. Enough to feed thousands of people for years. Hidden away down here. Some of the ravagers tried to hide behind those supplies, but Lilah and Nix, Benny and Chong found them.

Hunted them.

And they killed them all.

ALETHEA HAD TO TURN AWAY FROM THE SPECTACLE
of the man with the sword and the armored dog doing insane
amounts of damage down there, because things were not
going as well up on the catwalk.

Mrs. Cuddly went down with a knife stuck in her thigh
and lay there, gasping, trying to use her cleaver and meat tenderizer even while she was down. The guards on the wall were
mostly dead, and some civilians had climbed up to help. Alethea saw many of them go down, some dragged to pain and
horror by reanimating guards. Every now and then, though,
one of the fast-infected or an armed ravager would spin away
as another mystery bullet ended their lives. If it wasn't for
the shooter—whoever and wherever he was—the wall would
have been lost.

Alethea pulled Spider back and they stood above Mrs.
Cuddly, defending her as the dead closed in.

In the street below, Alice Chung stood behind the Chess
Players, holding her piece of pipe. She had no body armor,
and the old men had tried to tell her to hide. She did not.
Alice's mind was filled with the image of Gutsy Gomez and

her dog attacking and killing five *los muertos*. Five, and Gutsy was two inches shorter than Alice.

She gripped her pipe, determined to fight. Determined to make Gutsy proud of her.

Karen Peak led a team of guards and townsfolk in a rally to try to reclaim the town square. Adolf Cuddly was with her, his guns belching fire and his face remaining completely impassive, no matter what happened around him.

Karen held a Beretta M9 and her hands ached from all the recoil. She'd lost count of how many rounds she'd fired. When all her magazines had been spent, she'd taken more from dead guards, and even from dead ravagers. Her hands were powder burned and her eyes stung from smoke and tears.

"Here they come," she yelled as a new wave of fast-infected rushed toward them.

She raised her gun and fired.

The Chess Players were slowing down. They both knew it.

The street was heaped with the dead, but their weapons weighed ten thousand tons. Ford was wheezing and there were red blotches on his cheeks. His eyes looked fevered. Urrea had pains in his chest and down his left arm.

They tried to hold the line, but they were forced to give ground. Inch by bloody inch.

Captain Ledger loved a good fight.

This wasn't a good fight.

It was an epic fight.

His personal philosophy had always been that a fight was

won by whoever wanted it more, and he always wanted it more than anyone he faced. A lot of them probably *thought* they had the skills and drive and determination to win, but Ledger was still alive, and all his old enemies were dead.

He wondered, in his darker moments, whether when he died and went to where killers like him deserved to go, all the people he'd killed would be waiting for him. At other times he wondered if he'd go somewhere like the Valhalla of the Norsemen, where he would fight all day and feast all night, and that was how it would be forever. He thought that likely, or at least fitting, since he had never really known anything but war. A tragedy when he was a teenager had twisted him into a certain shape, forged him into a weapon, and that weapon had been called to use over and over and over again.

No rest for the wicked. That was how he saw it.

Now, he thought that this might be his last great fight.

An army of monsters all around him and no real plan for anything but inflicting as much collateral damage as possible. If he had to fall, then what of it?

His only real regret was that Grimm was going to die too. Ledger liked dogs a lot more than he'd ever liked people, and Grimm had been his friend for a long time.

They fought well together.

Up ahead he could see the ravager who he'd marked as the leader of this little shindig. A big bruiser of a guy who very much needed his butt kicked. Two or three times the ravager had ordered his thugs to gun Ledger down, but Sam Imura punched their tickets. *Bing, bang, boom.*

The leader leaped down from his hill and was working his way toward Ledger.

Fine, thought the old soldier, *if he wants to make a fight of it, then let's tango.*

For him it would be one last brawl to close out a life lived out in the storm lands, in the place where nothing but cold winds ever blew.

Maybe when it was over he'd find peace. Maybe that slim chance was possible, even for someone like him. He thought about his wife, Junie Flynn, who had almost certainly died on First Night. Junie with the tangled blond hair, sun freckles, and the bluest eyes Ledger had ever seen. Sweet-natured, smart, powerful.

Lost.

And their child. Lost. It did not matter to Ledger that their baby had been adopted. Who cared? Family was family.

What mattered was that maybe they would be waiting for him on the other side.

Maybe.

Maybe.

He swung the sword, and Grimm slashed with his spikes, and they fought on.

GUTSY STARED AT COLLINS BUT NOT AT THE GUN. SHE didn't really care about it. The world was ending anyway.

Dr. Morton stood holding a duffel bag, eyes wide, mouth open, shocked to silence.

Behind Gutsy, out in the hall, the soldier was screaming in a way that told them all that he was losing his fight with his former "pet." Good. Sombra had a lot of his own issues to sort out with the man who had beaten him so cruelly and forced him to fight other dogs.

"Bess," said the doctor, finding his voice, "Darren . . ."

"Darren's an idiot who can't even control his own dog," snapped Collins. "Who cares about him?"

"But—"

"Finish filling the bags. Do it now, Max, or so help me God I'll put a bullet in you."

The doctor flinched and began reaching for more of the records.

"Gomez," said Collins, eyeing Gutsy, "what did you mean when you said the base had blown up? Was that some kind of stupid joke?"

"It's the truth," said Gutsy. "I was there. It's destroyed.

So . . . where are you going to go now, huh? You have another bunch of Rat Catchers somewhere else?"

Collins smiled, but it was fragile, forced. "You're lying to me."

"Why the heck would I lie?" laughed Gutsy. "What's the point? I went out there to try and find you and beat your brains in because of what you did to my mother, but the Night Army got there first. It's burning, and I ran back here to try and warn the town before it was too late."

"You should have run faster," said Collins coldly.

"Bess . . . ?" said Morton. "What are we going to do?"

"We do what I said before," she snapped. "We get these records to the other lab."

"*How?* It's over a thousand miles from here. How will we get there without the vehicles at the base?"

"Let me worry about that."

The screaming in the hallway stopped, and Sombra came stalking back into the room. His muzzle was smeared with bright red blood, and there was an alien wildness in his eyes. For a moment Gutsy thought the coydog was going to attack her, but Sombra looked up at her and there was a momentary softening of his expression. It was as if he was aware of the line he'd crossed and it scared him. He whined and gave a sad little wag of his tail. Gutsy wanted to hug him, to tell him it was all going to be okay. Except, as she had done once before, she declined to lie to the animal.

Nothing was ever going to be okay again.

Collins was moving backward toward a big storage locker, her gun steady on Gutsy. "Come on, Max. We have to go. We'll find a way to get to Asheville. Get the bags."

With her free hand, she reached back for the locker door handle, but the doors suddenly opened outward and a ravager slammed into Collins with shocking force. The gun went off and a bullet punched the wall inches from Gutsy's head. Collins fell screaming with the ravager on top of her. Her gun flew from her hand.

Gutsy was suddenly in motion, swinging the crowbar at the ravager, but in the instant it landed on the killer's skull, Gutsy realized that the ravager wasn't moving.

The ravager wasn't alive.

The crowbar crunched through bone and Collins immediately shifted the body off her and snapped out with a powerful kick-sweep that sent Gutsy crashing to the floor. She fell hard and banged her head on the ground, but she kicked back and caught Collins on the hip, spilling the captain as she tried to rise. As Collins fell down, Gutsy swarmed atop her and began hitting the woman who had killed Mama and treated her like vermin.

Every bit of fear, every moment of indignity, every life destroyed and future stolen put iron in her muscles and shoveled coal into the furnace of her hate. It was no longer the cold hatred from back in the cemetery. Now she burned with it as she punched and punched. This was for Mama. For her friends. For the town. She hit and hit until she thought her hands were going to shatter. Collins may have been military, but she wasn't prepared for the speed and power of Gutsy's attack. Maybe she'd underestimated the little Latina. Maybe her own rank and status made her too arrogant to think this "rat" was any kind of threat.

She learned different.

But then someone looped an arm around Gutsy's waist and hauled her backward and off the captain, and it wasn't Dr. Morton.

"Enough!" roared a voice she had never heard before. Gutsy was dumped on the floor, and the person who grabbed her danced backward out of reach of the furious swing Gutsy launched.

Sombra leaped at the newcomer and clamped his teeth on the person's wrist, but those teeth did not bite through flesh.

The moment froze.

A boy stood there. Maybe fifteen or sixteen. Tall, strong-looking, wearing full body armor and a helmet with a plastic visor. Behind the visor were Asian-looking eyes. He had what looked like a samurai sword strapped to his back.

"If this is your dog," said the boy, struggling with Sombra, "better call him off. I don't want to hurt him."

Suddenly there was more movement in the corner, and Gutsy turned to see something that looked impossible. Three more teenagers stepped out of the cabinet as if they were stepping out of nowhere. It was like one of those old novels. Like the kids coming out of the wardrobe from Narnia or Alice through her mirror. They were all dressed in body armor, all splashed with gore. A second boy, also with Asian eyes, and two girls: a tall, stern-faced blonde and a short redhead. The second Asian kid had a compound bow and was drawing an arrow back, the weapon pointed at Sombra, who continued to slash and chew the first boy's wrist pads. The blond girl had a long spear and the redhead had another *katana*, though hers was in her hands.

"Last warning," said the boy with the bow. "I like dogs,

but I like my friend more. Well . . . maybe only a little more."

Gutsy tried to make sense of it. Failed.

But she said, "Sombra . . . no . . ."

And with great reluctance the coydog released his bite. He stood his ground, though, growling at the newcomers. In the corner, Dr. Morton was a statue, too terrified to move. Captain Collins groaned and rocked side to side on the floor, her hands over her bloody face.

"Who . . . who *are* you?" gasped Gutsy. "And where did you come from? How did you get in here?"

"The tunnel . . . ?" squeaked Morton. "God, are *they* in the tunnel?"

Everyone knew who "they" were.

"Only what's left of them," said the blonde.

The first boy held out a hand—very careful of Sombra—toward Gutsy. "My name's Benny Imura," he said. "We . . . um . . . well, we're here to help."

"Help what?" said Gutsy, getting up without his assistance. "We're losing. We're all going to die."

The boy grinned. "Maybe not. I kind of have a plan."

"You won't like it," said the other boy. "No one ever does."

As it turned out, Gutsy liked it just fine.

GRIMM SLAMMED INTO A PAIR OF RAVAGERS, THE blades on his shoulders shearing through their thigh muscles. A third ravager fell as a sniper bullet took him in the eye. Ledger leaped over his body and rushed at the leader of the wolf pack.

"Yo, Raggedy Man," he bellowed, "let's dance."

There was a flicker of confusion on the ravager's face, but then he was backpedaling away from the slashing blade. He turned and dove into a very smooth roll and came up with a rifle, but Grimm hit him hard and drove the ravager back and down.

Even so, the ravager twisted as he fell and drove a stunningly powerful punch into the side of Grimm's head, leaving a dent and tearing a cry of pain from the dog. Grimm staggered and fell, and the ravager scooped up the gun and swung the barrel toward Ledger.

Ledger was already there and he brought his blade down on the weapon, striking sparks from the barrel. The gun fell, but the ravager immediately kicked Ledger in the stomach. The old soldier went down hard, his sword spinning away. Then the leader and two other ravagers charged at Ledger, going for the kill.

• • •

Sam Imura had no more rounds for his rifle, so he abandoned it and took a Colt CM901 rifle from a duffel bag they'd brought with them. The burned-out old car he had been using as a shooting blind was now too far from the action. It was time to follow Ledger into the thick of it, as he had done so many times all those years ago. He slung a smaller bag, filled with as many additional magazines as he could carry, slantwise across his body, and stuffed his pockets with magazines for his Sig Sauer P226 handgun.

Then he was running.

He'd lost sight of Ledger when the big idiot tried to take down the ravager they thought was the Raggedy Man. There were infected everywhere, and they turned to face the running man.

Sam preferred the distance and solitude of a sniper's elevated firing position, but he was, first and foremost, a world-class special operator. That meant there was no kind of weapon he couldn't pick up and use. There were few weapons he had never fired. The Colt and the Sig Sauer were old friends. He knew how to make them sing dark songs.

They filled the night with the music of Armageddon.

On the wall, Alethea and Spider were running out of catwalk. Mrs. Cuddly crawled along with them as they retreated, leaving a slug's trail of glistening red.

"Behind you," she screamed, and Alethea turned as one of the fast-infected flung himself at her, fingernails curled into claws, mouth wide for a bite. Alethea turned too late.

Then the leaping monster seemed to freeze in midair as if it had hit an invisible wall.

Alethea saw the shiny tip of a knife protruding from between its broken teeth. There was a grunt of effort and a figure they had not seen before tore a long spear from the back of the infected's head, letting the body fall.

Alethea, Spider, and Mrs. Cuddly all gaped at the figure holding the spear. Tall, powerful, armored, deadly. And totally unknown to them.

"Stop staring and fight," said the figure in a ghostly whisper of a voice.

More of the dead rushed at them, and the tall girl turned to fight the ones behind her. Alethea and Spider exchanged a look, eyebrows raised.

"Works for me," said Alethea, and whirled to swing Rainbow Smite into the face of another monster. Spider laughed and joined his foster sister. They formed a protective triangle around Mrs. Cuddly, and whenever one of their enemies fell to the catwalk, injured but not dead, the meat tenderizer and the cleaver were ready.

"Get inside," gasped Ford, pushing Urrea toward the open door of the general store. They were both hurt, though neither had been bitten. Their pads had saved them so far, but now there were simply too many *los muertos* to fight. Alice caught Urrea as he stumbled and half carried the old writer inside. Ford kept swinging his ax to try to buy them enough time, but gray hands were plucking at his clothes, hooking around the edges of his hockey pads.

Alice pushed Urrea into the hands of the people huddling inside, snatched up Urrea's fallen sword, and tried to swing it, but it was too heavy and awkward and she fell hard onto her knees. A ravager rushed at her, his face split by a hungry grin of dark triumph.

A second later a ball of fire exploded in the center of the town square. The ragged clothes and withered flesh of the shamblers ignited and they staggered in all directions, their senses immediately useless inside envelopes of flame. A second explosion set more of them alight. A third burst among the fast-infected who tried to escape.

Ford and Alice clung to each other, reeling backward from the heat, but the fire was not aimed at them. They saw a figure standing on the roof of the hospital. A small woman or teenage girl—it was hard to tell with the armor she wore—was hurling plastic water bottles with burning pieces of cloth stuck in them. No, not water, Alice realized as she caught a whiff of gasoline.

The ravagers tried to make a break for it, some cutting left and others right to escape the conflagration in the center of the square.

Karen Peak and Mr. Cuddly were there on the left with the last of their defenders. Their guns cracked and the ravagers fell.

On the right, Alice saw another teenager dressed in armor. A stranger, and he had a sword in his hands that he swung with deadly precision. Ravagers fell screaming around him.

And fighting beside him, swinging a machete, was *Gutsy!* Her ugly dog was with her, lunging at ravagers and knocking them down within reach of Gutsy's blade.

Behind Alice the children were crying, babies screamed, but Mr. Urrea cheered. Ford got to his feet and hefted his ax. Alice rose too.

The battle wasn't over yet.

Sam Imura killed his way to where Ledger had fallen. He had no illusions about some miracle save that would allow Ledger to have survived. The world was not that kind, as had been proven too many times.

Then he heard a horrific roar and spun to see Grimm come charging past him. Half of his armor torn away, his helmet dented, blood streaked along the mastiff's sides, but the monstrous dog kept going as if no force on earth could stop him. The fast-infected and the shamblers did not even try to run; the ravagers who tried, failed.

"Welcome to the party," yelled a familiar voice, and Sam stared in true amazement to see Joe Ledger, as battered and bloody as his dog, standing with a sword in one hand and holding the hair of a severed head in the other. Ledger tossed the head at the closest infected. "Here, catch," he said with a maniacal laugh, and then stabbed the infected through the eye.

Sam could not help but smile. If this was all proof that his own sanity had finally cracked all the way through, then so be it. There were worse ways to go down than in the company of an old friend.

He shifted to stand with his back to Ledger and fired, fired, fired.

The dead kept coming. Maybe not as many as before, but enough. More than enough.

Sam caught sight of something flying through the air, and for a weird moment he thought he was back on some previous battlefield and the object was a fragmentation grenade thrown by an enemy combatant.

It wasn't. It was a bottle of gasoline with a burning rag. It struck the back of a shambler and exploded, dousing all the other dead around it in flames. Grimm began barking furiously and backing away in fear. Ledger whirled.

"What the—?"

Another firebomb splatted against the crest of the hill on which the head ravager had been standing, and burst. Two ravagers reeled back, clawing at fire on their hair and skin.

Then a third ravager—who had escaped the flame and was raising a heavy maul in preparation for striking Grimm—juddered to a sudden stop, dropping the tool. An arrow stood out from his left temple, the shaft still quivering.

Sam and Ledger both looked up at the wall. At the bunch of figures who stood there. A curvy girl with a baseball bat, a skinny boy with a staff. And two figures in full SWAT armor. A short girl with a whole basket of bottles at her feet, and a slim boy who was busy fitting another arrow to the string of his compound bow.

"No," said Ledger, his face nearly blank with shock. Then a huge grin spread from ear to ear. "Nix!" he bellowed. "Chong!"

On the wall, they jerked erect at the sound of his voice. It was immediately clear that they hadn't known who it was they were saving. They were just people helping people in the middle of a battle. Now they both began jumping in the air, punching the night sky with their fists.

For about one whole second.

Then the dead rushed past their burning comrades and attacked. Sam began firing again. Ledger swung his sword and Grimm attacked with his spikes. More fire rained down. There were many more arrows.

The fight raged on and on and . . .

SILENCE SWEPT ACROSS THE FLAT PLAIN THAT surrounded New Alamo.

Smoke curled upward from hundreds of smoldering corpses. Fire chewed at old flesh and leather and the handles of axes. Two figures stood in a field of death, dressed in tatters. One held a rifle by its stock because in the end that was all he had left for the fight. The other held a sword. Between them, lying on his side and panting with exhaustion and pain, was a huge dog. All three of them were covered in soot.

On the wall stood four teenagers, their shoulders sagging with exhaustion. There were no more bottles of gasoline in the basket by the short girl. There were no more arrows in the tall boy's quiver. The boy with the staff leaned on it as if it was the only reason he had not yet fallen down. The other girl bent and placed her bat on the catwalk, then stood and straightened her tiara.

Then Gutsy climbed up to the top of the wall, followed by Lilah and Benny. The white-haired girl pushed past her, grabbed Chong roughly, studied him with a harsh and critical eye, and then crushed him in a fierce embrace. Chong winced, but smiled, too. Benny went over to Nix and bent to kiss her, but she turned and pointed. He peered through the smoke and then his whole body went rigid.

"He's alive. . . ." He gasped. Then he leaped into the air and pumped his fists and roared out a name. *"Joe!"* Then all Benny's friends were shouting and waving. Gutsy went to the edge of the wall and looked down at the two scruffy old men.

"Who are they?" she asked. Spider and Alethea joined her.

Benny turned to her. "Friends," he said. Despite the grime and sweat and blood on his face, he was smiling.

EPILOGUE

One

GUTSY STOOD WITH ALICE, SPIDER, AND ALETHEA and watched as a tall, battered old soldier hugged the four strange teens. They were all crying. Another old soldier stood apart, watching with guarded eyes, silent and strange. It felt odd to watch this because it had nothing to do with her, her life, her friends.

Except that it did.

Without the arrival of the four teens, Gutsy would have died in the hospital. Now Dr. Morton and Captain Collins were tied up and in Karen Peak's custody. There was no more base and the Rat Catchers were gone, their power broken. There would be so many questions Collins would not want to answer.

But answer she would. Gutsy promised her that before Karen led her away to a holding cell. Dr. Morton tried to apologize, but Gutsy turned her back on him. He would have a lot to answer for as well, and word was already spreading around town about what he had done. None of the members of the town council had so far shown their faces since the fight began. They would all be found, those who were still alive. The power in New Alamo was going through a change. Everything about the town was changing. Gutsy wondered what it would be like in a week. Or a month.

The big gray-blond soldier, Captain Ledger, finally stepped back from the teenagers and wiped his eyes. He put his hand on the shoulder of the one who had introduced himself as Benny Imura.

"Benny," he said, "before I start yelling at you juvenile delinquents for disobeying every rule of common freaking sense and coming out here looking for me, I need to tell you something."

Benny grinned. "What's that?"

Ledger cleared his throat. "You know that your brother Tom and I go way back, right? We met not too long after the dead rose and I helped coach him, taught him some useful dirty tricks about how to fight and how to survive."

Benny nodded.

"You know that Tom had an older brother?"

"Sure. Sam. He was a soldier and died during First Night," said Benny. "I . . . never got to meet him. Why?"

"Don't ask me how," said Ledger, "and don't ask me why the universe is this weird, but . . ."

"What are you saying?"

Instead of answering, Ledger glanced at the other old soldier. A Japanese man in his fifties. Benny turned to look at him, nodded a hello, started to turn away, then stopped. A frown creased his face. He turned back to the Japanese man and studied him. The other three did as well. Slow realization changed the whole pattern of Benny's face. The hardness of a young killer seemed to fall away, leaving a kid staring in shock at something he did not, or could not, believe. Benny's eyes were huge and his mouth hung open.

The old soldier came walking over, very slowly, uncertainly. His lips trembled and tears fell down his soot-stained cheeks.

"Benny . . . ?" he said in a choked whisper.

"I don't . . . I don't . . ."

And then Benny flew to the older man and grabbed him, hugging him, and was hugged back. They began laughing. So did Ledger, so did the other teens.

After a moment, so did everyone there.

Two

The fires raged.

The dead burned.

So, too, did nearly half the houses in New Alamo. Whole sections of the wall were scorched, and the stacked tires around the gate entrances smoldered until dawn.

In the cold light of a new day, with a bloody sunrise splashed across the horizon and smoke rising in columns, it was hard to tell if the town had survived or if winning the fight had killed it.

Three

The following afternoon they all gathered in Mr. Ford's classroom at Misfit High.

Gutsy was there with Alice, Alethea, and Spider. They

were all clean but bandaged. Karen Peak was there, along with a few of the townsfolk she said could be trusted. The Chess Players were there, heavily bandaged and looking older than their years. Benny Imura and his friends were there. Sombra and Grimm lay on the floor near each other. Sam sat with Benny. Ledger stood by a map on the wall.

"So, this is where the base was," he said, making a mark. "This is New Alamo, and this is the forest where Sam has a cabin. Somewhere in this area over here is where Sam thinks is a big cache of weapons."

"Do we need them anymore?" asked Spider. "The ravagers are all dead. And so is that guy, the whatchamacallit?"

"The Raggedy Man," said Alethea. "Stupid name."

"Stupid or not," said Nix, "he's dead, right? Captain Ledger cut his head off."

"That usually does it," agreed Benny.

"Actually, kids, I don't know if that was him," said Ledger. "I killed some weirdo out there who seemed to be running things. But if that was the Raggedy Man, then he didn't live up to the hype."

"It can't be him," said Karen.

"Why not?" asked Urrea.

"Because from what you said, he was telling the ravagers what to do, but did he actually seem to be controlling the shamblers? Or the fast-infected?"

Sam and Ledger exchanged a look. "Not really," said Sam.

"What does it matter if it's him or not?" asked Chong.

"Because," said a cold voice from the other end of the room, "you have no idea who or what the Raggedy Man is."

They all looked at Captain Bess Collins, who was tied to a

chair. They had moved her from the holding cell to the school. It was quieter there, and none of them trusted anyone related to the town police or government anymore. Karen had helped them do it.

Collins's nose was swollen and crooked and she had two black eyes and a split lip. Even so, beaten and helpless, tied and captive, she retained her sense of power.

"Oh, so now you're finally going to say something?" said Alethea, puffing out her chest.

"Maybe," said Collins, "if we can make a deal."

"No way," said Spider.

"Yeah," agreed Alethea, "only deal you're getting is whether I kill you or Gutsy does."

"What kind of deal?" asked Urrea, ignoring that threat.

"You want to know about the project, yes?" No one answered. Collins nodded as if everyone had. "You want to know why we kept everything a secret from the people here? You want to know why we dug up all those bodies? You don't have to say anything. I know you have a million questions and I have all the answers. So, sure, I have a lot to bargain with."

"Going out on a limb here," said Ledger, "but I'm pretty sure Dr. Morton would be happy to talk to us. He looks like he's ready to unburden his soul."

"Max is a weasel."

"Maybe," said Gutsy, "but if he knows all this, then we don't need to make any deals with you."

"Sure," said Collins with a casual shrug. "Ask him. He'll spill his guts. He'll tell you everything *he* knows."

She leaned on the word "he," and everyone heard it. Collins watched their faces and nodded. Her expression was like that of an alligator. Cold, smiling, heartless, and confident. "He knows enough to confuse you all ten times as much. But, believe me or not, Max doesn't have a real clue. No one else in the lab or the base had the full picture."

"Just you?" asked Gutsy.

"Just me."

"What's your price?" asked Sam.

Collins gave another shrug. "I walk."

"You," said Ford, "are completely out of your mind."

"Why on earth would we even consider that?" asked Gutsy, truly perplexed.

"Because I know what you *need* to know." Again the emphasis.

"And what is that?" asked Urrea.

"I know who the Raggedy Man is," said the captain. "I know you haven't killed him. I know what he can do. And I know what's coming."

"Why are we even listening to her?" demanded Alethea.

"Shut up, fat girl," sneered Collins. "No one cares what you have to say."

"Hey!" growled Spider, taking a threatening step forward, but Alethea stopped him.

"She's just trying to be mean," she said. "I've been dealing with mean girls all my life. She's nothing."

"Keep saying that," said Collins. "You might even believe it after a while."

"Okay, *enough*," growled Gutsy. "What are you trying to say? What is it you think is so important that we'd ever consider letting you go?"

Collins smiled. "Do you idiots think that you actually *won* last night?"

"Um . . . yeah," said Chong. "Lot of toasted zoms out there."

"Then you're as big an idiot as the people in this town," said Collins. "That was the Raggedy Man testing you to see how tough you were."

"If that's true," said Urrea, "then he knows we can beat him."

"Oh, is that what he knows?"

Ledger walked over to her. "Listen, sister, let's have a perspective check here, okay? You're tied to a chair after getting your butt handed to you by a fifteen-year-old kid. So you talking smack doesn't carry a lot of weight. That's point one. Point two is that if you have information that we need to have, do you want to look me in the eye and tell me *I* can't make you talk?"

"And who are you?" she said with contempt.

He smiled. "Ever heard of the Department of Military Sciences? Ever heard of Rogue Team International? Yeah, I can tell you have. You're career military, so you definitely heard of both groups. Good. Then you've also probably heard of the guy who ran point for those teams. Psychotic kind of guy who looks a whole bunch like someone in this room."

The sneer faltered. "Joe Ledger . . . ?"

"Joe Ledger. Nice to be recognized, Captain. Now think back on every story you ever heard about me. There were some real doozies floating around back in the day. Yeah, I can see you remember some of them. Good. Think about what you heard me do when I went up against the bad guys. Now . . . go another step down that road and think about what I would be willing to do to protect the people I care about. Go on, let your imagination run wild."

Gutsy glanced at the four teen strangers. She could see from the looks in their eyes that they knew some—but probably nowhere near all—about what this man was saying. They knew enough that it turned their faces to stone. Sam Imura, the other soldier, met her eyes and gave her a single, small nod.

Captain Collins licked her lips. It was the first genuine sign of nervousness.

"I still want a deal," she said quickly.

"We'll see," said Ledger. "First you're going to tell me something that lets everyone here understand the value of what you have to trade. Tell us about the Raggedy Man."

She took a long time coming to a decision, and they all waited her out.

"Do you know the story of how the plague got started? Do you know about the pathogen?"

"Lucifer 113," said Gutsy. "We know."

"You know about Dr. Volker and what he did with that pathogen?"

"Yes," said Gutsy. "He gave it to a death-row inmate to make him suffer. But he wasn't buried and he woke up and started attacking people. That's how the plague started."

"Then here's something you may not know," said Collins, and there was no sneer in her voice now. She looked terrified. Maybe of Ledger, maybe about what she was saying. "The first infected, the patient zero of that plague, Homer Gibbon, wasn't a shambler. He wasn't like the fast-infected or even like the ravagers. He was unique. Supremely dangerous. And he could control the other infected."

"I never heard that part," said Sam, "and I was on the ground in Stebbins County."

"It's true."

"How do you know this stuff?" asked Spider.

"Because the Raggedy Man told me."

There was silence in the room.

"He was in our facility for years," said Collins. "We studied him, hoping to use his unique biology as patient zero. He was the purest strain. We hoped to learn so many things. To awaken the minds of the shamblers so they wouldn't hunt us. And other things. We wanted our own shock troops for use against the shamblers if that failed. But it didn't work."

"The ravagers?" asked Gutsy.

"The ravagers," agreed Collins. "You see, we were never able to control them, right from the start, because someone else already was controlling them." She looked around. "The Raggedy Man was like a god to them." She paused and corrected what she'd said. "He *is* their god."

"It doesn't matter," said Gutsy. "We destroyed his army."

"No," said Collins, and for a moment Gutsy saw the captain's professional calm slip, revealing the real person behind the soldier's face. Collins was terrified. Genuinely and deeply terrified. "What you fought was nothing. An expeditionary force. How can you not grasp that fact? He has *billions* of the dead. He has an army bigger than this world has ever seen, and he is their god, their king, and their general. He's going to come here and wipe New Alamo off the map." She looked at Benny and his friends. "He's going to find wherever you came from and devour them all." She leaned back and looked up at Ledger, trying to reclaim her facade of calm, but it didn't work. Not anymore. "He's already sent an army to Asheville. Maybe the city is still standing, or maybe everyone there is dead. Either way, time is running out. The research we were conducting here was getting us close to a real cure, close to a way to stop the Raggedy Man forever. Now . . ." She shook her head. "God, you idiots may have killed us all."

"Who is the Raggedy Man?" asked Chong.

Collins stared at him. "Haven't you been listening? The Raggedy Man is Homer Gibbon, and he is coming for us."

"How do we know you're not lying to us?" asked Gutsy.

Suddenly the air was torn by sirens from the guard towers. SOS.

Save Our Souls.

Gutsy ran to the window and opened it.

They could hear the screaming start.